Swinson

Nellie Mae Batson

Righter Publishing Company

Copyright 2002 by Nellie Mae Batson
All rights reserved

This is a work of fiction. All characters, events and circumstances portrayed in this story are products of the author's imagination. Any resemblance to actual people and events is purely coincidental. No part of this book may be reproduced without written permission by the author and publisher.

Righter Publishing Company, Inc.
PO Box 105
Timberlake, North Carolina 27583

www.righterbooks.com

Second Edition

March 2008

Printed and bound in the United States of America

Cover by Lynn Batson

Library of Congress Control Number
2008920007

ISBN: 978-1-934936-02-3
Swinson
By Nellie Mae Batson

Introduction

In the year 1858, Jess Swinson and his sons, Jesse and James, begin a journey from Ireland to America in hopes of reclaiming the family fortune and reuniting their family. As Jess stands on the deck of the ship, biding farewell to his wife and five children, he exclaims, "With God as my witness! I vow that an heir of my seed will one day reclaim the Swinson fortune and social standing."

The path that unfolds before the three Swinson men is wrought with trial and heartbreak as they slowly make their way to America, only to be separated once more, causing James to go his own way. Jess and Jesse make their way to the wilderness of North Carolina to start a new life. In Clinton, North Carolina, Jesse mets Colista Anita Batts, a young woman of courage and determination to match that of Jesse. The wide-canvas story that evolves will keep the reader waiting to see the end result.

Swinson is a story of great loss, great love, and the promise of tomorrow as Jess' vow is never forgotten and is passed down to his grandchildren and great-grandchildren after his death.

Nellie Mae Batson lives in Sneads Ferry, North Carolina. Nellie Mae is the mother of six sons and the grandmother of seven grandchildren. She enjoys writing, gardening and making quilts. This is her second published work.

Glossary on Page 348

Other Books by the Author

Lossie

Skeet Apples

Appreciation

A special thanks to Annette Squires for her help and urging me on and to Rina Hutchinson and Lona Lockhart for editing my story. An extra special thanks to my son, Lynn Batson, for this wonderful new cover.

Publishers Note

Nellie Mae Batson's stories are unique and she has a unique storytelling style. In addition to being fascinating windows to North Carolina's rich history, her characters speak in the dialects of their time and place. It is also a singular aspect of her writing that the narrator's voice is also in the dialect of the time and place.

The Publisher

Swinson
Chapter One

James Jesse Swinson, called Jess, walked alone down the dirt road from the town of Ardara, headed home to his wife and seven children. He was deep in thought as he plodded along the dusty road.

In the bottom of his trouser pocket were three tickets. The tickets secured passage on a cargo ship scheduled to depart the Loughros More Bay, Ireland, in four days.

It was 1858. The day was hot from the bright sun that beat down on the earth. Dust swirled around his feet as he walked to the shade of a near-by tree. The cool offered by the shade felt refreshing to his bone tired body. He removed a sweat stained, brimmed hat from his head. With a blue bandanna handkerchief, he wiped sweat from his brow.

He was quite mentally and physically weary. It seemed that the world had beaten him.

He leaned his back against the tree and sat on the ground with one of his long legs extended out in front of him and the other drawn up at the knee. The old sweat stained, brimmed hat rested atop his knee. He picked it up and twirled it around on one of his hands a time or two. That felt hat had been a gift from his mother.

His mind wandered back through the years. The Swinson family had lived for generations near the small town of New Abby, in the county of Kirkcudbright, Scotland. They were farmers and cattlemen. Grain and cattle were their two main means of livelihood. They were well educated and somewhat wealthy and a social asset to the area. Jess was the third born in the family of five children, which included three sons and two daughters.

The adjoining farm belonged to Liam and Colleen McDonald. Their daughter, Lillian, caught the eye of Jess when he was a young man in his teens. The attraction grew and a romance flourished.

They married and lived on a section of Swinson land. Jess, his father, and older brothers built the newlyweds a house three quarters of a mile from the main farmhouse.

He followed in the footsteps of his family and farmed the land, like his ancestors before him.

Their first child was born eighteen months later in 1844. He was a fine, fair-haired boy, who they named James. Two years after the birth of James, another son came along. Jesse was born in 1846. Jesse was a beautiful child. He was like a lap dog. He loved anyone that came near him. His laughter could be heard from inside the house or any area on the farm he happened to be. He was a joy and blessing to the family

Jess and Lillian farmed the land together. They shared the hard jobs, along with those of pleasure. Their love was outstanding in the county of Kirkcudbright.

Each year after Jesse was born a new baby arrived in the family until seven children filled the house with glee and laughter. All the children were healthy and alert, each one smart in their own right and fair-haired and light complexioned. There was not an ugly featured face in the bunch.

Soon after the birth of their last baby, Lillian's health took a turn for the worse. She had had too many babies too close together.

Jess didn't pay too much attention to her health problems at first. She continued to perform her daily duties, though at a slower pace, and she always seemed tired. He did notice that their lovemaking had slowed to a snails pace.

Jess was a good farmer. He had worked hard for the past nine years, and had added to his holdings on the farm.

When the baby was four months old, Jess knew he had to do something about Lillian. He could see she was failing almost daily. It tugged at his heart to see her in such a sad, run-down condition. He sent a letter off to Doctor McIntire in Edinburgh, requesting that he come to the farm. Jess got his reply from the doctor in three weeks later. Jess met the doctor at the station in Moffat with a horse for him to ride along with Jess back to the farm.

Lillian was so weak by the time they reached the farm, that all she did was sit listlessly in the big rocker.

Crusty old codger that he was, Doctor McIntire was a good man and a concerned doctor. Jess had complete faith in him, and listened to all he had to say.

After a lengthy physical examination and an hour or so of verbal exchange, the doctor decided that there was nothing wrong with Lillian, other than bad case of depression.

Her body was worn out and tired from the birth of her babies. Steady work on the farm, and caring for the children had increased her tiredness and her self-sympathy. The doctor felt, with proper medication and good loving care, she would overcome her depression.

He told Jess in private the results of his examination. She needed a change in her life. A different location to live would probably be one of the best things Jess could do to improve her health. If he didn't do something to get her out of her depression, she would die. Her interest in living was at zero at no fault of her own or those around her who loved her dearly. This sort of thing just happened to some women, where it doesn't bother others.

Jess and Lillian had a deep love for each other. It had started when they first met, and had grown richer through the years. Their marriage had been filled with passionate nights of making love, romping over the fields together, and picnicking on lovely cool days. Their lives had seemed perfect until the depression overtook Lillian.

Jess went to his father and told him what doctor had said. His father advised him he had to do whatever was best for his family. He would really hate to see them leave the farm and take the grandchildren away, but he would understand.

His father also reminded him that he too had left his beloved home in Sweden shortly after he had married, and came to this strange land here in Scotland. He also told him how his own father, Jess' grandfather, had left the shores of England to find his fortune in Sweden, which allowed them to survive and prosper.

Jess his made up his mind by the end of the week to go seek a new home for his family. With a few changes of clothing packed, he took each child, and hugged and kissed them with all the love he could muster. When he left the yard on horseback, he turned to look at Lillian as she sat in the rocker on the front porch rocking listlessly.

He had spent many hours talking to her, trying to get her to understand why he was leaving her and the children. She seemed not to care for any explanation.

He left of Scotland, on that long ago day, a sad man. To leave the family he loved more thananything, hurt beyond description, even though he knew they were in capable hands of his father, mother, and older brothers. Tears rolled down his cheeks as he turned and continued on his way to put distance between him and his homeland.

He traveled through the English countryside, through the counties of Northumberland, Durham, and Cumberland. He walked mile after mile, searching for the right property. He stayed in England for a full month before he decided he was not going to find what he was looking for and wanted.

How he missed his Lillian. His thoughts were on her a lot of the time, not only to find the perfect place for her to call home, but for her health reasons, and his love for her. He missed her closeness when he lay down to sleep at night. The occasion arose several times during his travels, where free sex was offered by wayward kinds of females but he remained true to his Lillian.

He found himself in Whitehaven, England, in the middle of October. He bought a ticket on a boat to cross the Irish Sea. A short stop at The Isle of Man was an interesting break in his journey.

He came ashore at Dundalk Bay, Ireland. He traveled inland to Monaghan. There he searched for property as he crossed the land.

It was forty-five days before he arrived at Ardara, Ireland. On his first day of searching in the area, he found exactly what he was looking for and it was a nice farm surrounded mostly by woods for sale.

He bought the farm and contacted a builder to renovate the existing house and outbuildings. There were enough animals and equipment on the land to get the farm cultivated and seeds in for the next crop.

Two families lived on the land in small houses located on different sides of the fields. They had worked the soil for many years and they called it home.

Jess kept the tenants. He needed the help the workers would contribute now that he was away from his father and brothers.

He went over to Ardara and found a couple of workers for the house. They could stay in the room behind the kitchen. A man and his wife, who were looking for work, were in a shop when Jess entered and asked the shop-owner to recommend someone for the job.

The tenant farmers were eager to please Jess and anxious to do good work on the land. They learned pretty soon that Jess was an honest and fair man to work for.

By springtime, the fields were alive with crops. Sugar beets, barley, and potatoes were the main crops. Allen and Mary, the recently hired house help, kept the big vegetable garden clean of weeds.

It was a beautiful spring. The house had turned out to be a showplace when the builders had completed their work. Allen and Mary had done wonders with the yard to make it a comfortable and a lovely place to call home.

Jess decided it was time to go back to Scotland and bring his family to their new home.

He made the journey back in a lot less less time than it had taken him to reach Ardara. As he traveled, thoughts entered his mind as to how he would find Lillian when he arrived at home. He had had little news from any of them since he'd left all those months ago.

The smaller children spotted him when he neared the edge of the yard. They went shouting toward the house, announcing his arrival.

Lillian came out on the porch, wiping her hands in her apron bottom. She peered in the direction from which he came. She was a vision of loveliness for the eyes of Jess. He had missed her terribly. She looked to be in much better health than when he had left. She ran down the steps as soon as she recognized him. With outstretched arms, she greeted him with warmth and some of the old expressions of love she used to use when they were young.

Jess knew from the expression on her face and the strength in her arms that their reunion would be a good one.

All the children were filled with anxiety and question after question. It felt so good to have his arms about them, to have them close to him, and be able to touch their skin with his hands. It made him feel a great pride to be their father.

Jess told his family over the supper table about their new home in Ireland. His description left nothing out. When he finished, they were all ready pack up and go.

After the supper dishes were washed, and the kitchen tidied up, Jess and his family walked across the field to his father's house. He related the details of the move to his parents and added that farming was still in the family.

They would be leaving in three days. Family travel preparations were all in order.

Lillian got the children off to bed for the night and waited for her husband in their bedroom. She wore a light blue nightgown. She did some embroidery work while she waited for Jess to join her. She was seated in a comfortable chair.

She rose to meet him when he entered the room. Her heart began to race and she was filled with passion for her husband again. Their lips met in a hungry, long awaited kiss. With his hands, Jess reclaimed her body through the silk gown.

It was good, their love making, but not back to where it had been in the beginning. Jess felt, that with time, she would be her old self again.

Their last meal in Scotland was with the Grandparents. It was a sad time and a time of excitement also. The good-byes were in progress when Jess' mother came to him and gave him a brand new, brimmed felt hat. It was a farewell gift.

Jess and his family left Scotland late in the afternoon on that early, summer day.

The trip to Ireland turned into a fun trip for the travelers. Lazy hours were spent on the deck of the ship while crossing the water with games to be enjoyed by the children, as well as adults. Nights of good restful sleep. The salt air began to liven Lillian up more after a few days out to sea.

The time spent traveling on land was tiresome and boring. It was hot and sticky. The children grumbled and complained from their discomfort. The sun tanned them as brown as berries.

When the farmhouse appeared in their view, they gasped with delight. It was a beautiful sight for their tired eyes.

Allen and Mary ran down the steps to help unload the wagons. Good smelling vittles were simmering on the stove in the kitchen. It was a warm welcome that they received when they set their feet on the soil of *Lillian Way*, the name Jess had given the farm.

Lillian took to Mary and Allen on sight and continued to improve daily. The children were happy and contented. Jess felt as though he was sitting on top of the world. Everything was perfect. He found a few minutes each day to stop and give thanks to God for his blessings.

The potato famine had hit Ireland in 1845. From then until 1847, rent-racked Ireland suffered a disastrous setback. By the year 1848, the population of Ireland had decreased by half a million due to emigration, mostly Protestants, to America, and starvation caused by the potato crop failure.

As time passed, Jess felt the results of the potato crop failure also. Even though he had not arrived in Ireland until 1852, he lost most of his lands due to the high rents. His tenant farmers left the land, along with Allen and Mary. They too, along with the farm help, emigrated to America.

The third youngest child fell ill. Doctor bills and enormous medical expenses nearly depleted the family funds. Jess held out, barely surviving until 1858.

He sat down and penned a letter to his father back in Scotland. He hated to have to fall back on his parents with a passion. It was either eat his pride and ask for help, or see his wife and children die of starvation.

His father sent him some money. It was his decision to buy the three tickets to America and leave the remainder of the money for Lillian and the children to survive on until James, Jesse and he reached America and could send for them.

He felt it would not take the three of them too long to earn the money once they reached the shores of the land known as "the land of riches and plenty."

He had gone to Ardara to secure the tickets. The only ship leaving within right away was a cargo ship. The captain offered him passage if he and the boys would sign on to work. The ship was short of crewmembers. If Jess agreed to work on the way over, the captain could set sail within the week.

Jess didn't particularly appreciate the arrangement, but considered it better than nothing. The reduced price of the tickets meant he could leave more money with Lillian. On his way home, he had stopped to relax for a few minutes beneath the shade of the tree.

When he got home, Lillian had the few possession packed that she and the children would need to survive. Jess had located a two-room hovel for them to occupy closer to town until they too could leave for the new homeland across the ocean.

Lillian and the wee ones walked the miles to Lougros More bay, where the ship was docked to bid fond good-byes to Jess and her two boys.

Jess and his two sons boarded after the tearful, sad farewells. It tore at his heart to have to leave them all standing there on the wharf. Lillian looked forlorn and destitute. How could he have let their lives come to this? Where had he failed?

He felt a jerk when the ship pulled away from the dock. James, Jesse and he stood side-by-side at the ship's rail. They watched as the figures on the pier grew smaller and smaller.

Jess was an angry man and a humiliated husband and father. He parted his legs slightly, raised his right hand high above his head.

With his hand clinched into a tight fist, he declared, "With God as my witness! I vow that an heir of my seed will one day reclaim the Swinson fortune and social standing."

Chapter Two

After the ship moved out to sea, James was assigned to work in the galley.

"Of all places, I despise messing with food and dishes. Aside from getting my craw filled." He spoke softly, so only his father and brother could hear his complaint.

Jesse was twelve years old one week before they set sail from Ireland. He was a handsome, robust young man with eyes so green they seemed to shine in contrast with his honey blonde hair. His mouth was filled with straight, pearly, white teeth. When he smiled, the expression lit up his entire face. He was a big youngin' for his age. He looked like a grown man. Working on deck, and being a jack-of-all-trades filled his days at.

Jess had to work below deck caring for the stowed cargo. The ship's freight consisted of precious Irish lace and Irish linen, the only free trade left to the Irish due to the penal laws enacted by the English.

At night, they slept in the same quarters. When they finally got to lie down on the berths, they were usually so tired they spent very little time in conversation.

Jesse learned the meaning of hard, tiresome work. His hands had blistered, healed, and re-blistered. The skin on his hands had cured into leather-like cowhide with hard thick calluses. The muscles in his arms, and those in his thighs, were hard as steel. He had picked up the crew's use of foul language within a month's span of working on deck. Gone were the days when he could talk without the use of profanity. The first time his father heard him spit out some of his newly learned words, he quietly stood by and just looked at his son. He shook his head in utter disbelief. He said not a word to the boy. It would not have done any good. Jesse was teenager now and had the build and life of an adult man.

Life aboard ship was rough, mean and downright cruel. Jess learned quickly that the life the boys had known back in their homeland of Scotland and that of Ireland was gone, probably never to return. They had experienced some hard times the last few years in Ireland, but nothing to compare with what they now endured.

James, too, had turned into a ruffian. So much so, that when he spoke to his father or brother, he spoke as a seafaring ruffian.

Jess found it hard to realize there would be no praying together. The boys, who had been brought up in the local Protestant faith, felt they had outgrown the need for daily prayer. Besides, if one of the crew should catch them on their knees, it would be the devil to pay.

"You go on and pray Paw. I can't think of a single thing to give thanks for right now. It seems to me the devil has done more for us lately anyhow," Jesse remarked to his father in a sassy manner.

The winds blew and the rains fell. On clear days, the sun shone bright. The combination caused the complexion of Jess and the boys to be ruddy, crusty, and dirty. This was true for Jesse more than the others, since he stayed out in the open more than the other two. They had not had a bath since boarding the ship. An occasional jump in the salt water was as close as they had come to a bath.

No one smelled the rancid odor anymore. They all smelled alike. Jesse's crotch had chafed and cured so many times, that the areas had finally toughened up to the point where it didn't hurt any more. He wore the bare necessities while at work: a pair of torn off trousers, solid shoes and an old piece of shirt torn and rolled into a bandanna tied around his head to keep his long hair out of his face. His hair had grown to shoulder length.

His father and James dressed about the same as he did. The father wore his shirt most of the time and hung onto his felt hat.

James took to stealing shortly after he learned the routine of galley work. He found that he could slip a tasty morsel of the best cut of meat in his pocket or in the cuff of his trousers, to later share with his father and Jesse. They had all suffered from lack of nourishing food before they left Ireland and now needed all the good food they could get. Extra slices of fresh fruit, as long as it lasted, turned up at night when no one was watching. They ate raw vegetables when possible.

The work was hard and seemed to be never ending. Jesse still found time to dream his dreams. He was anxious to get to the new world and find his fortune. If the rumors were true, he would work hard and be a rich man by the time he was forty.

They had been at sea for eight weeks. Jess met Jesse on deck one day and found a few minutes to fellowship.

"Son, it won't be too much longer now before we reach our destination. Well, I don't exactly know how much longer it'll take us, but we're on our way. To tell you the truth, I feel like I can't take too much more of this ocean. I'm ready for some solid ground beneath my feet."

"Me too, Paw."

They had been told that they would put in to shore at a place called New York Harbor.

"When we collect our wages at the end of this journey, we should have enough money amongst the three of us to find a small place for us to live, plus send a little money to your mother. We can get jobs and save up our money. It won't be too long before we have our family together again. I miss your mother, my wife. I miss her something awful son," he told James.

Later on that night, Jess was having a hard time going to sleep, so he eased out of bed and went topside. James lay awake in his berth and heard his father leave. He followed to see what his father's trouble was. They talked a while and then returned to their berths.

James arose and pulled his shoes on first thing the next morning. He slept in all his clothing. So did everyone else. He was supposed to be in the galley early. He always shook his father and brother before he left the area.

Dawn was just breaking. The sun was not yet over the horizon. James straightened up from shaking his father. He took a couple of steps away from the berth, when he heard the explosion. *Ka-Boom!*

All men that were in bed jumped out. The ship shook from stem to stern. For a moment, they stared at each other. Jess and Jesse grabbed their shoes and ran after James to see what the ruckus was.

When they crawled to the top of the stairs, the crew from a renegade Privateer's vessel met them.

"Out o' thar!" came the order from one of the privateers. "All o' ye move along!"

The command came from one of the meanest, ugliest looking human beings either of them had ever laid their eyes upon.

The cool, brisk air blew against the faces of the still sleepy men. It was difficult for them to realize and understand what was going on.

Jess and Jesse struggled into their shoes. With shoes still untied, they were ordered to move over and stand by the railing.

The ship's Captain and firstmate lay dead. All crewmembers that had the misfortune of being on deck were also slaughtered. Blood covered a big portion of the deck. Some of the crew were wounded and near death.

Jess took a quick glance around him. Only a handful of the original crew was still standing. He felt that at any moment he too would be down, with his blood running to meet that of those already dead.

Fear was a new sensation for the Swinsons. It took only a few moments for them to realize that the power of fear could control their very being. Orders were lashed out for the cargo to be transferred to the privateers' vessel.

"Easy boys, keep ye mouths shut," Jess mumbled under his breath to his sons.

He and the boys worked as fast and as hard as they had ever worked at a job. The blades of the robber's knives were never far from the backs of those who labored under the weight of the precious freight.

The cargo ship began to list heavily to the right, making it awkward to walk and carry a heavy load of linen or lace from the hold of the ship. Neither Jesse, his father nor brother said a word the entire time they toiled at the job.

The order came to abandon ship. "All hands onboard. Make ready to sail!"

They joined what was left of the cargo ship's crew, and followed the command to get aboard the pirate ship.

One grown man and two young men were scared beyond thinking for themselves. They were not allowed to gather any of their personal belongings to bring along with them. What they wore on their bodies was all they had.

The vessel pulled away in time to avoid the suction of the ocean water created when the merchant ship sunk to the bowels of the Atlantic.

The pirate ship sailed south with the Swinsons thankful for their lives, fully realizing that at any given moment, the lives they were thankful for could be snuffed out with one swing of a sword.

They learned to obey immediately when an order was barked out to them and to comply quickly, without so much as a moment's hesitation or thought of their own.

Rare were the minutes they could get together for a conversation among themselves. They had kept it a secret from the privateers that they were family. They never spoke to each other when one of their captors was within earshot.

If they had thought life was hard aboard the cargo ship, they learned in pretty short order, that being a prisoner on a pirate vessel was a life too hard to ever want to recall if they should be able to escape.

To escape was uppermost in their minds every hour of every day. As long as they were out to sea, the idea was only a vision. When they sailed into a port, they looked for a means of escape. But they were guarded at each port.

James and Jesse grew deeper and deeper into the ways of rough, rowdy, foul speaking young men. Jess watched as his sons became hard, mean plunderers of the sea to plunder and steal from seagoing ships.

Late one night they anchored off the coast of North Carolina. Jesse could see land if he stood and stared toward the horizon. The moon was full and the ships crew was preparing to go ashore to do some trading and pick up new supplies.

Jess sought out James and related to him the plans to escape while they were on land. James passed the message along to Jesse when he found him.

When they reached the beach, Jess lay down and wallowed in the sand. It felt so good to feel earth beneath his feet again. He arose and turned to see his boys taking strides on the beach, not caring to appreciate the land as he did. They each helped unload the longboats and trudged inland.

Time came to make their escape. Jess had included two of the other captured man in on the plan to get away. Jess figured that if he included more men in the attempt, the fact of him and his sons being family stood a better chance to remain hidden.

They made their lam and got to the edge of the woods before they were found out. Imperfect timing was the failings of a successful escape.

The five men were beaten and thrown into the longboats. When they got back on board the vessel, they were flogged to within an inch of their lives. Raw sores covered their backs for weeks. That was no excuse for not working. They still had to perform, wounded or not.

Jess lost weight and felt poorly most of the time. His thoughts were on and about Lillian and the babies that he had left in Ireland. What would become of them? It had been six months now since he and the boys had departed. He was in a situation where he could do nothing to help her or so much as send her any kind of message. He had no money and no way of getting any in the near future. It was a daily task just to keep alive and away from the wrath of the privateers. He seldom spoke to his sons. They nodded a greeting when they came within sight of one another.

James and Jesse adjusted to the life more readily than did the father. They learned to laugh at the boisterous jokes and gags as they went about their routines. After a fashion, each of them could out cuss and out brag any man on the ship. They dressed as a privateer would dress. They looked the part of a high-seas robber, but both boys and the father still had their dream to find the exact opening to make their escape.

Jess had lost all hope of ever reaching the original destination and sending for and getting his family together again.

They had been held captives on the vessel for such a long time when they reached the mouth of the Mississippi River. They realized at that point, that if they were ever going to gain their freedom, it would have to be in an area where there were plenty of woods near by, thick with under-brush to conceal their getaway.

Late one afternoon, all hands were gathered on shore. A deer had been caught and roasted on a spit over an open campfire. Jess and his sons were among those enjoying the tender venison. They sat on the ground beneath a moss laden oak tree. It was some time in the season around the New Year.

Jess lifted the piece of rare meat with the point of a whittled off branch he had pulled from a near-by tree. He stuck it in his mouth and as soon as his teeth clinched a good hold on the meat, he pulled the small twig away from his face. He twirled the makeshift utensil around in his hand.

While he chewed, he said to his son Jesse, who sat next to him, "You know son, we've been away from home a long time. I fret over the condition of your mother and those other children. Are they still alive, sick or hurting? What can I do caught up here in this world of ugliness and fear for our lives? We've got to get away from them, somehow, and pretty soon at that. If we don't, I don't know that I can go on much longer. I've kept the hope of getting our family back together as a means of survival all this time, but now I seem to have lost any hope of that ever coming about."

Jesse dislodged a piece of meat from his teeth. He spat it to the ground and responded to his father, "No need to worry about them now, Paw. They're either dead or alive. Not a thing we can do about it. Hell Paw, I want to get away as bad as you do, and we will, just as soon as we get up that big, wide river yonder, we'll do it." He rolled over, found a root for a pillow and went to sleep.

They spent another two months in and around the mouth of the river before the time arose to go up the mighty Mississippi. The contraband was transferred from the larger vessel to a smaller boat for travel up the river to be delivered in the state of Illinois, across the river from St. Louis, Missouri.

The boat sailed under the disguise of a merchant vessel. From the distance of a passing boat, no one could tell what traveled in the water with them. The area around East St. Louis, Illinois, provided cover for the privateers in the lay of the land. There were bays, inlets, and coves to conceal their movements.

On the journey north toward their destination, Jess caught James and Jesse off to themselves on the afternoon of the planned escape. It was one of the few times they had been alone. The boat was much smaller than the ship, so they had to be very careful when they spoke to each other or communicated in any way. The plan had been formed and gone over a dozen times in the last two months. All that was needed was the perfect timing to jump ship and swim out of hearing distance before they were missed.

In the spring of 1860, just before sunset the trio of Swinsons finalized their plans for the journey by water to the shores of America. If all went well, they would leave the contraband vessel as close to midnight as they could judge.

They ate their evening meal in silence. They kept quiet, for fear their anxiety would show. They still feared the Privateer rogues, even after all the time in captivity. Each time they had attempted an escape and been caught, the whippings got worse. No wonder they had a respect for the lash. Although, not enough to prevent them from trying to escape every chance they got.

They had been on good behavior for the past four months. Their hope was that by not creating any disturbance on their part, they could finally make their getaway.

The quietness of the night seemed to be the eeriest it had ever been. Only the snores from the sleeping men and the rustling sound the rats made while rummaging around through the cargo disturbed the stillness. Each Swinson lay dead still in their berths. Not a one of them slept, though they pretended. When the hour arrived, Jess eased the coarse covering from his legs. He watched as his sons followed his move. On hands and knees, they crept past the sleeping men. They took one guarded move at a time. Their hands braced the stairs to prevent the squeaks as they slowly worked their way out of the hole.

The fresh spring air brushed against their faces as they took carefully placed steps across the deck to the Illinois side of the boat. A rough movement in the water caused the boat to jostle and made them nearly lose their footing. They glanced about to see if the night crew had seen them. They could hear the rowdy talk and laughter of the men who were suppose to be on watch. At the moment they were gathered up on the opposite side of the boat from them. They remained still until they realized their safety. They had studied the noise the boat made when in the water and timed their steps to coincide with the noise provided to cover their movement.

They had no choice but to remove their shirts and shoes before leaving the boat. They had no clothing, other than their trousers and belts, no money and no personal identification.

Jess whispered to his sons, who were almost grown men. James was sixteen, while Jesse was fourteen. "We best slide over the rail feet-first. That way we'll make less of a splash when we hit the water." He took a firm grip on the rail and pulled himself up.

"Boys, try to stay together. If we get separated, there's no telling where we'll wind up."

They all slid down together. The water was cold... real cold. It didn't bother them too much. Their adrenaline glands were furnishing them with extra warmth and strength. They moved away from the boat as quietly as they could slide through the water. As soon as they cleared the vessel, they felt their days of slavery were over.

No one spoke, other than to call out now and then to assure they stayed close. James swam with ease, so did Jesse. Their bodies were strong and hard from all the strenuous work they had done in the past two years. Jess kept pace with the boys. He too was in good shape. When they felt they were far enough away from the boat, they rolled over on their backs and floated. The move gave their arms and leg muscles a chance to rest.

Three exhausted souls reached the riverbank at about the same time. Not realizing it, they had swum three miles to reach shore. They crawled up on the bank far enough to get under a low hanging tree branch. They laid down flat on the dirt. It was still dark as daylight was an hour or two away.

Birds flew overhead, singing and chirping. Rabbits hopped near their bodies to inquire about the intrusion of their territory. Other animals crept close to sniff the strange odors that filled their nostrils.

The tired souls slept on. The sun rose and shone brightly all day. The sun was hanging low in the western sky across the river from them when James stirred in his sleep and caused Jess to rouse and sit up.

A still tired man sat there on the ground and rubbed his eyes. He was so disoriented he just sat there and stared out across the water for a while. He couldn't recall a former time in his entire life when he had felt such hunger, plus the awareness of how tired a body could actually be. He started to get up and discovered the muscles in his legs were so sore he could barely straighten them out. So were the muscles in his arms. His back felt as if it had been broken and put back together in different sections.

In his effort to arise, his moans and groans woke both the boys.

"God Almighty! I feel like I'm a hundred years old this morning," he muttered. "Boys, time to rise and shine. Look there, the sun's well up in the sky and a beautiful day 'tis." He waved his hand out toward the river.

James sat still on the ground for a few seconds before he asked his father, "Paw, ain't that Missouri there across the river?" He pointed in front of where they were on the riverbank. "I be damned if we ain't slept the whole day through, the sun's going down, Paw, instead of rising."

James turned to his brother, "How you doing?"

"I'll do."

They took one last, long look at the river before they entered the woods. Not a single living being was in sight in any direction.

Chapter Three

The undergrowth of the woods was thick. The fellows' feet were tender and they felt every prick and nick from the stubble along the way as they walked.

James caught his little toe on a root that stuck out of the earth and it threw him to the ground. The pain was excruciating. He grabbed his foot. He fell to the ground in a sitting position.

"Damn it to hell! My toe is ripped off my foot."

He opened his hand that held the pained foot to look at the wounded toe. A tiny, hairline split was visible between the two toes. Blood oozed from the opening. He grabbed up a handful of loose dirt and rubbed it into the wound.

"I need something to tie around these toes to hold 'em together. The little toe itself feels like it's broke." He rattled off another string of profanity.

His father looked around and found a small vine growing up a tall bush. He pulled it out until he had enough to tie the toes together.

One of the smartest things they had done when they had departed the boat was to take strong sturdy knives along with them. Thanks to the swift hand of James, they each carried a knife. They had swum from the boat to shore with the knives tucked securely between their belts and waists.

Jess pulled his knife from his belt and, with one swift swipe of the blade, cut the vine free from the bush. He stripped all the leaves off the vine and walked over to where his son sat.

"Do you want me to do it, or you do it yourself?"

James reached for the vine and wrapped it around the toes several times and then tied if off. "Makes me so mad to do a hell of a trick like this when all we've got to do is walk." He stood up and put a little weight on the foot.

"Hey! It ain't too bad."

Jess knew he had to find and make some kind of covering for their feet. If not, their feet would be ruined.

The first thing on the agenda was to find food. The trees were tender with new spring growth pushing out new sprouts. Bark pulled from the tree trunks was also a tasty, juicy bite of eating if a person was hungry enough. They found a few tender roots sweet enough to eat. By the time night fell on them, they had filled their bellies and had found a cozy place to sleep the night through.

"We can't get too far from the river now, boys. We will have to have water. We can go without food, but not without water." Jess made the statement then he rolled over and went to sleep.

They had only been awake for three hours, but still so very tired from the long swim. All three of them were asleep within thirty minutes.

The chirping of a nearby bird woke them early the next morning. Jesse sat up with a pain in his gut that let him know his bowels were on the move. He got up quickly and ran for the nearest big tree. He dropped his drawers and squatted on the opposite side of the tree from his companions.

He found a soft wad of green leaves to wipe his behind with. When he returned to where his father sat, he wore a frown on his face. "My guts ain't handling the supper we ate last night none too well. You should o' seen what ran out of me." He reached around and rubbed at his bottom. "I think it took the hide off o' me! It burns like hell!"

By the time he got the statement out of his mouth, a large healthy looking rabbit appeared close to where they sat. Jess eased his knife from his belt. "Shh," he whispered. He looked the rabbit straight in the eye and raised his right arm slowly up over his head. With one thrust, the knife left his hand and sunk into the throat of the rabbit. The dead animal never made a sound; just lay over and quivered a time or two.

"Boys, our breakfast awaits skinning. I can taste him already." Jess went to retrieve his knife and picked up the rabbit. He weighted him by hand. "Yep, there's enough here for all three of us. Get the fire going while I skin 'em."

The fire was started by friction using dry twigs. As the rabbit roasted over the open fire on a spit made from green limbs, Jess cleaned the hide of the rabbit. He stretched it out and pondered aloud, "Will it be enough for two, or just one?"

Both the boys looked over at him wondering what he was mumbling about. He caught the questioning expressions on their faces and said,

"I was wondering if this hide would make one shoe, or two. Think I'd better try for one." He laid the hide near the fire to dry out.

The aroma of the rabbit cooking over the open fire was more than they could stand. They were so hungry, that they started to pull pieces off the carcass before it was done. By the time it had cooked through, they had picked every morsel of meat from the bones and gnawed the juices out of them.

"I was wrong. It wasn't enough to curb our hunger. There'll be another one along before too long. We'll fill our bellies and make each of us makeshift shoes from the hides," the father remarked.

Wild animals were plentiful throughout the woods. They were not used to having humans in their domain, so they were a little careless about wandering out in the clearings, making it somewhat easier for the hunters to kill them.

At the close of the fourth day, shoes of a sort were on each of their feet. Dried meat hung on vines from their belts. They got a little tired of rabbit meat, so on the second day they had gone for young deer and wild turkey.

They had used their knives to shape spears from strong, willowy limbs off low growing tree branches. The spears turned out to also be a dandy means to catch a fish, if they were patient enough and skillful with the spear.

Fish was a welcome change in their diet. One night, when they were sitting around the campfire waiting for the fish to roast on the spit, Jess made the statement,

"What I wouldn't give for a beautiful polished dinner table sitting right there," he pointed to a clearing in the nearby woods, "covered with a fine, Irish linen table cloth. On that table, there is a spread of Yorkshire ham, and finnan haddie. Oh, what I would give for a haggis."

The boys looked at him as if he had gone mad. "Paw, what ever in this world made you think of foods from the Gods?

When what we've got to eat, is grub from the earth?" Jesse asked. "A fittin' meal would probably make us all sick," he added.

They had remained in the same area of the river where they first swam ashore. They were rested up and fit for travel at the end of the fifth day. It was time to move on toward their future. They had shoes on their feet, food on their belts and a determination to conquer the world before them.

"If we walk with the river to our left we should be headed toward the east. East Saint Louis should be straight ahead of us. We'll have to be careful. I don't know how long the privateers were to remain here in the area. No more than ten days though. We'll only go to the river under the cover of darkness, in case they decide to look for us on their way back to New Orleans," Jess said to the boys.

They walked until they were completely spent. After resting and eating, they continued to walk. They had no idea how many days they had traveled. Each time they heard a noise they stopped dead still in their tracks until they learned where the noise had come from.

They were three ragged human beings. Their appearance was enough to scare another human into running. They had been on foot for several days when they approached a clearing. James leaned against a tree while the other two found a place to lay down to rest. "Looks like a family lives over there," he said nonchalantly. He reached up and yanked a twig from the tree he leaned against. He stripped the foliage from it, stuck it in his mouth, and continued, "Paw, you know I could slip in there and see if they have anything we could use. Maybe there are some shoes and trousers and a piece of bread would fit right nicely between my teeth, long about now. What cha say, Paw?"

Jess had reached a point in his life where he questioned his belief in right and wrong. He had lived an upright and wholesome way all his life. He had been his brother's keeper. He had worshipped, prayed, and tithed his earnings. He had done what his church had taught him to do. What had gone wrong?

He rubbed his brow with his hard-callused hand. "Do what you must."

They stayed in the thicket near the clearing for the remainder of the day. Under nightfall, James left the security of the woods and walked toward the house. His father and brother waited in dread for what would occur. They both realized that James had learned the art of stealing and, with the knowledge of thievery he had stored under his head of blonde hair; it should come in handy for him as he went on this dangerous trek.

James had spotted clothes hanging on a clothesline earlier in the day. He had also made a mental note that a smokehouse was located a hundred feet or so from the main house, where the unsuspecting family lay sleeping. The one thing he did not like about the situation was the dogs he'd seen hanging around the house. He had caught sight of two and hoped that was all.

Jess and Jesse heard the barks from the dogs and knew James had done his damage. They also knew the dogs were on the move. They noticed the vibrations in the yips as the dogs ran. Soon, they heard the sound of James' feet as they hit the ground. He ran with the speed of a cheetah.

The shotgun blast, echoed through the night, from the direction of the house.

James was several hundred feet ahead of the dogs. When he entered the edge of the woods, he found Jess and Jesse ready to greet the dogs. "Damnation and hellfire, stop 'em sons-of-bitches, now!" He was so out of breath, the words escaped his throat in gasps.

Jess and Jesse stood behind trees. When James passed them, they kept a sharp eye on the dogs in the pale moonlight. They each held a thick slab of a broken tree limb, raised high over their heads. When the dogs neared them, the limbs came down hard across the heads of the animals. The force of the blows knocked the dogs unconscious. Jess stooped long enough to check the animals. He would never hurt another man's dog if he didn't have a real good reason. The dogs were still alive, so he dropped his weapon and took off in a run to catch up with his sons.

The low growing branches and bushes tangled in their feet and tore at their flesh.

"Come on, Paw, run like the devil himself was after you," James mockingly chided his father.

When they decided it was safe to stop, they fell to the ground in a heavy sweat. Each man panted and took deep gulps of air to settle their lungs.

"James, me boy, you will be the death of me yet," Jess spat at his son.

James laid his loot on the straw in front of him. "This ham is what nearly done me in. When I closed the smokehouse door, the hinges squeaked. Up until then, the dogs had not caught scent of me. The noise roused them up to take chase of me. I all ready had these britches and this sheet." He spread out the stolen articles.

The sheet was a welcome sight. It could be torn into squares and used for handkerchiefs. The weather seemed to get warmer every day. Sweat was a bothersome aggravation, continually running down their faces as they trekked through the woods.

James lifted the trousers up and commented, "I don't know if they'll fit any of us or not. I didn't have too much choice."

There were three pairs of homemade trousers, all too big for them, but it made no difference. They put them on and tightened up their belts to keep them up. Their chests remained bare. "Next trip, I'll come back with shirts and, pretty soon, there'll be real shoes on our feet."

He brought out his knife and cut a plug out of the smoked ham. With it still on the tip of the knife, he offered it to his father followed by a chunk for his brother. The ham had been smokehouse cured to exactly the right degree, allowing it to be eaten without further cooking. The skin was tossed in the woods. The ham lasted for two days. They ate it for breakfast, dinner, and supper as long as it lasted. To have the taste of salt in their mouths again was heaven sent.

A big storm built up and it began to rain. The rain fell in sheets. The ground became soft and muddy. Their homemade shoes got slick, making it hard to walk. They had no idea how much farther they had to travel to reach their destination. They didn't even know what their destination was. Jess decided they should find a tree with enough foliage to shield them from the rain, climb up the tree, and wait out the storm. They sat in the tree until their tail bones felt as if they were cracked.

It was midmorning the next day, before the storm let up. They were soaked to the skin and chilled to the bone. The days were rather warm but the nights got rather chilly. They scaled down from the tree in a heavy shiver from the coolness.

Every stick and twig in the surrounding woods were soaking wet which left no way to get a fire going. The one bright hope was that the sun came out and began to warm them up.

They had made leggings from dried deer hide and fastened pieces of the dried hide to their belts to use as shoes when needed. The first thing they did when they reached the wet ground was to fashion new shoes. The ones on their feet were sloppy wet and stunk beyond carrion.

James continued to ranshack every home they came across on the journey. He took only those items they were in desperate need of. Jess and Jesse could not get up the nerve to boldly enter into another person's home and rob a man of his belongings. However, they didn't find it too hard to accept and enjoy the things James brought to them.

"Just tell me the difference. I do the stealing and you two enjoy the results. By damn, you're as guilty as I am. If one of us didn't pilfer and get a few items we have to have, what would we do? Just you go on and tell me. What would become of us? I'll tell you, I don't feel one minute's guilt about what I'm doing. As long as I don't get caught, I ain't worrying one damn little bit about it."

It took them a little more than two months to reach East Saint Louis, Illinois. When they entered the edge of town, they were dressed as proper men of the working force. Jess was clean-shaven, and each head of hair trimmed to a respectable length, which was the handiwork of James and his talents. It was a welcome sight to see and mingle with humans again. People they were not afraid of, for one reason or another.

They walked passed a cafe, with odors from the kitchen floating out into the street where they walked. It was all they could do to keep up their pace of walking.

"That's the first thing I'm going to do, when I get my hands on some money, is go in there and eat my gut full of good food," Jesse uttered.

Water drooled from his mouth he was so hungry. He licked his lips as if to savor the taste of the aroma.

As Jess and his sons walked a small group of young women passed by them. Jess had no interest in the female race at the moment. James and Jesse could not take their eyes off them. James ran smack into a post that held up a canopy in front of a street front business.

He reared back and rubbed his chest and head. "Damn it to hell that hurt!" He clinched his fist up and hit the post a solid blow. Blood oozed from his skinned knuckles. He licked the blood from his fingers and looked to see where the girls were. They had walked on out of sight.

Jesse was laughing. He'd seen his brother headed straight for the post and never said a word to warn him.

"Ha! Ha! Ha! I think you stayed in the woods too long brother."

He slapped the sides of his legs and laughed some more. Jess took it all in stride and continued to walk on. He was looking for a place to seek employment.

They each found jobs on the very same day they arrived in East Saint Louis in the stockyards. As soon as the boss learned that Jess was an educated man, he put him to work in the office. The boys with their strong, virile bodies were placed on the yard.

They slept in the open until receiving their first pay. On that day, Jess sent Jesse to locate rooms for them to sleep in. James was sent to the mercantile to purchase much needed clothing. Jess went to a local store and bought paper and pencil. He walked to a small park, not too far from the stockyards, and found a bench to sit on.

It had been so long since he had left his Lillian and smaller children, that he found it hard to put his feelings on paper. He penned the letter with emotional distress. He walked to the nearest post office. Before he sealed the letter, he slipped five dollars inside the envelope. He held it close to his heart for a moment. He then handed it to the man behind the counter.

Jess' work was not hard on his body, only his back and his mind. He had been outside in the fresh air for so long that he found it tiresome to sit indoors all day. He missed the sunshine on his back and the raindrops when caught in a sudden shower. Being indoors all day was a drastic change for him. He was still a farmer at heart.

Both the boys adapted to their routines with no problems. Each was a good worker. Earning his pay was a bit different for James. He tried and kept himself from pilfering while on the job. Jesse was just simply pleased to be back in civilization again.

They had not been at work too long before Jess decided he was not cut out for inside work. After two months passed Jess started looking around for other jobs for him and his sons. He had almost lost hope of ever farming again.

Summer turned into fall and the weather turned off cold early in the season.

Jess went to the post office every day after work. It had been about four months since he had mailed the letter to Lillian. Each day the postal clerk shook his head when Jess asked for his hoped for letter. The clerk had learned who he was and looked forward to seeing him and even calling him by name.

In early October, Jess pushed the door to the post office open to be met by a smiling clerk.

"Good evening, Mr. Swinson. It came today." The clerk extended his arm and placed the letter in Jess' hand.

"Thank you, and thanks be to God. I was so afraid there would be no letter." He glanced down at the letter in his hand. It was not Lillian's handwriting. His heart skipped a beat or two. A bold, self-assured hand had written the address on the envelope.

He looked back at the clerk. His heart sank. He thanked the clerk again and turned to leave the building. The clerk had no way to know the pain Jess felt when he walked away from him.

He tucked the letter deep inside the breast pocket of his coat. He then pulled his collar up around his neck to ward off the cold air.

When he got to the rented room, he found both boys there. They had stopped at the cafe on the way home from work and brought food with them for their supper.

"Boys, I got a letter today from Ireland," he spoke slowly. "I've not opened it yet. I'm afraid it's not from your mother."

He sat down heavily in one of the three chairs in the room and tore the flap loose from the envelope.

The letter had been written by the pastor of the church located near where he had left his family. Jess did not know the man. The letter told of how Lillian and the five babies had died. The house had caught fire during the night. They had perished; burned to death without any lingering suffering. It had happened about six months after Jess and the boys departed Ireland for America. The pastor they had known and loved had also died a year before Jess' letter had arrived from America.

The pastor went on to say that, the Irish postal service had tracked him down to see if he would write to the family in America and relate the news of their deaths. The money Jess had sent along in the letter to his wife had been used to help defray the expense of the funerals of his family members, though a little late, it was helpful to the church.

The pastor extended his regrets at having to send such sad news to him and the boys and signed the letter *Respectfully, Reverend Michael O'Hara.*

Jess sat there in the chair for hours before he undressed and went to bed. He was a broken man. The hurt he felt was beyond description.

When he had first come to town, he had quickly found a church, and had gone faithfully to the weekly services. He had volunteered his time to several activities in the church work field. He tithed his weekly pay. He urged his boys to attend the services with him when he first started to go, but left them alone when he knew they had no interest in the church or God. After the night he read the letter from Reverend O'Hara, he ceased all contact with the church.

The winter was hard, long, and the coldest weather they had ever lived through. Both brothers learned the number and street addresses of every brothel within walking distance of their menial home. They were frequent visitors to the houses of ill fame every weekend. They continued to drink alcoholic beverages and often times arrived home late at night for the father to put to bed.

Jess spent his hours mostly at home alone, reading books from the library or whittling. He took up the hobby of whittling when they had spent the month in the woods before reaching East Saint Louis.

On a clear nice day, he took walks back to the woods to find the right kind of trees to gather wood from to do his whittling. When he got a good number of figures whittled to his own perfection, he went uptown to the streets where small shops were located. He found a buyer for his wares. He sold all he could hand carve. The money he made from the sales he stuck back in a safe place.

He was quite thrifty. Really, he was tight with his money. He was determined to leave the job at the stockyard as soon as he could secure a better-suited position.

In late spring of the following year, Jess and the boys stopped off at a tavern on the way home from work one night. They had lived in the rented room for about a year and had become accustomed to a few of the local habits.

They sat and drank their brews in silence. From the other end of the bar, a conversation was in progress that caught their attention. One of the men was overheard to say that a surveyor company was in the process of hiring two crews of men to go out and make maps of the United States.

Jess' ears perked up to catch every word of the conversation. He finished his drink and then walked over to the other end of the bar where the man doing the talking sat.

"Where might a body get in touch with this company?" he asked ever so politely.

"Down at the docks. But unless you have the right kind of learning under your hair, there's no need to waste your time applying for the work," the rowdy, tough looking man replied.

Early the next morning found the three Swinsons waiting in line by the makeshift office of the Leeway Surveying Company. Jess' education, and what he had taught the boys throughout the years, paid off. They each got a position with the company. They were to report to work with their belongings packed and ready to mount the company horses at daybreak on the next Monday morning. That gave them five days to resign their jobs with the stockyard and ready themselves for a new outlook on life.

The next Monday morning found them at their scheduled places at the appropriate time. To their dismay, they learned that James had been assigned to the crew headed out west. Jess and Jesse were to go south.

There was nothing to do but go where they were assigned to go. Jess took his son James aside and said to him, "Son, I don't know what to do about this predicament. I never thought to request that we all three be put on the same crew. I failed to foresee this occurring. You are your own man as of today. You make the choice of whether you go west with the company or stay here. I hate this like the devil for us to be split up, but our family life is gone, never to return."

James' mind had to be made up quickly. Men were mounting the horses and the crews were ready to leave town.

James was a headstrong, hard drinking, loud mouthed, profanity speaking young man of seventeen and a half years old. He was strong in body, tall in stature, and quite handsome. He was a bit excited about the thought of heading west. He had heard stories of the growth toward California. He made a snap decision to go with the crew he was assigned to.

He took his fathers hand and drew him close to his chest. "Paw, I'm sorry our lives have taken this turn, but hell, Paw, we can't stop living just because we don't like the way things are going. I'll be all right. After a year of slinging horse and cow manure, I'm more than ready for some raw, exciting adventures." He released his father and turned to his brother. "Well little brother, it's time for us to make a parting of our ways. You take care of yourself and see to paw, now. He's not a young man any longer. We both know he lives with a broken heart. I don't know how we can keep in touch, but I promise if there's a way I'll find you one day."

Jesse got up on his horse and turned to James, "Remember the vow Paw made before God the day we left Ireland." James remembered the vow vividly and tipped his hat.

The crews got their horses on the move. Each man rode proudly in the saddle. When they got to the edge of town, James' crew rode toward the Mississippi river, where they would cross over to the western side, while the others turned left on the road that would take them south. Before they were out of sight of each other, they twisted in their saddles, for one final farewell wave.

The weather was on the way to becoming hot by the time they reached the borderline separating Illinois from Kentucky. Their work began when they reached the Kentucky state line.

The work was slow and time consuming, but very interesting to Jess and his son. It felt good to use their brains and muscles, all in a day's work.

They knew nothing about the detailed works of surveying or recording the information to apply to maps. They were each quick to learn. Within a month's time either one of them could have shown Sam Potts, the boss, a thing or two on how to speed up the work and be more accurate, but decided it best to keep quiet and follow Sam's way of doing things.

They lived in the woods when too far from a town or settlement. On a few occasions, they ran up on a family living in the woods here and there, scattered around on the mountainsides. Most of the families' means of livelihood was usually that of moonshiners making illegal whiskey.

Jesse relished in the news every time they ran up on a mountain man who ran a still. He recalled back to the first time he purchased a jar of the white lightnin'. He had taken a big swig and it nearly lifted the top of his head off, but, oh, how he liked the affects it gave him. Over a period of time his drinking continued and the sting was not near as strong as when he took those first drinks.

On one bright sunshiny morning, they were out early at work when Jesse tilted his head back and sniffed the air. "What in the name of God is that I smell?"

Sam too had caught the odor. As soon as Jesse asked the question, Sam threw back his head in a healthy round of laughter.

"My boy that is a pole cat and that is just his friendly aroma. You'd best hope he don't get close enough to you to use his green mist weapon on you."

Sam was so tickled that he continued to laugh for a while. Jess and his son held their noses to prevent smelling the odor.

There were five men on the crew and each man did all the jobs at one time or another. On this one particular day, it was Jesse's turn to shrub a path in the dense undergrowth for the tripods to be put in place. After Jesse had cleared a good swath, his father busied himself setting up the tripods. While he leveled it off, Jesse continued to shrub the path needed for their work. He worked his way through the bushes and small trees until his arms ached. He decided to sit beneath a nearby tree to rest for a spell. He lowered himself down slowly and let the bush ax lean against the tree trunk.

The bush ax started to slide, and before he could get a grip on the handle, it fell on down beside the tree where a stand of thick, low growing bushes grew.

"Dammed thing can't stay where I put it." He half stood and twisted to reach for the handle when the mist hit him. He had not seen the polecat, it had been hidden in the under brush at the base of the tree trunk.

He clinched his eyes tight and backed up. "Paw! Paw! Come a running. Something has sprayed all over me."

The fresh mist from the pouch of the skunk was so strong it reeked. Jesse didn't recognize it at first as the same odor he had smelled earlier.

He wiped his eyes and face with his shirtsleeve. When he opened his eyes they burned so fiercely, he snapped them shut again. "I be dammed if I don't think I'm blinded Paw. Paw! Where are you Paw?"

His father had smelled the odor when the skunk had first sprayed the mist. It was almost more than he could do to go to his son. He snatched his handkerchief from his back pocket and pressed it tightly over his nose. The strong scent penetrated the thin material and nearly gagged Jess when he neared the boy.

He stooped over and picked up a good-sized limb that Jesse had thrown to the side. With his tough, gloved hands, he stripped off all the twigs. He extended the limb out until it almost touched Jesse.

"Take a good grip on this stick." He touched his sons hand with the limb, "I'll lead you back to the supply wagon. I'll be danged if I can stand to get any closer to you boy." The stench was breath taking.

Father led son as slowly and carefully as possible to the wagon, where another man was stirring the stew pot filled with their noon meal.

"Whoa up there!" he yelled as soon as he got a whiff of the polecat odor. He knew in an instant what the scene had been with Jesse and the skunk. "Ha! Ha! Ha! I see one of them got 'cha. Grab a chunk of that lye soap over there. It's lying there on the tailgate. You'll find a rag hanging on a nail on the side of the wagon," he pointed to where the rag hung.

Jess held his breath and washed the boys face and eyes. After several rinses, Jesse opened his eyes and blinked them a time or two. They stilled burned like the dickens and his vision was somewhat blurred.

As soon as he got his eyes adjusted so he could see a little better, he literally ripped the clothes off his body. He stood there buck-naked before all the men who had gathered up to see what the commotion was all about. The men, including his father, were so tickled they could not control their laughter.

"Laugh, damn ya! I don't find one damn thing funny about the son-of-a-bitching mess I'm in."

He snatched the rag and lye soap up and headed for the creek filled with cold water running down from the mountainside. The water was cold… real cool to his body. He paid no attention to the temperature of the water. He sat down flat on the bottom of the creek with the running water sloshing around him. By the time he had worked up a good lather of soap on the rag, he was so mad he could be heard all the way back to the wagon. He put pressure on the rag as he washed the upper portion of his body.

"I'll kill every damn pole cat in the state of Kentucky! I ain't ever had such a stint stuck to me in such a nasty fashion. Damn it to hell and back!"

After he had applied soap to all parts of his body, he laid down the entire length of his body in the running water, allowing it to rinse over him. When he stood up, he could still smell the odor. He lathered and re-lathered himself three times before he was satisfied.

He walked up from the creek, dripping wet. He was still mad and fuming. He rummaged through the wagon and located his satchel, withdrew a fresh change of clothing and stepped in his trousers.

"Now I'll have to buy another round of work clothes."

Sam spoke up and said, "You shore will need new clothes. It's a well-established fact you can't wash the stench out of any kind of material. You may as well burn 'em clothes you got misted in right now. That's about the only way you can git rid of the odor." He laid his instrument against the wagon and poured a big cup of water from the cooling jug.

He took a big swallow and continued, "I've heard say, that the local Indians use pole cat oil to ward off the mosquitoes. It oughta be good for something, huh?"

Jesse picked up a long stick and started to push the offensive clothes into the fire under the stew pot.

"Hey! Wait up there young fellow! Don't put 'em under the food. Drag 'em off yonder away from camp to burn 'em," the cook of the day exclaimed.

It took days for him to overcome the ordeal with the skunk. Every time he heard a noise in the bushes, he stopped what he was doing and looked carefully in and around where the noise had come from. He got a whiff of the odor many times after that occasion.

He said to his father, "I'll never forget what a dammed pole cat smells like for as long as I live."

They stayed in the woods and forests most of the time. Sam told them that when the weather turned off cold and it rained or snowed, or other winter climates came, they couldn't do much work outside.

"That's when we go to the nearest town or settlement and get all the information we have recorded in ledgers. Now you men don't go and think that just because we're not in the woods there won't be work to do. There's plenty to keep your heads bent over those pages for days. Your nights will be your own."

Summer eased into fall with mild weather hanging on. The Swinsons marveled at the colors that abounded around them. Neither one of them was much of a beauty seeker, but what God did to the mountain side in the fall of the year was enough to make the toughest man stop for a few moments and admire the breathtaking view spread out before him.

Late October, they walked their horses into the town of Maysville, Kentucky. The crew of men was tired and dirty. The first thing they did was find a bathhouse and from there a cafe for a good hearty meal.

They rented three rooms in a boarding house where they were offered two meals a day and a change of bed clothing once a week. They would have to find their breakfast in one of the local cafes.

Two of the rooms were for sleeping with four men in one of the rooms. Two men were to sleep in each of the double beds. The boss chose to sleep alone in the smaller room. The largest room was used as an office for the many hours of paper work.

The first morning after sleeping in a bed, Jess woke up early. He got up and stretched.

"Wake up boy. It's time to get a move on. I myself could lay there and sleep a while longer. I had almost forgotten what clean, fresh sheets smelled and felt like."

He gathered up his dirty clothes and stuffed them under his arm.

"You need to do the same. Get you soiled clothes together and we can drop them off at the washer woman's house on the way to the cafe where we'll find our breakfast." He placed his hat on his freshly combed hair and headed for the door. "I'll wait for you out on the front porch. Get a fire under your laziness, you hear?"

Working inside all day was almost a welcome change from what they had done all spring and summer. There was still enough daylight left in the day after work hours to explore the streets and surroundings of Maysville.

It took Jesse less than a week to locate the house of ill fame. It was simply called *Marge's*. One night, when he came home a little earlier than usual from a visit to the house of Marge, he found his father home alone. "Paw, don't you ever feel the need of a woman? There's some of the best over at Marge's." He pulled a chair away from the wall and sat near his father.

He sat with his stomach against the back of the chair. "Come on Paw. Go with me next Friday night. It' been so long since you lay with a female. I'm here to tell you, it'll make a different man out o' you."

Jess was a tired man, not so much from the work he did, but from life itself. He spent many of his leisure hours in meditation, recalling his life with Lillian and those children who had lost their lives at such an early age. All burned alive. How his heart ached for the feel of her soft body close to him, her mouth pressed to his. At times, he could almost smell the scent of her. The aroma of a certain flower, or a bloom from a tree would put out an odor that reminded him of the scents she wore when she dressed up in her finery.

Something deep within Jess had died when he got the news from Ireland that she was dead. He hadn't paid it that much mind at the time, but since then he'd not felt the need or the want of another woman.

He looked directly at his son and said, "No, I can't say that I do need one of those trollops. Son, your mother and I had something wonderful in our marriage. Our love for each other exploded every time we came together in our lovemaking. I haven't found a woman that makes me feel even the tiniest bit like I want to roll around in bed with her. I don't know son. Maybe that part of me is dead. I've heard of it happening to men."

"Damn, I shore hope it don't happen to me. There's nothing greater on this earth than a good roll with a hot loving woman. They feel so good all cuddled up next to a man."

Jess was still a very handsome species of a man. His hair thick, while graying a little here and there. With all the fresh air and sunshine he had lived and worked in for the past couple of years, it gave him a look of brawn and distinction. He carried his body straight and proud, almost like that of a twenty-five year old. His muscles would match those of Jesse's at any arm wrestling bout. He had found a way to keep his teeth clean and sparkling way back when they spent the time in the woods after their daring swim to shore from the rogue vessel.

One day while he was gathering some wood for a campfire, he pulled a small branch off one of the larger black gum tree limbs. He worked it around between his fingers a time or two. He figured out that it was strong and limber at the same time. He lifted it up to his nose and the odor was pleasant enough. With his knife, he trimmed off the rough edges where he had torn it from the limb. He then cut the handle part to about the length of his hand He admired his work. Then skinned the green bark from the length of the twig and stuck it in his mouth. He wallowed it around in his mouth with the aid of his tongue for while, and then he decided to chew on it. Tenderly, he worked his teeth on the soft twig. The taste was only a little offensive but to his liking. He found the chewed bristle turned into a brush-like instrument. Voila! A toothbrush.

He used a little fine sand to work the yellowing slime from his teeth with a gentle slow movement of the toothbrush. He found that the sensation of clean teeth made him feel better all over.

The next time he made a brush, he heated the wood before he skinned it. That was all it needed to take the bad taste out of the wood. The boys each made toothbrushes for themselves and used the same cleanser that their father did. The sand was too harsh, so they only used it once a week. When Jess arrived in East Saint Louis, he bought a bag of salt and a box of baking soda. He combined the two ingredients to make the cleaner for their teeth.

From then on, when their store bought tooth powder ran out, they just fixed up a batch of Jess' mixture to keep their teeth clean and healthy. The remedy was passed on to Sam Potts and other crewmembers.

By the last week in February, all the paper work was completed and packaged, ready for shipment back to the home office in East Saint Louis. They took it to the railroad station and shipped it by freight.

Supplies were bought and new work clothes picked out, purchased, and packed in their satchels. The horses, which had patiently waited in the livery stables, were brought out and curried, hooves trimmed and taken to the black smith for new shoes. They had fattened up over the winter months from little activity aside from a Sunday afternoon outing now and then.

They left Maysville and worked their way south in the state of Kentucky. When they neared the border of Tennessee, they turned west and surveyed to the western border of Kentucky. From there they moved south, down into Tennessee. It took them until November to work across the state to the eastern border near Bristol, Tennessee. There in Bristol, they repeated the process of recording their work and got it shipped to the home office.

Jess had heard some 'Hill--Billy' music off and on throughout the time he had worked through the mountains, but nothing to compare with the amount he heard in Bristol. Some times when he sat and listened to the hum and whine of the banjo, mandolin and guitars, their combined sound reminded him of the bagpipes he had come to love while living in Scotland. At times, he would go to the house from where the music came, pay his five cents to get in, then sit and listen to the hum of the strings with his eyes closed. He would daydream of days gone by. Jesse also learned to like and appreciate the mountain music.

Jesse bought himself a handmade guitar and spent many an hour picking and strumming but he never accomplished the art. Not once did he get a proper tune to escape the strings of the instrument. He gave up the pastime by the time spring arrived the following year and sold the guitar.

When it was time to leave Bristol, Jess needed to be alone for a while. He took a long walk in the nearby woods. When he knew he was out of sight of every living soul, he undid his belt and pushed his trousers down enough to unfasten and pull out his money belt. He had purchased the belt in East Saint Louis. He had added cash to it since his first pay from the stockyard.

With all he had saved from his salaries and from the sale of the hand carved figurines, which he still continued to do while he worked in the woods, he was amazed at the amount he had collected and now counted. He would go to a bank when in town and change small bills for larger ones. That way, it took up less room in the money belt.

Jesse had no idea his father was saving money. He himself started to spend his money just as soon as he got to town. Oh, he would always buy his personal items and things he needed for work but whatever else money was left he spent on whisky and women.

It was a clear, crisp morning when they left Bristol headed east toward the border of North Carolina.

"Will these mountains never run out? I'm ready to walk with both my feet on level ground. I could never have imagined there were so many miles of mountains and hills in the entire world," Jesse complained a few days after they got into North Carolina.

Sam Potts explained to him that there were still plenty of those hills to climb yet before they walked on flat land again. "Oh, about halfway from here to the ocean, the hills play out and the land is rolling for a while. The closer you get to the ocean the flatter the land gets. Why I've been told that you can drop a ball and it'll stay right where you drop it."

"That's where I want to go and stay. I've had enough of these mountains to last me a life time," Jesse remarked. "How about them pole cats? Do they live in this state too?" Jesse asked with interest.

"You won't find as many of 'em here, but be on the lookout for snakes. They grow big and mean. Most of the time, you don't know they're about until you're right up on one. Just watch your step."

"Snakes!" Jesse shouted. "If it ain't one damn thing it's another. I'd go back to Ireland if I had half a chance."

He learned what snakes were all about before the summer was over. They had killed enough to stock a snake farm. They had quickly learned to keep an eye on the ground when there was a place large enough for one of the dreaded critters to hide.

With a lot of luck, none of them got bitten, though there were several close calls.

"I'd rather tangle up with one of these snakes any day compared to them pesky pole cats," Jesse stated one day, soon after he had shot the head off a big rattler.

The spring and early summer of 1862 passed with nothing much happening, other than mosquito bites, skinned arms, cheeks, and necks. It was hard to avoid the broken tree limbs, and at times one of the men got a nasty scrape from one of the branches.

While on an errand to the nearest settlement to purchase supplies, Jesse heard the news of the War Between the States. Before he loaded the wagon for his return to the campsite, he enlisted in the army to serve his new country and seek adventure. He felt there would be excitement on the road ahead of him while he served a term with the army. The young man was sixteen years old.

Upon arriving back at camp, his first words to his father were, "Paw, I joined the army today. I go back tomorrow to leave with the other joiners. I'm in Company L, Regiment 67." It was August 17, 1862.

He left early the next morning for his adventures of war. Jess was saddened to see the boy leave. He was so young, though aged for the times. Jesse was as big as any full-grown man.

Jess continued to work for the company. Jesse wrote to his father through out his term in the army, using the surveyors head office as an address to keep in touch with him.

At Jesse's return from the war, he rejoined his father and the company of mapmakers. He came home from the war with no scars of battle, only two years older. As an adult man, he took up his life almost where he had left off.

His father had kept all his clothes, hoping for the return of his son. The shoes fit his feet as good as they did the day he had left. The pants and shirts proved to be too tight. His body had thickened up during the time he was away. First on the agenda was a trip to the nearest town for new clothes that fit. Otherwise, the War Between the States did little to change their lives.

Chapter Four

Jess and Jesse sat talking quietly with each other late one afternoon when the work was finished for the day. "Paw, I don't know that I'm completely satisfied with this line of work we're in, are you?" He picked up a straw particle and broke it into tiny pieces.

"No," was his father's response.

"How are we going to find what we want, if we spend all our time climbing around in the woods from state to state? It's interesting enough work, and I do appreciate the pay that comes with it, but somehow I find that I want to do something else," Jesse continued.

"If we keep our eyes and ears alert, we might just hear about some land that we can get our hands on to build a small farm. That's what I want to get into again. I need to feel the earth in my palms. To see green shoots sprouting out of the ground from seeds that I put in it. What I wouldn't give to stand and look out over a field of green growth waving back and forth in the spring breeze. That is, on my own land, I'm talking about. I'd gather me up some animals and fill the yard with chickens. How does fresh eggs for breakfast every morning sound to you?" Jess asked his son as he dreamed aloud.

"Damn it to hell Paw, why does our lives have to be so messed up?"

Jess had long ago ceased to correct his son's language. He cringed beneath his skin each time he heard the foul words leave Jesse's mouth. It was as if the profanity was part of his learned language and he could not control the use of it.

Jess felt he knew enough perfect English words to carry on a conversation without the use of profanity. He never took God's name in vain, though he had failed to give the Lord any praise since the news of the sudden death of his family members.

The sun had begun its descent in the west and cook of the day had the evening meal almost ready to ladle from the pot.

Father and son continued to set on the ground, with their backs at rest against two large trees.

"I wonder where James is today." Jess asked the question out of thin air. "For some reason, he's been on my mind lately. I wish there was some way we could hear from him. I have a feeling deep down that he too, is lost to us."

Suppertime was called and they went to the makeshift table where they ate heartily of the rabbit stew.

The leaves had begun their annual change of color. It still took Jess by surprise that so much beauty could develop, in slow motion, over a period of a week or two. Jesse never paid much attention to the glorious scenery that surrounded them.

By the first week in November, they were ready to pack up and leave the woods for the year. The nearest town was Clinton, North Carolina. The ground was so much smoother in Sampson County than the areas they had covered since they had begun their adventure with the Surveyor Company.

Winter weather set in before the season arrived. A light snow fell during the first week of December. The crew spent all the day light hours confined to their work. There were a lot of figures and numbers to be recorded. Since the land had leveled out in areas, more territory had been covered than had been in the previous summers.

One night Jess went to the nearest cafe for his supper. Jesse had not finished his work for the day when his father got through, so Jess decided to go on without him. He was tired and quite hungry.

He stepped up on the porch of the cafe at the same time as that of a stranger to Jess. The stranger tipped his hat and said, very politely, "Evening to you."

Jess in turn did the same thing. "Evening to you, sir. Supper smells good tonight, don't it?" They walked on in and took a seat at the same table. A fine relationship developed during the meal.

Jess told his new friend what he and his son had done for the past several years. He went on to relate the story of his life and all their hardships endured throughout their travels.

"I'm tired now and need to settle down and get my roots set in. Live a life a man ought to have."

Jesse joined them in the cafe before they finished eating. He ordered from the menu hand printed on a big board that hung on the wall in plain sight. He ambled on over to where his father sat with the stranger. "How's the grub tonight Paw?"

"Not bad. I can always eat chicken and pastry. The dry beans ain't bad either." He lifted up a piece of the bread he had been eating and asked of the stranger, "What is this bread made of? It has a good and interesting taste to it." Jess wanted to know.

"That, my friend, is pone bread. It's made from homegrown corn. Ground up at the local gristmill. You throw a little flour and salt in the bowl along with the meal, that's what the corn is called after its ground up. Then you pour in enough water to get a good, smooth mixture. Pour it in an iron spider, greased heavily with hog lard. Stick it in a hot oven and bake it 'til its golden brown."

Jess savored the taste with a good-sized slab of fresh churned butter. "You know a man could make a meal from this, if he had a big pitcher of butter-milk to go along with it."

Jesse discovered that he liked the pone bread also. "I've eat a lot of different and downright strange food since we arrived on the shores of America. I found a lot of them to my liking. Others I'd just as soon not have ever again." He twisted the piece of bread around in his hand and added, "I think I'll remember the recipe for cooking this. It's good. Yea, it's good and tasty all right."

After they finished with their supper, the three of them walked out to the porch of the cafe and had a seat on the bench that sat on there year round. It was rather chilly, so they pulled their coats up snugly close to their necks and pushed their hands deep down into their pockets.

Jess looked at the stranger and wondered why neither one of them had introduced themselves. He pondered on it for a while and thought he might as well be first. He pulled his hand from his pocket and extended it toward the man, who sat on the other side of Jesse.

"My name's Jess Swinson, and this here is my son, Jesse." He spoke with a heavy dialectic brogue, a mixture of

Scottish and Irish dialect. Jesse's was more of the Irish brogue. He had lost most of his Scottish brogue, from his years of living in Ireland. They had picked up a new way of saying some of their words just in the few short years they had been in America. They found it easier to go along with the slur of the English language, like so many other people were doing in this new land.

The man shook his hand with a strong grip, "Glad to make your acquaintance. I'm Straw Wilson." He held on to Jess' hand and continued, "Well, that ain't my name, but am called Straw. My given name is Francis. I'd fight the man that called me that today. My ma gave me the nick name because as a youngin' I was always chewing on a piece of straw."

It got too cold to set on the porch any longer, so they rose to leave. "You want to meet us here for breakfast in the morning?" Jess asked before they said goodnight.

"Shore. I usually get here around six o'clock."

They ate most of their meals together for the rest of the week. After one supper hour, Jesse invited Straw to go along to the local tavern with him and his father. He agreed to go. The weather was cold enough to feel the need of a good stiff drink or two.

They sat and shared stories of good and bad times. Straw was a traveling man. Picking up work where he could find it. All he owned was a spare set of clothes, his horse and saddle, and a world of knowledge. He called it that because he felt he had done and seen all there was for a man to see and do.

At one point in the late night conversation, Jess brought up the subject of farming. They had had enough drink to feel relaxed and carefree. He spoke again of his desire to get back to working the soil for a living.

Straw listened all through his friend's conversation about farming. He had kept quiet about some land he knew about down in Onslow County. He had seen and walked over a big portion of the land earlier in the year. He'd had the notion in mind to settle down himself on the land. At the last moment, he decided he couldn't stand to be tied down in one place for more than a year at a time.

He rubbed the stubble of beard on his chin and thought, *"This would be the right man to tell about the acres and acres of land waiting for a good man to come along."* He took a big swallow of brew from the tin cup and offered the information to his newfound friends.

"I know where there's a place you can do all the tilling of the soil you want to do." He said no more, just waited to see what Jess' reaction would be.

The noise was so loud in the tavern that a person had to repeat a statement over at times to understand what another person had said.

"Tell me that again," Jess requested, in a loud voice.

Straw repeated what he had said and added, "It's yours, if you got the money."

Both Swinsons leaned back in their chairs and looked straight on at Straw with a look of disbelief on their faces.

"I ain't telling you no lie. All you gotta do is go buy the land and start plowing your farm."

Jess slept a fretful night after the conversation with Straw. He turned and twisted all night. He was more tired when he got up the next morning than when he had gone to bed the night before.

Over breakfast the next morning, he said to Jesse and Straw, "I think maybe I'll mosey on down to Onslow County and have myself a look at the land you told us about."

He went to Sam, his boss, and asked for two weeks off the job. "I'm going to look at some land I might can get for farming. You've know all along that farming is in my blood. If I'm ever going to settle down and do what I want to do, now seems like the right time to get a start at it."

He borrowed his workhorse from Sam and promised to take good care of the animal. The Leeway Surveyor Company had furnished all equipment and animals they had worked with since their start with the company.

Sam trusted Jess and loaned him the animal with no questions asked. "I shore do dread the thought of you and Jesse quitting me. You've been two of the best workers I've ever had on the job. But, I won't hold a man back from what he feels he must do."

It was a long, lonesome ride for Jess to arrive at his destination. He traveled through Duplin County in the rain. He was beginning to think that it would never cease. All day and through the night, it continued to rain.

When he passed through the small town of Richlands, he felt as if he was almost there, not knowing he still had so many more miles to go. Straw had given his instructions on how to reach the area a few miles north of a small community called Maple Hill.

"Now don't cha even think about taking a shortcut. If you do and git lost, you're liable to wind up in the biggest swamp you'd ever want to see. Man I'm here to tell ya, if ya git tangled up in that swamp, we've seen the last of ya. Follow the instructions I give you and you'll have no trouble. Look for a Garganus family."

Jess went straight to the one family that lived in the area. Straw had given him good directions. A Garganus family had settled in the area four years earlier.

The dogs began to bark, announcing his arrival, long before Jess was in sight of the house. Mr. Garganus was standing on the front porch of his house when Jess emerged from the one lane dirt road that led up to his farm.

"Evening Sir. I'm Jess Swinson. I've come this way to look at some land here close by you. I was sent by a Straw Wilson," he tipped his hat in a greeting to the man who stood on the porch.

"Evening to you. Get off your mount and come set a spell with me and the madam. Have a bite to eat with us. We're just about to set down to the supper table." He shook the hand of the welcomed man. "I shore hope you do decide to settle down here. Me and my family like living here, but it's so lonesome for the womenfolk. All the female companionship my madam's got is with our girls."

Jess took a liking to Mr. Garganus that very night. He spent the night with them and early the next morning, the two men left on horseback to ride over the land Jess was interested in buying. Before the middle of the day Mr. Garganus thought this had gone far enough.

"Just call me Cyrus," he said to Jess.

Cyrus gave Jess directions on how to get to the county seat to take care of the purchase of the acreage of land he wanted. Cyrus had been a big help at showing Jess where the best land for clearing was located within the acreage. He also showed him where the stream of water ran through the property and the areas that were no good except for animals to roam.

When Jess had done all he could do toward starting his farm, he gave Cyrus a hearty farewell. "I'll be back just as soon as I can get back here with my son."

Jesse had continued to work on the job while his father was away. At times, he worked seven days a week. With his father gone, Jesse tried to carry his work and that of his father. He'd worked late into the night several days a week.

While he was on a dinner break one warm Saturday, he had finished his meal and stood on the porch of the cafe where he and Straw carried on a hardy conversation. He noticed a handsome buggy coming down the dirt street toward them.

When it neared the cafe, Jess noticed the proper young lady who sat beside the stiff, older looking man on the seat. She stole his heart at that very moment. He stood up erect and watched as the horse pulled the buggy past him in a slow trot.

He grabbed Straw's arm and shook it vigorously, "Who in the hell is that?" He twisted to watch the buggy as it turned the corner and disappeared from his sight. "Tell me Straw, who is she?" He was to the point of shaking the man bodily, who stood and enjoyed the look and actions of the young man who had just seen a fine lady.

"Easy there. She's outta your reach. She's from some other town. I don't rightly know where. I heard say, she's here visiting her grandfather, the rich, old Greek. You might as well forget that one."

"Like hell I will. That one will be my bride. You wait and see." His entire body was in turmoil. "Did you see the way she lowered her eyes at me when the buggy went by? I sensed the meaning in that look as plainly as if she had given the invitation out of her own mouth. Yes sir, that's my woman."

He made it his business to find out exactly who she was and where she lived at the moment. It didn't take him too long to locate where she resided.

Gus Solomon was a big landowner in Sampson County and one of the wealthiest men in North Carolina. He was a descendent of Dionysius Solomos who was noted for his famous contributions to Greek literature.

Gus had been shipped off to America to hush and cover up for a shameful deed he had committed in Greece. He and his new bride arrived in America and changed their name from Solomos to Solomon. With family money brought along with them from Greece when they came, they set up a family life in Sampson County, on the outskirts of Clinton, North Carolina. They prospered and raised a family.

Colista Anitia was the daughter of their youngest daughter who was also their youngest child. Colista visited with her Grandparents often now that she was a grown-up young woman. She liked the luxury their lifestyle afforded.

Her hair was dark black and her skin creamy, soft olive white. Her eyes were the color of a faded field of grass that sparkled when she laughed. She was natured up to be kind and gentle. Her manners were of the best that the excellent finishing school in Boston, Massachusetts, could offer. She could cook, sew, weave, tend to animals, and manage money.

She was an unmarried maiden, which was of some concern to her parents and grandparents. She had been almost to the point of marriage once, but had pulled away to take an extended trip across the seas.

The same Saturday that they first laid eyes on each other, Jesse showed up on her grandfather's front porch before nightfall. The young colored boy heard Jesse's horse galloping toward the house and ran to meet him. The boy's job on the weekends was to stay close to the front of the house to take care of the horses when guests arrived on the farm.

"Thank you. That's nice of you to take care of my mount. Do you know if Miss Batts is home?" Jesse spoke in a soft, polite manner.

The young boy nodded his head, indicating for him to go on up to the front door. It was a strikingly handsome man who walked the length of the porch. The sound from his surefooted steps echoed off the roof of the porch.

He raised his arm to pound on the door but, before he could knock, the door opened to reveal a dark skinned man standing before him with a pleasant expression on his face.

"I've come to call on Miss Colista Anitia Batts. Will you kindly tell her I'm here?" The manservant nodded his head and ushered him into the parlor then disappeared inside the house. In less than five minutes, Gus was in the room.

Their eyes met. An instant dislike for each other formed at the moment.

"Joshua said you are here to see Colista," Gus uttered the words with a harsh voice and without as much as a formal greeting.

"Yes sir." Jesse stood as tall as he could. He sensed the dislike that the man he stood before radiated to him. He caught the sarcasm in the grandfather's voice, but he was determined to stand his ground and see the most beautiful lady he had ever laid his eyes on. "I'd be much obliged if you could send her here to me, sir."

"Who are you? Where do you come from?" Gus was angry at the gall of this young whippersnapper. "You stand here, in my own parlor, and demand to see my precious granddaughter?"

Jesse's anger had begun to rise to the boiling point as soon as Gus asked his first question. He decided it might be best if he controlled his temper and went along with the demands of the older man. He shifted his hat from his right hand to his left and extended his right hand out toward Gus,

"Well sir, I'm Jesse Swinson. I'm looking for a wife, and decided your granddaughter is the right woman to fill my needs. So if you don't mind, will you fetch her for me?"

Gus ignored the outstretched hand. He was angry enough to skin the young man alive as he stood so brazenly in front of him.

"You think that's all there is to it, young man? To simply march yourself in here, in my home, and announce you're here for a wife?" He walked from one end of the room to the other, pounding his cane sharply on the floor as he walked. "Who in the hell do you think you are, Mister?"

Jesse jumped from the loud clang the cane made as it hit the floor. What had he said wrong? Why was the man so irritated? He glanced down at his attire. Maybe the man didn't like the way he was dressed. No, he looked as fine as any gentleman in the entire county.

This was Jesse's first attempt at asking for a lady's hand in marriage. He thought he was going about it in the right way. Maybe he wasn't. He had never seen a man ask a woman to be his wife. He knew they got married, but knew nothing of the details. After all, the only contact he'd ever had with the female gender was located in Brothels.

Gus couldn't quite make out the reasoning the young man had in mind. If he truly wanted to court his granddaughter, why didn't he do it properly? Why would he show up here on his doorstep, acting the fool, with no warning? He made his mind up without a moment's hesitation. With his cane pounding a rhythm on the polished hardwood floor, he began to walk out of the parlor.

"Come with me," he ordered. Jesse's face lit up with a hopeful smile.

When they reached the front door, Gus tucked his cane up under his arm and reached for the doorknob. He pulled the door open wide. With the cane, he motioned for Jesse to go through the open door.

"Don't you ever come back to this house. Don't even put a foot on any of my property." He slammed the door sharply. The downcast Jesse walked slowly down the many steps leading off the porch.

Colista was standing by an upstairs window at the front of the house when Jesse rode away through the yard. He stopped at the edge of the yard where the giant oak trees formed a shaded path in the summer time. Something compelled him to twist around in the saddle to look back. He spotted her where she stood. It appeared that she was making signals to him. He could not quite make out her message. He gave no visible sign that he had seen her, in case he was being watched from the interior of the house.

He straightened up and continued to ride until he was out of sight of the house.

"Whoa up there, boy." He sat dead still in the saddle thinking over the signals he had seen from the window. "Hot damn, she was telling me to meet her in the direction she pointed."

He pulled on the reins and urged the horse into a fast trot through the woods. He headed in the direction she had suggested with her signal. He rode until he was halfway around the property, secluded in the woods, but with a full view of the house.

Daylight was just about gone. He felt that if she didn't show herself soon, he had gotten the wrong message. He sat patiently astride his horse and whistled. He was far enough from the house not to be heard.

When there was just enough light left in the day, he spotted the back door of an outbuilding open. He strained hard and saw that it was her. She wore dark clothing and walked as calmly as if she were on her way to a picnic.

When she got to the edge of the woods, he stood on the ground to greet her. "Hey," he said, excitedly.

She stopped just short of him. The moon was not up high enough to cast enough light for her to see him clearly. "Hey."

She smelled so good to him. That was the first thing he noticed about her. All he could see of her was that she was bundled up in a heavy coat. It was cold.

"I come a courting you today and got run off."

"I saw you before you ever got to the house. I eased down stairs and stood and listened to the two of you talk in the parlor. I nearly broke my neck getting back up those stairs without grandfather knowing I had been snooping on your conversation. I was beginning to think you were not going to turn and look back while you rode off from the house."

He reached out and clasped her hand in his. He pulled her close to him. "Stand here, it'll be warmer. What kind of a man is your grandfather? I doubt if he will ever allow me in the house again. He was a mighty mad man when I rode off the place late today."

He lifted her hand to his mouth and blew his warm breath across her cold fingers.

"My name is Jesse Swinson. I saw you in town today and knew that you and me are destined to be together." He waited for a response from her.

"You know who I am. I heard you call my name when you first arrived. I'm like you. When I saw you today, something moved inside me, something that has never moved before. I've thought of nothing but you since then."

The scent of her made his head do funny things to him. He fought to keep from tightening his arms around her to draw her close to him. She sensed the same sensation and leaned in close to him. That was all it took to make him draw her into the circle of his arms. She tilted her head back and he crushed her mouth with a kiss that made her go weak in the knees. It was a long, passionate kiss, filled with emotion they shared with each other.

He took his mouth from hers and placed his hands on either side of her face. He could barely see the outline of her features. He knew she felt warm and strong in his arms. Yes, she was strong for a woman. She was exactly the right height and shape for him. "Woman, I've got to have you for my wife. What do you say about that?"

She felt secure in his arms. She knew nothing about the man that held her close to him and made her feel so good. She felt the want, the pull, to be with him all the time. At the moment, she didn't want to leave the embrace of his strong arms.

"You don't waste any time with the little things that usually go along with courting, do you?" She put her hands up on his and slid them up and down. She looked at where she thought his eyes should be located.

It was quite dark by the time she spoke again.

"Yes, I'll be your wife. How do you propose we make it come about?"

The horse whined and trampled about near them. It was cold and the horse was ready to go home and get in his stall for the night. The only way he had of letting Jesse know his needs was to neigh. "Whoa there boy," Jesse cooed to the horse.

"When can I see you again?" Jesse asked anxiously.

She lowered her hands from his cheeks. He placed his around her waist and pulled her as close to him as possible, so he could taste the sweet flavor of her lips again.

"Oh, you take my breath away. But I love for you to kiss me."

She seemed to be out of breath when she answered him, "Do you know where the curve in Willow Creek is located? A great big oak tree stands in that curve. I'll meet you there tomorrow at two o'clock in the afternoon."

No, he didn't know where the curve of the creek was. That was no problem for him. He'd make it his business to find out exactly where it was. He realized he should work all day tomorrow to catch up for taking half the day off to find her. No matter, tomorrow was Sunday anyway.

"I'll be there."

He kissed her one last time before parting, with all the emotions he could bolster up. He didn't want to let her go. She felt so right in him arms.

The moon had risen high enough to throw a little dim light on the field when she turned to go back to the house.

He mounted his horse and watched until she was out of his sight. The heels of his boots dug into the lower belly of the horse. Rider and animal went swiftly to the stable in Clinton.

At dawn the next morning, Jesse was hunched over the paperwork. He hoped to get most of the workload completed by the noon hour. He did stop long enough to go to the cafe and eat a big breakfast, with Straw as his companion.

"Say Straw, do you know where Willow Creek is?" he asked matter-of-factly.

Straw thought on the subject for a few minutes and had to admit, "Nope, never heard of the creek." The one thing he hated most in this world was when he did not know the answer to a question when it was asked of him. "Maybe the cafe owner can tell us where it is." He couldn't let the situation go without giving Jesse advice on the matter.

Straw was right. The owner gave them directions to find the creek.

"It won't take you more'n three quarters of an hour to get there if you're on a good horse."

Jesse worked up until twelve o'clock straight up. He went to the local bathhouse and scrubbed his body until it stung. He dressed with care and rode out of town filled with anticipation.

When he approached the oak tree, he saw her standing beside the creek. She turned to greet him when she heard the horse's hooves pounding on the ground. Her face lit up in a beautiful smile, "You came!"

"Damn right, I come. Told you I would, didn't I?" He swung his long legs off the horse and landed on both feet when he hit the earth. He held the reins in his hand as he walked toward her. His face was all smiles. "You are the prettiest thing I've seen in a long time ma'am. I don't have many dealings with the Lord, but I'll have to give him credit for leading me here to this place. Did you know that He had you here, just waiting for me to get here?" He circled his arms around her and tugged to bring her close to him.

They walked together to the tree where she had her horse tethered. There is where he tied his horse.

"Burr, it's cold out here this afternoon."

He began to gather up twigs and large sticks. She walked with him. She bent over to pick up a piece or two of scrap wood for a fire.

"I can do this," he said, before her hand touched the sticks.

She gave him a look that let him know she was no sissy. "And I can help you. You might as well learn right now, I do what I can do. I'm no soft, dainty, little ole lady. I never have been one to sit back and let others do everything for me. Oh, I like my niceties as well as the next one. But don't go telling me what I can and can't do."

She took the handful of twigs from his hand and leaned back from him. Her smile was the sweetest one she could give him.

He bent over to collect more scrap wood and mused at this female he was in the company of. He had never met up with a woman before who got so riled up over such a small thing. He finally had enough dead branches to start the fire. He walked to the oak tree and squatted far enough away from the trunk to prevent heat damage to the bark. He liked spunk in a woman. If he were to go with his father to dig a farm out of the woods, he'd need a strong woman, in more ways than one.

They sat with their backs resting against the tree trunk while the fire warmed their nearly frozen feet. The crackles and spits provided by the fire added to the romantic mood of the hour. It amazed Jesse that he could sit there snuggled up next to her and continue to be and act the gentleman. It felt good to sit and do nothing other than be next to her.

Their conversation moved from one subject to another, just small talk to fill the time.

"Tell me, why is your grandfather's house still standing intact? I've seen so much damage from the war all over the southern states that we've worked through and when I was in the army. How did he avoid ruin?" The Civil War ended in March of 1865.

"We don't exactly know. There were a few homes left standing after the fighting, and we just happen to be one of them. Maybe it was because the house was out of their path. We feel blessed that it was spared."

He almost dreaded to tell her where his father was and why he was there. He blurted out, "How do you feel about being a farmer's wife?"

"I've lived on a farm all my life, except when I was away at school or on extended trips. It's a good life and a lot of hard work. Why?" She asked as if she had no idea what he had in mind.

"When we wed, that's how we'll make our living. Pa is down in Onslow County right now looking over the land. If he likes what he finds, we'll go there as soon as he returns to Clinton. Do you want to marry here or wait and wed in Onslow County?"

"Let's wait. We can have a heap of fun between now and then."

"I got a work 'til Paw gets back. I slipped away this afternoon. There won't be much time for us to be together."

She tickled his nose with a broom sedge straw and said in a teasing manner, "We'll see about that."

The afternoon hours slipped away all to fast. After a few moments of silence, Jesse asked, "Who owns all this land here around us?" He moved his arm in a sweeping motion to indicate where he meant.

"As far as I know, it's unclaimed. Grandfather's land boundary ends back there a ways." She pointed in a southern direction from where they sat.

"I don't want any one to slip up on us. I suspect your grandfather would shoot me on sight if he should catch us together, especially if we were on his property."

Gus was at one of the neighboring farms. "Today he is at one of his weekly poker games, and Grandmother never leaves the house on Sundays. That's why I chose this place for us to meet. No one comes here, unless it's a traveler passing through."

The sun was lowering in the west and Jesse thought it best if she got back to the house before pitch dark. He got up and helped her to rise. He relaxed his arms and brought them down to encircle her.

She pushed the cape from her head and stretched up to meet his kiss. He suddenly realized they had been together all afternoon and this was their first kiss. It was a meaningful expression of emotions that flowed from him to her. Sometimes the message of silence was better than a conversation filled with thoughtful words. "I love you, my little southern Blossom." He uttered as he helped her mount her horse.

They rode side by side until it was time to take different routes to reach their destinations. "See you soon. I love you, too," she whispered, and goaded her horse to a full gallop.

Jess returned to Clinton three weeks from the day he left. "Good news son, we're the owners of two thousand acres of land. We'll be leaving here as soon as we can get things squared away with Sam and the jobs."

Straw was in need of work. Jess recommended him to Sam for one of the positions left open by his son's and his departure. Straw got the job.

In the meantime, Jess had purchased a horse and buggy, a wagon and two mules, two plows, bush axes, pitchforks and several other implements to use at their work, on clearing the new ground in Onslow County.

Jesse confided with his father the news about Colista.

"I don't know about taking a woman with us boy. It's going to be rough and mighty hard for me and you. A woman is another worry added to the ones we now have. There's nothing on the land except trees and underbrush and, of course, a nice creek filled with water. Don't you think it'd be wiser if we go on, just the two of us, get something started and then come back for her?"

"No Paw, I don't like your idea at all. She goes when we go, or there is no us for you and me. Paw, I can't live without her. Just you wait 'til you meet her. She is one fine woman, Paw. A lady, she is."

After they talked on the subject for a while, Jess agreed to allow Colista to join them on this exhilarating adventure. There was not one thing he could do about it anyhow. He'd learned that once the boy made up his mind about a thing, it was useless to try to persuade him away from it.

On Friday before the Swinsons were to leave Clinton, Calista was in town on the pretense of going to see her dressmaker. Straw told Jesse he'd seen her when she rode into the outskirts of town alone in the buggy, and that he had watched her until she had entered the dressmaker's shop.

Jesse left the boarding house and entered the dressmaker's shop by the back door. He stood just inside the doorframe until he spotted her. He whistled their signal they had worked out the day they had met beneath the oak tree.

She heard and excused herself from the seamstress.

"I probably won't be back today. I'll come in one day next week to finish the dress measurements." She left through the front door and hurriedly walked to the rear of the shop.

Jesse explained the details of their leaving the very next morning.

"Can you meet me halfway into town from your grandfather's? I'll be meeting you with the buggy. I will not take one thing of your grandfather's with us. You meet me on horseback; the horse will go on back to the farm when you turn him loose with a smart whack to his rump."

She was so excited when he told her, she could barely wait to get back to the farm and get her few things packed. She packed wisely, nothing fancy. She had enough sense about her to realize there would be hard long hours of work in her future. There was one thing Jesse would take that belonged to Gus. At least Gus' money had paid for it. Jesse would not know about it until he looked at the results of her foresight.

She met him as scheduled, a little after dawn, on the dirt road that lead into Clinton. She pulled back on the reins when she saw him approaching. She was on the ground when he reached her side.

He got out of the buggy and took her satchels off the saddle. He hooked the reins loosely on the saddle horn. Then got a grip on the bridle and turned the horse around. "Smack!" The sound echoed in the still morning air. The horse galloped off down the road toward Gus Solomon's property. He put the bags in the buggy. He took her elbow as gently as he could. When she stepped up to get on the seat, he held back.

"What's the matter?" she wanted to know.

Those were the first words that had been spoken between them on this cold winter morning.

"There's something we ought to do before we go any farther," Jesse said in a serious, hushed voice.

She placed her foot back on the ground and straightened the skirt part of her dress. When she looked up at his face she asked, "What?"

"What if we don't like each other, uhm... uhm... you know, uhm, in bed? Wouldn't it be hell to pay if I got you all the way down there and then found out that we don't match up?"

"Well! I never heard such!" she spat at him. "But you know something? You do have a point there. I'm willing and more than ready to do the experimenting. You name the time and place."

She never changed the expression on her face the entire time she uttered the words.

He reached in the buggy and pulled a blanket from under the seat. He grabbed the reins from the whip cradle, motioned to her with his head to follow him, and led the horse into the woods. He found the clearing he looked for and tethered the horse to a tree. He then spread the blanket out on a bed of pine straw and dried leaves.

He gathered her in his arms and captured her mouth in a strong, passionate kiss. He lowered their bodies down on the blanket. They lay down and Jesse pulled the loose part of the blanket over them. He tugged on her skirt until he had it high enough. She worked herself out of her under drawers while he unbuttoned his trousers.

They were each one ready for him to enter her. The sky opened up. Thunder exploded in the heavens. Lightening struck. Music filled the air.

She dug her fingernails into the material of his over coat so hard that he felt the pressure on his back.

They relaxed and Jesse rolled off her. He threw the blanket aside. There was no need for it now. They shared enough heat to ward off the cold.

"God Almighty in heaven. Woman, you are all I will ever want."

Before she moved, he saw the blood. "What's that?" he asked.

"I was a virgin. That happens the first time a woman has a man. It's nothing to worry about, and it's the only time it will occur." She sat up and tried to arrange her hair back to a respectable condition. She got up and worked at getting her clothing back in the best shape she could. Then she propped her hands on her hips and demanded, "Well, do I get to go with you?"

"Lord have mercy yes, but I haven't heard you say if you liked me or not."

She tied her bonnet snugly beneath her chin and walked toward the buggy before she answered. "I knew before the test that I was yours. I suppose us womenfolk have a way of knowing things that men aren't capable of. Come on get in the buggy, times a wasting."

Chapter Five

Jess waited in the street out in front of the boarding house for Jesse to return with his lady. He had completed the task of loading everything they owned and meant to take with them. He was impatient to get on the road to start the new phase of their lives.

He spotted the buggy when it rounded the curve at the edge of town. He didn't know how he would take to this new member of the family. He knew it was really none of his business who the boy took for a wife, so he might as well let well enough alone.

"Paw, meet your first daughter-in-law. She will be as soon as we get to Onslow County and find the marrying man. Well Paw, to tell you the truth I don't rightly know if she's your first one or not. For a minute there I plum forgot about James."

Jess removed his hat and nodded his head forward, which was a courteous and polite way of greeting in the area.

"Hello, Mr. Swinson. I'm pleased to make your acquaintance and so happy to be going along with you to our new home." She smiled and his heart melted. She had a friend in him for the rest of their lives.

The journey was long and tiresome. They stopped around sunset each day where they found water to make camp for the night. Colista set in to cook supper that first night on the trail. It took Jesse a little by surprise. He had always done the cooking when they had traveled, before she entered the family. "Oh, there will be things for you to do yet, sir. I'm not too good at skinning wild animals. Really, I just don't like to do it. I can shoot one in a minute though." She spoke as friendly as she possibly could and hurried along with cooking their supper. Each one was hungry. None had eaten a bite since an early morning breakfast.

It took them four weeks to reach the County Seat in Onslow County. The wagons were heavy and it tired the mules too quickly to move along too fast. If Jess had of used his head, he would have waited until he got to Onslow County to purchase the needed supplies and equipment rather than haul it all those miles over cold and frozen ground. He realized the fact before their journey ended.

Jesse expressed his desire to stop in the small town where the County Seat was located. "My need to find a parson or a preacher is pressing hard on my list of things to get accomplish first."

It had been a long, long month since he and Colista had done their testing to see if they matched up with their sex desires. How he had made it this long, he didn't know. She would not allow any more tomfoolery until after the wedding ceremony.

With difficulty, he tried to focus on the daily chores he was responsible for. Having her so near to him nearly every minute caused him to ache for her. He wanted to lay with her, to feel her soft skin as it touched his.

One day as they jogged along, both perched atop the wagon seat, Colista mumbled under her breath. Jesse did not understand what she said. "What was that you said, my dear Colista?" Every time he spoke her name, he faltered at the pronunciation. His tongue tangled up trying to roll over the syllables.

She laughed at him each time he used her name. "I said I don't know what to call your father."

"Call him anything you want to."

"Do you think I could get away with calling him Paw like you do? That's what I'd like to say when I talk to him or about him."

"Go on and call him that. It'll make him feel good and proud. The next time you talk to him, call him Paw and see how he reacts to it."

"I'll wait until after we're wedded. Don't you think that would best?"

He nodded his head in agreement with her and kept silent for a while.

She leaned over close to him and nudged her elbow into his side. "Now, what are you thinking about?"

"I've had something weighing heavy on my mind for some time now. It's your name. I have a hell of a time saying it correctly. Your name is as pretty as you are and I hate to mess up the pronunciation every time I open my mouth to speak to you. I've been thinking about a pet name for you. One that I can say easily and still has meaning for us both. I've come up with exactly the right one."

She waited to hear him say the name. When he continued with his silence, she asked, "Well, what is it?"

"Brister."

"Brister?"

"Yes, Brister."

"Where in the name of goodness did you get that from?"

"There is a stone I heard about, some time back, called Bristol stone. When it is highly polished, it is called a Bristol Diamond. You are my Bristol Diamond. I can't very well call you Bristol, so I decided on Brister. From now on you are my Brister to me and me alone."

She had not thought too much of the name, when he had first begun to talk. After she heard his definition, she felt all tender and warm for him. She pulled his face close to her and kissed his cheek. "You are a precious dear, do you know that?"

"While we're on the subject of names, Paw is having trouble with your name too. Think up something for him to call you."

When she was a little girl, her grandfather had called her Listy Ann. Why couldn't the name follow her to her new home and life? "I've got the perfect one to tell him about." She would leave out the part of her grandfather's original use of the name.

Two days before Christmas Eve, 1868, they arrived at the County Seat of Onslow County. It was so cold that clouds of condensation escaped their nostrils when they breathed or opened their mouths to speak.

Not a soul could be seen on the roads of the small community. Smoke billowed skyward from every chimney in view. The wheels of the buggy and wagon made an awful noise as they crunched over the frozen ground that served as streets.

Jess drove the wagon on this day with Jesse and his lady in the buggy. Jess pulled on the reins to the right and stopped the mules at the hitching post in front of the general store. Jesse did the same thing and helped Brister from the buggy. "Come on, let's get inside and warm up." He held her arm while they entered the store.

Inside the store was warm. Several local residents and a few farmers sat huddled around a wood stove while they talked. The cold blast of air that blew in when the door was opened caused them to hush their talking and turn to see who had entered the building. When they noticed a lady was among those entering, they each arose and opened up a path for her to get to the source of warmth, each doffing his hat. "Evening, ma'am," the store's owner spoke up first.

He then turned and nodded a greeting to Jess and Jesse. "What brings strangers out in this kind of weather?" he wanted to know.

Jess had ambled over to warm himself, too. He turned and, while everyone in the place listened, he explained to them why they were in the area and who they were.

"The first thing we need after we thaw ourselves out is a preacher to marry up my son there," he gestured toward Jesse, "and his fine lady."

"You're in luck there, Mr. Swinson. The preacher should be here sometime early tomorrow if he don't freeze trying to get here. Another young couple are to be married around ten o'clock." Charles, the storeowner, introduced himself and the others in the store to the newcomers. He had given the much-welcomed information that the preacher was on his way.

"While we're here in the store, let us gather up the supplies we will be needing to take with us, on to the land. We'll be in the need of enough to carry us on through the cold months," Jess said to those around him.

Colista's ears perked right up when she heard Jess mention supplies. She walked over close to him and asked, "May I suggest a thing or two while you make your selection?"

"Yea, that'll be fine."

She cupped her chin in her hand and thought. She'd need a wash pot, scrub board, a box or two of lye and several sections of homemade lye soap she'd seen in a box at the end of the counter, and some needles and thread. Several pieces of the men folk's clothes were in need of repairs. She had thought to toss her thimble in her satchel before leaving her grandfather's, but neglected to bring along other necessities. She had been in too much of a hurry when she had literally thrown her clothes in the bag in preparation to leave.

"I'd really like to have a few of those spices too, if you don't mind." All she'd had to season with while they traveled was salt and pepper. "And one of those Grier Almanacs, please." She casually walked about the store and looked at others items she'd like to take along to her new home, but decided she had better not ask for too much.

The last items Jess asked for was three bars of sweet soap. He knew Colista would never request anything personal for herself. He thought the soap for her face would be one little thing she could claim for herself. She did not notice when he tucked it in with the other supplies.

After all the supplies were loaded, the three of them walked over to the one cafe in town. Each one was in the need of a good meal. While they sat at the table,

Jess talked to his son about going on over to the government office and get his name on the papers for the acreage. "No need to mess around and come up with a problem later on." He took several more bites of his meal and asked, "Son, do you have enough money on you to pay the preacher for tomorrow's service?"

"Yea, Paw. I still have all my last pay wages."

The preacher showed up as expected and married Jesse and Colista pretty soon after the ceremony of the other couple. When Colista turned to Jess, she put her arms out toward him. He came to her. They hugged and she said with a big smile, "Hello Paw." It was December 24, 1868.

"Hum!" he muttered and smiled back at her. "Yea, I like that. It has a good ring to it, the way you make it sound."

"Paw?" she said his name in the form of a question.

"Yea?"

"I've noticed you have a little trouble with my given name. You can call me Listy Ann from now on. Will that suit you all right?"

"Listy Ann. Listy Ann." He wallowed the name around over his tongue a time or two. "I like the sound of that and it suits you a heap better than that tongue twister your name really is." He hugged her again. They all went to the cafe for a filling late dinner. While in the café, they made new acquaintances, and sat and talked for several hours. Up in the afternoon they went to their rented rooms for the remainder of the day and night.

The room was toasty warm to Jesse and Listy Ann when they closed the door behind them to spend their wedding night together.

Inside Jesse and Listy Ann's room was a small wooden heater with a kettle of hot water steaming on the top, a box of firewood stacked over in the corner of the room, a washstand with a bucket filled with water and a washbasin resting on the stand. Towels and soap, to go along with bathing needs were also supplied.

She filled the basin with hot water and added enough cold to create warm water, then refilled the kettle from the water bucket and placed it to the back of the heater. She took the washbasin, rag, and soap to the small dressing room off the main room. It was chilly in there, but she felt the need of privacy to prepare for her wedding bed.

Jess slipped out of the room and found a bathhouse still open. When he returned to the room, he was clean and fresh smelling.

She pulled the cloth draped across the door of the dressing room aside. She came to him in a soft batiste gown.

The sight of her astounded him. The dim glow from the kerosene table lamp provided enough light to enhance the aura she possessed. Her long, thick, black hair flowed loosely about her shoulders. Her cheeks were highlighted with a hint of rouge. The gown fitted snugly at her waist to accent the fullness of her breasts. The expression emitting from her eyes matched that of her appearance. She was as ready for him as he was for her.

"Humph, damn! Come here woman."

The bang on the door at the break of day the next morning aroused the newlyweds. "What?" came the sleepy response.

"Times a wasting. Get up. Get your traveling clothes on. Let's get on the road. I'll wait on you over to the cafe." Jess rapped loudly on the door once more, "Get a move on now!" He walked away from the door, mumbling to himself, "There's still about ten more miles to go. Then I'll be home one more time." He hoped forever.

They had been on the road about three hours when Jess pulled his pocket watch out to check the time. "We'd better stop for a while and allow these mules to rest. They're hauling a heavy load and it won't do to ruin them before we start clearing the land." He pulled back on the reins, "Whoa up there, boys. Time for a rest. Jesse, you get a bucket of water from the barrel and water up the horse and mules. Then unhitch them and tie 'em off to that tree over there. I'll get a fire started. A good hot cup of coffee will warm our bones while we wait on the animals to rest."

He looked back over the dirt road from where they had come. "Will you look at that, not a rut cut anywhere. If the ground was not frozen, we'd of not gotten this far. The wheels rolled over the frozen ground much better than if it was wet and muddy. Burr," he shuddered. "This cold is enough to freeze us all to death if we don't take precautions." He looked around and studied the area they were resting in. "I'd say we're just about half way to our destination."

The coffee smelled good boiling over the open flames. They huddled around the fire to warm their hands. The minute they removed their gloves, the cold made it almost impossible to use their fingers. Jesse brought up some old pieces of dead logs for them to sit on.

Listy Ann got tin cups from the wooden crate that contained the cooking and eating utensils. She poured the steaming liquid and handed the first cup to her father-in-law. "Here, Paw. You come first today. I love your son more than anything I know of, and I love you too. That's what warrants you being served first."

Her convincing smile told him she was a good woman, a woman of worth, and good breeding. He wondered, under his breath, if his son knew exactly what he had in the woman he had chosen for his mate, and from what Jess had picked up by observing her, she would be an equal mate for Jesse. She was no sniveling "yes sir" person. Yes, Jesse had himself a woman.

"Thank you kindly ma'am," he replied, and sat down on one of the old logs Jesse had made possible. He blew steam from the top of the cup with air blown from his nose and sipped the scalding coffee at the same time. "That's as good a cup of coffee as any man needs."

Jesse crossed his legs that were outstretched toward the flames. He cupped both hands around his cup and asked, "Paw, where'd you get the cash money to pay for all these supplies, there on the wagon? The thought has been with me for a few days now."

Listy Ann had finished her coffee and excused herself before Jess could answer his son's question. "I've got to go find a private place in the woods." She reddened in the face when she glanced at her father-in-law and caught him looking at her.

"There's still a lot of good use in the old catalog over there under the buggy seat." They used the pages to wipe their behinds after a squat in the woods. It could be crumbled up and made softer to the flesh. She reddened more as she walked away.

Jess stood up and went to the fire where the coffee pot sat. He filled his cup and turned to face Jesse. "Son, all the time we've worked, beginning with the stockyards back in Illinois, I've saved every dollar I could, while you and James threw yours away on liquor and loose women. I knew that we would one day find somewhere to call home again, or least I hoped for it to come about. I saved all my wages above my living expenses, and every single dime I made from the sale of my wood carvings."

"I've wondered at times what you did with all them figurines. So you've been selling 'em, huh?"

"I've got the money set aside for the closing out of our land deal which we'll go back in the spring to get settled up. We'll be getting our deed at that time. There is very little money left for us to survive on through these winter months. We'll have to live off the land until we can get a crop grown and harvested for market."

Listy Ann came back to the campfire. She drained the few remaining drops of coffee from the pot. With water from the barrel, she rinsed the pot before storing it back in the crate. She had overheard the conversation between father and son. She joined the men who rested on their log seats. "Woo, I feel better."

Jess looked at her and wondered if he should ask her about what had been on his mind for a while. He decided to just go on and ask her. "Listy Ann, where do you come from? Who's your father? We don't know a thing about you, or at least I don't. It won't make a bit of difference in my feelings about you. I have a habit of asking questions to get the answers I can't figure out for myself."

She herself had been wondering, too, when one of them was going to question her about her heritage and family background. "My father and his family farmed in Sampson County. He met my mother when she was only fourteen years old. They ran away together and married. They got a small piece of land to farm over in Lenoir County. They still live there. I am their youngest child. Randolph Batts is his name. My mother is Tammie Batts. I have two older sisters and five older brothers. They are all scattered out around the state with their families. I have all the education I could possibly want. I have studied in Boston and at schools in England and France. I love to help work on a farm more than any other occupation I've tried. I have experienced a few. I love seeing things sprout out of the ground and grow. I love tending to them while they reach maturity. I love hearing chickens while they scratch around hunting for food. I am a farmer at heart. Jesse is the first and only man I have ever been to bed with."

She looked off into the distance when she made that last remark. At times she wondered where some of the things she said came from or where she got the nerve to utter them from. She'd think a thing and before she realized it, the thought would be in the form of words. She looked back to see the reaction on their faces to her explanation of who she was, where she came from and where she hoped to go.

Jess rubbed his rough, stubbled chin. He tried to conceal the grin that tried to surface. "That's a pretty good answer to my question." He was a little taken by her frankness. In the long run, he felt it best to know a little about her so he would know better how to approach her on any given subject if, and when, it arose.

Jesse got a kick out of his father when he got a little to inquisitive. He leaned backwards and let a loud roar of laughter escape his throat. "Ha! Ha! Ha! Paw, did you like what you heard?"

"Yes, I'm satisfied."

It was time to get started on the move again. Before they got on their respective seats, Jess said to the others, "I told Mr. Garganus that we'd stop off at his place on the way in. If it's all right with the two of you, we'll go by there before we continue on to our place. By the way, Merry Christmas to you both," he said and then sat down heavily on the wagon seat.

"Same to you Paw. Ain't this a hell of a way to spend our first Christmas together?" he remarked to his Brister.

Mr. Garganus came out of his house when he heard the wagon wheels moving over the frozen ground. He had ventured out into the yard by the time they got to him. He stuck his hand out to Jess, "Glad to see you made it back. You shore did pick a cold time to do your traveling. Get down, all of you, and come on in the house. My ma'am is just getting our Christmas meal on the table." He went to the buggy and assisted Listy Ann down. "Howdy ma'am, my women folk is going to be mighty pleased to see you."

He called two of his boys out of the house to assist Jesse while he took the animal loose from the buggy and wagon. "Turn them loose yonder in the lot with ours. Let them eat and water up. They'll find their own place to shield off the cold. They'll be easy enough to bridle when you're ready to leave."

The Garganus Christmas table was an unbelievable and welcome sight to the tired new comers. A golden brown turkey, filled with stuffing, graced the center of the table, surrounded by bowls of homegrown vegetables, cornbread piping hot from the fireplace oven, and sweet potato pie. It was enough to enlighten the appetites of the gods.

"My man shot the turkey at daybreak this morning," Mrs. Garganus said to Listy Ann.

The Garganus' had been settled in the area for four years. They had almost twenty-five acres cleared with cotton being the main crop and the running of turpentine as a secondary income. The woods were full of pine trees, which made the gathering of turpentine easier. It was hard work and took long hours to collect, but well worth the effort.

When it was time for the Swinsons to say their goodbyes and thank yous, they knew they had made good and lasting friends. They felt that they would need these neighbors if they were to survive here in these woods.

When Mrs. Garganus could not persuade them to spend the night with them, she packed a basket with enough food for their supper.

She handed the basket to Listy Ann. "Now you come on back over here and sit with us. It ain't far from your place to here. You can walk it in no time a tall." She grabbed Listy Ann and hugged her so tight it hurt. "Child, I'm so pleased you're here."

Jess clucked to the mules and they began their pace once again. To the surprise of Jess, he found a path had been cut from the main dirt road all the way to the exact spot he and Mr. Garganus had stood when Jess had proclaimed, "This is where I'll build my house." A small cleared area welcomed them upon their approach. The wood from the hewn trees lay stacked in a nearby pile. Close to that lay another pile of cured wood. Looking over a ways, Jess spotted a campfire laid out. Dried grass had been crammed beneath the wood. All one needed to do was stick a match to it.

They knew who had done the work. Jess was tired and when he stepped down from the wagon, he turned to his children with tears in his eyes. "This is what I'd call a real neighborly deed." He wiped his cheeks and sniffed his nose.

Jesse took a sulfur headed match from his pocket and, upon swiping it across his buttocks, the flames swirled around the head of the match. He stooped and stuck it to the grass. The fire caught and within seconds, small pieces of wood were in a full blaze. Jesse took a few steps backwards, "What the hell?" In an excited voice he asked, "Did you see the way that wood caught up in flames? I've never seen such fast action in a piece of wood." He looked around and found a smaller pile of rich looking wood. It was all cut into small slender pieces. He went over to the pile and picked one of the pieces up. He held it close to his nose and took a whiff.

"It smells like it's got oil in it. I wonder what it is. One thing for sure, I'll find out tomorrow. That is if I get a chance to get back over to their house."

Jess took the bolt of tarpaulin off the wagon first and told Jesse to get the axes down. "We'll cut down enough small trees before dark to get post for the lean-to so we can sleep under a roof of sorts. We all need a good nights rest before we get started in full force here."

The roaring fire put out enough heat to warm them when they went to stand by the flames.

Chapter Six

The warm sun on Listy Ann's face, caused her to stir, which in turn made Jesse open his eyes. He was not yet familiar with the warm body folded within his frame. She opened her eyes to find him looking at her.

"Good morning my love, ready to get up and tackle this new world of ours?" He teased her as he leaned over and kissed her forehead.

She snuggled down in the covers and muttered. "No, I don't want to get up. It's too cold."

Their conversation, though hushed, roused Jess. He threw his bedroll back and got up. He still wore the clothes he had worn the day before. He picked up his coat and shoes and walked over to where the campfire smoldered from a few coals that remained in the ashes. He stirred the ashes with a piece of the oil-wood and threw it into the hottest area of the ashes. He leaned over and blew gently on the oil-wood. Presto, the rich wood caught ablaze. He added bigger pieces of wood and the fire was going good within a few moments. He sat on the cold ground and pulled his shoes on. He stood up and warmed the coat before he pulled it on his back. He walked off toward the woods. Both of them in the bedroll knew where he was going and for what reason. They took the time of his absence to catch up on a little love making.

When Jess returned to the fire, they were both up and dressed with their coats tucked in close to ward off the cold. Listy Ann took her turn to go to the woods next. "Lord have mercy," it was cold with her clothing pulled up enough to allow her to pee, "I wonder if those men know how lucky they are not to have to get half undressed to rid themselves of a little water waste?" she spoke to herself as she straightened up and went back to the warmth of the fire.

The coffee pot was sitting in the edge of the fire when she got back. Jess had to break the ice in the water bucket before he could dip out enough water to fill the pot. Listy warmed enough water by the fire to wash her hands and prepared a little breakfast.

Their first meal cooked on the place was flour bread, pork side meat and syrup. The syrup was so stiff they had to warm it before it would pour from the jug.

It was a beautiful day, but the air was so cold it almost hurt them to breath. That did not stop them from doing the work they planned to get done on their first day.

It was December 26 when Listy Ann stood in the clearing and marveled at the small world that surrounded her. She crossed her arms beneath her breasts and surmised that there was a lot of hard work lying ahead of her and her men folk. Gone were the days when she could go to her grandfathers and have the servants do her bidding.

She was eighteen years old and Jesse twenty-three. Paw was nearly forty-eight. He had a birthday coming up on February 3 of this year. They were all healthy and of sound mind.

Listy Ann cleared up the cooking utensils while the men unloaded the wagon and buggy. They stacked each item in piles that would be easily gotten to when needed.

Listy Ann decided to get some of the clothes washed early so they would have time to freeze, thaw out, and dry before nightfall. Jesse helped her get the wash pot set up. They each took peck buckets to the creek and made the many trips until the pot was filled with water. The water was frozen near the edge of the creek but out in the middle the water ran freely.

Jesse went on back to help his father and Listy started the fire under the pot. When she turned away from the pot, a thought popped into her mind. She walked to where the men were and said, "You know something? I forgot all about washtubs. I can't scrub a lick at these filthy clothes with no tubs. We got everything but the tubs. Now what am I going to do?"

Jesse slapped the sides of his legs and threw his back in a healthy round of laughter. She propped her hands up on her hips which the men would come to learn was a signal for her anger to turn loose on them. It was near the time of the month for her flow of waste blood to appear. It always made her nervous, edgy and a little on the mean side.

"Well, I'll tell you something. I don't think it's all that amusing. We all smell like we've wallowed with Mr. Garganus' hogs and there's not another piece of clean clothes on this place. Do you realize it's been five weeks since there was anything washed?"

She dropped her hands, turned around and returned to the pot. She kicked at some dirt that had thawed out up against the black wash pot that smoked like it was on fire while the new was burning off the pot. She looked back at the men to see if they had watched her and saw they had. She tried to control her anger, but at times, it got away from her. She came toward them with a big smile on her face.

"I'm sorry, but just to show you being forgetful sometimes isn't all bad, let me tell you about something I haven't forgotten. I was just going to let you find out from Mr. Garganus but now, I've decided to tell you myself."

She went to the pile of what they called oil wood, and picked up a handful. She stuck them out in front of her and asked, "Do you see this? I could barely keep from laughing aloud when you two were admiring the oil-wood yesterday. Well, sirs, it's only an old pine tree that's been dead for years. The outer part of the tree decayed throughout the years and fell away, leaving the heart, which is this." She extended the items farther out to them. "They are called splinters. Made from the heart of pine, we call it fat liteard. You can find it all over these woods. And I just might know a few more things that you don't think that I know."

Jesse came to her with his arms outstretched. "I'm sorry, too. You looked so out done when you made the statement about no washtubs. I was really laughing with you, not at you." He put his arm around her shoulder and said, "Come on Brister, let's see what's in the wagon."

Jess cleared his throat to remind them that he was still there.

Jess walked with them. When he pulled the bolt of white homespun from the wagon, Listy Ann's face lit up. "Gracious sakes alive Paw, I'm glad to see this. It'll be the answer to a lot of things. It will make pillowcases, sheets, towels to wipe our faces with, dishrags, shirts. Oh, the list goes on and on." She grabbed the bolt of material and hugged it to her face.

When she turned back from placing it on one of the piles, Jess spoke, "Little lady, I thought you may like to have a small delayed Christmas gift. Here," he extended his hand out to her with the gift, "I bought these when you weren't looking."

When she saw what it was her mouth flew open in a surprised, excited way, and her breath intake was so loud, the men feared she would strangle before she caught it again.

"Oh Paw! You are a sweetheart. This is the best gift you could have given me. I'm going to use it very sparingly." She held it up to her nose and closed her eyes as she savored in the aroma of the sweet soap. She stuck the bars of soap down in her pocket. When she brought her hand out, she smelled of her fingers. The odor of the soap lingered. It smelled so good and refreshing.

She noticed that Jess had pulled a big three-legged cast-iron stew pot from the wagon. "Give me that, and I'll get some dry beans on to cook for our supper. It'll take 'em all day to get done on the open fire. I saved that fried meat grease from breakfast. It'll help season the beans along with some salt." She left them to finish unloading the wares and got the beans on to cook.

The young couple were astounded at the amount of things Jess had stored on the wagon: tools for farming, corn for the horse and mules, a big tow sack filled with Irish potatoes, more smoked meat, seeds to get in the ground as soon as they got enough cleared to plow and make rows. To Jesse's surprise, there were two pairs each of bibbed overalls for him and his father. Jesse had never owned a pair of overalls, but had seen other men wear them and thought that he may one day get him some.

"Thank you Paw, these will wear good and keep me warm at the same time."

At the close of that day, Listy Ann had three pillows made from the homespun, stuffed with dried grass she gathered in the nearby woods. All their clothes, still dirty, hung from pegs she had made and stuck in the cracks of the lean-to. Some of the supplies were stored in wooden crates that the men had nailed together for her. She had lined them with Tarpaulin to keep the rain out. The food was stored safely away out of the reach of wild animals.

The men, too, had accomplished much through the day. Three stalls had been erected, one for the horse and one each for the mules. Each time a tree had been felled, they decided what it would be used for. The long straight ones were put aside for the making of their cabin. The scrubby trees were used for the out buildings and firewood. Before they stopped for the day, a toilet stood at the edge of the clearing.

Each time Listy Ann heard a tree fall, she looked in the direction of the noise to make sure her men folk were all right.

She was so pleased to have the toilet in place. She hated to have to go to the woods and half undress every time she had the need to pee.

When they fell into their bedrolls that night, it took them moments to fall asleep. They appreciated the fresh smelling pillows to rest their heads upon for the night.

The next morning began about as the day before. By ten o'clock the sun had burned the frost off the ground and each person felt as if they had done a days work. Listy Ann brought them water to drink. Jess wiped his mouth with his sleeve and said, "It shore is nice of you to stop your work and tend to our needs. Thank you."

She had decided early on in the day to go on and wash a few pieces of their clothes. She could prop the washboard up on a piece of wood to do the scrubbing and rinse each piece separately in one of the peck buckets. Jesse took enough time from his work to whittle a stirring stick to use for poking the clothes while they boiled in the pot.

She was taking the first batch to the nearest low growing tree when she heard the blast of the rifle. She jumped so that she dropped three pieces of the wet clothes in the dirt. "Damn! Damnation to hell and back." She turned quickly to see if either of the men had heard her foul language. She had vowed never to use another word of profanity the day she left her grandfather's house. Here she had spit out a mouthful before she realized it.

No such luck, they had both heard her. Jesse stood straight up and gave her a thumbs up sign. "That's my woman!"

he yelled out, so she'd be sure to hear him. "Get the stew pot on. Paw just shot a rabbit for our supper."

Jess stopped his work in the woods long enough to skin the rabbit. Listy Ann went on to the tree with the remaining pieces of clothing. On her way back, she picked up those from the ground. After she rinsed the dirt out of each piece, she hung them out to dry also. Before she could continue the washing, there were more trips to the creek for clean water.

The rabbit stew was a treat for supper that night. She had used some of the spices to flavor it up. With some potatoes and corn bread dumplings dropped in the pot, it was a meal to put strength back in their tired bodies.

When they had been on the land for three days, they were all working out in the woods. Listy Ann would go to help them as soon as she got her little bit of chores around the lean-to completed. She pulled branches out of the way, carried small trees to their designated places, and any other job the men thought she could handle. She was a worker. It amazed the men folk at the things she could do in a day's time and never complain.

They had been at work a couple of hours or so, when they heard a hearty, "Hey-o the Swinsons." It was Cyrus Garganus on horseback riding toward the clearing. They were so pleased to have company that they dropped their tools of labor and went to greet him.

He was off the horse by the time they reached him. "Good morning to you, sir," Jess was the first to speak. Cyrus shook Jess and Jesse's hands and tipped his hat to Listy Ann.

"Thought I'd mosey on over here this morning and see how you folks are faring. It's been right smart cold and I didn't know if maybe you'd all of froze by now."

After a few grunts and a big smile Jess said, "We're coming along pretty fair." Then he added, "Come on over by the fire. We'll make a pot of coffee and sit a spell."

He, with the help of Jesse, had put together four rough chairs made from some of the smaller tree branches. The chairs sat pretty well, too. It beat sitting on the ground or finding a stump to rest on.

Cyrus admired the chairs and recalled aloud how well he remembered his days of cutting his farm and home out of these woods around them. "It won't take you too long to have things on a comfort level. With three of you to do the work, it'll surprise you how quickly things fall into place for you." He sipped the scalding coffee and licked his lips to remove that which had dribbled from the cup.

They enjoyed the fellowship for a while longer and then Cyrus got up to leave. "I'll be going for supplies tomorrow. Thought I'd drop over and see if you needed anything or wished to ride along with me."

Jess got up and walked with his neighbor to the tree where his horse was tied. His mind was working faster than it had recently. Yes, it would be kind and thoughtful of him to spend the day apart from the newlyweds. They needed time to share alone. With them all sleeping in the same lean-to at night, it put a cramp in their lovemaking.

The few extra minutes he gave them in the mornings when he stayed in the woods longer than he needed to, was not much time. He often wondered if they knew why it took him so long each morning.

"You know, I think I will go along with you. It won't hurt a bit for me to rest up my back and arms for a day. I'll enjoy your company also. There are so many things I need to ask you about. Such as ways to get jobs here on this new land accomplished the fastest way, and when to dig and when to plant. I know farming, but that was in another country."

They shook hands and Cyrus heaved himself up and straddled his horse. "Come on over to the house by daylight, if you can. We need to leave early because it'll take us all day to get to Jacksonville," a small thriving settlement located on the east banks of the New River, "do our bargaining, and get back home." He waved a farewell and rode out of sight on the path he and his boys had cut before the Swinsons had arrived.

Jess was up before daylight the next morning. He fed and watered the horse and mules and added wood to the smoldering fire. Without any breakfast, he saddled the horse and rode away without disturbing the sleeping pair. He had told them the night before that he would most likely be gone all day.

Jesse and Listy Ann stayed in their bedroll until the sun was way up in the sky. It was wonderful to be alone and to be able to talk aloud to one another and to say loving things to each other without whispering.

When Jesse and his bride were sexually satisfied, he got up and rekindled the fire. She rolled over and snuggled down in the warmth of the cover, she relished in the fact that she could lay there for a while and daydream. After they ate their morning meal, Jesse went to start fires around a few of the tree stumps. What part of the stumps that didn't burn out, would be blown out with Dynamite later. "If you need me for anything, holler and I'll come to you," he said to her as he walked away.

She felt so good and contented. All she needed was a satisfying, completed love making with the man she loved. She hummed as she tidied up the breakfast remains. After she straightened the bedrolls, she decided to go to the woods and cut gall berry bushes to make a yard broom. She had seen a patch of them growing near the path on the way to the creek. The yard area around the lean-to and campfire was scattered with debris from wood scraps and other trash and she did not like a messy place.

Just as she started to leave the yard, Jesse came running up at a fast pace. "Quick! I got to get the rifle. I just saw a great big old tom turkey. If I can get back and shoot him, we'll have fowl for supper tonight."

She continued on to the woods in search of the gall berry bushes. Jesse hurried back to the woods, where he had seen the turkey. She was on her way back with her arms full of branches when she heard the shot ring out followed by a loud, "Whoopee!" She knew that he had zeroed in on his target.

The wash pot was filled half full of water and a fire built beneath it in preparation to scald the turkey. Jesse learned it was a lot easier when you had a woman to help do a job. While they worked together, he told her the stories of how they had trapped turkeys and other wild animals on their way to East St. Louis. "These tricks you have for cleaning a bird is a whole lot better than how we did it. Of course, we were about to starve by the time we caught anything to eat, so it didn't matter too much if it was done the right way or not."

Within two hours from the time Jesse shot the turkey, an aroma was floating up from the stew pot that hung over the campfire as the contents boiled over the open fire. It would be enough for the three of them to eat off for two or three days.

Jesse went on back to his work in the woods and Listy Ann got her branches trimmed down good like she wanted them, enough to make a good sized handful, and stood there holding them. At times, she forgot that everything she did had to be done from scratch. Now, where would she find a string to tie the branches into the broom she hoped for? She thought for a moment and remembered the homespun. She hated to use the new material to make a string, but realized she had no other choice.

When Jesse came up for dinner, he noticed right away the clean swept yard area. "Sure does make it look better around here. I like things clean too. Where did you get the broom?"

She explained the makings of the broom and pointed to where it rested against the lean-to.

The turkey was not quite done enough for the noon meal, but the giblets were. She had stirred up a few corn meal dumplings and dropped down in the broth to cook. "I sure would have loved to have had some rice to cook. This broth would go good with rice," she commented.

They wound up back in the bedroll soon after they ate. "You are a sight, Jesse Swinson. Do you suppose you will ever get enough?"

"Never, as long as you are alive."

They went for a walk through the woods later on. They came up on a patch of tall, dried grass. "Look at that," she stated as she stopped and dropped her hand from his.

He looked all around and couldn't see a thing that was impressive at the moment. "Look at what?"

"The grass, that's just what I need to stuff mattresses with. Let's go hook up the team and wagon, come back here, cut, and gather this grass. I'm tired of sleeping on the cold hard ground, aren't you?'

"Um-huh, shore am."

Smoke billowed skyward from several tree stumps and from beneath the iron stew pot. Jesse had cleared away all trash and debris from the stumps, so there was no danger of the woods catching fire while it was unattended. They added wood to the fire under the pot before they went for the grass.

It took a lot of room to turn the mules and wagon around. Jesse drove on until he found a clearing that seemed to be big enough. Before he completed the circle, they came upon a well-worn footpath. He pulled back on the reins and halted the mules. "Now Listy Ann, that looks to be a path that is used daily. Wonder who travels through here? I'll have to ask Mr. Garganus about this just as soon as I see him. I don't recall him mentioning anything about any folks living between us and the big swamp. Do you?"

It seemed to be a puzzle to her as well. "No. I don't."

As the sun eased over the tree tops, Listy Ann sat by the fire on one of the homemade chairs with enough of the homespun cut for a single mattress. She stitched with sturdy, self-assured fingers and sang a song her mother had sung to her when she was a little girl. She looked up toward the path when she heard the sound of a wagon approaching. She lay her sewing aside and ran toward the woods where her husband worked. "Jesse!" she shouted.

Before she got to the woods, she turned back and recognized her father-in-law. He rode his horse while Cyrus sat on the wagon, and drove the mules that pulled the wagon.

By the time she felt safe, Jesse had raced in to answer her call. They walked over together to greet Jess and the neighbor.

"Come see," Jess beckoned to Listy Ann.

"Wash tubs, good gracious, I'm glad to get these. What else did you bring Paw?" She was like an anxious child, waiting for an expected surprise.

She remembered her manners. "How are you Mr. Garganus?" she asked of him.

"Fine, ma'am."

Jesse went to help his father get the things off the wagon. When he lifted off the large sack of rice, Listy Ann winked at him and said, "See, I'll have my rice for supper now."

There were spring onion sets and mustard seeds, plus other items they needed.

Cyrus went to the back of the wagon and lifted off a basket filled with eggs, and a tow sack filled to the brim. "My madam sent this over for you. She thought you might enjoy an egg to go with your rice for breakfast in the morning." He handed her the basket and then gave her the tow sack.

She opened it enough to peek inside, "Collards! Oh boy, I haven't had these in such a long time."

Her husband and father-in-law looked on in amusement. They had no idea what collards were. They never even heard of them. They had wondered what was in the sack, but decided to remain quiet. They would learn soon enough. As excited as Listy Ann was, she wouldn't keep it a secret very long.

"Mr. Garganus, please tell her how much I appreciate all this, and let me add my thanks to you for clearing the path for us and all the other things you did. That was so thoughtful and nice of you."

Jesse spoke up with his thanks also.

The man felt a little embarrassment for all the gratitude paid him. It was such a little thing to do. He didn't know exactly what to say, so he removed his hat and said, "Something sure smells good a cooking."

"Can you believe? My husband shot his first turkey today. That's what you smell now. We ate the giblets with dumplings for dinner. It's still stewing in the pot," she volunteered the information proudly. "Won't you stay and share supper with us?"

He declined gracefully, because his wife had his supper ready for him back at his house. "I'll be getting on back there to the house now."

Jess walked the horse to the stall, removed the saddle, and took the bridle off. He whacked the rump of the horse when he turned him loose. He felt the tiredness that engulfed him. As soon as he fed and watered the animals, he went to the fire and drug up a chair. "I've done enough for today," he stated as he leaned back and propped his feet up to the fire to warm his toes.

Listy Ann had put her sewing away and had supper pretty near ready to eat by the time he sat down.

They were up and about early the next morning. Jesse asked Listy Ann what she wanted done with the feathers from the turkey. He had learned that she threw nothing away.

"Just leave 'em in the bucket. I'll take care of 'em after a while."

She sewed steadily on the mattress during the first part of the morning. It took many stitches to sew the length of the mattress. When she tied the knot after taking the last stitch, she took the mattress cover to the wagon and stuffed as much grass in it as she could carry back to the lean-to. Now, how was she going to get enough of the straw over to where she needed it? She got a piece of the tarpaulin and piled grass on it, then dragged it back to where the mattress was. When she had stuffed enough grass in the mattress for the right firmness, she sewed up the hole she had used to do the filling of the mattress. She took Jess' bedroll and hung it on a tree to air out. She then laid the mattress down on a piece of the tarpaulin where he slept.

She looked, washed the collards, and got them to boiling in the biggest pot they had, along with a piece of the smoked middling meat. The men were not too far, from the boiling pot of collards. When the odor floated out to where they were, they both stopped their work and straightened up to sniff the air a time or two. Jesse looked at his father, "What in the world is that smell Paw?" They sniffed the air several more times and looked around to see what was in the woods that would put out such a stench. "Paw it don't exactly smell like a polecat. Do you think?"

Listy Ann stood and watched her men folk. She had been waiting for the scent to reach them. She had seen people before who had been introduced to collards for the first time. The odor was very offensive. Like no other odor, but comparable to anything that smelled bad. She called out to them to come up by the fire. The closer they got the fresher the scent was to them.

"Brister, do you smell something terrible?" he questioned. "It seems to be stronger up here by the fire than out there in the woods."

She was laughing so that she could hardly explain. She pulled her dress tail up to wipe her eyes and pointed to the pot of collards.

"It's the collards cooking." She continued to laugh and clapped her hands in glee. "I wish you two could see yourselves."

"You mean to tell me you eat that? Why, it smells as bad as one of them Kentucky skunks. Phew, woman that's rancid." Jesse rubbed his nose to wipe away the odor.

"It will become one of our staple foods for the winter. It's one of the best tasting vegetables you can ask for. It's filled with vitamins and just wait 'til you take a taste of it. You will be quite surprised." They went back to their work thinking they'd never learn to like something that had an odor like that.

They started digging a well that day. Cyrus had suggested they dig one before warm weather set in. The water in the creek would dry up except for a trickle from the heat unless there was a heavy rain.

It was a hard task to dig with only a shovel and a pick. While Jesse dug, Listy Ann hauled the dirt away a bucket full at a time. Jess rigged up a pulley with cut tree limbs and some of the rope he had purchased back in Clinton. He built a frame over the space where Jesse dug. When a certain depth was reached down in the ground, it would be easier to haul the dirt up in one of the buckets tied to the pulley. Then Listy could go back to her chores.

When Jesse reached about a seven foot depth, Jess noticed clay-like soil in the bucket. "Hey Jesse," he leaned over the hole and hollered down to his son. "This is the kind of clay Cyrus told me to look for to make our bricks out of. I'll put it in a pile all by it's self and when we have enough we'll stop digging and work up a few bricks.

Listy Ann called out to them. "Come on up and get washed up. Dinner's ready."

They were ready for a rest and both hungry as bears. They knew they would have to sample the collards and neither looked forward to the experience.

"Do you suppose it'll kill us to eat it?" Jesse asked his father. He had his back turned to his wife when he asked the question. He didn't want her to hear what he asked.

She had stirred up some pastry to cook in the turkey broth, just in case they wouldn't eat the collards. At least the pastry would fill their bellies if not with collards.

Jess lifted a forkful of the greens to his nose and inhaled deeply. "Say, it don't smell nothing like it did cooking."

He eased the fork into his mouth, closed his teeth on it and pulled the fork out. With his tongue he wallowed the finely chopped, drained of all juices, greens around in his mouth, chewed, and then swallowed. He discovered a very interesting taste. He tore a piece of the boiled middling meat off with his fork and added it to the next mouthful of collards.

"Go on boy, eat some. Like she told us, they ain't bad. None of that odor we smelled ain't in them now." He ate hearty of the vegetable. So did Jesse.

"The pot likker, which the collards boiled in, is the best laxative you could ask for, and when we get a dog, I can make his meals from the likker. Just add corn meal to it, and boil a little while. That's called mush. If we should get hungry enough, we can survive on mush, at least for a good while." She offered the information with a smile.

Jess excused himself early and retired for the night. Soon after he lay down, he hollered out, "Hey! What's this?"

Listy Ann knew what he meant. "That's your new mattress Paw."

He stretched out to his full length and wiggled around on the softness. It felt quite comfortable. "Thank ye me gal, but shouldn't you and Jesse be laying on it?"

"I'm working on one for us Paw. It'll be ready by tomorrow night."

"It smells so clean and fresh. I even like the sound the crunch makes when I move. So that's why my bedroll was airing out most of the day?"

They often sat by the campfire after Jess turned in for the night. It was a time for small private talk and fondling.

In the bright sunshine of the next morning, Listy Ann was gathering dried straw to add to the brick makings. She had stooped over to gather up an armful when she straightened up. She felt the dampness in her straddle. "Oh gracious, I knew this would happen about now." She dropped the straw and walked to the lean-to.

The bolt of white homespun was of good use again. She got scissors and cut sections to be rolled and fitted to her need. She went on and made enough to last her through the week, then stored them in her satchel. She went to the toilet, and carefully put one of the cut folded sections of the homespun in her under drawers to absorb the flow of blood. The rag was pinned to a string made from the homespun tied around her hips.

She came out of the toilet, straightened up, and went back to her chore of gathering straw as if nothing had happened.

That night when Jesse snuggled up to her she whispered to him, "That's all we can do for the next six or seven days, is snuggle." She hoped Paw didn't hear her message. She explained to him that it was that time of the month for her.

He didn't know a whole lot about the workings of a woman's body, but had learned that much a few years ago. He tightened his arms about her, and they slept soundly on their new, crunchy, straw mattress.

For the next month, they worked from dawn until dark. The well filled with good tasting, clear water, which was a delight for each of them. It meant no more heavy buckets of water to be brought up from the creek. The bricks turned out pretty good too. They had followed Cyrus' instructions on how to make them. They had used a rack made from small tree limbs to lay bricks on to help dry them by the fire, and the warm sunshine was a great help.

With the two men cutting and saving the logs needed, there were enough long, straight logs to erect their cabin. Listy Ann had spent many an hour stripping the bark off all the logs. She would be so thankful to have a roof over her head again.

Jess used a ripsaw to fashion out enough shingles to cover the top of the structure. Jesse notched the logs as soon as his wife cleared the bark away. With three of them working in unison, they were ready to start work putting the cabin up by Jess' birthday.

It had not rained since they had first arrived. The wind blew like it was angry with them at times and it stayed so cold.

Cyrus and his family came over on the day the roof was to be added. His wife brought food enough for everyone to enjoy. To Listy Ann's delight, there was a chocolate cake.

"Oh, Mrs. Garganus, that looks so good. I can't wait to eat a slice. You and your family are such fine neighbors. I don't know what we would have done without you."

"You would have survived, we did. And me with small children," the older woman said back to her.

After they finished their meal, Jesse turned to Cyrus and asked of him, "Sir, do you know anything about a well used path over south of us? Listy Ann and me, we found it a while back and I keep forgetting to ask you about it."

Cyrus leaned back in his seat and rubbed his chin. "Well, yes I do. I really should have mentioned it to you folks before now, but seems to have slipped my mind." He had everyone's attention as he continued his story.

"They're Indians that use the trail, as they call it. They've been over there for many years. They were here when me and my family moved in. There's not a mean one in the lot. They are friendly as a newborn kitten. Seems that they are of the Iroquois Nation, from up in the state of Ohio. When they were forced to leave, from what I gather, it was back around 1667. From the best I can recall, they were headed on down to South Carolina and for some reason a small scattering of them broke off from the main party and ended up over there, just this side of the swamp, where they still live. They too are farmers of a sort. They have several acres cleared and mostly they grow corn, beans, and squash. They have a few chickens, and a few animals, but no horses or mules. What they plant, they work with hand tools. The last time I was over there, I took notice that the tribe had just about diminished, and that was a few years ago. They're dying off and not many babies being born. They bury their dead the same way we do. Their graveyard is located not far from their village."

He stopped with his tale long enough to lift the tin cup to his mouth and empty it of water. All that talking made him thirsty.

"Now Jess, Jesse, the land you're buying, part of it is where they have settled. They have the right to live there as long as they choose to, even though it will be your land. They won't bother you at all, but if you decide to visit them, you'll find a welcome out for you at any time. They speak enough English so that you can converse with them."

When Cyrus and his family left for home later on that day, the roof was on the cabin and the chimney was almost completed. Cyrus and his boys had joined in with the work to help the Swinson's with their roof.

The cabin was as long as the logs were. At one end, Jess had sectioned off a small room for Jesse and his bride. The larger room would serve as his sleeping quarters, kitchen, and sitting room. There was a door in the front and one in the rear, no windows in the small abode, and the ground served as a floor.

Late February brought showers of rain and warm days, sounds of birds in the trees, frogs in the creek and tiny buds pushing out from trees and underbrush.

The men had made a bed frame to fit each mattress, all from rough wood, but filled their needs at the moment. A table big enough to seat four people accompanied by four chairs, stood in the kitchen area. Listy Ann had cleared the bark from all the wood used to make the furniture. She used sand along with a piece of the homespun to polish the wood until it felt smooth to the touch.

She did the cooking in the fireplace but still, on warm days, she cooked outside. She looked forward to the day she would have a cook stove to cook on. Jess had promised to purchase one just as soon as he could.

At the end of one particular day, as they sat at the supper table, Jess said, "We're out of money. We're simply going to have to live off this land until we can sell some turpentine."

They had gone to Cyrus and learned how to slash the pine trees and make the containers to catch the drippings. Every day one of them, and sometimes both, went to empty the sticky liquid. With the weather getting warmer daily, the turpentine would run more freely. Most of the pines in the area ran their sap faster in the spring.

"Paw, I still have my last wages. All I spent of it was what I paid the preacher for marrying us."

"Do you know how far that money will go when you start buying farm needs? You hang on to what you have. You'll need it when we go to closeout buying this place."

It was a warm afternoon. They had quit work a little earlier than usual. Listy Ann had supper ready to eat by the time they watered and fed up the animals. Their meals fell in the order of breakfast in the morning, dinner at noon and supper at the end of the day.

There was still enough daylight coming in through the open doors to see clearly. Listy Ann could sit on her secret no longer. She excused herself and arose from the table. She entered the prized little bedroom she adored. When she came back to them, she laid her one good dress on the table in front of them. "Here, I want you to see my dress. I brought it along just in case I'd get to go somewhere and need it. So far I haven't needed it Look it over and tell me what you think of it." The dress was floor length with a bustle. She had a hat with a wide brim, flowers, and ribbons for decoration to wear along with the dress.

Both men looked at her with questions on their faces. Yes, it was a dress all right. They each reached out to feel the material. What could she have in mind by putting the dress on the table like that? The though ran through their minds.

"Go on, pick it up. Feel the weight of it. With all that bustle added to the back there, you men never realize how much weight we ladies have to carry around when we get all frocked up." She was impatient for one of them to lift it up off the table.

Jess took a handful of the material and lifted it slightly. "You're right, it is sorta heavy." He moved his hand up and down to judge the weight. When he let it get too close to the tabletop, he and Jesse heard the clunking noise it made when it banged lightly on the tabletop. "What in the world have you got in it to make such a noise?" her father-in-law wanted to know.

He laid the dress down and felt around over the material. Jesse was feeling around on the dress also.

She could stand it no longer. She leaned over and spread the dress out over the table, so the hem was between the two of them. "There, open the hem up. Go on, pull that thread right there, out."

Jess' fingers were rough and scaly from so much hard work. They snagged on the fine material as he worked at the thread. Jesse too, found his fingers snagged on the soft dress. Jess finally grasped the thread and pulled at it to open the hem. When he saw the money, he let his hands fall away and rest beside the opening.

Jesse's mouth hung open as if he was transfixed, in that shape.

Listy Ann stood with her arms crossed below her breast, pleased as she could be at what she looked at.

Jess ran his hand over the money. It was the most he had seen in a long time, maybe ever, at one time.

To Jesse's knowledge, he had never seen so much at one time. He looked up to see the sneaky smile on his wife's face. She winked at him.

"Brister?" He tilted his head back in the way that she had come to love. "What?" it seemed his mouth would not form the question that sat on the tip of his tongue. "Where?"

Jess was also dumfounded. "Little lady, what is this?" He did not take his eyes off the money while he asked. He did not want it to disappear. He had stretched every cent of his money as far as he could and it had not been enough to carry them through until they could sell some of their farm products.

"That's five thousand American dollars. It's my inheritance from my great grandfather. He died in Greece several years ago and left it to me. I have found no need to spend any of it until now." She looked straight into her husband's eyes, "I know you told me to bring nothing of my grandfather's with me. Well, in a sense, this money came through him, but was never really his. The reason I've kept quite until now is, I know you are both proud men. Sometimes I think too proud for your own good."

Jesse pushed his chair back from the table a ways. Listy Ann sat down in her chair. Neither said a word.

Jess was trying to absorb what this all meant. There was a lot, an awful lot, of cash money lying on the table in front of him, but to take a woman's money? That would take some considering.

It was as if she was reading their minds. She gathered up the money and stacked it up in a neat pile in front of her.

She patted the top of it and said, "I know what you both are thinking, but let me tell you a thing or two before we go any farther: this is a new world we are in. We have to make a lot of the rules we live by daily. There is no social standard to compare with what we do." She nudged at the money and moved it out to the center of the table. "Here's the money. We need it desperately. I bring it into our marriage just as I bring my hands. With my hands, I help you dig out a living from this ground. With my body, I hope to give you sons and daughters. With this money, I give us a chance to move along faster and less hungry toward our goal of surviving in this wilderness."

She paused in her statement to see if one of them would respond.

"Hhhmmm!" Jess cleared his throat.

Jesse reached over and fondled a handful of the money. "This shore does put a different light on our situation, don't it, Paw?"

Listy Ann was a woman light years ahead of her times. She was a woman of strength, determination, boldness and she was an honest human being. She was tall of stature for a woman and shaped like a Greek Goddess. Her hair was black. Her complexion was of a light olive shade, smooth, without a blemish. She had full rounded lips that showed pearly white teeth when she smiled, which was often. Her eyes were a pale green, filled with mischief, when she was in the right mood. Her fingers were long and slender. They were graceful hands that could play the piano and pump organ. She loved to paint and draw pictures. Many pieces of her work hung on the walls of her father and grandfather's homes.

In this wilderness, where she and her new family called home, there was no place for many of her talents. Her mind and interests were active in doing her share of the work as well as being creative in this new life. She had channeled many of her knowledgeable talents down to suit the situation she found herself in. When she saw a task that needed to be done, if she didn't know how to do it, she sat with it for a while until she figured out the procedure of doing the job.

As for the money, she'd brought into the marriage, she had sense enough to know had she revealed it before there was a desperate need, they would have denied her offer to pool her money with theirs.

She had been wise in her decision. Jesse was thrilled on sight of the money, while Jess held back with his acceptance.

"It will make a big difference in our growth here on this land. But I hate like the devil to take your money, Listy Ann."

"Paw, it's not my money, it's our money. Just think of it as part of me that you have welcomed to your bosom. If you don't use this money, what will become of it?"

"Let me sleep on it. It sure does look good, laying there before me. I'll have to be honest and tell you that much."

Listy Ann got up from the table and went to the fireplace where the coffee pot sat in the hot ashes. She took the pot to the table and refilled their cups with the steaming black coffee.

The sun had settled in behind the trees for the day. When Jess finished his coffee, he excused himself and went to his bed. He always cleared his throat to let his daughter-in-law know it was time to turn her head while he removed his outer clothes. Soon after he lay down he said, "I'll tell you again how good this mattress you made for me feels when I lay upon it. I think about it every time I lay on it." He turned toward the wall and was asleep in no time at all.

It was a restless night for Jess. When he arose a little before daylight the next morning, all was well in his mind about using the money. During the night, he had mulled over all the things Listy Ann had said concerning the use of the money. He realized she had been wise in the things she had said.

Jess prepared to go to town the second day after the money was revealed. "Anything particular you want from the store?" he asked of Listy Ann.

"Yes, I need two flat irons. I'm tired of seeing you men in wrinkled clothes all the time. Please, if you can find a cook stove, get one. I'd really like to have a sewing machine, too. It takes me forever to sew up anything on my fingers. We also need another bolt of white homespun. Both you men are in need of under drawers." She didn't mention that she too needed slips and new brassieres. She could not stand to wear the brassieres she had which were sewn into the tops of her corsets. Farm work was no place for corsets. She'd learned that within the first month being on the land. She felt like she could design and sew up the brassieres if she put her mind to it. She would be in the need of more teddies pretty soon, too. The homespun would be used for many needed items.

With a cook stove to use it meant a different length wood to be cut. They knew it would take most of the day for Jess to complete his trip to and from town. So Jess and his Brister got busy with the cutting of the stove wood. They used a crosscut saw. She kept up with his every pull of the saw. The rhythm of the sawing got them in the mood to enter the cabin and try out their mattress one more time.

Jesse went and got fires started around several more stumps. It would be planting season soon and they needed all the cleared land they could get. Then he got his materials together to begin work on the construction of a chimney to hold the cook stove flue, while Listy Ann found herself a good sturdy chopping block and began to split the wood into small pieces to fit inside the firebox of the stove. She wanted to be ready should Jess come home with a stove. She chopped enough wood to last for a week before the noon hour. She stacked the wood in neat stacks. She made a square of four pieces and built the stack upward to her own height. In that order, it allowed the wood to dry much faster.

Darkness fell and Jess was not home. "Jesse, what do you suppose could have happened to him? He should have been back here hours ago." Listy Ann stood in the open doorway of the cabin and looked toward the path he would be using to come home.

Jesse was worried too, but tried to keep his concerns from showing. "I think I'll hitch up the horse and ride over to Mr. Garganus'. Maybe Paw stopped there on his way out and mentioned what his plans were for the day."

Jesse rode up to the cabin door on his way out and asked, "Do you want to go with me? You've never been left here after dark before."

"No. I'll be all right. Just hurry and come on back. You hear?"

Jesse met his father just after he crossed the creek. He turned his horse around and followed him back to the cabin.

"I'm sorry to be so late, but I got to talking to a man about setting up a saw mill out here and time got away from me before I realized it." He got down from the wagon and told Jess that they'd unload the supplies the next day.

"There'll be light then so we can see what we're doing."

Listy Ann could hardly wait to get her hands on the sewing machine. "What kind of machine did you get me Paw? Did you remember to get thread that will run through the bobbin?"

"Why, a Singer of course. The man said it was the best on the market today." He went on to stable the mules after he answered her.

Just as soon as Jess entered the cabin, Listy ladled his supper of rabbit stew on his plate. He talked of his interest in the sawmill while he ate. "If we can get it set up, we can have enough planks sawed to get the main house framed out in about two weeks. I went on and bought nails today."

Early the next morning the stove was set up in the cabin near the fireplace. The first meal cooked on it was fried potatoes, fried pork and piping hot biscuits. "These are fine biscuits Listy Ann. I haven't had one since Christmas day over at the Garganus'. Now you have pleased my belly with yours. How do you get them so fluffy?" Jess complimented her as he drug crumbs of a biscuit through syrup.

Jesse and Listy Ann enjoyed the end results of owning a cook stove also.

"Paw, you just wait until you sample one of my cakes or pies. I can make a tasty custard, too."

She realized she'd have to wait to cook many of the dishes she wanted to, due to the lack of ingredients not yet on the pantry shelf, because she did not have a pantry shelf, only a good-sized sideboard attached to the cabin wall.

Jesse whittled out grooved blocks of wood to set the sewing machine wheels in to keep sand from ruining them. It too was kept in the cabin to be carried outside on the days she planned to use it. The light was so much better out in the yard than in the cabin.

Late one afternoon, Jess went to his satchel and took out paper and pen. He searched around in the bag until he found the inkbottle. The writing material had been purchased before leaving Clinton. He went to the sewing machine, drug up a chair and placed an oil lamp on the sewing machine. The machine made a fine desk for him to do his writing.

He had finally remembered to ask Cyrus about the mail system here in Onslow County a few days earlier. He had been told that the mailman came about once a month from Catherine's Lake, North Carolina, a small farming community nearest to them in miles, where the post office was located. "If there's a piece of mail coming this way, he'll bring it on before his once a month trip is scheduled. Otherwise, he comes around only once a month, to see if we have any going out."

Jess wrote to his son, James. A very short letter, expressing his love for him and the terrible void his absence had cause in his heart and in that of his brother. He explained of their settling on the land, and the progress they had accomplished since their arrival. The news of Jesse' wife was the last item he entered in the letter. He addressed the letter to his son in care of the surveyor's company they had worked for, to the home office in East St. Louis, Illinois.

Early the next morning he saddled the horse and rode over to Cyrus' house. "I've brought a letter for the mailman to get. It's to my son, wherever he is. All I know is he headed out west with the job he was on. Will you hold it until the man comes? I'll appreciate it."

"Be glad to oblige you. He should be getting here any day now."

When the mailman did come, he rode on over to Jess' house to say howdy and let the Swinsons know how welcome they were in the county. "Good day to you, Mr. Swinson. I'm John Wooten, your mail carrier. When Mr. Garganus told me you and your family lives back up in here, I thought I'd ride in and make you welcome."

They shook hands as soon as John dismounted. Jess invited him to walk on over to the well with him for a cool, fresh drink of water.

Jess lowered the wooden bucket he had handmade down into the water. When it filled, he drew it up with pride. It made him feel good to offer his new thirsty friend a drink. It was good tasting water and the well casing and overhang was professionally constructed. John made a comment on what a good job Jess had done there.

Spring was finally bursting out and it was a warm day. The trees were filled with buds and green could be seen all around in the woods. It was a welcome sight, too, because the cold weather had been hard on the new settlers.

When John finished the water, he returned the dipper to the bucket with a remark as to how good the water was and then added, "You folks have come a long way on clearing your land here abouts." He looked all around at the headway they had made and swung his arm around to indicate where he meant. "Do you have any seeds in the ground yet?"

They walked toward one of the fields and continued to carry on their conversation. "Yes, we've started. We got the cotton in and early garden vegetables. Cyrus up there has been quite helpful guiding us along. That's a fine man, Cyrus is."

John knew of some things he thought he'd pass along to this new farmer. There's a man travels around selling his wares.

He's called the Watkins Man. He gets his goods from up New York way and comes around every six weeks or so. His line runs from liniment to flavoring. "If you'd like, I can tell him to stop over here to allow you to see what he has to offer."

They had walked back up to where the mail carrier's horse was by the time he finished his helpful hints. "There's also a fisherman who will come to your house to sell you fish. I'll send him in here also, if you'd like me to."

"Jess took his hat off and wiped his brow with his sleeve. "That's right neighborly of you. A good mess of fish would taste mighty good to all three of us about now. I know Listy Ann will like for the man with the products to come by here."

Jess went on to tell his new friend about the letter he was sending off to his son. "Do you suppose they will forward it on to him, if he's still with the company?"

"That's the way a lot of today's mail gets around. It might take a year or so for you to get an answer from him." He pulled the letter from his bag and looked at the address. "Shouldn't be no problem." He secured the letter back in the bag again and climbed up on his horse. "I'll be back. God bless you and your crop."

He rode away and Jess felt good about mailing the letter. He put his hat back on and went to hitch one of the mules up to a plow. Jesse was already in the field plowing with the other mule. When they had plowed enough new ground to feel safe about the woods not catching on fire from the blasting, they were to blow the remaining stumps out of the ground.

The land they had cleared, and were still clearing, was all east and northeast of the original clearing toward the Garganus farm. Their aim was to clear all the timbers between the two farms so there would be a visible view from one farm to the other.

Listy Ann was busy with the weekly washing. She had recently finished her monthly period and had the rags she used for pads soaking in one of the peck buckets. She always washed them out when the men were away from the house, either in the fields or busy in the woods with the turpentine or cutting trees down. It was just one of those jobs she preferred to do in privacy. It was a nasty, dreaded chore that women had to put up with. If she threw the rags she used for pads away, she would soon run out of material, and that would never do. Each month she soaked them until she finished her bleeding and then washed them out, then added them to the regular wash.

When they were hung out on the clothes line that Jesse had finally took the time to make for her, they were hung with discretion, under a bed sheet or any item of clothing large enough to conceal them from an onlooker. All her underwear was hung on the line in the same manner.

On this particular morning, after she had finished the breakfast dishes, she pulled her poke bonnet on her head and tied the strings snugly beneath her chin. The bonnet was always on her head, whether it be winter or summer, when she went out for a long period of time. She glanced toward the new ground where the men were at work, and decided it was safe to start her wash, beginning with her pads.

She filled the wash pot and got the fire going. When the water heated up she got busy scrubbing the rags on the scrub board. She had her mind on making a flowerbed around the cabin and did not hear Jesse as he approached her. He was on his way to the well for water.

He walked by where she was bent over the washboard and said, "Hi lovely lady." She jumped and splashed water on the front of her dress.

It irritated her to have her clean dress soiled with the dirty water. "You damn fool, what's the matter with you, sneaking up on me like that?"

"I didn't sneak up on you. I came up here the way I always come up here. I need water from the well. Me and Paw are getting hot and thirsty out yonder in the sun. We couldn't get your attention to have you bring it to us, so here I am." He stood for a moment and looked at the water she worked with. He had never seen her do the chore before.

"What in the name of hell are you doing there?" he had a snarled expression on his face, and was curious as to what she was up to.

She explained what she was doing and why. "Now you go on about your business and I'll tend to mine, if you don't mind."

He leaned in close to her and kissed her gently on the cheek. "I'm sorry I startled you Brister, but I love it when you get testy with me; shows me that I've got a woman who will stand up to me and still fulfill my needs in all other areas. I love you Brister. I never knew what love could do for a fellow until I met you. Once when Paw and I were talking about my mother, he mentioned how a woman could make or break a man. Now I know what he was talking about. You are the best thing that has ever happened to me."

In March of 1869, the first transcontinental railroad was completed, and Jess stepped across the ends of cotton rows. The seeds were pushing the earth aside, sprouting, and pushing the new growth upward reaching for the sunshine. The rows were lined up perfectly straight in the acres of new cleared ground, and a cast of green could be seen all across the field of cotton.

The cornfield was showing new shoots, cracking open the soil that held the corn kernels, waiting for a good spring rain to soak the ground and give the sprouts growth.

He felt proud when he looked out over his first crop. He turned and walked toward the acre that had been planted in garden seeds. "It won't be too long before we can grace our table with some of these vegetables grown right here on our very own land," he said aloud as he squatted and pulled a small, tender onion from the rich, loose soil.

It was still early in the day when he returned to the house where Listy Ann was putting breakfast on the table. While they ate, Jess spoke to her in a sweet, friendly tone. "How do you like the idea of me bringing back some baby chicks when I come back from town today? With all the grass coming up, it'd make good food for them. There's plenty of bugs and worms in the ground for them to keep busy scratching. Feeding them won't be a problem. I'd like to have eggs and chicken on the table once in a while to eat. Wouldn't you?"

She arose from her seat and went to stand behind him, "That will be a good and smart thing to do Paw." She placed her hands on his shoulders and massaged the muscles of his neck and upper back. It always relaxed him and made him feel loved when she showed him a little attention.

Jess left shortly after he ate. He was on a trip to purchase needed supplies and to see about finalizing the deal to get the sawmill up and operating.

Jesse and his Brister always enjoyed the times when Jess was away for the day. It had become their private time to learn and explore with each other. Most of the days when Jess was away, some of the farm chores lay undone. They took long walks through the woods. Listy Ann found and marked trees she wanted to transplant to the new house area. The fall season would be a good time to move the young, tender trees from their original stand.

Her favorite was the gracious, stately oak. She found and tied a piece of homespun string to each tree she wanted to transplant. She knew before hand the amount of leaves that would have to be swept up in the autumn. The leaves would be a worrisome thing to be put up with, but the benefit the trees provided during the hot months with shade, was worth the aggravation.

At about nightfall, Jess returned from town with the wagon loaded with sawmill equipment, a rooster, and five hens. One of the hens came with eight baby chicks, which Listy Ann called biddies, three sows and enough feed to carry them until the corn and peanuts, which Listy Ann called ground peas, were harvested to feed the animals with.

The chickens were allowed to have the run of the yard and field during the day, and to be confined in a coop during the night. A row of nests was built to run along the length of the coop. The hogs were marked with a series of cuts on one ear to establish ownership. They ran free in the surrounding woods. They soon learned to come up when it was feeding time. One of the sows was expected to have a late litter of pigs in a few days.

When Jess thought of his mark to put on his hogs he used three long, straight, clean cuts, to the left ear of each hog. When a person ran up on a hog in the woods or in a field, they would know whose hog it was by the mark it carried on the ear.

The rails for the fence to enclose the crops were cut from the heart of pine. The centers of the trees were apt to last for years without decaying. Jess and Jesse had several lengths cut and laid in a zigzag pattern, but had a lot more to cut and lay before the field was encircled. The fence was to keep the hogs from rooting up the crops. On occasion, a hog would root beneath the fence and enter a field. It was soon rounded up and returned to the woods. When the crops were harvested, the hogs were allowed to roam the fields, rooting and eating the ground peas and left over corn to fatten them up for the cold weather slaughtering time.

It would pose a big problem to keep the hogs out of the field, so the men worked at break neck speed to complete the job of rail splitting and laying the rest of the fence.

It was work from before daylight until after dark, each and every day. When night fell, it wasn't too long before the three Swinsons were in bed sound asleep.

The first morning after the rooster arrived, they awoke to a new and wonderful sound. The rooster was still in the chicken coop but let it be known he was on his new turf and the hens were his harem.

Jess had constructed the coop the day after he brought the chickens home, out near the toilet. All the chickens took to it after Listy Ann shooed them in it a couple of nights. They went to roost between sunset and nightfall.

The eggs tasted very good to them, when there were enough to cook. They'd only had chicken eggs when Mrs. Garganus had been so gracious as to send or fetch some over. Listy Ann decided not to have chicken to eat until the biddies grew large enough to eat. They had eaten many turkeys. Since the turkeys roamed wild in the nearby woods it was easy enough to shoot one when needed. A few times the men would run up on a turkey nest and bring the eggs to the house. Sometimes they would be rotten and other times eatable. A turkey egg is very small so it took more of them to fill a man's stomach.

When the sawmill was up and running, they realized they could get more work done on it in a day, than they could in a whole month before by hand.

The rail fence was finished all the way around the farm and planks lay stacked neatly in a pile toward erecting their house. They had the site picked out for the house. All three of them were satisfied with the location. It was to be built one half mile from the cabin, across the creek, nearer to the Garganus farm.

The reason for the location was the creek. When it rained a lot, the water rose, making it hard to cross. Since clearing the land on both sides of the creek, it stayed wet and muddy for a long time near the creek.

The cleared land now reached well past the creek on up beyond where the house would be located. Ditches had been dug in the low areas to allow the water to drain from the fields into the ditches, which flowed into the creek.

With the weather getting warmer each day, Listy Ann got her flowerbeds worked up. She used the hoe and rake to loosen up the soil. There was no need for fertilizer because the dirt was rich and pliable.

She went to her satchel and drew from it the treasured seeds she had taken from her grandfather's supply before she had left his home. She knew and remembered what Jesse had told her about taking nothing from her grandfather, but felt he wouldn't make too much ruckus over a few flower seeds. One of her passions was lovely sweet smelling flowers. She had enough seeds to make a bed in front of the cabin and a good-sized patch close to the water well.

Three days after Jess had returned from town with the sawmill he was hanging up his coat and remembered the papers he had tucked in one of the breast pockets.

"I plum forgot about this. I got it when I was in town the other day for you two." He handed it to Jesse who sat at the supper table.

It was a handbill, advertising that a theater troupe would be at White Store, a small thriving community located between Wadesboro, North Carolina, and the South Carolina state line, about thirty miles east of Charlotte, North Carolina.

"I thought you might think about taking a week or so away from this place with nothing but work, and go on up there for a few days rest and entertainment. The man that gave it to me said it would be well worth the time it'll take to get there. I also gathered up the train schedule for you to look at. If you decide to go, I can take you to the Verona depot and go back to get you when you return." He sat down and filled his plate like that of a hungry man.

Listy Ann was too excited even to think about eating her supper. She stood behind Jesse's chair and read the words on the handbill over his shoulder.

"Oh Paw, can we really and truly go? I used to go see things like this all the time. It is fully entertaining to sit and watch the shows." She continued to read and pointed her finger at the last name on the page. "Oh look, Lily Sattler, the opera singer is performing. I saw and heard her when I was in France a few years ago."

"Set down Brister and eat your supper. I'll give this to you as soon as I finish reading it. I don't know about going to hear one of them opera singers. I went to hear one when we were still in Ireland, went with my mother. I didn't like it then and doubt I'd like it now. Just give me some good old down to earth singing."

"Oh, you don't know what fine music is, do you?" she spat at him.

"Yea, I know what it is. I may not look like a social fellow today with my bibbed overalls and dirt stuck to my shoes, but I remember a few things. Mother was into all that stuff when I was a little fellow back in Ireland."

The mention of Ireland always put thoughts of remorse in Jess' mind. He still had his days when the memory of what he'd had in Ireland and lost, was almost too much for him to bear. He pushed his chair away from the table and excused himself. "If you don't mind, I think I'll go on to bed. It's been a long day and I'm tired all the way through my being."

Listy Ann was so excited about the trip to White Store that she sang all the next morning while she got her chores done. She drug out her one good dress and hung it in the shade of one of the trees to air out. She fluffed her hat and rearranged this and that on it until she got the results she wanted.

"It's going to be a fun trip for us Jesse," she said, when the men came to the house for dinner.

The crops in the fields were at a stage where they didn't need constant attention. Jess told them he could handle things around on the land while they were gone. He had arranged with the oldest Garganus boys to come over and help with the sawmill work.

The first of April, Jesse hooked the horse up to the buggy and the three of them headed off to Verona. The trip would remain in their memories forever.

While they were gone, Jess worked hard and long hours. The moon was at its fullest. Several nights he worked on into the night. The moonlight was almost as bright as day, without the sunshine.

Lewis Cyrus, Jr., called Lewis, was nine years old and a big help to Jess. The boy was big for his age and could do a man's job at that age. Jess paid him ten cents a day for his work.

In May, the rains came and filled all the creeks and ditches to overflowing. The land needed the water, but not quite so much at one time. Jess walked the fields and decided there was a need for more drainage ditches. He and Jesse would get to it just as soon as the water level lowered enough to start the digging.

The temperature had risen to a new high for so early in the season. Jesse came to the house one mid-morning, wet with sweat that dripped from his face. He found his woman and said to her, "Come on, go with me. We're going swimming down in the creek. That place where the water has washed out a good-sized hole. It's filled with fresh, clean water. Just right for a good swim."

"Swimming! Where in the world did you get that thought?"

"Just stop what you're doing Brister and come on. It'll be fun. Paw is in the back field ditching, he knows where we're going. He won't be bothering us so hurry up and come on."

When they got to the creek, they stopped in the shade of one of the trees that lined the creek bank. It felt good to their hot back to stand there and allow the cool shade to cool them off a little while they watched the water flow along the creek.

Jesse took every stitch of his clothing off and stood before her buck-naked. She had not seen him in that state before. The weather had been too cold to be taking clothes off the body. The intake of her breath almost startled her. Her hands covered her mouth. Her face reddened in excitement and anticipation of what his body could do to her and for her.

She stood still while he flexed his muscles and did a few poses for her. "Brister, take your clothes off. What are you waiting for?"

It was strange that she hesitated to take her clothes off. Actually, she had never undressed in front of a man before. It took a little nerve to just step out of her clothes as easily as he had.

He laughed at her while he moved closer to her. "It's only me, honey. I may not have seen all of you, but I sure have felt of everything you have under that frock. Don't you think it's time we looked at each other?"

"Well yes--eh--but eh -- oh, all right." She undid the front of her dress, and it slid to her feet. She wore no underwear beneath the frock and when she stepped away from the dress, she too was in the nude.

Jesse, a grown man, nearly swooned at what stood before him. She had the perfect shape. Her breasts were firm and tilted at the nipples. Her waist was tight and narrow as if it was tied with human skin. The skin of a goddess covered her, smooth and creamy. Her hips rounded at exactly the right angles. She reached up and took the pins from her hair, allowing it to hang free. With her hand, she fluffed her loose hair, allowing it to hang freely about her shoulders and over her breasts.

Jesse forgot about the water for the moment. He gathered her up close in his arms and kissed her with all the love he had. She returned his kiss with passion filled with fire from her needs.

He picked her up and slowly carried her into the running water of the creek. He pulled his lips from hers and looked deep into her eyes. He turned and walked back to the creek bank.

The robins sang from the treetops. The blue jays squawked while they fought each other, fluttering from tree branch to tree branch. Rabbits hopped around them at a safe distance. A few white fluffy clouds sailed quietly in the heavens as the two lovers made love at the edge of the water.

He rolled away from her and stood up. He lowered his hand toward her and assisted her to rise. "You are the best lover I have ever known," he smiled as he pulled her close to him. "Ready for that swim?"

She felt so good, relaxed and pleased with her world. She realized she was a long way from the life style she had known all her life until Jesse entered. The social events she had enjoyed through the years were a thing of the past. She wouldn't trade that life for this one for anything in the world. The love she had for, and shared, with Jesse was the greatest gift she had ever received. She smiled her brightest and nodded her head in response to his question.

They frolicked in the cool water. The area was not large enough for them to do any real swimming but plenty big enough for them to play like they were a couple of carefree teenagers. "You crazy man, you're going to drown me right here in this little bit of water if you don't stop that." She cleared the water from her face and laughed as she warned him not to push her under the water anymore.

He grabbed her around the waist and nudged gently against her until she lay with her back on the ground at the edge of the water. "Have you ever made love while you were in the water before?"

Afterwards, they splashed in the water for a while longer. Then Listy Ann got the lye soap she'd brought along and lathered up her hair. The lye soap did wonders for her hair. When it dried, it had a softness and shine that she liked.

When she had all the suds rinsed from her hair, she walked out of the water. She stood on the bank patting and fluffing her hair while the sun dried it. Jesse still sloshed about in the water.

"You'd better get out and get your clothes on. Paw will be coming up pretty soon for his dinner. Lordy mercy, I forgot about dinner. I'd better get to the cabin and get something on the stove."

Jesse got out of the water and while he dressed, turned at such an angle that she got a good view at his back. The scars from his days on the ocean were still vivid.

"Jesse, wait a minute. Let me have a look at your back. What are these scars from?" She ran her hand across his shoulders and back. "Who did this to you?"

He said nothing until he had all his clothes on. He leaned over and picked a green straw from a bunch of grass growing near his foot. He sat down and rested his back against a tree. He stuck the straw in his mouth and began to tell her the story of the years the privateers had held them captive aboard the ship.

"Paw and James carry scars just like I do. It was a mean, hard time on that ship. I try not to think about it. I was just a young thing, but I recall every hour of it. We were lucky to escape with our lives in tact."

It broke her heart to see the scars he would carry all his life and to hear the story of their hardship coming to America. She had been born here, and never thought too much about the sufferings of those who chose to leave their homelands to make America their new homes. There must be a lot more for him to tell her about their trip, but would have to wait until a later time to ask him. Time was at hand to get dinner ready.

"Can we come back tomorrow if the water is still deep enough?" he asked.

They walked away from the creek not knowing the seed of their love had taken root. A new life had begun to form within Listy Ann.

Chapter Seven

It was a hot summer. By the middle of July, the men had the crops in the fields laid by and were working on the house. The foundation was constructed of large heart-of-pine sills, resting upon round heart-of-pine blocks. The floors and walls were of oak. Following Cyrus' advice, they never drove a nail into a plank until the moon was on the shrinking side. He'd told them, that if they followed his instructions, the plank boards would never curl or twist.

Jess did not know why the house was to be built so high off the ground. That was the custom the other farmers in the surrounding county had used when they had built, so the Swinsons followed their examples. One day Jess intended to inquire as to the reason for the space between the earth and the floor.

The frame of the house was completed and rafters were in place for the roof. It was a big house. Three bed rooms, a front room and a large space for the kitchen all on one floor. A small porch was located on the back of the house and an L shaped porch hugged the north end of the house, and ran the entire length on the west side to provide shade on the hot days of summer. The bricks had all been made, and lay stacked nearby for the double fireplace and kitchen stove flu outlet.

Both men were nailing shingles to the roof when they heard the screams coming from the cabin area. They looked toward the cabin to see smoke billowing skyward.

Jesse leapt from the roof in one bound. He mounted the horse bare backed with one leap over its rump. He left his Paw still on the roof. Jess climbed down and went to where the mules were tied, still hitched to the wagon. He untied the team, jumped in the wagon and ran the mules as fast as they'd go toward the cabin.

Jesse's heart was pounding so hard, he found it hard to breath. He could not see Listy Ann when he got in view of the cabin. "Where is she?" the words were barely out of his mouth when he pulled back on the reins to slow the horse. He was off his mount before it came to a stop. "Brister! Brister?" he yelled for her. There was no answer. He ran to the door of the burning cabin and found the heat too fierce to enter.

He ran on to the corner and when he started to turn, he spotted her at the well, drawing water. She had tried to douse the flames when she had first seen them. The roof was simply too high for her to get the water up to the burning area.

He raced to her and grabbed her in his arms. He crushed her to his chest. "My Lord Brister, when I couldn't see you, I thought you were in the cabin."

Jess arrived and was on his way to the well with the foot-tub. "Grab a bucket boy and let's get this fire out before it spreads. With everything so dry, it'll be in the woods in no time."

With all three of them working at the fire, it was under control after a while. Everything in the cabin burned. The cook stove could be cleaned up to be usable again.

The smoldering ashes would hold the heat for the remainder of the day or longer. It was a heartbreaking experience to stand and watch all their personal possessions burn. They could all be replaced except for a few personal items with sentimental value, which were gone forever.

"Do you know how the fire started?" Jess asked of Listy Ann.

"I don't really know Paw. I got the cook stove fire going with a pot of dry beans boiling on the top. Everything seemed to be all right as usual, so I came out here to get more of the washing done. A noise made me look toward the cabin. That's when I saw the flames shooting out from around the chimney up there on the roof." She was so nervous and upset she could barely get the words out of her mouth. She was smutty and wet from water splashing back on her. Her hair hung loose on one side of her head. The pins had fallen out somewhere and she had not noticed. She flared out her hands and exclaimed, "Well, there goes everything. Now what're we gonna do?"

Jesse had walked all around the wooded edges of the clearing to make sure no coals had reached the dry area there. He got back within earshot in time to hear her plea. "No, Brister all is not gone. We'll just simply pick up our shoulders and continue. Me and Paw? We've got the house well on the way. It won't be much longer before we can sleep under a real roof." He gestured his hand out toward the burned cabin, "That was only a few logs and rough furniture there." He felt he knew what she was talking about, her sewing machine, hairbrushes and some of their clothes.

A frantic thought clamped onto her mind. "Paw! What about the money? Was it in the house? Oh Lord, now you just tell me what are we going to do?"

Jess walked over and stood next to her. He opened the pocket on the front of his bibbed overalls and withdrew his long change purse. Both of the on lookers smiled when he opened it and revealed the money. "Usually, I take it out as soon as I return from town and lay it up there on the mantelpiece. For some reason, I sorta forgot about it and it's been here against my chest ever since I put it there a few days back." He stuffed it back down in the pocket. He along, with his children, was thankful he had the money tucked away safely on his person.

Listy Ann glanced at the place where the flowerbeds had been along the cabin front. "My flowers! Look, every one of them burned up and gone. My beautiful, beautiful flowers." The flowers had flourished and had been in full bloom on either side of the cabin door. She dropped her head in her hands and wept.

Jesse went to comfort her. With his arm around her shoulder he cooed, "Don't cry Brister. It'll be all right." It was the first time either man had seen her cry and it pulled at their hearts to watch her. It amazed both of them that it took the loss of her flowers to bring tears to her eyes.

"Look Brister, all is not lost." He pointed to the bed of flowers that stood swaying in the breeze by the water well "see, you still have those."

She sniffed her nose, pulled her apron bottom up, and wiped her eyes. It made her angry to allow her emotions to get the best of her, and to go so far as to cry was inexcusable to her pride. "All right," she muttered.

"You look a mess. Come on over to the well with me, let's wash your face." Jesse took her by the arm and walked beside her.

She glanced up at his face and burst out in a hearty laugh. "You could use a little tending to yourself. You look like you slid down the chimney."

He drew up a bucket of fresh water and poured a wash pan full, for her to use. She was drying her face when they heard the racket made by wagon wheels, moving fast over the ground. They looked to see the entire Garganus family riding up in their wagon, the mules in full gallop. When they came to a stop, they all got off the wagon. "We saw the smoke and heard your shouts. We knew you had trouble. We've come to help. Though, looks like it's too late for the cabin. Anybody hurt?" Cyrus asked as he panted for his breath. He walked on over to the well where they stood.

"No one hurt. Thank you for being concerned and coming over to see about us and to give us a hand. As you can see, all that was lost was the cabin and what was in it. Thank goodness, Listy Ann had most of our wearing clothes outside to wash. We at least have a change of clothes," Jess stretched out his hand and shook the hand of his neighbor.

Mrs. Garganus went to stand by Listy Ann. She didn't like the color in her face. "Do you feel all right, honey?" The two women had become best of friends and the age difference mattered not. The men had walked off while they talked.

Listy Ann released her hold on the towel and it dropped to the ground. She grabbed at her stomach with both hands and uttered a piteous, "Ooohhh!" She collapsed to the ground in an unconscious state.

Jesse was by her side within the moment. "Brister! Honey!" He scooped her up in his arms and looked at Mrs. Garganus, silently pleading for her help.

The older woman had taken notice of the blood on the ground and on Listy Ann's frock. "Cyrus!" she spoke calmly to her husband. "Take the children to the wagon, now." Children were not allowed to know much and see less, if the parents had any control over matters.

"Is she with child?" she asked bluntly.

"No, not that I know of, anyhow." Jesse answered.

She instructed him to carry her to the wagon, and lay her down gently on the bed of it. "Let me take her home with me and tend to her for a day or two. She'll not be needing to do any work for a while, only rest and nourishment. It won't be long before she's back on her feet."

Jesse did as he was told, and wondered how the older woman knew what was wrong with his wife. She'd not said a word to him about having a baby.

Jesse laid her motionless body down gently. Mrs. Garganus had gone by the clothesline and grabbed a sheet on her way to the wagon. She tucked the sheet in close to Listy Ann, where she lay. "Are you sure she'll be all right? She looks so pale." Jesse was concerned for his loved one, he cared not who saw how worried he was. "I'll get the horse and follow you home."

The children sat on the edge of the wagon. They looked on, but didn't say a word or ask a question.

She regained consciousness at about the time she was laid on one of the children's bed. "What?" she looked around, trying to find where she was.

"Now you just lay still and behave yourself. I'm here to tend to you." Mrs. Garganus cooed, in the accent of her native tongue, when Listy Ann stirred.

Mrs. Garganus got busy cleaning her up. She removed the bloody clothes and put one of her own, old frocks on her. "I feel fine now ma'am. I think I can get up."

"No dearie, you must lay there and be quiet for a while."

Listy Ann placed both her hands on her stomach and looked at her friend, with a question on her face. "The baby, was there a baby? I had only missed one monthly." A tear or two trickled from her eyes, as she waited for a reply.

"Yes, and it's gone love. The excitement of the fire and with you rushing around, slinging the water as hard as you could toward the roof, was more than your body could handle. Sometimes it's best to go on and loose the little one if there is a problem. I know it's hard for you to realize that what I'm saying right now is the truth, but in the long run, it could be a blessing in disguise. Now try to get some rest. Sleep if you can. Me and Cyrus, we'll take care of your men folk for a day or two."

As soon as Jesse knew that she was all right, he kissed her tenderly on the cheek and went back to the smoldering remains of the cabin. He found his father sitting on an old stump beneath one of the trees at the edge of the clearing. "Are you all right Paw?"

"Yeah son, I just felt the need to stop and rest a while. We're not ruined completely, but it's a good setback. Every bit of food we had was in there." He stretched his legs to their full length out in front of him and added, "It was mighty nice of the neighbors to help us like that. We'll go in first thing tomorrow and get supplies to restock the pantry. Well, the pantry I speak of is up yonder in the new house." He faltered in his words for a moment, "How did you leave the wife?"

"Paw, she was carrying our child. She was only about six weeks along and that's why she had not said anything to either of us about it. Mrs. Garganus assured me that she would be up and about in a short time, but for right now, she needs complete rest. Paw, why did I get so scared when she fainted? I felt like I was going to die before she roused up. I have never had that feeling before. I'm telling you Paw, I don't know what we would have done if Mrs. Garganus had not been here."

The father sat a while longer before he answered his son's question. It had been a long time since he had sensed the feelings his son spoke of. Yes, he remembered the anxiety he felt when his Lillian took sick, all those years ago. Really, he had to stop and think even to call her name. It seemed to have been in someone else's lifetime. Was that really him that he remembered? So much had occurred in the time span since he and his little family were secure in their happiness on the farm there in Scotland.

He got up and walked close to where the chimney stood. He could still feel the heat. The fire had burned every piece of wood away from the bricks. He turned to his son and said, "When you find a woman to love, and she loves you in return, it is the greatest thing on this earth to have possession of. There is, and never will be, anything better than love to share with a woman that loves you. You become a part of each other. When one hurts, the other feels the pain. You saw her wither and collapse. Your heart went out to her, and you didn't know what to do to help her. That's what caused your ache."

There was nothing more they could do at the clearing after they gathered up all the clothes that were dry, so they went back to work on the new house. They had no dinner, but felt no hunger. The excitement of the fire and Listy Ann's troubles had seemed to kill their appetites.

They had been at work for an hour or so when they heard the familiar sound of wagon wheels. They looked up to see Lewis bouncing atop the wagon seat. "Ma sent you over some vittles for your dinner. It's a bit late, but she thought you ought to have something in your guts." He hopped off the wagon and lifted the pail that held the food and walked over to the sweating men.

It was hot weather, very hot. Jesse took his shirt off and sat on the ground in the shade of the structure. "Thank you Lewis, you're a fine lad to bring this over to us." He shook the young boy's hand and knew he had a friend in the young lad. He opened the pail to find a steaming pork stew, filled with potatoes and other vegetables from their garden.

Lewis handed them each a spoon from his overalls pocket and from the bib pocket he pulled out warm squares of pone bread wrapped in cloth. "I'd better be getting on back to the house. Pa told me not to tarry over here very long." His bare feet stirred up the dust when he walked back to the wagon. "I'll see ya'll later," and was gone as soon as he turned the wagon around.

Within two weeks, Listy Ann was up and around like nothing had happened to her. She had not felt the need to get in contact with her parents or grandparents since she had hurriedly packed her few things and scribbled off a short note to her parents and to her grandparents before she had left her grandfather's house to meet Jesse. She had left her parents message with her Grandparents to be delivered. Since the day she had had the miscarriage, her thoughts traveled to her mother often. The urge to write her mother was most important, these days.

Jess reminded her to make a list of what was needed both on the farm and around the house, on the day after she returned to them from the Garganus' house. They had moved in the new house and made do with what was there. Her personal writing materials were foremost on the list.

Jesse and Listy Ann went along to town with Jess that day. It was the first trip the three of them had taken together since they had made their way from Clinton to the farm.

It turned into a relaxed, enjoyable day for them. To go to a cafe again was a special treat for Listy Ann that she had almost forgotten about. She ordered a nice big steak, cooked medium rare. She savored every bite as it passed over her taste buds.

They walked the roads of Richlands and shopped in every store in town. She bought yards and yards of material. Different laces for her good frocks, ticking for pillows and mattresses, denim for heavy aprons and needles and thread. The list went on and on because there was a need for all the necessities for keeping a house and running the kitchen. A brand new Singer sewing machine was strapped securely in the wagon bed.

At the end of the shopping spree, they sat in the cafe and totaled up the receipts of all the purchases while they enjoyed coffee before heading back to the farm. The amount was startling. "Listy Ann, without your contribution of funds, we would not have been able to restock and get all these things we desperately need. Let me say again how much I appreciate the money," Jess spoke lovingly to her.

"Think nothing of it Paw. What's mine is yours, too."

The wagon was fully loaded when the mules were hitched to it for the long, slow ride home. It was just before dark when they pulled into the yard of the new house. If felt strange to them all to stop before they reached the cabin in the clearing. The old cabin had become home and they felt as if they were deserting an old friend by stopping at the new place.

They slept on the plank floor inside the structure in the bedrolls again. The roof was completed and the outer walls were up.

Since the cabin had burned, it had put Jess' mind to thinking about how quickly it went up in flames. He pondered on separating the kitchen from the main house for several days before he mentioned it to Jesse and Listy Ann. They agreed that it was a very good idea. The kitchen construction was started fifty feet west of the house. It was a completely separate building with two rooms, one for cooking and one for dining. A double chimney was situated in the dividing wall. An open fireplace was built in the dining area and a flue put in the cooking area for the stove.

The more Listy Ann thought about the separate building arrangement, the more she liked it. The fire safety for the house was number one on her list. Second, the heat from the cook stove would be contained in the kitchen, rather than heating up the entire house. In hot weather when she fired up the cook stove, it put off a lot of heat that kept the rooms hot for hours. At least they could sleep in a cooler environment. Yes, she was glad they had decided to go for the two buildings.

The room that was to have been the kitchen in the original house was turned into a sewing and craft room for the lady of the house. Hopefully, one day, to be used as an extra bedroom for some of the many children they planned to fill the house and yard with. They each loved children and looked forward to the day when the sound of their children, Jess' grandchildren, would ring out from the land they proudly called home.

The outbuildings were under construction at the same time as the living quarters. Every piece of board was used.

A smoke house would be needed for their meat supply. It should be ready by the time hog killing time arrived. The chicken coop, surrounded by a wooden fence, all ready housed the chickens. Listy Ann loved those few fowl. She talked to them and kept the nests clean. She threw fresh, tender, green sprouts in to the chicken yard every morning for the chickens to peck at. She savored every egg the hens dropped. She loved to hear the rooster crow every morning at daybreak. Many a morning she was up, busy at the stove when he called out his first announcement of a new day.

The cookstove had been set up out in the open while the kitchen had been under construction.

A corncrib had to be built to store the corn when harvested in the fall for food for the animals and chickens, plus corn to take to the gristmill for grinding into cornmeal for human consumption.

A barn to house the horse and mules and, hopefully, later on, cows would be included. A big lofty barn was what they had in mind, with five stalls running along each side. A huge airway was to run through the length of the barn. The buggy house would stand beside it.

A large lot area was set up around the barn for the horse and mules to run freely when not hitched to a plow or a riding vehicle.

It was hard work, carving out a living from the earth and surrounding woods. Their work was a continuous struggle. Their hands were toughened and callused. Muscles developed hard and strong. They ate big, nutrition filled, meals. Three times a day they ate, and felt hunger again when it was time for the next meal. They rested an hour each day after the noon meal and slept soundly through the night. Their survival lay in the land.

The work never got too steady for Jesse and his Brister to take time for each other. At least once a week they romped through the woods or walked over to visit the neighbors. On occasions, they saddled the horse and rode double back over the land to explore and find new places to make love.

On some of the rides, they found wild huckleberry patches and briar berries growing. Kirnchberry bushes grew plentiful in the area. The kirnchberry was right tasty to eat but filled with too many large seeds to mess with much cooking. Listy Ann made a mental note of where each berry bush was located so she could return when the berries ripened for the harvest.

Their love and respect for each other grew as the year progressed. Listy Ann loved the quiet times they spent together, whether it was in the woods, or sitting beneath a tree near the house enjoying the shade.

She had often wanted to ask him about his mother and siblings left in Ireland. All she knew was there had been a family that no longer existed. On one of their rides, she decided to approach the subject. "I know it hurts for you to recall the terrible loss that took them from you, but I'd like for you to tell me about them."

He pulled on the reins and the horse came to a stop. He dismounted and assisted her as she slid down. They walked through the trees at a slow pace while the horse stayed tethered to a tree.

"It's been so long that I find it hard to remember the little ones. They were all so sweet and innocent."

He stopped for a moment, reached down, and plucked off a shoot of wild growing broom sedge. He stuck it in his mouth and wallowed it around with his tongue. It hurt to remember those cute little girls with their laughing eyes and the many questions they always had for him when he got home from anywhere.

"I sometimes find it hard to believe they are gone forever. One of the boys looked just like me. He had the same coloring and the same hair. If I close my eyes and concentrate, I can envision them standing there on the porch waving a greeting to me and James when we approached the house." He was quiet for a while and then smiled the sweetest smile at her, "You would have loved mother. She was a grand lady. She always smelled so good. I used to love to hug her, just so I could inhale the freshness of her. My mother was a beautiful, friendly lady. She was known by all the people in our county and was paid the respect due a lady of her standing.

"We lived near our Grandparents when we lived in Scotland. I don't remember too much about that life. They came to visit us a couple of times in Ireland, but you don't get too much from short visits." He went on to fill her in on all the adventures and misadventures of his travels to get to Onslow County. "We were wealthy once." He stood up and threw the straw aside He slapped the tree he stood beside. "You'd never imagine that today, would you? We lost everything we owned due to the potato famine and being captured by the privateers.

I've not had a day's schooling since we left Ireland." He turned and took her hand. Together they walked to where the horse grazed on tender grass. "Brister, all those babies and my mother perished in a fire, shortly after we left them."

They stopped and he put his arm around her. "I'm so glad I met up with you Brister. I know there was no proper courting. There was no time for that. We had to move in a hurry." He kissed her as tender and lovingly as he could. "We can make up for all the courting we lost out on while we grow in our marriage, if that's all right with you."

She stretched up on tiptoes and reached her arms around his neck. "You big man, I love you. I didn't need to spend time on courting. I knew that first day you were the man for me. We don't have to make up for anything. Just being with you day after day is all I ask for. I like it here where we live. I like the adventure of grubbing our living out of the soil. To plant seeds and watch them sprout and grow makes me feel alive and useful. When I put food on the table and know I had a part in getting it there, it gives me pride." She returned his kiss.

They found a soft comfortable place on the ground and united their bodies in lovemaking as if it was for the first time.

In the months they had been on the land, they had accomplished a lot. Jess was proud when he walked over the fields before breakfast each morning. He had established a routine for himself. When he arose in the mornings, he went to feed the animals and draw up water for them. The hogs had learned at about what hour their food was put out and usually showed up at that time.

As soon as he had those chores completed, he walked the fields to inspect the progress of growth and find out if the hogs or any other animal had broken in to root at the young plants.

He usually got back to the house about the time Listy Ann was putting breakfast on the table. "How did everything look today Paw?" she'd ask of him.

"That cotton will be ready to pick before to much longer now. It's going to be a job for the three of us to get it picked and hauled to the station. I hope the rain stays away until we get it harvested." He sat down at the table and remarked, "This meal smells and looks mighty good this morning. Sometimes, I think you're the best cook in the world. With no more than you have to work with, you lay out a pretty table full of food. This home is blessed to have you here. By the way, where's Jesse this morning?"

"He's gone to check on a swarm of bees he saw fly over just after we arose. He thought maybe he could snare them by cutting the limb they land on. Those three hives you and him made last month need to be filled." Bees were a necessity on a farm for pollination.

Jess had finished eating when he heard his son call out to him. He went to investigate and saw Jesse walking very slowly toward the hives. He held the tree limb high over his head. "Take the top off the middle one Paw. I think we've got a rich swarm here. If I can get them inside before they scatter again, they'll stay with us." From that one swarm, the hives filled and more hives were built.

About a week later, the men folk were in the far side of the field. Listy Ann was behind the kitchen, drying snap beans for their winter supply. Her mind was on nothing in particular, she hummed to express her happiness. She stopped her humming when she heard the familiar area greeting from a stranger, "Hey-o the house."

She wiped her hands in her apron tail as she walked around to the front of the kitchen. Her mouth fell open and she found no sound in her throat. She stared at the darkest colored man she had ever seen. He sat atop a wagon seat with a woman as dark as he was beside him. She held a baby no more than a year old on her lap.

He remained on the wagon seat and tipped his hat, "Mornin', ma'am." He said no more, only smiled and waited for her to respond to his greeting. His teeth shone through his dark, friendly smile. She knew there was no reason to feel fear. Then why was she glued to the ground, standing there like an idiot, without a tongue?

The colored woman saw the state Listy Ann was in and handed the baby to its father. She started to get down from the wagon. "Ma'am?"

The sound that escaped Listy Ann's lips was hair curling. "JESS-AAA!!!" she hollered as loud as she could. She then clapped her hands over her mouth in embarrassment. What was wrong with her anyway? She realized what she had done and started to walk toward the wagon.

"I'm so sorry. I guess seeing you sorta startled me there for a moment. Please forgive me for being so very rude." She was standing beside the colored woman when she completed her apology. "Good day to you." She stretched out her hand and tried to make her smile and handshake appear real and trustworthy.

The man remained on the wagon seat. He didn't know if he wanted to be near that crazy woman on the ground. The baby whimpered and he cuddled it close to his chest, "Dare, dare Ander, it be a'right."

Jesse arrived, panting from the run up to the house, wanting to know the reason behind his summons. "I don't know. Something inside me just let loose. I haven't seen a colored person in a long, long time. It simply startled me there for a moment, that's all. I'm so ashamed of myself."

The colored man got down from the wagon and handed the child to its mother. He nodded to Jesse and waited for Jesse to extend his hand in greeting before he did. He and his wife were new in the area. They had some acres of land, five miles southeast of the Swinson Farm. The mailman had told them about the other farmers in the area. They had used part of the Indian trail to reach the Swinson's farm.

They had been released from slavery down in Georgia four years previously. They had married shortly before their freedom. They had been on the move for three and a half years when they learned about the land in Onslow County. It had taken all their money to purchase the land. They had been on their land a week and decided to come over and see if there was any work they could do for the Swinsons for wages.

They were hungry and had next to nothing to live on. They owned the mule and small wagon, a few cooking utensils and a change of clothing and some seeds, treasured from the slave days he had carefully hoarded, and a few pieces of farming equipment.

"My name's Jasper Moore. Here's my madam, Miss Marcy. Our son here, he be Andrew, dough we calls 'im Ander."

By this time, Listy Ann had regained her wits and said to Miss Marcy, "I'm so glad to see you. Come on with me. There's food cooking on the stove right now. It'll be ready to eat in a short while. I know you're hungry. I can see it in your eyes. That odor coming from the kitchen smells good, huh?"

Miss Marcy took Ander and followed her. "Ya'sum it shore do."

Listy Ann didn't realize how true her statement was. What little food they had had went to the child for the last two days. Miss Marcy's mouth watered and her stomach growled in anticipation of eating again.

When Listy Ann called dinner, Jasper insisted they, he and his family, eat separate from them. "Why?" Jesse wanted to know. He had heard about the eating arrangements the colored and whites had in the south, but with him coming from a different part of the world, he knew nothing of it first hand.

"It jist best if we eats apart frum you white folks," the proud colored man stated.

Jess noticed the plea in his voice and told his son to leave the man alone. "Go on and set up another eating area. You can use the edge of the porch for right now."

After they ate, they all sat on the porch and talked through the rest period. Yes, there was work for the new family to do, yes, plenty of work. They could not have showed up at a more convenient time. The cotton was almost ready to be picked, and the corn was just about ready for harvest. More work was needed on the house and kitchen buildings. Yes, there was plenty of work.

Jess and Jesse talked with a heavy accent from their native tongue. Jasper along with his wife had their own way of talking. Each amused the other with their style of speech. Listy Ann found both dialects interesting. She had to ask Miss Marcy to repeat some of her words at times, when she could not catch the meaning.

While still sitting on the porch, Jess taught Jasper the method of getting turpentine from his pine trees. He had plenty of scrap boards to let the man have to build the troughs to attach to the trees for catching the liquid. "You've got a lot of hard work ahead of you Jasper, you and your woman. It will all be worth it. Me and my family will be here to lend you a hand."

When the hour of rest was up, Jess arose and so did Jasper. "Do you want to start to work today?"

"Yas'sir."

Miss Marcy was to stay at the house and help Listy Ann. Jasper went to the fields with the men.

The baby fascinated Listy Ann. She rocked and sang to him while he fell asleep. It felt so good to hold a small one in her arms.

Miss Marcy washed up the dishes while her baby was being taken care of. "I had me three babies afore Ander comed along. They all died frum one thang or another. I pray to God that this'un lives to be a man. It's hard when your child dies. We had no place to live during dem times. We moved frum one farm to another working other folks land, barely staying alive. We wuz headed north when we heard about the land here. I shore do hope you white folks don't mind us living so close to you."

Listy Ann laid the sleeping baby on a pallet made from a folded quilt. "Miss Marcy, I never did hold to slavery, though I was raised with it. Times change and folks might as well go on and do some changing with it. It may take a lot of years for the change to come about. No, we don't mind where you live. We're more than glad to have you as our neighbors. I know you will like the Garganus family. They were, and still are, a lot of help to us. Just like I hope we can help you and Jasper. Some times, I wonder where we would be, had not the Garganus family been here to give us a helping hand. Come on and we'll get to work while the baby sleeps."

At quitting time that day, the Moore's went home with enough food to feed them for the next week, and hay for the mule. Listy Ann fed them supper before they left. "You say we can expect you back tomorrow to do more work?" Jesse inquired.

"Yas'sir."

Jesse didn't exactly know why, but it made him feel good for the older man to say sir to him. Jasper was maybe three years older than Jesse.

The two women sat and sewed the next day, making bags for holding cotton when it was picked. They used the homespun, with tarpaulin attached to the side that would drag along the ground. The bag hung on a strap from the shoulder that reached the waist and was big enough to hold the cotton from down one row and then back up the next.

Listy Ann found it very interesting to have another woman to talk to while they worked. Miss Marcy was a smart and thrifty person, too. She hesitated many times before she would suggest one of her thoughts to Listy Ann.

Miss Marcy could bake the best cakes and pies. She could do just about anything there was to do, but her talents were best applied in the kitchen. Listy Ann gathered up a storehouse of recipes by observing Miss Marcy at work, plus ways to make shortcuts in the daily chores around the house.

Ander was kept in a wooden box while he was awake, that is, until he learned to walk. He was a good natured youngin' and entertained himself most of the time with little wooden toys that Jess whittled out for him. Jess was one to not waste time. Most of the time, he had his knife out whittling on a piece of wood while he talked or chose to be quiet.

The rain held off until the cotton was picked and taken to the station, and the corn pulled and stored in the crib. The money they made felt good resting down in their pockets. The fodder looked good and smelled better, stacked in rows out in the field.

Instead of being paid with money all the time, the Moore's took supplies. They needed the supplies more than they did cash money at times. Jess also sawed Jasper's trees into planks at the sawmill in return for his work on the land.

The colored family was coming along slowly on their house and out buildings. They worked three days a week for Jess and four days on their own land. To work solo was a time consuming task.

The men from the Garganus and Swinson families donated a few days of work to help Jasper get a head start on the cutting of the trees and blowing up stumps. Then more days later on, with putting rafters up and jobs that was hard for a man to do alone.

The first week in September, all three Swinsons made a special trip over to the county seat to finalize the purchase of the land. With money put aside, especially to pay for the farm and surrounding acres, they walked away from the county seat with a clear deed. The land was purchased from a Hosea Marshburn on September 25, 1869.

The next week Jess, Jesse and Listy Ann packed up for a trip to the ocean. All the crops were harvested and chores around the farm were at a place where they could be left undone for a while. Lewis was to tend to the feeding of the animals and chickens while they were away.

It took them all day to reach their destination, a fifteen miles or so journey. Fishing was the object of their trip to the Atlantic Ocean.

The weather was still warm enough to be nice. Jess slept in the wagon at night. The young couple chose to sleep on the beach on a double bedroll. The cook stove had been disassembled and brought along, with enough dry stove wood to last throughout their stay at the beach.

They ate fish or some kind of seafood every day. Listy Ann had brought food supplies from home to go along with the fish. She washed dishes in salt water. Drinking and cooking water came from the water barrel attached to the side of the wagon.

They didn't want to spend the entire day fishing, so Listy Ann and Jesse walked the beach and collected shells. They collected a large amount to adorn her flowerbeds. Jess chose the time to catch up on his sleeping.

At night, Jesse and his Brister sat on the beach at waters edge. They had the time to talk like they had never taken before. It felt so good for her to sit on the sand, her back at rest against his strong body, for hours at a time. They took moonlight dips in the nude just off shore in the surf. They made love up in the dunes.

One night, while they were fooling around on the dunes, Jesse said to her, "Look yonder, down the beach. That looks like a man coming toward us." She strained to see what he pointed at in the dimness of the night. It did look like a man.

As it neared them, they decided it was the biggest man they had ever seen. He took her hand and they walked quickly to the wagon where Jess was asleep. He shook his father by the feet, "Wake up Paw, and get the gun! There's something coming down the beach toward us. I think it may need some attention."

Jess crawled out of his bedroll and sat on the tailgate of the wagon, the gun in his hand. "What's your trouble son?"

Listy Ann had become nervous as she watched the large shape approach them. "I think it's an animal, look at the way it lopes as it walks." She got behind Jesse and held on tight to the back of his shirt.

The mules got scent of the intruder and reared up, snorting at the displeasing odor of the shape almost upon them.

"It's a damn bear, look out!" Jess pulled the trigger of the gun. The shot cleared the bears head, just high enough so that the wind created a loud enough noise as it passed, to startle and deafen the animal. It was probably the first gunshot the bear had ever heard in all its lifetime. It stopped and stood straight up on its hind legs, the full length of its body, then bellowed so loud that it frightened man and animal within earshot.

They couldn't see exactly the size of the opened mouth, but knew that they were goners. Jess tried to reload the gun, but in his haste from nervousness, could not get the thing loaded again. "Paw! What are we gonna do? The dam thing is right on top of us."

The bear dropped down on his front feet, turned, and galloped up and over the dunes. He left behind three very frightened humans and a team of mules. Jesse went to the mules and tried to comfort them. They had dug holes in the sand beside the wagon where they were tied. It must have been after midnight when Jesse got them settled down.

Jess, Jesse and his wife sat on the tailgate of the wagon and discussed their feelings about the experience they had just shared. Neither one of them felt any need for sleep at the moment. "I've been told that there are bears in these parts, but to tell you the truth I did not believe the tales. After tonight, I reckon I'll have to change my beliefs on that subject. Humph! That was a big son-of-a-bitch. Wonder what made him dart and run off like that?" Jesse stood and stretched his legs after he completed his statement.

"It was probably the blunder-bust noise of the shotgun going off so close to his head," Jess answered as he got off the tailgate and turned to lay the gun on the bed of the wagon. "I'm glad that thing was loaded," he made mention of the gun.

Listy Ann remained on the tailgate, "Paw, I'm ready to leave here, if you are." She offered her thoughts freely.

They had been on the beach four days and had the fish boxes nearly full. The fish had been gutted and salted down, with the scales left on to preserve flavor, then packed down firmly in the boxes. The fish salesman that made his rounds in their area had instructed them on how to put their catch up. Jess, himself was ready to go home also. The wind had burned his nose and cheeks to a brilliant red.

He turned to Jesse and asked, "Son do you suppose we should fish one more day to try to fill that last box?"

"I'm with my wife Paw. I've had about enough of this wind and sand. If we stay much longer, our skin is going to peel off our faces, though I've enjoyed every minute of it, up until tonight." He was quite for a moment or two then added. "You know we can give Jasper the box not filled. His family is smaller." Their aim had been to fill three boxes of fish.

They began their packing and, by dawn, Listy was cooking breakfast over an open fire. "Men-of-mine, have either of you noticed how rough the surf is this morning?" By the time they had finished eating, they noticed scattered clouds was building up in the southern sky.

They had completed the packing and were well over the dunes by sunrise. Within a couple of hours in their travel, the sky became filled with angry clouds and the wind blew in gusts.

"Maybe it's a good thing we decided to leave when we did. There's bound to be heavy rain in those clouds," he pointed toward the heavens.

When the rain started, they got out their slickers and got them on before they got wet. The mules didn't seem to mind the rain falling on them. The rain cooled the temperature down several degrees and Listy Ann felt the chill clear down in her bones.

It was almost nightfall when they pulled up in the Moore's yard. Jess hollered out the familiar greeting to let them know they had company. Jasper emerged from the house wondering who was calling on him in such weather. As soon as he recognized them, he threw up his hand in a welcome salute.

He knew they were off on a fishing trip, but had no idea they would be bringing him a box of fish. "Sir, dis is mighty fine of you. Me and my ma'am like eatin' fish. The little un do, too." He rubbed his chin and helped get the box off the wagon. "Yas'sir, dis be all right indeedy." It was a small blessing for Jasper and his family. They would be able to eat fine for days. "Won't chu come on in de house and rest up a spell?"

"Thank you, but no, we'd best be getting on to the house. It'll be plum dark before we get there now. We'll see you before long. Good night to you," Jess said as he crawled up on the wagon seat.

Cyrus heard their approach and was standing on the porch when they reached his yard. "Glad to see you home again." It was the first time Cyrus had had such an unsuspected gift given to him. He was almost flabbergasted with gratitude.

He helped get the box on the porch and turned to shake hands with Jess. "You are a good neighbor, Jess Swinson. My whole family loves fish and now look what you've gone and done. You'll not need to pay the boy anything for tending to your place while you were gone. These fish are payment enough."

Jess didn't say anything about not paying Lewis. That bargain was between him and the lad. He did say, "The fish were biting plentifully and it was a joy to catch them. Some we caught with nets and others we hooked. The weather cooperated up until this morning. And then it tried to wash us away on the journey home."

"It's most likely going to be one of them gre'nor-easters, from the looks of things," Cyrus said.

"We'd best be on our way. It'll be right late now when we get on to the house. Tomorrow is another work day." He flipped the reins and remembered, "Hey Cyrus, remind us to tell you about what happened to us last night."

Cyrus pulled the fish box up next to the house and muttered to himself, "They're good people, good folks." He went back in the house as the rain continued to fall and the wind blew harder.

Early the next morning Listy Ann woke up sore all over. "Do you suppose it's because I slept in a nice soft bed again?" They all got a good laugh out of her comment. It was a terrible day weather wise. The fields were forming puddles and when they took time to ride down to the creek, they were amazed at how high the water had risen up on the land. It took them a whole week to clean up the destruction caused by the storm.

After the clean up, they thought it was a good time to do work on the inside of the house. Jess realized winter was coming on and the cold weather would blow in if the work was not done.

By the end of November, the work was completed. Soon after Listy used the new wooden steps for the first time to enter the house, she remarked to the men, "Lordy, it sure does feel good to walk up sturdy steps instead of those wobbly old stumps."

Jess was proud of their work. Each plank and beam had been cut to precision and nailed into place with accuracy. Both the buildings stood erect, solid and weatherproof. When he glanced up at the chimneys, he felt special pride in that accomplishment. To build a fireplace and, have it draw properly, took extra talent. There were three fireplaces in the house and one in the dining room part of the kitchen, plus the cook stove flu for the smoke to exit. The extra bricks were used to line the walking area around the well that had been dug near the back of the kitchen so it would be easier for Listy Ann's use. The wash shelter was located a few feet from the well, and the clothes lines were out at the edge of the yard.

The wood used to build the home was beginning to weather cure and turn a grayish color. So were all the out buildings that were made from the same kind of wood.

The smokehouse, corncrib and chicken coop were all made of logs. Only the limbs, knots and bark had been removed.

The first week in March 1870, Mr. Wooten came down the lane to deliver the mail. He stopped the horse and dismounted.

All three of them went out to meet him. It was the highlight of the month to see him coming to their house. To their delight, there were two letters and one handbill. He opened his bag and said, "I think you may have news from your son." He handed Jess the letter. "And for you too, Listy Ann. I bring you a letter also."

She took the letter from him and looked at the return address. "It's from mother! I've been waiting for news from her and the family ever since I mailed my letter off to them." She carefully ran her finger beneath the back seal and removed the contents.

Jess had opened his letter and read the bigger part of it by the time Listy Ann squealed. "They'll be here the second week in June."

The men could easily tell by her actions that she was thrilled to get the news from her family and learned that her parents planned a visit.

When Jess had read all the words in his letter, he reread it more carefully a second time. He folded the pages and looked up at them with a smile on his face. "He's well. He lives in a small community called Greely, out west in Colorado. He has a wife and a small son. They call the boy Jesse. They expect a second child in the spring. He works on a cattle ranch, near where they live. He and his wife have homesteaded land and are building their own herd of cattle." He wiped at the moisture that had gathered up in his eyes. "I'm so glad to hear from him. Pleased he is well and has a family to love and to love him back." It was a day of rejoicing.

Shortly after Mr. Wooten left, Listy Ann called out to get the men's attention. She was not certain of her news but felt confident when she asked, "Can I add a little more joy to all our good tidings we have received this day?"

Both men looked at her to hear what she had to say that would make them feel any better than they did from the news received from James.

"I'm with child!" She took her hands from her hips, crossed them beneath her breasts and waited for their response.

It took several minutes for her news to sink into their heads. "Yahoo!" Jesse took his hat off and sailed it across the yard. He rushed to her, picked her up, and whirled about the yard, dancing and kissing her. "I'm gonna be a Paw! I'm gonna be a Paw!" He sat her down on the edge of the porch and asked, "When?"

"I think about the first week in December."

Listy Ann's parents and grandparents arrived on a Friday afternoon. They sat in the oversize buggy and looked around the small, and, in their eyes only, crude way of life their heir had taken on for herself. It was hard for the grandfather, Gus, to imagine his precious little Listy Ann working the soil and tending the chickens, doing the menial chores that should be done by the hired help. His wife sat on the seat beside him. She saw and sensed his reaction to what surrounded them.

She took a firm grip on his elbow and cautioned him, "Gus, you are to say not one word of what you're thinking right now. You are here for a friendly visit, nothing more than that. I mean what I say to you. Keep all your advice and suggestions silent. Do you hear and understand exactly what I'm saying to you Gus Solomon?"

Listy Ann's parents, Randolph and Tamma sat in the back seat. They quietly listened to the conversation between the older adults. They wondered how the weekend visit would progress. How well they remembered how it had been when the old man found them shortly after they had eloped. Randolph had been a young man and not as strong as Gus.

They had married and been living in Lenoir County for four months when the old man found them. He bellowed out his demand that his daughter return home or he would get the law to see that she did return. She was under age and Randolph knew the old man could carry through with his threats.

Tamma pleaded with her father to let her stay. She cried and begged her mother to help her. Her mother had learned shortly after arriving in America that Gus was the ruler in the family and it seemed that no matter what she said, it carried no weight; however, she learned through the years that there was ways to get around his bossiness. At the time her daughter pleaded for her help, she only nodded her head in agreement with the father.

When Tamma was sure that she could not change her father's mind, she looked him straight in the eye and asked, "Well, what am I going to do with the child I'm carrying?"

That put a different slant in the thoughts of Gus' mind, "A child?"

"Yes father, I'm going to have Randolph's baby."

After much thought on Gus' part, he discussed his plan with Randolph and Tamma. If they would allow him to fortify their farm holdings, buy more of the surrounding acreage to add to the amount of land they all ready owned, let him hire field help to assist Randolph and help for the house to lessen Tamma's burden, he would allow her to remain with Randolph and raise their child together.

Randolph knew he was in for a lifetime of orders from Gus the minute he agreed to the rules put before him. He didn't particularly like the man when he first met him, he still didn't care for him. That was the reason behind him and Tamma running away to marry. If the only way he could keep Tamma by his side as his wife, was to go along with her father's suggestions, then that's the way it would have to be.

Gus was an old man now, in years, but as domineering and as manipulative as he had been when he had first married his wife. He had made their lives productive and successful as far as finances and having the best part of life, that money could afford.

As Randolph listen to his mother-in-law talk so boisterous to Gus, while they still sat in the buggy, he felt as if he wanted to add a few words into the conversation, but from years of holding his tongue, he sat quietly and said nothing.

It was only a moment or two before Listy Ann emerged from the kitchen and saw the buggy. She cupped her hands around her mouth and yelled out to her men folk, who were in the barn at the time, "They're here!"

She walked toward the buggy and wondered if either one of them would suspect that she was carrying their grandchild.

She knew from the expression on her grandfather's face what he was thinking, and was determined to hold her own ground. This was her home, where she lived with her husband, whom she loved dearly. She was not going to allow the old man to cause any strife within the lives of those she loved and herself.

"Grandfather, get down and let me hug your neck. It is so good to see you all." After she greeted him, she walked around the buggy and helped her grandmother to the ground. "You are a dear to come all this way to see me Come on, give me a big hug."

She glanced to the back seat of the buggy at her parents. "Good day to you both. Hurry up and get out of the buggy. I need to hug you both also." While they got off the buggy, Listy Ann continued, "Father, you and mother sure do look good."

Both the Swinson men stood in the entrance of the barn and watched. They wanted to give Listy Ann enough time to greet her family properly before they made an appearance. "Come on Paw, it's time to go make their acquaintances, though I don't one bit look forward to this visit."

As soon as they approached the company, Listy Ann introduced everyone. "And grandfather, of course you know my husband Jesse Swinson." Jesse had no desire to show his grandfather-in-law the respect of calling him Mister, so he stuck out his hand, and when Gus took it Jesse said, "Good day to you Gus. I'm pleased you and the family have come to our home." He in turn called her father Mr. Batts when he extended his hand to him.

When Jesse and Gus' eyes met during the handshake, they saw in each other's eyes the understanding that they would hold their peace while in the company of the one they loved mutually.

Jess caught the feel of friction between the two men and wondered what was going on between them. Jesse had always used proper manners. Now, to be as rude as to call the man by his first name, rubbed Jess the wrong way. He decided to wait until a later time to question the boy. He had never been told any of the details of how Listy Ann and his son had met.

Jess greeted the company and helped unload their luggage. He then took a grip on the horse's bridle and led the animal to the lot. He turned the horse loose in one of the stalls and then filled the water trough and bin with fresh corn. He threw hay at the feet of the horse. When he went to put the buggy under the shelter, he noticed the containers filled with green growth in the back of the buggy. He sat them on the ground at the edge of the barn.

Every thing on the place had been cleaned and polished until it possessed an air of freshness. The wooden windows were opened and hooked to the outside of the house, allowing the fresh air to flow through both buildings. The yard had been swept clear of the tiniest particle of trash. The sideboard in the kitchen was laden with fine desserts. A big pot filled with a young rooster, donated by Mrs. Garganus, was on the stove simmering to keep the chicken and pastry warm. Yes, the in-laws faired mighty good at the supper table that night.

Soon after supper, the men went out to look over the animals and the cleared acres under cultivation and the crops that were swaying with the wind. Jess took Gus to see his pride and joy, the sawmill. One could look at Jess and know the pride he had in the farm. He knew it was a good place to farm and felt like a complete man here on this land after so many years of humiliation and hurt. "Yes, I think we will do alright here. If the weather holds, and we get the crops gathered in, there should be no problems ahead for us this season," he said with pride.

A person could tell that Gus thought their holdings to be less than proper for his heir, though he held his tongue. There was a certain aura about him that let Jesse know how he felt, even if he never expressed any of his feeling aloud. Jesse simply ignored the man. He wasn't rude or disrespectful to him, aside from that first greeting.

The womenfolk were left in the kitchen to tidy up. They sat on the kitchen porch afterwards and talked. They caught up on each others lives and what had happened since they'd last seen each other. It made Listy Ann feel good to learn about all those she had left behind.

Tamma remembered the shrubs just before it got completely dark. The three women walked out to the barn together. "I brought you these because I remember how well you like the blooms they produce." There were two China Berry trees, two altheas of different colors and a healthy looking wisteria vine.

Listy Ann was tickled to get the shrubs and tree. "Oh mother, thank you. I can almost smell the aroma the wisteria will put out next spring in my yard."

When they returned to the house, Listy Ann got her almanac out and found the day she wanted to get the plants in the ground. "There, next Tuesday is exactly the right day."

The men had returned and sat on the house porch to talk until bedtime.

Breakfast the next morning was later than usual. It was seven o'clock before they sat down to eat. Gus spoke up with, "Listy Ann you were always handy in the kitchen, but I'll have to admit, you have improved with your cooking since you've married. I can see the result of long-term work here on the table before me. I know how much work and how many long hours it took all of you to get this kind of fine meal on the breakfast table. Farming is a hard life." Gus held the rest of what he had in mind to say in his throat when he felt the toe of his wife's shoe crack against his shin beneath the table. It wasn't often that his wife laid down an order for him to follow. He decided he had better heed her warning this time and keep the remainder of his words to himself. He sipped at the hot coffee and cast his eyes across the table straight into her eyes where he read, "Good for you."

It turned out to be a very good visit. The weather cooperated to the fullest to help provide the perfect atmosphere.

Mid-afternoon on Sunday, Gus asked his granddaughter to go for a walk with him. "All right, let me get my bonnet."

They walked slow, stopping now and then to observe and discuss objects along the way. When they approached the bridge that spanned the creek between the old cabin and the new house she asked, "Would you like to see where we first lived?"

"Yes, I'd like that."

They came upon the remains of the old chimney, all that was left of their original dwelling. Most of the yard was now overgrown with wild weeds. It would soon look as if no one had ever lived there. She described the horrors of the fire that destroyed the cabin.

She glanced over toward the water well. It was nearly filled with debris. Her men had continually dumped trash in the hole when they had a cart full from clearing new ground. Among the weeds and grass growing around the well casing, she spotted several zinnias proudly waving their blooms, trying to survive in the crowd of tares. "Look grandfather, there by the old well, my flowers, or what's left of them. Come on. Let's go over for a better look."

Yes, old Gus thought, just like you. You are a pretty blossom out here in this God forsaken place, to wither and finally let the tares take over.

Gus kicked at the crumpled pile of brick before they found two solid stumps to sit on. He crossed his legs and spoke. "Your grandmother cautioned me severely when we first arrived against interfering in your life, but I need to talk to you about a few things. Can I?"

She grabbed up the hem of her dress and fanned the dust at her feet. "Yes, grandfather, you can say anything to me, and I in return, will say something to you if I feel the need. Is that fair enough?"

He cleared his throat and began, "Are you happy here in this wilderness? It looks so lonesome and forlorn. I can barely stand the thought of you eking out a living from the dirt, working from dawn to dusk. You were not brought up to live so lowly a life. Does not the social life interest you at all? All you have to do is say the word and I can have this place fixed up in no time.

Build you a big comfortable house to raise your babies in. They will be my great grandchildren you know. Are you to deprive them of the things I can do for them? Girl, you cannot molt away here in these woods and turn into a weather worn old farm wife to be buried at your death in this God forsaken land. You just can't."

"Grandfather, you know I love you, don't you?" She waited for him to respond by nodding his head. "Well, I love my husband more than anyone else on this earth. I could not have imagined the happiness I now possess. Leave me alone grandfather. Don't do anything to rile up Jesse. He's a very proud man. He's smart, very smart. Like his father, he does any job he wants done. Just look around you. All this was nothing but woods a little over one year ago. All the furniture in the house and kitchen Paw, err, Mr. Swinson made every piece of. You will have to admit it is as fine as any piece in your house, which you paid such a high price for. I'm so happy, I cannot describe to you how happy. If you mean what you say when you say you love me, let us live our lives the way we want to.

"Yes grandfather, I've witnessed what your meddling has done to my parents. You don't like to hear it, but you broke my father's sprit all those years ago. I grew up knowing that fact, but I still loved you. Some of my love was for what you could buy me. I'm ashamed of that now, but it's the truth. I enjoyed all the luxuries you provided me throughout my youth and early womanhood. Now grandfather, I'm a fully grownup woman. I like who I am and what I'm doing. You know you can spoil everything here with your bossy ways and not caring who you hurt with the things you say. I don't want you to interfere in any way, do you understand what I'm saying, and asking of you?"

The old grandfather had never been talked to in such a manner in all his life. She was truly blood of his blood. He smiled beneath his breath. He didn't want to reveal to her how proud he was of her. Yes, she was a woman now, her own woman. She had no need for him or his money. If he knew what was best for him, he'd leave her and her way of life just as she wanted it to be.

He rubbed his chin before he spoke. "I do believe you mean what you say to me. Alright, I'll keep my distance if you'll promise me one thing: if ever the time should come that you, Jesse or your father-in-law gets in need of anything at all, you will send me word. Will you promise me that? Give me your word you will let me know."

She got off the stump and went to him. She took his hand and pulled to help him get up. "Yes. I give you my word. I'll do just that. But don't you wait around to hear that we have need of you."

They walked back to the house by way of the outskirts of the entire field.

When the company packed up to depart on Monday morning, Jess came to them with a beautiful magazine rack. He had spent hours on the hand carved decoration bordering the rack. "I know you have a house full of furniture, but I wanted you to take home something from our house."

Gus shot a startled glance at his granddaughter. Then he smiled a friendly smile and accepted the rack. "Why thank you Jess. I know we will enjoy this." For the parents, Jess gave them a handmade bellows for their fireplace.

Listy Ann went to her mother. She handed her several jars of homemade jelly tucked down carefully in a decorative bag. She had spent tedious hours to complete the fine needlework that accented the bag.

She turned to her grandmother and handed her an identical bag. "All these jars are filled with wild berry makings. I picked every one of the little rascals." She hugged each woman and added, "I'm so pleased you all came to visit us. Be careful on your journey back to your homes. Think of me when you eat from the jars. I love you all."

She backed up away from the buggy and stood beside her husband and father-in-law to wave their good-byes until the buggy was out of sight.

Jesse had his arm around her and felt pride to stand beside her as her husband. "You know something Brister? Old man Gus ain't quite as awful as he makes an effort to be." She kept quiet about the conversation she had had with her grandfather.

The next day the trees and vine were put in the ground. Listy Ann chose the northwest corner of the porch for the wisteria vine. Jesse brought stable manure from the barn to add to the holes before the vine was put in. "We'll have to water it every day, some times twice, since we're getting it in the ground right here in hot weather. Both the trees, too," she added her thoughts.

She picked up the shovel and he reached for the rake. He placed his free hand around her shoulder as they walked to the barn to put the tools up. "Jesse," she murmured.

"Yes, darling?"

"Not a one of them know that I'm with child. For some reason I had no desire to tell them."

Listy Ann ceased to keep in contact with her parents and grandparents. She never saw either of them after that visit.

Chapter Eight

They had come a long way at making the land a comfortable home and productive farm. One day Listy Ann was standing in the middle of the yard between the two buildings. She looked up at the smoke billowing skyward from both chimneys. She smiled at knowing who was in the house dozing while sitting in a chair, her husband, warming himself up before returning to the outside chores. The weather had turned off right cold for October.

"Listy Ann!" She jumped at the sound of her name.

"Paw, you startled me."

"What are you doing out here in this cold? You'd best get back inside before you catch you death of cold."

"Oh, I'm all right Paw. I was hot from standing near the cook stove. The temperature gets on up there when the stove is fired up for baking. Come on in and let me pour you a cup of coffee. I just boiled a fresh pot. It'll warm you up."

Jess had been busy out in the barn. Since the crops had been harvested, he had turned one of the stalls into a workshop. He had put a floor in before he began work on his projects. He was making a crib and chest of drawers and a rocking chair in preparation of the coming grandchild.

He was proud of the table and chairs that sat in the dining room. The day he had brought them in, Listy Ann nearly swooned.

"Paw this is a very good job you've done here. It looks like a professional job." The minute the words left her lips, she realized what she'd said. He was a professional when it came to working with wood, whether it was trinkets or a table. "Paw, I'm so sorry. I meant to pay you a compliment, and it came out the wrong way." She ran her hand across the top of the lazy-Susan style table. The table had four tiers. The bottom for the place settings of plates and drinking vessels, the second for bowls of food, the third for salt, pepper, and smaller items such as jellies, pickles and so forth. The top tier was just large enough to hold the kerosene lamp. They had shortened the name of the table and simply called it the "round table."

Jess had found an old walnut tree growing wild on the property and had collected the nuts. He had saved the outer hulls for the staining of the furniture he made. He soaked the hulls in a tub of water until he saw the color he wanted appear. He applied the stain to the wood before it cured completely, so it would look natural.

The table would seat ten people. He had made twelve matching chairs, for when company came, and when the family grew in number.

There were two corner cabinets. One was a safe for storing left over food and the other a pie safe. Another was a buffet type cabinet for storing dishes and silverware. Each piece of furniture matched. Yes, Listy Ann liked the looks of her dining room.

In the cook house sat a small table where they ate breakfast and Listy Ann did most of her preparation of food before cooking it. Jess sat at the small table to sip the hot coffee and talk to her for a while. "What time is our company arriving? You've got this kitchen smelling mighty good, it makes me want to nibble."

The Garganus' were expected over to share the midday meal with them. "They're supposed to be here around one o'clock. Everything is almost ready. All I have to do is get cleaned up and put my good frock on."

She wore her calico dress with the lace trimming. It fit snugly. The fullness of her breast due to her pregnancy made the dress fit a bite tighter than she liked, but it would have to do, she had no dress bigger. She wore calico in the colder weather because the material was woven heavier and the colors were plainer and darker. In the warm weather, she chose gingham to sew up her clothes from. The colors were softer and more cheerful and gingham was a lighter weight material.

As the weeks passed, the baby grew healthy and strong within Listy Ann's body. She could tell it was an active child by the pressure of the movements. She experienced no nausea or ill temperament. She did find that sleep was a necessary time to rest. Never before had she taken a nap in the afternoon, until the pregnancy demanded it. Her appetite was ravenous.

She had never paid much attention to the rules of carrying a child, and as her progress developed, she had to learn most of the needed activities to go along with becoming a mother.

Often times she asked Mary Garganus for advice if she felt uncertain about one thing or another.

"You may not know now what to do, but I'll grant you one thing, you'll learn and remember what there is to being with child and giving birth to it. This is a hard world we are thrown in. We have to learn to survive or we are lost back to the dust," Mary told her one day.

The weather turned very cold the latter part of November. Cold enough to freeze an inch thick in the water bucket that sat on the water table in the kitchen.

The animals blew clouds from their nostrils when they met Jess for the morning feeding. "Good morning there, old fella. Do you like this cooler weather better than those hot July days out in the fields?" He rubbed the bridge of the horse's face and scratched beneath his jaw. The horse had become accustomed to the feel of Jess' hand. He would nudge him if he forgot to follow through with his personal touch.

Jess left the stalls and went to feed the hogs. He always started the rhythm of his hog call while he filled the bucket with corn. If he had the time, he tore the kernels from the cob by raking the butt of his palm down the length of the cob and giving it a twist. He could clear all the kernels off with four rakes of the hand.

"Tch! tch! tch! Souie, souie, souie, tch, tch, tch." He made the 'tch' sound by dropping his tongue from his top front teeth, in a fast movement. The hogs had learned the call and came running with their 'oinks' and 'squeals.'

The young hogs, to be slaughtered for meat, had been penned up and fed twice a day to fatten and make the meat more tender. If they had been allowed to run the woods with the older ones, the meat would be tough and sinewy. If the weather stayed cold enough, hog killing time was set for the month of February.

The third day of December was cold, a real cold, winter day. Listy Ann did little more than sit and fan herself. She couldn't imagine fanning herself in the dead of winter. Her body was so big and heavy that it was a struggle for her to move from one place to another. She seemed to be hot all the time. She did manage to get the meals cooked and on the table. Other chores around the place were left until Miss Marcy arrived. She tried to come to the farm every other day. She was to help deliver the baby and felt the time was near at hand. She was with child again, but would not mention it until Listy Ann delivered.

About four o'clock in the afternoon the sky darkened and clouded over, it looked like a storm was under foot. Listy Ann decided to fix supper a little early and said to Jesse, while she waddled from table to stove, "Please go feed the chickens and gather up the eggs. I don't think I can get that done today." Soon after he left the kitchen, she felt a wetness between her legs. She went to the back door and opened it. The cold blast of air did not hamper her. She pulled up the front of her frock and saw what looked like watered down blood oozing down her legs. She felt no pain, but knew that the baby was getting ready to make its entrance into the world. She noticed the rain had started to fall.

When Jesse stepped back in the kitchen, he took one look at her and he knew right away that something us up. He was as wet as a drowned chicken but paid it no mind. He threw up his hand at her and ordered, "Wait right there woman! I'm going for Miss Marcy." He was so excited he didn't know what to do next.

"No, Jesse. It's not time yet. Go to the house and get Paw. Tell him to come on over here to the kitchen, we'll go on and eat our supper early and get it over with. I feel fine right now, but there will be need for anxiety before this night is over, or at least by early tomorrow. Now just go on and get Paw." The supper dishes were left unwashed, but stacked in the dishpan.

The darkness came earlier than usual due to the nearness of the storm. Jesse walked from one room of the house to another. He had filled the kettle with water and placed it near the fire to have it hot and handy if needed. He watched the storm and he watched his wife. "Brister, honey, don't you think it's about time I went for Miss Marcy?"

"No Jesse, not yet."

They all went to bed early. There was nothing else to do aside from read by the kerosene lamp and talk to each other.

Their minds were not exactly on conversations or the subject matter of a book.

Listy Ann tossed and turned. Jesse lay awake, pretending he was asleep, when in truth, he felt her every move.

A little past midnight a pain eased through her lower back, a pain like she had never experienced. It lingered only a moment or so. She waited, with her eyes wide open, as if she would be able to see the next pain when it came. It came all right, with the force of horses pushing within her back. "Oh! God," she moaned, and rolled to her side.

Jesse was out of the bed in seconds. He reached for a sulfur match, and quickly lit the kerosene lamp. "Can I go for Miss Marcy now?"

She had never felt such pain. She tried to get out of the bed. She had the urge to use the chamber pot. It felt like to her, that she was going to pee all over the bed.

"You stay in the bed. I'll go wake Paw." He pulled his overalls on and realized he had them on backwards. "Damn, babies pick a hell of a time to arrive."

"Oooooh," Listy Ann cringed with the pain.

Jesse went to her, but there was nothing he could do. "Hold on Brister, I'm going for help right now. I'll get Paw in here before I leave."

Jess lay in his bed wide-awake. He listened to what occurred in the other part of the house, recalling in his mind the memory of his first child's birth. He had decided to stay in the bed until his son needed him. Sometimes, too many men at a birthing could get bothersome.

"Paw, Paw! Wake up. Listy Ann's time is on hand." By then he stood by his father's bed. "I'm leaving to get Miss Marcy. Tend to her Paw. Don't let nothing happen to her. Paw, why am I scared to death?"

"Son it's only natural that you feel that way. It happened to me and will happen to you again." He had risen and had pulled his overalls over his shoulders. "It is a great event for a child to be born. Now you take notice of where you're going. I know you'll be taking the short cut through the woods. It you don't be careful, you'll wind up in that swamp, we'd never find you. Don't fret about your wife. I'll take care of her until you return."

Jesse galloped the horse at break neck speed ignoring his father's advice.

Miss Marcy had had her satchel packed for days, filled with all her remedies and needs for the work ahead of her. She heard the hoof beats of the horse when Jesse raced into their yard hollering, "Hey-o the-house!" at the top of his lungs.

When he leapt from the saddle, he saw light appear inside the house. Jasper opened the door to let him in. "Howdy Mr. Jesse, come on in out of the weather. My madam will be ready shortly. You sit here in the living room while I go hitch up the horse and buggy."

When he returned to the house, he said to Jesse, "If you'll trot de horse on de way back, you'll make better time, dan if you tries to gallop her. You can't see good 'nough to travel fast. Leave your horse here. Ander and me, we'll fetch him home fer you on tomorree."

When they got back to Listy Ann, she was sitting up in the rocking chair. Between the two of them, they got her back in the bed. Miss Marcy commenced to spread necessary items needed on the center table located near the bed, for the task coming up. She seemed to pay no attention to the woman in the bed or the loss of her own personal sleep.

Four hours, Miss Marcy sat in the room patiently waiting and watching. She nodded off in sleep a time or two, when her patient dozed between pains. She had attended enough births to know when the time was near.

When time came for the baby to make its entry, Miss Marcy stood by the bed. She pushed Listy Ann's hair away from her face and wiped sweat from her brow. She cooed and tried to console her through the last of the ordeal. The young woman looked up and asked, "You're not one of them conjuring women, are you Miss Marcy?" She was earnest in what she asked.

The colored woman shook her head as she smiled. "No ma'am, I left all dat behind me, when I left de plantation down in Georgie. I knows how to conjure. I never liked to perform dough. My mammy, she said dare was a little some'um wrong wid me. Don't you worry yore pretty little head now missy, everything I does, you'll understand and agree wid."

The baby was born a little after five a.m. The wind howled around the corners of the house as the unbiblical cord was snipped and tied off. The smack applied to the little fellow's rump announced his arrival to the waiting men folk.

Dark skinned hands placed the baby by its mother's side. "You'll have nothing but trashy looking liquid for him to suckle for two or three days. He needs it to get everything inside him working and in order. You'll know when the milk enters your tits. There's always a certain amount of pain and soreness. It's all natural, nothing for you to fret over unless a thing out of the ordinary happens. If it do, tell me 'bout it soon as you notices it. You got a fine boy youngin' there. I'd say round nine pounds." She opened the bedroom door and beckoned the father to come in.

She stood at a distance while Jesse went to look at his son for the first time. She always relished the expression shown on a man's face when he first looked at the little image of himself. "He's so little."

"He'll grow. Look at the wide spread of his hand," Listy Ann responded as she fingered the small pink hand.

"How are you, Brister? I began to think this night would never end." The day light was just beginning to open up the day. "Can I hold him?"

Miss Marcy came to the bedside, scooped up the baby, and placed it in the father's arms, who acted stiff and nervous. "He won't break Mr. Jesse; you can even nuzzle him if you wants to."

When Jesse went to leave the room soon after the new mother went to sleep, Miss Marcy handed him a bundle. It was the afterbirth, wrapped in an old rag. "Ask your Paw what to do with this."

Jesse took the bundle, "What is it?"

"Just git on, do as I say. Mr. Jesse, he'll explain to you, now git on."

The bundle felt warm to his touch. For some reason, it made a chill run up his backbone.

It was complete daylight when he walked out of the room. He found his father on the kitchen porch, drinking a cup of hot coffee. "Paw, Miss Marcy handed me this bundle. She said you'd tell me how to take care of it. What is this Paw?" He weighed it in his hand.

"Son, you have there in your hands, the afterbirth. It's your job to go out behind the barn, dig a good, deep hole and bury it. The job will be yours every time a child is born to you and your wife."

While Jesse took care of the chore, he felt his chest swell with pride, a son. Of course, a daughter would have been all right but a son!

When he returned he found Miss Marcy in the kitchen preparing breakfast. "Is it all right to leave her and the baby over there in the house alone?" he questioned her.

"Ye'sir, she be fine now. She and de little'un are sleeping. Missy will sleep de bigger part of the next day er so. She done a big job. She tired, real tired. It up to you to see dat she stay in bed for thirteen to fifteen days."

"Fifteen days. Why so long? Are you sure everything is all right?"

She put more wood in the cook stove and, with her apron bottom, she lifted and shut the firebox lid. "She need de time to allow her body to heal properly. If she git up and about afore the parts used to make the baby heals 'n get back to where dey belongs, she'll mess up her insides. Therefore, she'll have trouble dat you don't wants. I knows it be a hardship on you men folk, but it got to be. She need to eat good, too. Her milk be dropping in a day or so, and her body will demand plenty a nourishment. And Mr. Jesse, do you need to be told to leave her alone until the bleeding stop?" It took all the gumption she could bolster up to speak to him so boldly.

Just then, they heard the sound of the cart that brought Jasper and Ander to the place. Thank goodness, it distracted them away from the subject that seemed an embarrassment to both man and woman.

Before the Moore's left the farm that day, Miss Marcy had washed all the bedding and other items used in the birthing.

Little Ander watched in amazement while his maw changed the hippin' on the newborn one last time before she left.

At the close of the day December 4, 1870, Jess took down the family bible and recorded the birth of his first grandson, James David. He was a happy man to have come so far as to see his grandson born. He would never get to see or cuddle the children of James. He tried to keep his mind off those he had lost, but still the memory crept in ever so often.

Before the week was up, the baby had been dubbed with the nickname, 'Dave,' to follow him all his life.

Their first Christmas in the new house with a baby was a joyous time. They all went over to celebrate with the Garganus family.

It was a cold crisp morning and Listy Ann was busy making mattresses for three more beds. Jess had two of the bedsteads put up in the room, three to the room. She had been saving corn shucks since the fall before, when the corn had been harvested, for stuffing mattresses and pillows and maybe a few other things too. When there were enough shucks to fill the wash pot, she boiled them for half an hour and then spread them out on one of the porches to dry. She was careful to choose a day when there was no wind blowing. When the shucks dried, she trimmed off all the hard places then stuffed them down in a sack, made from the homespun to be ready when she got the ticking material sewed and ready to stuff. The shucks were soft and pliable after the process of boiling and drying. It was a long, tedious, time-consuming job, but well worth the effort. She kept all this in her workroom.

She found and cut dried sedge for her broom makings. The sedge grew in two heights. She chose the taller one for her brooms. When she finished construction of the broom, it was a good four feet tall and five inches around, a good-sized hand full to hold onto while sweeping. She made two brooms at a time, one for the house and one for the kitchen. The broom usually lasted two to three months.

For a scrub mop, she got Jesse to saw her a wedge of oak wood, one inch thick and fifteen inches long. The short width was cut on a slant. He used an auger to bore seven holes down the length and three across the width. There was one hole at an angle in the thicker side of the wood for the handle. She took whole corn shucks, after boiling them to make them soft, and then she screwed one entire shuck into each hole. The shuck locked in and stayed put for the duration of the time it lasted. There again, there was a mop made for each building. It took about six of the mops to last through the year. The wooden mop head lasted for years.

She used lye to scrub the floors. With the shuck scrub mop, her hands never touched the strong, hot scouring water. After months of scrubbings, the floors took on a bleached effect and smelled, and looked, quite refreshing as soon as they dried from a cleaning.

The baby was never far from where she was at work. If he was in a good mood, he was in a special wooden box Jess had built for just that purpose. When the men were around the house, they helped tend to the baby, which gave the mother a breather.

She sat on that cold morning, stitching up the last seam on the ticking and mused at all they had accomplished. When she broke the thread from the sewing machine, she gathered the empty mattress up and moved over so she would have room to work. She began to stuff the shucks into the mattress, handful after handful. It took almost as long to fill the mattress with the soft, crisp shucks as it did to sew the ticking together to make the tick. She used a needle and thread to sew up the opening she had crammed the shucks through.

The mattress was heavy when she finished. She pulled on it once and decided to call Jesse in to assist her in getting it on the bed. She went out on the porch and called to him, "Can you come to the house and help me a little while?"

"Be there, directly."

He carried the mattress to the room and dropped in on the bedstead. He tugged on her until they fell together atop the mattress. "Come on Brister, let's break it in. Paw's way out yonder in the barn."

When he left the house to return to his work, she straightened up her hair and worked with the mattress until she had all the shucks even and smoothed out. She put fresh sheets on and continued to work at it until it was ready for sleep. That was the first regular mattress she had completed and naturally it went in Paw's room. He worked hard and deserved a few favors.

Jess had completed all the bedsteads for the house and a bureau for each room. The frames for the mirrors were empty until he could make the journey to town for the purchase of mirror glass. Chair frames for the house and porches were ready for Jasper to put in the cane woven bottoms.

Jasper also made baskets for the Swinsons and Garganus family. He had learned the trade of weaving while still a slave and found it to be a useful bit of talent. He made baskets for eggs, corn, bread, and for gathering vegetables. He often swapped the baskets for food or to get one of the Swinson's to do some sawing for him.

One night at supper In February, Jess said to his son and wife, "I think I'll ride over to the Moore's tomorrow morning, since we've not seen nothing of them in nigh on to two months. I want him the cane those chairs and it'll soon be time to kill hogs."

The day after the visit to the Moore's they all decided to go to Pin Hook. A community of farmers had settled there. One of the farmers grew trees and shrubs for resale. The time was right to transplant the young trees and other growths they wanted to get in the ground. The mailman had brought the advertisement flyer to them back in the fall. They had spent some time during the coldest months deciding what plants and trees they thought would thrive best on the land.

On a cold, crisp morning, the three of them hurriedly did the chores on the place and dressed warmly to make the trip. It was ten to fifteen miles to the man's farm. It would take them all day to get there and back.

On their way out, they stopped at the Garganus' farm to see if they wanted anything from the tree farm. "No. I thank you very kindly for the offer, but I don't think we need anymore," Cyrus told them. He had his farm pretty well landscaped with all the trees he felt was necessary.

They found the trees and shrubs to be a delight. Listy Ann would have liked to take everything the man had for sale home with her. They chose to purchase a dozen pecan trees, six apple, four peach, two pear and two healthy looking grape vines.

The grapes were scuppernong, one white and one black, each good for making wine and the makings of jelly. Both species very tasty to pull from the vine and eat when ripe, which was early fall. The art of enjoying one of the grapes took a small amount of talent. To place the part of the grape that clung to the vine against slightly ajar teeth, then push the grape with the fingers while at the same time sucking inward with the mouth. As soon as the pulp enters the mouth, swallow it all in one gulp, then spit the hull aside. If a person loved grapes enough, they could stand under a vine and swallow the pulps until they could feel them in their throat when they swallowed.

Two of the trees were June apples. They put off ripe apples in late June that where big with red streaks running from stem to blossom end. When a bite was taken from one of them, juices seeped from the corners of the mouth. They were also good for those first fruit pies of the year. Three of the trees bore their fruit in hot weather. One tree, a skeet apple, ripened after the frost laid on it a time or two. All the trees were chosen with productivity in mind. As well as starting new trees from seeds and cuttings.

While in Pin Hook, they went to the only cafe for a bite of dinner. It was always a special treat for them to dine away from home, not to say that Listy Ann was not a talented cook, by no means. To sit down and have the food placed before them, with none of their efforts applied in the preparation, was on their part appreciated.

Listy Ann went to the general store for the purchase of material for sewing up some frocks and baby dresses. She had found a need for more white homespun. The baby seemed to need more hippin'. It took a change after each wetting.

They loaded up the wagon, which was full, and headed toward home in time to arrive before darkness fell. The sun was to their backs. Since Pin Hook was located to the west of their farm, they rode in an easterly direction. The warmth felt good on their backs as they jogged along on the wagon. The baby slept all the way home.

They stopped at the Garganus' long enough to drop off several cans of peaches for the children. The children loved each Swinson in their own right. The boys made Jesse their idol while the girls adored Listy Ann. Jess was the grandfather figure.

It took them the better part of the week to get all the trees and vines in the ground, each one planted when the sign was right, according to the almanac. Earth and water signs were best for trees and shrubs. The pear and peach trees showed tiny sprouts forming when planted. "It's a good thing we didn't wait any later in the season to get these in the ground. Another two weeks and there'll be blooms," Jess stated, when the job of transplanting was finished.

Jesse straightened up with the shovel clutched in his hand and asked, "Brister, how come you never transplanted one of them pine trees up near the house? There are some pretty ones around in the woods.

"Why, didn't you know, that to have a pine tree in the yard is an omen that there will be a sickly child in the family?"

The weather provided plenty of rain for the new crop of trees. When the Swinsons awoke the next morning, it was raining a slow drizzle of a rain. It continued all day and on through the night.

The fourth week in February was time to slaughter the hogs. Jess borrowed Cyrus' scalding vat. He had not taken the time to build one for his farm yet. He and Jesse built the gallows frame for hanging the hogs, after scalding and scrapping off the hair, to split open through the belly to remove the innards. The gallows was made from small-bodied trees that would be easy to disassemble when the hog killing procedure was completed.

The pit was dug and the vat placed securely over the open hole, with a flue stuck in the hole at one end of the vat. Dirt was tamped around the flue and vat so no air could enter. In that manner, the fire would draw correctly and heat the water to the degree needed for scalding the hogs. At the other end of the vat, an open space was left to build a fire and push under the vat as far as possible.

On the day to kill the hogs, Jess was up at daylight to get the fire going under the vat. He answered the call when Listy

Ann called out, "Breakfast is on the table." He had already worked up a healthy appetite.

They had just finished eating when they heard the noise wagon wheels make when moving over cold, hard ground. Jess and Jesse got up from the table and went to greet their neighbors, both white and colored, who had come over to assist with the hog killing.

The women gathered up in the kitchen when the men went to the hog lot to begin their day's work. Miss Marcy instructed Listy Ann right away that she was not to touch any of the sausage makings. "What in this world are you talking about woman?"

"It be a proved fact, dat if you helps in working up de sausage whilst you are wid child dat sausage will spoil fer shore, 'stead of curing like it oughta."

"Where did you get such a thing from? I'm not with child again."

"Yes, lovey, you are." Miss Marcy replied, and continued. "I'm living proof dat de sausage will ruin. My mammy tried to warn me bout it. I didn't heed her word and de sausage spoiled."

Listy Ann stared at the colored woman in disbelief. She couldn't be expecting again, and Dave only months old. "Now Miss Marcy, tell me, why did you say I'm carrying a child again?"

"Why, sugar all I has to do is look at cha. Yore sides are thickening up, and you walk a bit different. There's a certain glow about your face. Oh, dare's ways of telling when a life is begun in a woman's body. Miss Mary dare can tell you de same thing. Why, just de other day, me and her wuz talking bout you." Miss Marcy turned to put some of the breakfast dishes away and added, "I lost another baby six weeks ago."

At that moment, Cyrus called out to the women that their help was needed. A table had been set up beneath the wash shelter for the women to trim fat from the hog guts for the rendering of lard. He turned toward Listy Ann, "The liver, heart and lights are ready, if you want to get your hassit on the stove." The organs had to be eaten within a week or so after the killing or they would spoil. They were divided three ways at the end of the day for the hassit which was a delicious stew made from mixing all the organs, then simmering for a couple of hours over low heat.

Listy Ann took Miss Marcy's advice and did mostly fetching and running errands for those who worked steadily. She took over the job of baby tending for both Ander and little Dave. She cooked a big dinner, which was savored by all present.

When Mrs. Garganus and Miss Marcy trimmed all the fat from the guts and maw, they took them to the creek where water ran briskly. They stooped and washed the insides of every gut clean of any unwanted matter. A gut was held open at one end and filled with the running water. Then each end was pinched closed and the water was sloshed from one end of the gut to the other, by moving the hands up and down. The insides of the guts flowed on down the creek as soon as they were dumped out. This was done until the gut appeared to be rid of all substance. When the creek washing was finished, the guts were taken back to the wash shelter where they were washed several times in clean well water, then dumped into the wash pot, salted down good and boiled for the amount of time it took to make them tender. A certain number of the guts were left raw, salted down and packed away until they were needed to stuff sausage and liver pudding in.

Lye soap was made from the scrap pieces of meat along with all the kidneys.

It was a long, hard day of work for all involved, no matter what the job. At the close of the day, Miss Marcy and her little family went home loaded with a good supply of fresh pork. So did the Garganus family. "We'll be back tomorrow to help with drying up the lard and grinding and stuffing of the sausage." The hog feet were left until every other job was done. When salted down and packed in a tub, they would keep for a week or more without spoiling. The feet made very good eating on a cold winter's night. The meat on the feet turned into a jelly like substance, when chilled.

Jess let the meat stay salted down in the saltbox, located at the rear of the smoke house for three weeks. Then he and

Jesse washed it thoroughly with warm water to remove the excess salt. The meat was then strung with a blade of bear grass through a slit made with a sharp knife at one corner of the side meat, and near the end of the small bone on the hams and shoulders. It was then hung on a wooden peg attached to bare rafters near the top of the smoke house. When the sausage was stuffed, it too hung in the smoke house, as the meat did.

The meat was smoked with a smoldering fire, which was never allowed to blaze up, for five to six weeks. The meat was then ready to supply the family with pork, hopefully until the next hog killing time.

The bear grass plant grew wild in certain areas of Onslow County. Several of the plants grew beside the dirt road that was part of the road from Jacksonville to the area where the Swinsons resided. Bears had been seen as they scratched their hides on the edges of the plant leaves. No one knew the correct pronunciation of the plant so they simple called it 'bear grass.' The road became known as the Bear Grass Road.

One April morning Listy Ann was in the chicken coop. One of her setting hens was about to become a mother. She lifted up the spread of hen feathers and watched as the tiny nebs cracked the shell. It was an amazing sight to watch. The baby chick wiggled and squirmed until it worked its way free of the shell to lay gasping and wet on the straw filled nest.

"You darling little creature," Listy Ann cooed, as she gently lifted the used up shell from the nest. All seven of the eggs hatched before nightfall. As soon as the baby chicks dried, they were carefully lifted from the nest and placed in a box beside the row of nests. From that day forward, they were in the care of the mother hen, with a little help from Listy Ann, who threw out food for them every morning.

By the end of the week, all the eggs under the two other setting hens had hatched out. Thirty biddies ran peeping and scratching about the chicken yard. Each mother hen keeping her chicks close by her while she clucked and showed them how to scratch out a place on the ground to rest beside the coop on the shaded side when the sun warmed the ground up.

The farm had come alive with new growth. All the seeds were in the earth for the crops. The young saplings of trees had new growth sprouting from the tender branches. The pear and peach trees were filled with blossoms that added color to the almost bleak surroundings. Listy Ann admired the blooms every time she got within eyesight of either of the trees with their aromatic fragrance.

"I could stand right here and inhale the mist from the flowers all day long. Don't you notice the beauty they add to our farm?" she asked Jesse one day while he was chopping at some wild dog fennels, an aggravating weed that grew to be five feet tall, if left to grow through the season. The foliage was like fine fur that grew around the stalk, two to three inches in width.

"I ain't paid much attention to colors." He stopped the action of the hoe and propped his arms on top of the hoe handle to watch her as she went on about the blossoms.

"I do wish you'd take a little time to appreciate the beauty of things, when you work so hard to get a thing done. Part of the results is what you can see and marvel at." She tried to get him interested in some of the things she had an interest in.

"Right now all I can see is these damn dog fennels. If I don't get the roots out, they'll be back up next spring bigger than they are this year." He glanced at the trees in bloom and smiled at her. "Oh, all right. I agree with you. They do make a pretty sight for the eye to rest upon."

She was a vision of loveliness in his eyes. She wore one of the dresses she had sewn to accommodate the growth of the baby. The color was soft and becoming to her complexion. Strands of her hair had worked free from her hairpins and were blowing gently about her face and neck.

She stood erect. Her middle showed the small amount of gained weight. She didn't feel as if she was with child. It seemed to Jesse that she was even more beautiful now than when he had first seen her on the streets of Clinton.

"Jesse, do you know what Miss Marcy suggested we do?"

"No, I don't."

"That we cease sleeping together until after this baby comes. 'Why Miss Marcy?' I asked her. 'I see nothing wrong with it as long as it doesn't hurt.' Her reply was. 'You best refrain frum relations wid your man during de time of your regular bleeding time. It has been known to cause a mother to loose de child. The truth be known, it be best if you slept in separate rooms.'"

"What did you have to say about that advice?"

"I replied, 'Oh my, I don't know about that. My man, as you call him, rather likes sleeping with me.' She then told me to do as I thought best."

Listy Ann and Jesse slept in the same bed.

On August 30, 1871, Hosea was born. He lived three days. He was laid to rest across the creek, near the site of the original cabin. Only Jess, Jesse and Cyrus attended the burial. Jess recorded Hosea's birth. When he put down the death date, his heart was breaking.

Chapter Nine

One day in early September, Listy Ann had the baby in a wooden box that sat at the end of the row, while she picked field peas. Jess had built the box especially to accommodate the size and safety of the child. Dave was about two and a half years old, and a good baby boy, if his stomach was satisfied and his bottom dry. He slept long hours, right there in the box, allowing his mother to accomplish many chores around the house and field.

Jasper had given them the pea seeds. The peas were clay banks, a good pea for eating fresh, canning and drying to store and have for the cold months. The peas had been planted in the cornrows so the vines would run up the corn stalks. The clay bank field pea matured about the first or second week in September. The dry vines added nourishment to the corn stalks when cut and stacked as fodder, winter food for the animals.

She had filled her basket and was preparing to lift the baby box when she heard Jess call out to her. "Yes Paw, do you need me?"

He took the box with the baby and hooked it on his hip. They talked while they walked to the house. "I met up with, and talked to the mail man today. He says we've got new farmers in the area for neighbors. A family of Blake's. They're northeast of us, been there about a week now. Mr. Wooten said they're a fine family, about your age. What I've come to you for, is to see if you want to ride over with Jesse and me to welcome them to the community. Jesse is up to the house now, washing up."

"New neighbors! That's good to hear Paw. Did you fix up a welcome basket to take along with us?"

He assured her that it was ready. "It wouldn't hurt none to add a peck of those peas you got there to what I've all ready put together. I want to go by and check the chicken coop. See if there's enough eggs to carry along a few with us. I recall what a help it was when Cyrus and his family lent us a hand when we first arrived. Do you remember how good those eggs were?"

It was a joy to Listy Ann to meet the new family. When she was introduced to the wife, she took an instant liking to her on the spot. There was one young son named Jeremiah, affectionately called Jere.

Robert, the father, was a farmer from a long line of tillers of the soil. His wife had been brought up in the city, but was adjusted to being a farm wife.

Robert also owned and operated a gristmill. He had brought all the equipment with him to the new location to set up and operate for the families already established in the area and for those who would come later to make their home in the community.

The three existing families were very pleased to see the gristmill come to the area. They had been going all the way to Catherine's Lake to get their corn ground into meal. Yes, every family that moved into the area brought improvement.

Through the next two years, new ground was cleared and more animals were secured. Life on the farm prospered.

November 16, 1873, John Austin is born. Miss Marcy came and helped as she had done with Dave. Another son added to the family. When Jess recorded him in the Bible, he ran his fingers down the length of the page. "I hope this entire page will be filled with the names of my grandchildren," he said to Jesse, who sat in the rocker holding Dave on his knee.

Jess went over, took the baby from his son, and used the other rocker to rock and lull the baby to sleep. It felt so good for old Jess to have young life about him again. At times, when he held the little fellow on his lap, it would surprise him to feel the warmth creep along his thigh. "Why, the boy has peed on me again." Listy Ann always laughed at the sound of that expression offered up in the strong accent of her father-in-law.

Dave at three could follow his GrandPaw through the fields, if it wasn't too unleveled, but most of the time, he wound up on Jess' hip on the way back to the house area. In the summer time, he wore the little pinafores his mother had sewn up for him. They were short sleeved and came down to just above the knees and opened at the back. No underwear was ever worn by the babies in warm weather until they were toilet trained. In the cold months, it was a different story. They wet in the clothes they wore. Listy Ann tried to keep them as dry as possible. It meant a lot of extra hours under the wash shelter to keep enough material washed and dried to use for hippin's when there was two untrained babies.

August 12, 1874, a baby boy was stillborn in the Swinson family. No name was given to the child. The neighbors gathered up to build the pine coffin for the little fellow. He was laid to rest near his brother.

October 16, 1875, Jesse rode on horseback to fetch Miss Marcy. Listy Ann was to deliver their third child. It was another boy. Big strapping youngin' he was too. They named him Jacob Edward. The three boys had all been born with light complexion and blond hair. It looked as if Listy Ann was to be surrounded by blond headed males. Where were her girls? She often wondered. Maybe the next one would be female.

In the spring of 1876, news came that more families had moved into the community. Joshua Pierce bought land in a northwesterly direction from the Swinson's farm. Joshua had two daughters. It was rumored that their mother was full-blooded Indian. The Moore's had two families move in close to their farm, a family of Fishers and a Pickett family.

All the folks in the area were farmers by trade. That didn't mean that they did so by choice. It was a means of survival. There were many different talents among the settlers. What choice did they have, other than plow the ground? They had to eat and feed their families. Some of the men had already become embittered by their surroundings.

Jess saw it happening and was glad he had not allowed his misfortunes to affect him. He too could have been a bitter man by the time the grandchildren started to bless his home in North Carolina.

The farm grew in acreage each year. More ditches were dug to accommodate the runoff water when the rainfall was heavy. The land was low in several areas, and if it did not run off, it would be stagnated and become a breeding hole for mosquitoes. The smell of soured, standing water was offensive to Jess' nose.

Other areas continued to grow along with the increase of children. Two cows were purchased, one with a young calf. Milk was now more in demand than when there had only been adults to nourish. Listy Ann learned to milk, the one chore that Jesse and his father despised to carry out. They each knew how to milk, and would if she was too tied up with something else to attend to the milking. The cow could be left with the udder full just so long.

    The two oak trees they had transplanted from the woods to the yard had grown by leaps and bounds and provided ample shade, one to shade the kitchen and one for the house. The grapevines produced grapes every fall. Jellies and jams lined the pantry shelves. Wine was stored in the smoke house where it was cool. The pecan trees had put off a few nuts. They were slow growers and would take years to reach full productivity. All the fruit trees bore beautiful apples, peaches and pears. Listy Ann canned jar after jar of fruit from the trees.

    The chicken flock had grown until there were eggs for every need and plenty of pullets and young roosters for the eating table, when desired. The eggs that were not needed for food in the kitchen were taken to the nearest store and sold or traded for needed supplies.

    Jess still loved to hear the old rooster's crow in the morning. He often took one of the boys out to show him the rooster while he stood on the top rail of the fence to announce the breaking of day. He would tell the grandchild about how he had vowed, on that day so long ago, that one of his heirs would one day reclaim their family wealth and standing. "Do you reckon, it'll be you little fellow?" He never mentioned the vow in front of either parent. He also told them stories about their grandmother, aunts and uncles they would never know. When they left the scene of the rooster, he always lifted the child up and straddled his little legs around the back of the grandfather's neck to ride there on the way back to the house for breakfast.

    One day Listy Ann and Jesse stood at the wooden window, all the windows were made of wood, and watched. "I wonder what he talks to them about, when he takes them out there." Jesse wondered aloud.

    "I've wondered the same thing myself. He does it with all three of them. I even asked him once about it, and all he'd say was, "Oh, it's just men talk."

Spring-cleaning on the farm was a family oriented job. It was a known fact that a house built from untreated, unpainted wood got chinch infested due to the corn shuck mattresses. A cinch is a little fetid insect, brown in color and destructive to corn crops if allowed to get a good hold on the crop. The chinch was also famous for getting in bed mattresses, pillows and linens. Listy Ann had seen no signs of the little devils, but as a preventative measure, the house was emptied out each spring. The walls were scalded down with hot water to which a small amount of kerosene was added. Every piece of furniture was wiped down with the solution. If the chinch got a good start in a house, they liked to suck blood from the sleeping body, causing hours of lingering itching.

The job began at daybreak. When Listy Ann went to the kitchen to cook breakfast, the men went to feed the animals and get the fire going under a filled wash pot. By the time she got the meal on the table, the men had started removing things from the two buildings. If a child was big enough, he too joined in and did what he was big enough to handle. No idle hands were allowed on spring-cleaning day.

The day was chosen carefully. If a storm should come up during the day, it meant everything got soaked. Listy Ann hated it when a storm surprised them. Jasper Moore could pretty well predict the weather. Jesse was in the process of learning all Jasper would teach him in the knowledge of forecasting from signs in the sky or in the wind. A rack of clouds that hung in the sky, the way a tree leaf hung from a branch, even certain bird calls had it's meaning, and the stinging insects showed Jasper a sign to forecast by also.

Jesse wrote down every bit of information he learned from Jasper. He in turn taught his sons when they were old enough to start learning their school lessons how to farm the soil, to cut their wood and to kill their animals. Everything they did to make a living off the land was done according to the sign that best suited the situation.

At the close of the day, when the house was back to its correct order, everything smelled so good and refreshed. Every soul in the house was tired. Every muscle cried out in pain.

By the end of 1876, there were enough feathers from the wild turkeys and chickens to stuff two ticks to fit a standard bed and four big fluffy pillows.

Every third year the old shuck mattresses were emptied out. The ticks were turned inside out, washed and allowed to hang on the clothesline all day to dry and air out. Then they were refilled with fresh shucks.

The boys had wet the shuck mattresses for a while before Listy Ann got tired of so much washing and airing out. One day an idea popped right into her head that she liked. She hunted up some of the old tarpaulin. After mentally measuring off the amount she thought would do the job she wanted, she cut it and went to the bed that the little ones slept in. Next to the mattress, she laid the tarpaulin and covered it with layers of white homespun, then smoothed the sheet over that. "Now why didn't I think of this when Dave was little? All the time I've wasted washing out pissy sheets and bedding."

Jesse came in the room just as she spoke. "Smoothing out another mattress, are you?" A big smile opened up his face.

She knew from the glint in his eye why he had made the trip to the house from the field, here in midmorning at that. Their lovemaking had grown with the years. Times when GrandPaw had the boys busy, Jesse hunted up his Brister.

Some of the times, Listy Ann did the hunting up. She'd be busy doing one chore or another, in whatever place on the farm the job took her to. Her mind would recall a special hour with Jesse and the urge would cause her to go hunting him up.

They were always very discreet at their trysts. Not once did either of the boys or Jess walk up on them. All it took was careful plotting.

Another son was born on July 2, 1881. He was recorded in the Bible as Zedick Calvin. He looked exactly like the three brothers born before him, same color hair and skin.

By the time Zedick was born, Jacob was called Jake. Jake was a mean youngin'. When there was a scrap between the three boys, Jake always won. He seemed to have no judgment to the amount of harm he did to his older brothers. He liked to win at an early age, whether it be an argument or a game they played.

His mother paddled his bottom more than the other two boys put together. The punishment never affected his behavior. He had his good points, but his roguish attitude overruled the good in him from the age he had learned to speak.

It bothered Listy Ann that Jake was so unruly. Her love for him was as dear for him as it was for the others. "What makes him want to be boss all the time over the other boys?" she asked the grandfather one day.

None of the older man's children had presented such a problem to him. James had been the strongest minded, but could be kept under control with the proper discipline. He rubbed his long gray beard and ran his fingers through the coarse hair. "It's rightly hard to tell what makes the lad act the way he does. Jake's a good youngin' as long as the others don't cross him. He'll be alright with you as his mother. By the time he's grown, you'll have forgotten the ugly side of him."

"I sure hope you're right Paw, because if he continues on like he's started, we're all in for some trouble. I can feel it in my bones."

During the fall season of the year 1881, it was decided that a school was needed in the area. There were five families located in the community since the Cooper family had moved in. With thirteen children of school age, the men got together and worked out the plans for getting a teacher and building the school. The location for the school was on Jess' property, at the southeast corner. He measured off an acre for the purpose. The Moore's lived a few miles on down the road, east of the school. Word was left in Catherine's Lake, Richlands and Jacksonville, for the need of a teacher. By springtime the following year, the school was in session. Simon King had applied for and got the job as teacher. Two toilets were built out back, one for girls and one for boys. A water well had been dug to supply the needs of the teacher and the students. It was decided that each family would supply the firewood one month at a time during the cold weather. The teacher boarded at the Garganus home. The school was known as the 'Angola School'.

As spring turned into summer, Listy Ann kept her eye on her beloved flowerbeds. Through the years, she had nurtured the plants and saved the seeds from year to year, until she had a variety of colors and different sized plants. Those seeds that she did not have, the neighbor ladies had shared with her from their yards. The flowerbeds were Listy Ann's outlets. She found her personal peace of mind from the daily routine of the hard life on the farm during the time she spent with the flowerbeds. She never found the time to complain about the never-ending chores that arose with the sun each morning.

One early summer morning she was bent over one of the flowerbeds when two of the smaller boys came careening around the corner of the house, one chasing the other, barely missing her rump that stuck up in the air. "Boys, you know what I've told you about my flowerbeds. You will get a switching!"

"Yes'um maw," was the response from one of the down cast faces.

"Now run on about your playing, and be careful of these beds." She lifted up the tail of her apron and wiped sweat from her face. It was one hot day. She stood still for a moment to survey the beauty of the surrounding yard and mused that the boys had stayed clear of her flowers. Because there was always some kind of action going on around the outside of the house, during the daylight hours no matter what the weather was.

Later on in the day, about mid afternoon, Listy Ann was placing pieces of stove wood on her folded arm in order to take it in the kitchen. The wood box had to be filled each afternoon. She was lifting a piece of the wood from the wood pile when she glanced up to see Jake had his toy gun, whittled out of wood by his grandfather for a Christmas gift, slung over his shoulder. He was accompanied by two of the family dogs. He walked straight and tall like the hunter he hoped to be one day. "Jake, where you off to this fine afternoon?" she asked.

"Me 'n my dogs goin to get a mess of squirrels for supper maw." He continued walking on around the corner of the kitchen.

"Good luck son," she yelled out to him as he disappeared from her view.

Listy Ann called supper and the family began to gather on the back porch to wash up. There was always a bucket full of water sitting on the wash bench, along with the wash pan and soap. The drying towel hung on a nail drove into the wall near the door. Jake was not missed until John asked where he was. Listy Ann heard his inquiry, walked out on the porch, and looked around. He was not in sight. "Jake!" she called out. No response. "Jake, Oh Jake!" Still nothing. She went back in the dining room where everyone had gone and stated, "Jesse, go find that youngin'. He's off daydreaming somewhere again."

Jesse grumbled as he pushed his plate away from him and stood. "I'm hungry and got no time to be messing with that boy." He looked at his wife and figured he may as well go and get his son.

In a few minutes, he was back in the kitchen. "I can't find him nowhere. Paw, any of you boys seen him in the last little while?"

Listy Ann arose from the table and looked at the table surrounded with hungry eaters. "Stop right there, there'll be not one bite eat 'till my youngin' is found." She left the kitchen and stepped off the porch steps into the yard in a fast walk.

Each family member filed out into the yard behind her. They all started calling out his name. "Where could he be? He's never failed to come when it's time to eat," Dave commented.

"Hush up Dave and go look behind the barn. John, you check out the chicken coop and yard. The rest of you fan out and cover the fields." Listy Ann barked the orders out and they all knew she was serious. The smaller boy tagged along with different ones because he didn't know what else to do. No one had ever been lost before.

No amount of calling the dogs got any response from them.

Jesse got the gun out and fired three rounds into the air, the signal meaning trouble amongst the community.

By the time the last rays of the sun lowered behind the treetops, father, mother, grandfather and brothers were in a state of disbelief. Where was he? The familiar sound of cartwheels on the path caused them all to look that way. It was Cyrus. "We heard the shots, what's the trouble over here?" He had several of his children in the cart with him.

"It's Jake, we can't find him." Listy Ann spoke before either man could. At the same time she grabbed her forehead and cried out, "My God, oh my God, when I was getting stove wood together up in the afternoon, he came by me with his toy gun. Two of the dogs were trailing along with him. He said he was going hunting for squirrels. Do you reckon he's lost out there in the woods somewhere?" She paced the length of yard between the house and kitchen. "Jesse get the horse, we've got to find my boy. He's only seven years old."

"Horses? Brister you can't ride a horse in the woods at night," Jesse made the brisk statement.

"I don't mean go in the woods with the horse. Let Lewis round up the other neighbors on horseback, and join the hunt with us. Hurry, it'll be plum dark soon."

Jesse took off in a trot to the barn, Lewis close behind him. It took very little time to get the horse saddled. The rider took off in a gallop in pursuit of help.

An hour or so later Listy Ann decided to put the younger boy to bed. He had become cranky and was whimpering and snubbing. "But maw, what about my supper?" Supper had been forgotten since the time Jake had come up missing.

She took him in the kitchen and lit the kerosene lamp. The little fellow filled his belly with a cold supper. His mother put him to bed for the first time in his life with the dirt of the day still clinging to his body. "Good night son. Your brother Jake will be found and be here to greet you in the morning when you rise for the day." She took the time to kiss him and tuck the covers in around his shoulders before she left the room. She always showed her love for the boys.

She returned to the yard where John and Dave waited, along with several other boys from neighboring farms. She sat on the edge of the porch and hung her head. Her worry was too intensified to let the boys see. She heard a shuffling noise and look to where the sound came from. It was the dogs that had been with Jake. "Mercy on us all, the dogs are here. Run boys! See if Jake is following them." She grabbed the lantern from the porch and went to look for herself. Not knowing from which way the dogs had entered the yard, left no clues as to which way to look. "Jake! Jake! Where are you son?"

No sign of the youngin' on the place.

The men searched through the night, making trips back to the house every so often, to see if any sign of the lad had been found.

Daylight dawned on a sad household. The neighboring men folk returned to their own farms to take care of the morning chores. "We'll be back just as soon as we finish up and get a bite of breakfast." Jess and Jesse went about their feeding and watering of their stock. Listy Ann went to the kitchen to start breakfast.

The sight that greeted her was sickening. All the remains from the forgotten supper met her full in the face. She raked the food into one big bowl and went out the back door. When she called the dogs, the two that had been with Jake were missing. "Now what?" she asked herself, aloud.

She reentered the kitchen, got a fire going in the stove, and put a kettle of water on for boiling. The dishes would have to be washed before she could cook. Her mind was not really on what she was doing. She had not shed one tear, but the time was near.

She had the firebox lid of the stove open in order to add more wood when she heard, "Maw! Maw!" She thought the boys were still in bed. The older ones had been put to bed, including the neighbor boys who waited on their fathers when the hour had gotten so late. She closed the lid to the stove and started to walk toward the front door of the kitchen. She may as well go on and see what the boys were up to, when from the back door of the kitchen she heard, "Maw, I'm so tired maw."

She whirled around to see a droopy Jake standing in the doorway, with his trusty little gun still clutched in his hand. She was on her knees in front of him before he finished the words. "Son, my son! Where have you been? We've looked for you the night through." A mother's relief came in the form of racking sobs, and tears she could not control. She hugged him close and rocked back and forth while still squatting on the floor. "Thank you God, for sending him back to us," was her utterance of thanks.

The sun had not come up when the neighbors began to return, bringing their families with them. Jasper and Miss Marcy was among the first to arrive, with looks of surprise and relief when they saw Listy Ann sitting on the kitchen porch steps, with Jake fast asleep on her lap.

A couple of the women went to the kitchen to prepare breakfast for the Swinson family, while Listy Ann continued to hold her sleeping son. The men sat around on the porch talking. "Jesse, what did the boy have to say for hisself?" one of the men questioned.

"Don't know a thing as of yet. All I can say right now, is he showed up with the dogs soon after dawn. I reckon they went back to where they left him last night and he followed 'em on back home."

Jake slept for a couple of hours, right there in his mother's arms. "Listy Ann, let me go lay the boy in the bed. Your arms are going to be ruined." She disregarded Jesse, with a nod of her head.

A few of the neighbors remained out of curiosity, to hear Jake's story when he roused up.

No one questioned him until he was cleaned up and fed. He kept shifting his eyes from one person to another, while he ate. Deep down inside of him, he knew there was trouble brewing for his absences, even though, up until now there had only been hugs and kisses.

They all sat on the porch listening to Jake's tale of his adventure. "Well, all I done was go huntin' for 'em squirrels. I was jist a gonna hunt the edge of the field when the dogs runned in the woods. I went too. First thing I knowed, I couldn't see the fence rails no more. Them dogs, they runned around so, dey got me lost. I walked and walked and tried to find the fence and couldn't. It got dark, so I set down to rest a while. The next thing I knowed the dogs wuz licking my face. I got up and comed on home wid 'em." He wiped a few tears from his cheeks. "Maw, I was so sceared." He sat with his back resting against one of the posts supporting the porch roof, with his arms folded around his drawn up legs. In his little mind, he feared the worst beating of his young years. He had made many a trip out to the wash shelter in the last year or two.

No one said a word. Punishment for the boys was a private concern for the Swinson family. They waited until all the neighbors had gone home before calling Jake to them. "Jake I think you've gone a little too far this time," his mother spoke first. "Whatever your Paw does to you is well earned. I'll not step in and interfere with his judgment this time." She whirled around, walked across the yard and went inside the house.

She stood just inside the door to hear what went on. It was not too long before she heard the wails. Jake screamed and carried on as if his Paw was killing him. He did get a pretty good licking. All his brothers sat on the edge of the porch, with their heads bowed, each one of them glad as could be to see him take the beating. They had gotten to the competitive age and were pleased when one of them got a good lashing, whether it be physical or verbal.

Listy Ann busied herself in the house. She had so much trouble controlling her temper toward Jess and Jesse when they corrected her boys. It seemed that she usually found a reason why one of them did what they did. Now, if she did the punishing, it was all right, but let one of the others do it without her knowledge and she would fly into a rage. Through the years, the father and grandfather had learned to leave most of the discipline up to the mother to avoid her wrath, which was wrong for them to do. With that many boys on the place, some of them entering their teen years, it meant problems and trouble just waiting too happen, in the future. Listy Ann was a possessive mother and thought her sons could do no wrong, most of the time.

The sorghum crop was planted in the spring of 1885, their first try at growing the crop for making syrup. The crop grew and was tended to just like corn. It looked like a field of corn to the untrained eye.

Cyrus had the mule powered cane mill and offered to let the Swinsons have use of it. Jess thought it a good idea to try the syrup making for a year before he invested in a mill of his own.

In September, the seed head of the stalk was cut off. The action was referred to as 'topping.' Then all the leaves were stripped from the stalk. The stalk was cut with a bush ax, just above the ground. When all the stalks were cut and loaded on the wagon, they were hauled to the mill. The stalks were fed into the mill to grind and press the juice from the stalks. The mule hooked to the leads connected to the lever that allowed the grinder to turn, went into action when the mule walked around and around the mill. The process was continued until all the stalks were pulverized. A worker removed the stalks with a pitchfork. The juice was stored in containers for the next day's cooking. It took about eight gallons of juice to produce one gallon of syrup.

The juice was cooked until all the water evaporated out of it. While it processed, a worker stood by the cooking vat and stirred with a long handled spoon. The impurities were dipped off and discarded. When the water cooked out it got syrupy. If it overcooked, it turned to sugar. A person had to know exactly when to remove it from the fire. Cyrus was kind enough to come over and help watch the last hour of cooking.

Their first try at sorghum harvesting, yielded nine gallons of iron-filled syrup. It was a long process from the time the seeds were dropped in the ground, until the syrup sit on the eating table. Many hours of hard labor went into the food source before it was devoured by the growing family.

One week after the syrup was stored for the winter, Jesse went for Miss Marcy. It was September 2, 1883. When he got back with her, little Montique had begun his entry into the world. "Lord God!" exclaimed Miss Marcy when she walked into the room. She threw her satchel down, and rolled up her sleeves. She stuck her arms in a bucket of rather hot water, prepared by Jess. She didn't notice the heat in the water or that Jesse stayed in the room.

She failed to shoo Jesse out of the room. It was his first time to see one of his children born. "Don't stand there man, hand me them rags. Move over there by her side of the bed and hold her hand." She didn't like what was happening here. The baby was coming too fast. "Wipe her face, Mr. Jesse! Keep her hands away from the area down here where I'm working."

Then it was all over. The child was big. Almost too big,

he tore the inside of his mother's vagina on his way out of her. Listy Ann screamed, but waited until she knew the child was out, before she passed out.

When her hand went limp, Jesse's concern peaked. "Miss Marcy!" He waited a second, "Miss Marcy!" He started patting his wife's face, and shaking her by the shoulder. "Brister! Brister, wake up, Brister."

The midwife was busy with the baby. When she got him to squall from the smack she applied to his bottom, Jesse glanced in her direction. All he asked was, "Miss Marcy?"

She knew that Listy Ann had only fainted, but didn't have the time to explain to Jesse until the baby was taken care of. She laid the baby down in the crib Jess had made for the babies. When she was sure the baby was all right, she returned to the bedside of the mother.

"Sir, your wife, she be all right. She simply in deep rest from big job she do. Give her time, she be fine." She went to work at getting the after birth. "You kin stay and watch iffen you wants to," she told him.

He decided to stay. He had all ready seen enough to know that he never wanted to give birth to a baby. He left the room when she handed him the warm bundle of rags to dispose of. On the way out, he stopped by the crib to look at his fifth son.

When Miss Marcy finished her day around the house, she found Jesse and asked, "Will you takes the clothes off the line tomorree? Dey won't have time to dry afore dark, today."

He had not been back in the room since he had experienced the birth of his son. "You'n go on in dare any time now. She still drowsy, but she talk to you. I put healing salve on her where she tore. It need takin' care uf, so's no infection set in. Come and let me show you how to put it on, when I not here. I be back in a day er so."

"Miss Marcy, whatever in this world would we have ever done without you and Jasper? I would have lost my mind, gone absolutely mad, if you had not been here this day."

The first of October was sweet potato harvesting time. Listy Ann was still in no shape to help much with any of the chores. So it was left up the men of the family to do all the digging and preparing them for curing. They stored the potatoes in mounds made from laying a thick layer of pine needles on the ground. Then the potatoes were stacked on the needles. The stacks were in teepee shapes, about hip high, and then covered with more needles. Then a good layer of damp dirt was packed all over the mound. The very top of the mound was left open. A piece of wood or tin was placed over the hole, and weighted down with a brick. An opening was left on the South side of the mound for removing the potatoes. The opening was covered with a piece of the tarpaulin to open in the style of an Indian wigwam.

When the job was completed, and they started to walk away, Jesse looked back at the nine hills of potatoes and remarked, "Boys, there lays some good winter eating for us all. Your maw will be baking pies and making puddings out of them tatters afore too long."

Dave was only thirteen years old but did many jobs around the farm. So did little John.

The week following the potato harvest, a heavy cloud built up. It looked like a good rain was on the way. Jesse always chose a time like this to clean the chimneys out. He filled the fireplaces with fat liteard. He bided his time until the rain soaked the roofs well before he stuck a lighted match to the liteard. The roar of the flames when it got to going good was frightening. It was the sound of a train traveling down the track at a fast rate.

The chimneys had to be cleaned out every fall to prevent a tar build-up inside the chimney. Jess had suffered through two fires and that was enough to last him a lifetime. He took all precautions of safety to prevent fires and taught the boys as they grew.

Listy Ann sat and sewed on her quilt squares until she was able to get up and get about to doing her business again. She saved every scrap of material from her sewing to make quilt blocks out of. She often sat by the fireplace on winter nights, after the boys were all in bed, and sewed on the squares. When she had enough sewed for a quilt top, she put them together with a lining made from the white homespun that most of the time she had pre-dyed. She had found that pokeberries made the perfect dye. Poke grew plentiful around the farm. It was a wild aggravation for the men. No matter how much they chopped down, it sprang right back the next spring, healthy as ever. Listy Ann tied the material in knots at different places and dipped the knots in the pokeberry dye solution. It was a change from the plain, beige colored white homespun.

For the batting, she used cotton from the field. Each year at cotton-picking time, she saved out enough for quilts she thought she could put together during the winter. It took many hours for her to card the cotton by hand, to get it pliable enough to use in the quilts. She stitched the quilt to the frames and got Jesse to help her hang the frames on the four attachments that had been put in when the house was built, right into the ceiling of her work, storage room. They were especially made for hanging quilts from in order to be quilted.

Soon after the quilt was hung, invitations went out to every farm wife in the community to come to her 'quilting bee'. The gathering of the local women folk was a time of relaxation, gossip, changing of ideas and to catch up on the latest family news.

Refreshments at one of the bees was always a fresh baked chocolate cake, with several jars of homemade sweet pickles, a pot of coffee for the ladies and milk or water for the children. Usually the quilt was completely quilted by the time the ladies left for home, and that was in time to get home and have supper on the table by nightfall.

The children always enjoyed a quilting bee. They got to play with all the children of the area for as long as the women worked at the quilt. They anxiously anticipated the cutting of the cake. They all liked the combination of chocolate cake and sweet pickles.

There was at least one quilt made a year on the Swinson farm. With the family growing in number, the cover was needed for the cold nights.

The day that Listy Ann returned to her motherly duties full time, after the birth of Montique, pronounced Mon-ti-key, later to be called Monty, she discovered several cold biscuits in the kitchen. "Mmmm, these will make a tasty bread puddin'." There was never a morsel of food wasted in her kitchen. She also made puddings from left over rice. They had rice every single morning for breakfast, unless the supply ran out. That meant that if she saved all the left over rice and biscuits, they could have pudding maybe twice a month. At times, she threw in a handful of raisins, fruit or pecans if they were in season.

The smokehouse hung full of smoked hog meat. Sausage hung beside the meat. Souse meat was kept in there too until it was needed for the kitchen table. The souse would usually keep until the weather started to warm up in the spring. Cracklings, made from the rendering of the lard were stored in a lard stand in the pantry.

It was a treat when Maw made cracklin' bread to sop up the syrup with. They could make a meal out of cracklin' bread and syrup along with a big, cool pitcher of milk.

The pantry shelves were crowded with jars of every vegetable that grew on the farm except okra, collards and potatoes. Irish potatoes lay shoulder deep in one of the barn stalls. Jess had put a floor in the stall for storing potatoes through the winter months. Collards remained in the garden. Unless it was an extra cold winter, the hardy collard withstood the cold, provided fresh greens throughout the season, and produced tender sprouts and seeds when the warm days of spring touched them. The sprouts were a tasty treat to have on the eating table.

The okra was a summer vegetable for them. Listy Ann had tried canning the okra, but they turned out too slimy when the jar was opened.

Jasper had brought over a bucket full of okra the first year he had made a crop. He and Miss Marcy had saved the seeds from their days on the plantation. It was a vegetable from their homeland. They liked the taste of the okra well enough to hoard the seeds until they had land of their own to plant.

None of the Swinsons or Garganuses had seen any okra until the Moore's introduced them to it. The day Jasper brought the okra over, Listy Ann ran her hand across a pod and quickly jerked her hand away, "Jasper, it stuck me." The pods are covered with short, spiny barbs.

He slapped his thigh with his old straw hat and laughed. He was a friendly sort of man, filled with love and compassion for his neighbor. He took a liking to Listy Ann the first time he had laid his eyes on her. During his life, he had dealt with many white women, but had never taken to one quite like he had to her. He would do anything within reason for her. His smile revealed large teeth and his eyes sparkled when he spoke to her. "Missy, you will love 'em pods, if you cooks 'em right. My madam, she show you how. I be bringing you seeds come springtime, so as you can plant 'em in your garden."

Jasper had been correct in his prediction. All three adults liked the okra upon their first eating of them. The boys were experimenting with the taste. The okra could be cooked several ways. Their favorite way was to cut it in small pieces and fry it in hog meat grease, with nothing added except salt.

The cornfields were dotted with stacks of drying fodder, food for the animals during the cold days of the year. The corncrib was filled up to the door with ears of dried corn. A little hay was in the loft over the stalls. It was hard, tiresome work to get the hay cut. It was cut by hand, so there was less hay then fodder. Fodder was cut corn stalks, stacked together and tied near the top to keep the stack from falling apart. It was left in the field until needed.

By late fall the farm was ready and waited for the cold weather to arrive. It made Listy Ann feel secure to stand in the front door of the kitchen when she took a breather from cooking, and look at her children at play in the yard between the two buildings. They had five dogs now, and the boys played with them a lot. The dogs were allowed to lie around on the porches, but never inside the living areas. Listy Ann had gotten some kittens several years earlier and through breeding, still had three that kept her company. The cats were not allowed inside either.

She would stand in the door at times to keep an eye on the boys and recall times when she was a spoiled, carefree young woman. Was that really her? The woman she remembered wasting away money like it flowed freely from an unending source, living in the lap of wealth afforded by her grandfather. She compared the wealth of her youth to the wealth she was surrounded by now. She would not have swapped for any thing.

June 12, 1885, another boy was born to Jesse and Listy

Ann, assisted by Miss Marcy. They named him France. The child lived a total of seven months. He was buried beside his two brothers.

In midsummer of 1886, the Garganus' held a picnic and invited every farmer and his family to come. Jasper and Miss Marcy showed up. They had four girls to add to their one son. It was a fine little family. None of the other colored families showed up, though they were invited, and welcome.

The men sat and talked over different ideas concerning the area. One suggestion brought up was the penning up of the hogs. There were so many running through the woods now that they could get out of hand if something wasn't done.

It was a beautiful day for the picnic. Everyone had a wonderful time in fellowship. The food was outstanding. They decided to have one of the picnics every year, to be hosted by different farm families.

It took the bigger part of the summer to catch all the hogs and get them to the rightful owner's pens and lots. When one of the hogs was caught, the mark on the ear showed who the hog belonged to. It was delivered to the owner.

Each farmer planted a certain amount of acres in ground peas. The peas made good eating when fresh dug and boiled, and parched when dried. Hay was cut from the ground up, adding a little flavor to the hay by including the ground pea vines for the horse, mules and cows. The root of the vine was left in the ground for the hogs to root up later on in the fall.

All the hogs were turned out of the hog lot when all the crops were harvested to roam and root the length and width of the fields. They cleaned up every bit of food left by the harvesters, plus all the ground peas out of the ground. Then the hogs were penned back up two to three weeks before time to kill them.

There was a picket style fence surrounding the house and yard to prevent the hogs from rooting up and destroying that area.

A good-sized flock of guineas had free run of the farm. Jasper could again take credit for the presence of the fowls on the farm. The guinea is a native fowl of Africa. Jasper had secured his small flock from a mail order house. It enabled him and his small community of colored families to feel good and to have a few of the things they had heard their forefathers tell stories about, when they had lived as slaves.

Listy Ann was on a visit one day to the Moore farm and thought she would like to have some guineas for her yard. She made the comment in front of Jasper. He made a mental note of her desire and when the next spring batch of guinea eggs hatched, he took two females and one male guinea biddies to her just as soon as the mother released them from her care. "Bless your old heart Jasper. You remember me saying I wanted some guineas, didn't you? I'll take good care of them. You are a fine man Jasper."

The guinea is a peculiar looking sort of fowl. Its head is as bald as an old man's and it is dark in color with white spots all over the feathers. A guinea is as good a watchdog as any four-legged dog ever was. They roost in the nearby trees at night. When any disturbance out of the ordinary occurred, the guinea is the first to take notice and warn all other inhabitants on the farm of the intrusion. The female calls out her alarm in a two syllable "Buckwheat, buckwheat, buckwheat, buckwheat." While the males call, is "Quit, quit, quit." The two calls added together in harmony created a sound to arouse the soundest sleepers.

On occasions, Jesse had threatened to kill every guinea on the place, when he had been awakened in the middle of the night. Only to discover he had been aroused because a wild animal had taken a short cut through the field, too close to the house. "One of these days, we're going to have one big pot of stewed guinea. Then maybe we'll be rid of that damn racket."

Guineas did make a tasty bit of eating. The meat had the same flavor as chicken, with a much better taste, a delicacy among fowl. Their eggs were smaller than that of the chicken, but a delicious treat to serve on the eating table.

When the crops were laid by the next spring, the Pierce family held the community picnic on a warm June Saturday. They had two daughters, Caroline and Elizabeth, about the same age as the Swinson boys.

A year-old shoat roasted above an open pit, dug the day before. A table had been erected at the edge of the yard, beneath and oak tree, to accommodate shade for the crowd.

The women sat around in clusters. Some of them did needle work, consisting of sewing quilt squares, crocheting lace trim for spreads, or patching torn clothes. Patching was an around the year chore. It seemed to the women that there was a tear in some piece of clothing in every week's washing.

The children who were old enough more or less took care of themselves for the day. The babies, there were always babies under foot, demanding attention from the mothers. If it wasn't to be placed at the breast for feeding, it was a nasty bottom to wash up and then find where the child had dropped the hockey, the term used to describe the bowl movement. Since no baby wore anything under their dresses in warm weather, it was a constant job for the mother to keep up with where the child left it. Nothing made Jesse any angrier than to step in a pile of fresh hockey.

The number of children had increased to twenty-three in the community. The number included the colored children, too. Listy Ann laid her mending down and commented to Mary Garganus, "Did you ever imagine there would be so many youngin' running around? I'll be adding to the number again in October."

Mary looked at her with a sly smile on her face. "I didn't know you were expecting again. You sure are carrying it well within your frame. Maybe this one will be a girl for you."

"I really hope it is a girl. I need one to help me around with the household work. Paw and Jesse have enough boys to supply them with workers for years to come."

Children were needed to work the land. If a farmer had to hire hands to work the fields, he would fold before he ever got a good start. The more children born to a farm family meant more hands to work the fields.

The men folk stood around the roasting pork. One of them would turn it and apply the sauce every so often. The sauce had been made especially for the occasion. It put out an odor that tempted the palates of every one that got a whiff. "This ought to be ready to eat, say about three o'clock," Cyrus commented to no one in particular, since they were all standing around him as he put the last strokes of the sauce to the meat.

All the men decided to walk to the barn lot and look over the Pierce's livestock. Two cows had dropped their calves and were in the pen together. Each calf suckled on the udders of the mother cows. It was interesting to watch how the calf drew milk from the udder for a while and then nudge the udder with enough force to joggle the mother cow. "Can you imagine what it would be like to be that mother? Looks to me like that punch from the calf would hurt. I reckon it don't though," Robert Blake offered his thoughts to the men.

Everyone gathered up in the middle of the afternoon to enjoy the meal together. It took a while to get all the children quieted down and their plates filled. Some of the babies were tired and cried for attention. It was not unusual to see a small child perched on the side of the mother, hooked securely on the hipbone. It was a wonder the women didn't develop a permanent sway as they walked from toting so many babies in that fashion.

Before the crowd scattered just before sunset, it was decided that the gathering would be with the Swinsons next year.

The third week in October, Jesse went at breakneck speed with the horse and buggy to fetch Miss Marcy. It scared him every time Listy Ann told him to go for Miss Marcy. His father told him that he would never get over being nervous when it was time for a baby to come into the family.

October 21, 1886, Charlie Thomas was born before sundown; four hours after Listy Ann had felt the all too familiar twinge of pain in her lower back. That one signal let her know it was time to get the birthing bed prepared and send for the midwife.

"Well Missy, you got yo'self another faired haired 'un," the midwife cooed to her.

"Is it a girl?"

"No, no luck in that die-rection. But he's a big, fine boy." The baby let out a shrill, "Waa! Waa!" just as the words cleared her mouth. "He's light skinned like the other'ns. Only the hair takes after you. Maybe there's no girl babies in you. Sometimes a family winds up with only one sex chillens. You and Mr. Jesse shore are headed there. Six boys, straight in a row. All as pretty a sight as any eye could desire to look upon."

Each time a baby came into the family, Listy Ann grew more impatient to get up and about her duties as wife, mother and housekeeper, before the fifteen days were passed. "It seems like such a waste for me to lie in this bed when I feel absolutely fine."

When she made the statement in front of Jesse one day, he reminded her of the warning Miss Marcy had laid down when Dave was born. "Now you know Brister, we can't have you messing your insides up. If it takes that long a time for you to heal, then you should follow the rules. I love you my sweet Brister, and I want you well and healthy. We have many years to spend together yet."

It always made her feel so good to hear his words of love, spoken from his heart. Very seldom did the name Listy Ann leave his mouth. When she heard the name from him, she knew he was upset over something she had said or done. Like the time she had whacked him across the back with the yard broom.

He was angry with one of the boys for not carrying out one of his instructions. He had failed to listen to the young ones explanation for why the job had messed up.

Jesse had the boy, John, by the arm, literally dragging him across the yard toward the wash shelter. Under the wash shelter, was the place where the boys got their whippings.

The boys had come to recognize the expressions on the faces of their father and grandfather that meant a trip to the wash shelter.

Listy Ann was in the side yard sweeping when she heard the pleas from the scared boy. "Please Paw, I didn't mean to let the milk jug drop. It was all Jake's fault. Don't beat me Paw! Please."

Jesse jerked on the boys arm and let a string of profanity escape his mouth. He took long strides as he walked, dragging the petrified youngster beside him.

They rounded the corner of the house and almost ran into Listy Ann. She raised up the yard broom and brought it down across Jesse's back with the force of an irate mother.

Jesse let go of John's arm and straightened up his back. He flexed his back muscles to ease the pain from the sharp whack of the yard broom. The broom was made from gallberry bush branches. When the gallberry branch dries, it is still strong and gets very willowy near the end of the branch where it is crowded with small twigs, which is what she hit him with. There must have been fifty of the keen little twigs to come down across his back. It hurt like the devil. He turned sharply toward her, with his teeth clinched together, he ground out, "Listy Ann, what in the name of hell do you think you're doing?" His back hurt, it hurt for him to move a muscle.

She dropped the broom and propped her hands on her hips, "I've told you over and over again not to cuss these boys. You're a grown man and you know enough English words to talk to them without the use of profanity."

"You go to hell, Listy Ann Solomon. I'll talk to them any damn way I please. How in the hell do you expect me to discipline these boys if you split my back open in front of them? Taking up for them is what you're doing."

When he called out to her and used her maiden name, it irritated her to the point of anger. "What kind of discipline do you call what you're saying to the child? Is that the way you want him to talk to you?"

He was so mad that he drew back his arm in a motion to strike her.

"You'd better not do that fool," the expression in her eyes was cold and piercing.

"Why not? Didn't you just knock the hell out of me?"

"I had a good reason. I've warned you, but you pay no heed to my warnings. Yes, you correct the youngin' when he needs it, but leave off the cussing. Do you hear me, now?"

Jesse felt the ooze of dampness seep down his back, but said nothing. He'd not give her the pleasure of seeing him cringe or complain another time. "You'd just best not attack me agin with that yard broom, Listy Ann. I'm giving you fair warning."

All the boys that were old enough had stopped what they were doing to get near enough to hear what was said between their parents. All that could be seen of them were their foreheads and eyes peeping around the corner of the house. Seldom did they witness any friction between their father and mother.

By the time Jesse collected enough of his thoughts to

remember what he was going to do John had joined his brothers around the corner. "John, come here boy."

As much as the little fellow hated to leave the safe place the corner provided, he walked toward his father. He drug his bare feet through the dirt with every step.

He stopped in front of his father, "Yes sir, Paw?" Tears seeped from his eyes. He knew he was in for it, even if his mother had made an effort to save him.

Jesse's own pain was so penetrating that it surprised John to hear, "Go on about your business this time son. You keep in mind that this will not happen too often."

"Yes sir," John responded. Before he left he cut his eyes to his mother. "It wern't my fault, maw. Jake stuck his foot in my path and tripped me."

"Run on and play," she said, without any emotion to the boy. She would never take side with one of the boys against Jesse. He was a good father to the boys. He took time to play with them, and show each one how to do chores around the farm. He did so with patience and love. It was his use of profanity, toward and around the boys, which upset her to the point of interfering.

They stood and stared at each other, not saying one word to ease the pain that squeezed at the hearts of the two adults who loved one another dearly.

She stooped to pick up the broom. When she straightened up, she noticed he had begun to walk away from her. She saw the dark stains on the back of his shirt. She felt so bad about what she had done, but was still so angry with him that she only said, "Jesse, wait up a minute." He turned to look at her. "Come on to the kitchen with me Jesse. I need to tend to your back."

It was quiet at the supper table that night. Even the baby sensed the tension. Jess knew there had been a misunderstanding between his son and daughter-in-law. He had learned years ago to stay clear of their squabbles. They always passed. This one would too, given enough time.

Before Jesse and Listy Ann went to sleep that night, they apologized and made up. It was a sweet night of lovemaking.

Jake was a sweet and lovable child if everything went his

way. At times, he created a rift between the other boys. No matter what the occasion, or what he had done, he denied it every time. If he got caught red-handed in the act, he would look either parent or his grandfather square in the eye and say, "It wern't me. I didn't do it. It must a been Dave." He would use any name that popped in his thoughts.

The poor little thing got a whipping two to three times a week. Listy Ann tried other forms of discipline, but in the end, it always took physical punishment to make him listen.

Jake was a good worker. He always did what he was supposed to do. His punishment was never applied for him not doing his share of the chores. It was misbehavior amongst his brothers, or daring deeds around the place. It was nothing to see him in the very top of an oak tree, or perched on the tip most part of the barn roof, or in the hog pen chasing the young pigs. He loved to hear them squeal, while he was hugging them. If there was any place on the farm he had not investigated and plundered through, he was bound to find it before he was a teenager.

Yes, Jake at ten and eleven years old was filled with energy and inquisitiveness. His mother watched him at times and wondered where he got all the energy. She had heard the old wives tale, that he would outgrow it as he aged. "Lordy, I do hope so," she remarked to Jesse one day soon after she had pulled the youth off Dave. He was trying to take a carving knife that GrandPaw had given Dave, to learn how to hand carve with, away from him. Jake did have his own little knife, but had misplaced it.

October 29, 1889, Jesse went for Miss Marcy. It was a warm autumn afternoon.

GrandPaw knew what was about to take place, so he gathered up the boys, all six of them and took them to the hayloft. The baby, Tom, was three-years-old and had to be watched every minute. GrandPaw hung him over his hip and carried him in that fashion while the older boys dug in the hay for dried ground peas.

When the dry hay had been brought to the hayloft, cured ground peas clung to the strands of hay, and made a tasty mouthful for the always-hungry boys. The rule had been laid down that no child was to go up in the loft without an adult, so they were anxious to get started on their hunt. It was a time of fun for the boys to scramble around in the hay, so carefree and happy. Of course at the ages Dave and John were, the hayloft had lost some of its pull for them.

Jesse arrived back with the midwife to find his wife in dreadful pain. When they entered the room she was in, she uttered, "I think I'm going to die this time. Never has there been this much pain." She squeezed the words out between the hard labor pains that engulfed her entire body.

She had had so many babies, and her body was worn out. She tired too easy. There was not enough spunk in her to fight the pain as she had with the delivery of her other children. "Lawdy Miss Marcy, do something to ease me off. The child is killing me." She cringed with the pain.

Miss Marcy sent Jesse from the room.

There was nothing she could do to help the suffering woman aside from wiping the sweat from her brow.

The hours passed slowly into the daylight of the next morning. Listy Ann dozed between the pains. It seemed to Miss Marcy, upon examining her patient that no progress was taking place. She began to fear the worst for mother and unborn child. She, herself, was beginning to tire from the long hours of anxiety.

Just before sunset, the air was opened up with a scream of pain from the throat of the suffering woman, who pushed with the pain of birth with all the strength she could use from her spent body.

Miss Marcy jumped from the chair she dozed in, and came to full attention, performing her duties as the baby emerged from the birth canal where it had labored for so many hours trying to become a member of the already large family of boys.

When the child was completely free of the mother, Miss Marcy snipped the cord and tied it off. She took care of the babies needs as quickly as possible, all the time she kept a close eye on the mother, who lay gasping and moaning from the long ordeal of giving birth to her seventh child.

The gentle hands of the colored woman laid the small bundle into the nearby crib. Her back hurt and her muscles felt the pain of too many hours bending over while she assisted with the birthing.

She turned to Listy Ann and said, "You have finally got yourself a dark skinned, dark haired child. Tell you something Missy, almost too dark. He'll lighten up some with fresh air, I feel lack. Do you want to have a look at the baby?"

"What is it Miss Marcy?" she asked in a low hushed voice. "Is it a girl? Oh please let it be a girl."

"No'am, it's another boy. He's as healthy looking as the others. A fine son you have here. Don't you want to hold him? The little tyke needs a bit of snuggling. He worked jist about as hard as you did to get into dis world."

Listy Ann was too tired to hold her newborn son. She knew there would be plenty of time for snuggling later on. Right at the moment, she needed rest more than anything else.

The midwife began the clean up of mother and bed. It was all Listy Ann could do to stay awake while being cared for. She felt so safe in the care of such a trusted friend, as Miss Marcy. It took a while to complete the finishing touches of the birthing.

Jesse answered the summons when he was called to the room. Upon entering, he walked over to the table where the kerosene lamp sat on the bedside table. From his pocket, he removed a sulfur headed match. He lifted his right leg and crooked his knee, causing the denim of his overalls to tighten across the lower part of his behind. With one swift swipe across the material, the match came alive with flames.

He lifted the lampshade with his free hand and touched the flame to the wick. The wick caught the flame and Jesse replaced the shade. He blew gently on the match and the tiny flame flickered and died.

He then looked at the woman he loved so dearly. It was a hard thing to stand and look at her. Her hair lay snarled and tangled about the pillow, damp with sweat. She lay so still and quiet, only her eyes seemed to have any life in them. Her face was pallid and clammy feeling to his touch, when he reached out his hand to caress her cheek. "Brister," he murmured.

She smiled. It was a weak expression, but it made him feel a little better. "I'll make it. First, I need to rest. I don't know when I was ever so tired Jesse." She took several deep breaths of air and continued. "Look there in the baby bed. I've given you another son." Her eyes closed and he thought she had fallen asleep.

Miss Marcy handed him the warm bundle of rags he had become so familiar at receiving after the birth of a child. He knew all too well what to do with it by now. "How is she this time Miss Marcy? She looks like death is trying to claim her."

"I don't rightly know sir. She done a heap o' hard work dis time. Let's give her a-day-or-so and see how thing go. You got a fine son to add to your family of boys. A mighty fine un."

Jesse left the room after one more look at his exhausted wife, who lay so still.

The next morning found Listy Ann sleeping peacefully. Her condition had improved during the night hours under the watchful eyes of Jesse and Miss Marcy. Neither of them had gotten one wink of sleep all the night through.

After breakfast was over and the boys all where they were suppose to be, Jess went to the writing desk and picked up the pen to record the birth of Jesse Gaston, October 30, 1889. The boy was named for his father and grandfather.

The fact that there were three Jesses on the place didn't seem to pose a problem for anybody. There was Jess, Jesse and the latest one would be referred to as baby Jess through his young years.

In the fall of 1890, Jesse called on Miss Marcy to come again. Listy Ann was about to give birth to yet another child. Soon after the child arrived, Listy Ann asked the question again, "Miss Marcy is this one a girl?" There was a silence in the room that bothered Listy Ann. "Miss Marcy! Is my Annie here?"

Marcy Moore turned from the area where she had been working with the child, wrapped snugly in the blanket. "Yes Missy, your little Annie has finally arrived." She laid the bundle in its mother's arms. She then called Jesse in for his bundle of warm rags. She shook her head at Jesse as he left the room. Something was not right with the baby girl. Listy Ann was too tired to notice anything out of sorts. She was elated beyond belief that a girl had finally arrived to nestle in her arms. Little

Annie died within the hour of her birth.

When Annie was lifted from her arms, the mother wept. She had lost too many babies to death. There seemed to be no emotion left in her, aside from tears to express. She turned her head and cried until she slept.

When Miss Marcy finished dressing the baby for burial, she handed the child to her father. She was laid beside her brothers.

Miss Marcy returned to Listy Ann's bedside. "Missy, Missy, I knows you is not asleep. Open yore eyes, look at me. I needs to say a few things to ya fore I leaves." She tucked the covers in close around her friend's shoulders while she spoke. It was past the midnight hour.

Listy Ann opened her eyes. "I saw signs when the girl was being born that told me there'd be no more babies for you and Mr. Jesse. Don't axe me to explain my words to you. It's part of the training I got from me own mammy, years back when she learned me to do mid-wifeing. She made me swear that iffen ever I seen the signs, I can't reveal what they is. I can tell ya they'll be no more little 'uns for you." She looked away from the tired face for a moment. She had hoped for some kind of response or statement.

Listy Ann laid still, not a word left her mouth. Not a muscle flexed within the whole of her body. Her thoughts were moving too fast to allow anything else to be effective at the time.

Could what the woman had just said be the truth? Never had she ever heard any more welcome words. Dear God in heaven let the signs be telling the truth.

She knew that Miss Marcy never lied about anything. She would not be saying such soothing words if there was not truth in them. Seven sons were enough of a family to be pleasing for any father and grandfather.

The exhausted colored woman continued to clean up the room. All the while, she kept the conversation going. "You and Mr. Jesse can get back to yore night time tangling as soon as you heals and not worry 'bout no more little 'uns." The only signs of life from the bed were the movement of eyeballs behind closed eyelids.

Thoughts raced through Listy Ann's mind as she tried to comprehend and get what Miss Marcy had said to sink down into her enough to lay there and rest in her state of being.

She had given birth to eleven children. Ah, those years were heavy on her mind. At times when she suspected that she was with child again and there was still a baby at her breast, she would wean it immediately. Folklore taught her that to continue to breast feed would poison the child within her. She had no reason to believe otherwise, since all knowledge of what she did toward bearing and rearing children came from handed down information. So, a sugar tit was constructed to aid the weaning process. The tit was made by cutting a round piece of white homespun, then place about two tablespoonfuls of sugar in the center, gather it up into a ball and tie if with a length of sewing thread. Dip it in warm water until the sugar softened, and pinch up enough to make a small amount to fit into the baby's mouth. It took a little while to get the baby used to the sugar tit instead of the mother's warm breast, but it worked every time.

Miss Marcy and Mary, she had finally gotten to first name bases with Mrs. Garganus, had passed along to her most of the rules and regulations she followed for her babies.

Listy Ann held each one of the boys on her lap at mealtime, when they were old enough to start eating solid food. She chewed the food until it was soft and pliable, then with her fingers she placed small amounts in the babies mouth. Before long, the baby was eating hardy on its own. She spoon-fed fresh cow's milk to them before they could handle a cup. The sugar tit was placed in the child's mouth after a meal for sucking that the child needed and used as a soothing aid to induce sleep. The child was usually weaned from the breast by the time it was one and a half years old, unless she was with child again and it had to be removed before that time.

She lay motionless as thoughts continued to crowd her head. It seemed that something was tugging on her. She cleared her mind of past thoughts to see who was interrupting her.

"Missy, Missy," it was Miss Marcy standing by the bedside. "Open your eyes Missy. There's still work to be done here. See if you can help me roll you over. These sheets need to be changed again. You're bleeding too much and de bed is soaking wet again. I need to change 'em fore I leaves." She pulled on the sheet as gentle as she could, trying not to disturb Listy Ann any more than necessary to get the sheets changed. "I'll be the rest of the night getting these things washed up and on the line." She was no more than mumbling to herself. She realized that the woman she worked with had no interest in what she had to say at the moment.

No matter what time of the day or night a baby was born, the clothing and linens used during the birthing, were washed and hung on the line before the job was over with. She had decided to stay through the night any way. She was concerned for Listy Ann's condition. Her temperature seemed to be rising and she thrashed about on the bed too much.

Listy Ann had always snapped back soon enough after the boys had come along. This time things were occurring differently. It set Miss Marcy's worries on edge.

GrandPaw had kept the boys entertained out around the barn for two nights and the one day in between. They slept in the hayloft. Jesse had brought their food out to them. Of course, the older boys knew what was going on but dared not to mention it in front of the younger brothers. They all thought it was a great adventure to do no chores and play with GrandPaw all that time.

When they came in for breakfast, they knew that it would be back to work and school when the meal was over. "Where's maw this morning?" piped in little Monty

"Yo' maw's in de bed, in de house. She feelin' poorly. Ya maw, she be up-n-bout fore too long," Miss Marcy answered his question while she ladled food on their plates.

By the end of her fifteen days in bed, after the loss of the baby girl, Listy Ann felt more alive than she thought she would feel again. The one thought that sustained her through the convalescence was the knowledge she was through with her childbearing years. She was thirty-eight-years-old, Jesse forty-three.

Chapter Ten

In 1891, the railroad was completed between Jacksonville and Wilmington, North Carolina. That same year, Parmalee Eclelston Lumber Company ran a railroad out from Jacksonville to the farming area to collect turpentine. In 1892, toothpaste was invented and the farmers started taking their cotton to Wallace, North Carolina, to market.

An air of calm, peaceful existence hung over the farm. Life was filled with good living, good food and happiness. The boys grew in size, and knowledge of farming the land. Each year a small amount of new ground was cleared. It was a time consuming task to get the land prepared for dropping seeds in the soil. At times a tree stump decided to become a stubborn problem to be removed from its comfortable place.

Dave was the studious son, who was quiet and thoughtful of all his brothers and never presented a problem for anyone. He spent all his free time reading or drawing. On one occasion, he got the idea in his head that he could handle the Dynamite used for blasting the stumps out of the ground alone. After all, he was twenty-three years old. He felt it was time he exercised his right to be an adult.

His job for the morning was to clear away as much debris from around the stump as could be moved, to prevent spreading of fire. So that when the older men were ready to do the blasting, they would not have to stop to do the clearing. He made a trip to the pack house where the Dynamite was stored and took what was needed back to the field with him, unnoticed. He carefully placed the charge and attached the fuse. He stood up and looked toward the sawmill where he knew the male parents were busy cutting lumber for one of the neighbors who planned to build a pack house. He knew the rules for doing the job. For several years now, he had assisted in the blowing up of stumps. That the older men were busy was no reason for the job to be put off.

He took one last look toward the sawmill and stooped to light the fuse. He ran as fast as his legs would move, like he had done when he had helped with the job before. Everything was going exactly as it should. When he was several yards from the stump, he twisted his head around to take a quick peek at the process and from the opposite side of the stump he saw Jake ambling toward him. He carried a water jug in one of his hands.

There was not enough time to get to Jake to get him out of harms way. By stopping, he put himself in danger also. He screamed with everything in him, "Jake!"

The noise from the explosion caused every soul on the place to stop what they were doing and go to the noise. The sound was not an unfamiliar one, only an untimely one.

It was an eerie sight to see the field filled with runners, appearing from different areas of the farm. Listy Ann had been stirring clothes while they boiled in the wash pot. She held the poking stick in her hand as she ran across the newly upturned earth. It was a task within itself to make any time while running across fresh plowed soil. It didn't seem to hinder the runners too much, because they knew when they looked toward the stump and did not see Dave, that in all possibility he was in trouble, and that he was responsible for the explosion.

Just before any of the family reached him, he got up from the ground where he had fallen. The blast from the bursting charge sent out a sheet of powerful wind and had caught him, knocking him to the ground. He rubbed his eyes to clear the thoughts in his head. Jesse got to him and grabbed him in his arms. Dave could not remember a hug that seemed to crush his ribs before. "Son, my God son, you nearly scared the life out of us. What in the hell do you think you're doing?"

Dave looked at his father in puzzlement and stammered, "Jake, whur's Jake Paw?"

Jake had decided on his own to take Dave a jug of fresh water. It had gotten hot out in the sunshine where Dave was using a bush ax and pitchfork. He didn't much like the job he had anyway. Cleaning out the chicken house was not one of his favorite things to do. He would use the excuse of taking the water out to Dave to get away from the stench for a while. He left the water well and walked the outer perimeter of the field on the way to where Dave was. He walked the pattern of the zigzag rail fence. He was in no hurry to get back to the chicken coop job. He failed to see Dave take off from the stump in a fast run.

Jake was studying the ground around where he walked. Rabbit warrens were scattered about in the soft dirt and at times young rabbits could be spotted. The boys had learned to chase the rabbits as youths and still found it exciting to stir up a warren and do the chase. Even though he was a big boy, it was still a sporty chase. He never heard Dave's frantic warning.

"Jake? What do you mean, where's Jake?" asked his mother.

"I saw 'im. He wuz oer dare. On tuther side of de stump. I called out to warm 'im." Dave had his hand lifted up shoulder high pointing at the place he had seen Jake.

They scanned the area, trying to spot him. Jess gave stern orders for all the younger boys to stand beside Dave and to keep the dogs with them. Some of the dogs usually followed the children wherever they went on the farm. "Now do as I say, stay right here!" he barked the command to them, and they knew from the tone of his voice they had better heed his words.

The three adults took steps in the direction Dave had indicated. Every heart was heavy with dread. The blast from a charge of Dynamite could blow a body apart. Jake stirred and moaned about the time they caught sight of him. He was face down in the soft dirt. When he raised his head up, his face was covered with blood.

When Listy Ann saw him, the mother instinct urged her to move faster than the men. With a scream that could have lifted the stump from its resting place, she sped to the side of her son. She fell to the ground on her knees, which made large holes in the dirt from the force of the fall. "Jake...! Jake, baby!" Her arms cradled him around the shoulders. Seldom did she cry around another family member, but the tears flowed freely when she felt his breath on her cheek. Like the time she had wept when Jake returned from his hunting trip.

Jess and Jesse knelt down beside mother and son. "Let's have a look at the lad," Jess stated.

The blood, still seeping from the cut just below his eye had covered the bigger part of his face. Listy Ann reached for the hem of her long petticoat. With a gentle motion, she began to wipe the blood away. Soon they saw what had caused the bleeding. A small splinter from the tree stump had been blown into his face, flat into the meaty part of the cheek. It was about an inch long. Jesse opened up his pocketknife and removed the splinter from the flesh. It wasn't a big wound but had caused excessive bleeding.

By the time he was cleaned of the blood, Jake had regained full consciousness and stood up on wobbly legs. "Who knocked me de hell down?" He still did not know what had happened to him.

He became quite upset when he noticed the water jug laying in pieces on the ground. "Now jist lookie dare. Dey went n broke de jug too." His fists formed and anger showed on his face.

Before he could carry through his anger, his mother explained what had happened. He was checked over to see if he had any more damage done to him. When everything checked out all right, she took his hand and they started to walk back to the house together. The family fell in line behind them.

Jess walked with his arm around Dave's shoulder. He knew the young man felt bad about what had happened, and was feeling pretty low.

When they reached the house, Jess said to Jesse and the boys, "Let's sit on the porch for a while, here in the shade. It's time we had a good talk." Jess usually let the parents handle the situations with the boys, but today he felt the need to take care of this one.

While Listy Ann had finished doctoring up the wound on Jake's face, the talk began. GrandPaw turned to Dave and said, "Son what you did today could have ended up with this family loosing two of our boys. You know that, don't you?"

Dave had not spoken one word since he had asked of Jake's whereabouts. He nodded his head and tried to utter a response.

GrandPaw continued, "To work with dangerous materials calls for a partner. Always get a body to help you, even though you know how to do the job." When Jess got concerned his accent was so heavy it was hard for the boys to understand all of his words. "I take full blame for what went on out there in the field. I've tried to recall a time when your father or myself warned you of the danger of working alone like you did today. We neglected to teach you that part. If you notice, I never work the sawmill alone. There's too many things that can go wrong if one person tried to work it." He paused for a moment and looked at his family of two adults and grandsons. He felt pride swelling in his chest when he saw so much love around him.

"I think we have all received a good, stern lesson here this day." He glanced over to his son and tilted his head, to let the father know that what he was about to say was what was to be. "We've all had enough punishment from this deed. The scare and lesson combined will suffice all else for this day." He looked around the group, expecting a few agreeable nods.

Both parents agreed with the older, wiser man. They both stood up together. "Let's all get back to work. There's plenty of work to be done before dinnertime. Enough to get our minds off the near disaster we all just experienced," Jesse added his authority in those words.

Listy Ann took Tom with her back to finish the washing. Baby Jess still slept in his wooden crate beneath the wash shelter. It was on days when the weather was nice that she taught the boys how to count and spell their names. Each piece of wood added to the fire around the wash pot was counted until that son knew how many pieces of wood lay in the fire. The clothespins were counted while one boy or the other handed her the pins, one by one. She made a game out of learning. A boy was included in each trip to the chicken coop to collect eggs. It meant a slower process of gathering the eggs by counting each egg as it was put in the basket, then recount when they were removed from the basket inside the kitchen to their storage bin. Sometimes an egg got cracked by the unsteady hand of the child. The mother never argued or complained over a cracked egg, there was always a recipe waiting to use up all the mistakes.

When the boys were old enough to speak clearly, the teaching lessons began. A smoothed off space in the yard between the house and kitchen was used for printing their ABC's, learning to add numbers and how to write and spell their names. Every day of the week, except Sunday, some kind of educational time was spent on the boys by one of the three adults in the family. Today was Little Monty's turn to be taught.

It tore at Listy Ann's heart to hear the slurred words leave one of her son's mouths. It was seven against three when it came to teaching and learning proper English and the use of it. The first time she heard 'twixt' used between two of the boys, she grabbed both sons, sat them down on the porch, one on either side of her. She asked for an explanation of the word. "Why maw, you're sittin rye cheer twixt me and John rye now. Don't cha know what it means?" Zedick replies and asked. His expression was so cute and in earnest, that she threw back her head in a good hardy round of laughter.

As the boys aged, their use of undistinguished language increased. Phrases put together by the children of all the farmers in the area created a mode of language for the community as a whole. The parents tired of fighting the act of regression and slowly joined partly in their manner of speech.

There were so many different dialects spoken in the neighborhood, that to allow the children to make up and use their own seemed to present no problems amongst them. The two Swinson men spoke with their heavy Swedish-Irish brogue. Cyrus Garganus used his native accent. There were the Pierces, Blakes and Coopers, and of course the colored folks had their own way of using the English language, too. Mr. Blake was the only one who had difficulty with English, but he seemed to get his message across.

It was enough to amuse a person to attend one of the community gatherings, just to sit and listen to the different expressions and use of the English language. Most of the adult males had acquired the use of profanity and used it more when the men got together for a conversation. Each man seemed to have a need to out cuss the other. It's hard to determine why a grown man feels the need to act and talk tough to feel big among other men. Old Jess was the only man in the neighborhood who could talk with other men and not use any swear words, but his brogue was so heavy it appeared at times that the roll of his tongue impaired his ability to express himself.

At times, Listy Ann found herself sitting quietly alone at one of the happy gatherings just to listen to the commotion created by the men while they talked and discussed the matters on hand. She loved the way her men folk drug out an emphasized thought or expression. She never tired of their brogue.

It amazed her, but she did grasp the reason why. Not one of the children in the area spoke with even a hint of their parents' accents. They were all too busy creating a language of their own.

One day, when Tom was learning his numbers while stacking stove wood with his mother, out of the blue popped the question, "Maw, why do Paw and GrandPaw talks funny?"

She realized it was time for another background lesson on the history of their heritage. She knew very little of that history, though she had probed and asked questions throughout her marriage. Jesse would always change the subject early on into the conversation. Jess seemed more interested in helping her teach the boys of their Swinson heritage. When a lesson was due, she chose a time when Jess was in a mood of nostalgia. He was apt to spend more time on the subject if she found him in the right emotional condition. After a period of his reminiscing of things and events he thought they would be interested in, he always held a question and answer session. It flabbergasted him to learn that all the boys, and Listy Ann herself, were filled with questions.

"How jew stand the treatment 'em nasty ole men give ya?" Jake inquired. He was the one that always wanted to know more about the days spent on the vessel and adventures of life on the ocean.

Back in the recesses of Jake's mind was the notion to one day go to sea, but under different conditions. When he listened to the tales his grandfather related, he immediately let his thoughts wander to a dream filled existence with him as the captain of the sea-going vessel. Never could he imagine the hardships and misery his Paw and GrandPaw endured while making their way to America.

It made Jess feel good to have the discussions with his family, while Jesse shunned away from the talks as much as possible.

Once in a while, one of the boys caught him off guard and asked a point blank question, that he found hard to avoid. "Did you e'r cut one of 'em old mean pirate's heads off, Paw?" John wanted to know one day, while his father was teaching him to plow a straight furrow in the field where corn was to be planted.

Jesse still felt such humiliation when he was reminded of the way he, his father and brother had been treated as slaves, and as no more than animals. It was so hard for him to explain to his sons without bringing resentment into his talk. "No son, I never had a knife with the blade long enough to do the job properly." He walked along beside the boy and was quiet for several minutes then spoke, "Son, those were days that are best left forgotten. Should I dwell on them too much, I just may get lost in 'em. I'd much rather live for today with you boys, your GrandPaw and mother."

"I wish I'd'a been dare wid ja and GrandPaw. I'd've' showed 'em a thing er two." The boy did a little bragging on his growth. He had developed arm and leg muscles before Dave and never let his older brother and other family members forget it.

Dave was thin and willowy. He always appeared to be somewhat underweight in his mother's eyes. It seemed to the brothers that she was always giving him the better portion of certain foods. "Now you know Dave needs to have this, so he can go on and fill out," she would remark when one of them would grumble about it.

Dave continued to be slim all his life. Jesse commented, "It's the Greek bloodline running through your veins." Some of Listy Ann's relatives remained slender throughout their life span.

There were days when it seemed to Listy Ann that all she did was stand by the cook stove and prepare meals. With seven growing sons, some more grown than she wished to think about, and three adults to sit down to the table three times a day, it took a lot of food to fill the hungry bellies. She did love to cook and try out new and different recipes on her family now and then.

There was a large variety of foods grown on the farm, so her choices were wide and to her choosing.

The day she decided to pick the young, tender poke salad greens was one that would remain in her memories for years to come. The tender shoots had to be plucked from the main bush before they were no more than three inches long. If allowed to remain on the bush any longer, the shoots became bitter and the word was, that it was then poison to a human if eaten. She picked a nice apron bottom full that early spring morning. She washed it several times and stewed it down like that of mustard greens. It put out an awful pungent odor while steaming in the pot. The smell was a lot worse than a pot of collards cooking.

When it was tender enough to suit her, she drained it to get all the liquid out, then she put it in an iron spider, added a little hot meat grease, salt and pepper and half a dozen beaten eggs. It was heated until the eggs were done. The dish was tempting enough looking when she added it to the table, laden with the rest of the meal.

She had gone outside and pulled on the dinner bell cord twenty minutes before dinner was ready. It took the men and boys that long to come in from the fields and stable, feed and water the mules, then get themselves washed up in order to get to the table in time to eat the meal while it was hot. Nothing seemed to rile Listy Ann any more than to get the food on the table and her eaters not show up on time. They had learned to get there on time if possible, to avoid her tongue-lashings.

As soon as they walked in the kitchen and smelled the poke odor, their noses flared out and questions rolled from each of them, either orally or by expressions from the eye.

"Now every one of you just sit yourselves down and at least try it. You'll never know if you like it or not, unless you try it. Why, I remember well how cook, back at my grandfather's, served poke salad every spring and how everybody looked forward to the occasion." She sat down at the table and waited for the first mouthful to be taken.

She knew right away that the poke was not going over very far here with this bunch. GrandPaw eased the fork up to his mouth and removed its contents into his mouth. Other family members followed suit and took a bite along with Jess. She looked around the table and a rumble of laughter quivered in her lower stomach.

The expressions on their faces were impossible to describe. Every one left the table in a hurried manner and went to the back porch where they spat the poke from their mouths, then went to the water bucket that sat on the water shelf attached to the porch. After rinsing their mouths out good, they joined in with the laughter that came from the table.

It was one of the days that the chickens were allowed to have free run of the yard and soon gathered up in mass to peck at the discarded poke. "Shoo, you damn chickens. I don't want your eggs to come flavored up with that awful stuff," Jesse hollered at the fowl before he returned to the table.

Listy Ann was so tickled she could barely control herself. She continued to have outbursts of laughter throughout the meal. "If it's all the same, it'll be all right if you never serve that again, as long as any of us remains alive," Jess offered the information and it was agreed upon by all.

Listy Ann laughed aloud for several days after the poke salad meal, whenever the thought crossed her mind.

Chapter Eleven

Through the years, many, many bones had been broken. When a leg or arm bone got broken, Jess and Jesse held the boy while Listy Ann set the bone and applied a splint. The splint was made from material found handy on the land. As the boys grew, they fought among themselves with a vengeance but let an outsider pick on one of them, and they joined forces to protect each other. At times, noses were broken, to heal with no attention paid to it and a crooked nose to be carried for life being the end results.

All the boys were tough young men, each tall and strong in his own right, with muscles built hard and strong from the years of cultivating the land and working the woods for their survival. Many acres of new ground had been cleared along with the growth of the family, for farming and grazing.

The sawmill had proven an asset to the growing community. The animal lot was filled with horses and working mules. A well had been dug near the barn shortly after the main house had been finished for convenience. To carry water from the house well was too far to tote water for the animals.

As they grew older, the boys learned to use the horses for transportation. It was their only means of getting from one place to another without use of the buggy or walking. The older boys found a delight in wooing the young girls when they got up old enough. Jake had met up with a young Miss from the Haws Run area, a community located several miles east of their farm. He took a fancy to her and made many horseback trips to visit his 'Miss Emma Jenkins.'

In the spring of 1894, Dave met a young lady, Della Casteen, a full-blooded Spanish young woman, from up in the Pin Hook area. They married in midsummer. Since they had no home of their own to move into, Jess stepped off what he judged to be nine acres of land for their house and farm to be built. The acreage was located southeast of the home place, toward Haws Run. The newlywed couple lived in the house with all the Swinsons until their house was erected.

About a year later, Jake was over for a visit with Dave and his wife. Della's sister, Clara Susan, was there for a visit, also. Before the visit was over, a friendship had sparked between Jake and Clarry. They married on January 2, 1896. Jake was twenty-one-years-old, and Clarry twenty. With her mother's help, she handmade her wedding gown. She married in a dress styled in the fashion of the day: a simple frock with a tight waist, smooth fitting long belled skirt, snug high-collared bodice, leg of mutton sleeves, bulging at the shoulders and hugging the forearms. They held their wedding in the front parlor of Clara's parent's home. They also moved in with Jake's father's family.

Again, GrandPaw Jess stepped off nine acres of land for them, east of the home place, abutting the north side of Dave's land. By the time they moved into their house in 1897, she was affectionately called Clarry, her nickname since childhood. Their house, in the Coastal Cottage style, was built on heart-of-pine pillars, two feet off the ground. It was a four-room house with a long kitchen. A dogtrot porch connected the house to the kitchen. The two buildings were in an "L" shape. The one-piece wooden windows were closed at night. Two wells were dug, one near the back of the kitchen and one out close to the animal lot.

Gold was discovered in the Yukon that same year.

Brother John met Pean Horn, also from Pin Hook, later that year. They married shortly afterwards. They followed the same pattern as the other married brothers and built their home west of Dave on nine acres of land stepped off by Jess. The lane, formally used as the Indian trail, separated the front acreage of the two brothers.

Dave and Della had their first child, a son called John Dave, in 1897. Edouard, called Ederd, Jake and Clarry's first child, was born February 11, 1898. Clarry had suffered a miscarriage the year before. John and Pean were blessed with a son one month later. Henry was born on March 2. The Swinson clan kept enlarging by leaps and bounds.

John was the one that had the business head of all the Swinson boys. He started buying more land from his father and grandfather, plus the land that came available in the surrounding areas. He saw early on the value of owning the land for future resale. On May 2, Jake bought thirty-four and a half acres of land from John for one dollar per acre. "Dammed brother charging me a dollar a acre. He'll be a rich man by the time he's thirty years old." He paid John in full on the day of the purchase. A road was cut out of the woods to run along beside Dave's property, from the edge of Jake's field over to the old Indian trail road. Dave and John's farms affronted the same road that Jasper Moore lived on. John was located between Dave and the original farm. All one lane roads ran to and through that of the home place on out to the Bear Grass road.

Then on June 6 of that year, Jake purchased a portion of the old Cooper place from Alex Surcey, a twenty-five acre tract of land that had been formally owned by the Coopers. The trail that was used during the Civil War, and was still used as a road, ran the length of the south side of the property through the woods over to the old Indian trail road. The road was referred to as the old Ashe Road, named for the Civil War Officer-in-charge when the road had been used by the army when it was moving through the area. Jake's land holdings now totaled sixty-eight and one half acres. His state taxes for the year of 1898 were $2.70. "Beats all I ever heard of, charging me a small fortune for nothing." The Sheriff, L. W. Hargett, came to collect, and told them that taxes would be collected every year from then on.

Jake and Clarry's second child, a girl, was born June 14, 1899. She was named Estella, called Ella. As the family grew, so did the need for more acres of land to be cleared. The few acres that were under cultivation would not feed and support a growing family. Jake bought his third tract of land from J. R. Marshburn. That tract of land was one hundred and five acres in total. It lay in between the old Cooper place and what Jake already owned. All the acres he possessed were joined together. Several acres affronted the Bear Grass road. His farm and wooded area now contained one hundred and seventy three and one half acres. On November of the year, he paid a total of fifty cents for County taxes.

Ederd was a timid and very shy child, who took to sucking his thumb before his mammy weaned him from the tit.

He would not take to the sugar tit. He chose to use his thumb instead. He wore dresses, just as his father had done before him.

A terrible tragedy befell the Swinson family in the Spring of 1900. When Jess failed to come to the kitchen for breakfast, Listy Ann sent Tom to see about him. When he returned, he was in a highly agitated state. "Maw, GrandPaw jist lays dare. I think he's died."

"Hush up your mouth boy. I've got no time for your foolery."

"But maw, I ain't messing round. GrandPaw's hand is real cold." The fourteen year old didn't know exactly what else to say.

Jess was buried at the site where his grandbabies had been laid to rest. The entire community turned up for the funeral. Since no preacher was in the area, his dear old friend and neighbor Cyrus, read some scripture verses and said a few words over the pine box coffin before he was placed down in the soil he had labored with and where he had become a contented man. He was missed by his loved ones more than they wanted to admit.

Later on around the middle of November that same year, another tragedy struck. The schoolhouse caught fire and, before it could be put out, burned to the ground. Thank God all the students were able to get out with no one being burned. "Grab your books!" shouted Mr. King as they fled the burning building.

"That old school has served this area for many a year," Dave said to one of the neighbors.

When the smoke had been spotted by the community farmers, every one of them that saw it or smelled the smoke went hunting the source. "We'll have to find temporary housing for the youngin's to finish up the year," John stated.

It was decided to use the Surcey's brand new pack house. The Surceys were the latest family to move into the community of farmers. The building was located across the dirt road from the land Jake had bought in 1898. The school age children lost one week of school.

A third child, James, was born to Jake and Clarry on December 26, 1900.

In the Spring of 1901, Alonzo Hewitt came to the community looking for land to purchase. He had heard the news that a school and teacher were needed. He found the land he chose to buy, situated about half way between the Pierce and the Swinson farms. He, himself was to be the teacher and build the school on his land. No college degree was required to teach children of the area, just a need to teach. Simon King had taught for many years and was getting on up in age. He felt the need to retire from teaching. He had remained a bachelor all through his teaching years.

Alonzo, with the help of the local farmers, built a one-room cabin for him to live in. The schoolhouse, when erected, was larger than his living quarters. The house was located on the corner of the road that ran from the Burnt Shoe on out to Cypress Creek. The road the Pierces lived on intersected Hewitt's house where it joined the Burnt Shoe Road. Alonzo met, and later married, Hattie Garganus, one of the local girls. By the time of their wedding, he was referred to as 'Lonzo.' It wasn't long after they moved into the cabin that more rooms were added on to the house to accommodate their growing family. Lonzo farmed a few acres around the house and out buildings. School months were few. They ran from October through February.

Jake took a dislike to Alonzo during the time the school was being erected and found fault with everything the new schoolteacher did or said.

Jesse and Listy Ann's grandchildren kept coming. It seemed that one to three was born each year. John's second son was that of twins, a boy and a girl, Isaac and Ida.

Listy Ann began to wonder if there would be many girls to fill the area around her knees. "Two granddaughters amongst all them boys, can you believe that?" To date there were five boys.

Jake and Clarry had very little love for each other. It was a marriage of Jake needing a wife, and old man Casteen needing to find his daughter a husband. They were civil to each other at times. Other times, Jake was down right mean to her. He continued to seek out loose women, and thought himself to be God's gift to them. He rode over to Haws Run at least twice a month to pay Emma a visit just like he was not a married man and the father of two children. Emma knew his circumstances, but cared not what anyone thought about her relationship with Jake.

One day while Clarry and her mother-in-law, Listy Ann, were in a conversation about unfaithful husbands, Clarry mentioned the fact that she knew what Jake was doing.

"You don't know one thing of what you're talking about, young woman," Listy Ann came back at her. "If he got what he needed at home, he'd not be the butt of your anger. Don't you be making little of my boy, when it's you not woman enough to handle him and take care of his needs."

Listy Ann still defended her boys in everything they did, whether they were right or wrong.

Poor Clarry hung her head in fear of her mother-in-law. She silently prayed that word would not get back to Jake of what she had said. Jake had taken to knocking her around a little if she went against anything he was into. The two small children were present most of the time when the abuse took place.

Still the children came. Jacob was born March 29, 1902. Jake had been to town to pay his 1901 county taxes of $2.95. He decided to save the sheriff a trip. His dad had gone with him to register to vote in the Angola precinct. Angola was the name given to the big swamp. Upon their return home, they found Clarry had delivered another boy, aided by Miss Marcy.

Jesse and his father had not interfered enough in Listy Ann's discipline of the boys through the years and now the results were beginning to show up in each of the boys except Dave. He continued to be the gentle, kind, loving person he had been all his life. All the brothers, except Dave, drank liquor, cursed and fought each other. Maybe not as often as in the past, but usually during a gathering of family members, there was always a scrabble leading up to fistfights before the departure time. Marriage had not taken any of the mean spirit out of them. The women that had become their wives had taken many hours of verbal and physical abuse so far. The wives dared not complain to anyone, except among themselves.

A devastating set back for the growing little town of Jacksonville occurred in 1903. The train depot burned, along with the wooden merchant stores on Main Street.

A second daughter was born to Jake and Clarry on May 10, 1904, also delivered by Marcy Moore. The baby was named La Vinia, nicknamed Vinnie shortly after her birth.

There was a lull in Jake's farm work the last week in July after Vinnie was born. He went over to his brother John's farm and asked to work a few days there with him. "A little cash to stuff my pockets will help me and the babies eat a little better if you'll put me to work." He worked five full days and earned $2.50. The first expense from the wages went for a pint of moonshine from the local still owner. The remainder of the earned money was spent on food.

Later, along about the second week in August, Harry Congleton came to Jake's farm looking to purchase live turkeys. Jake was more than ready to sell them. "I got some right nice turkeys out yander in the pen. You wanna go take a look at 'em?"

Turkeys roamed wild in the surrounding woods. It was up to a person to either go shoot or catch one for himself, or buy from those who did the rounding up and cooping of the turkeys. "What's the going price these days?" Harry asked. "I was wanting about half a dozen."

Jake knew what he wanted for the fowl, but rubbed his beard stubbled chin to make it appear that he was considering giving the buyer a good deal. "Tell ya what; I'll let you have 'em for seventy-one cents each. How's zat sound?" The turkeys were loaded on Harry's truck and hauled away. "Dammed fool, he coulda got'em fer fifty cents a head."

The next week Jake made a trip to town for supplies. Clarry gave him a list of things to bring back for her use. Among the items was shirting material, three yards of apron cloth and eight yards of checkered homespun. She, like that of her mother and Listy Ann, made every stitch of clothing the family wore except the overalls, sock and shoes, and of course, the old felt hats.

Johnny Casteen, Clarry's younger brother came to work for Jake in October of 1905. He lived right there on the farm and stayed in the house with the family. His salary was $6.25 a month. The boy was raggedy and in need of clothes when he arrived on the farm. Jake made another trip to town. He bought a pair of overalls, shirting material and a pair of socks, the total cost was $1.00. "Will prices never cease to rise?" he asked of Johnny, when he returned and handed the items to the young man.

The fifth child of Clarry and Jake was born on December 26, 1905, the same date as little James had come along back in 1900. Miss Marcy stayed all day and all night trying to get the child to be born. Jake didn't pay too much attention to the whole process.

"That's woman's work, getting 'em babies borned and taking care of 'em."

He went on about his business as if nothing out of the ordinary was taking place. Soon after he was assured that Clarry and the baby were alright, he saddled his horse and rode on over to Haws Run. He had trotted over there each time a baby was born to romp with Emma. He made several trips to Emma while Clarry's body recovered from giving birth. The baby was a boy named Stephen, to be called Steve.

In 1906, Jake found the time to work for his father at the sawmill for four days, earning one dollar a day. A little later on, he also worked at cutting cypress trees from a lower field for John, at the same salary. For the job with John, he took his wheelbarrow along. He received thirty-five cents for the use of it.

Taxes continued to rise. That year he paid $3.84 to Sheriff W. C. Mills when he came to collect.

When school started in the fall of 1906, Ederd was one of the students. He walked the four to five miles to the Hewitt schoolhouse. He swung an old gallon syrup bucket while he walked, that held his dinner. He was met at the end of the lane that led from the farm out to the Bear Grass road, by a couple of the Blake boys. The Blake boys were a few years older than Ederd, but made safe companions to walk with. Other children joined the walk to school along the way. Ederd still held to the habit of sucking his thumb. He tried to remember not to do it in front of anyone, but before he knew it, the thumb would be in his mouth. He took a lot of teasing from the local children before the need for thumb sucking left him completely.

The sawmill continued to be a means of bringing in cash or tradeoff work for Jesse and the sons still living at home. The James family, from over colored town way, did a lot of work at the sawmill, earning a dollar a day for their work. John James was the father. His sons were Cagy, Ransom and Simon. One of Cagy's payoffs was 514 feet of lumber at one and one half cents a foot.

On one of Jake's trips to town, he ran into a group of people in a heated discussion. He moseyed on over closer to catch what was being said. A committee had formed the Southern States Missions. The local town folks were at odds as whether to support the mission or not. Jake reached in his pocket and donated eleven cents to the cause. For what reason, he did not know. The receipt he received was signed by the president J. A. Barrett. When he got home, he showed the receipt to Clarry. "If it ain't one damn thing taking my money, it's another." She stored the receipt for eleven cents in the family trunk where all of the important papers were kept.

A baby girl, named Tamma, was born on May 25, 1907, to Clarry and Jake. She, along with her brother James, took sick during the summer. James died at the age of seven in August. He was buried in the old Indian cemetery, now part of John's farm, nestled in between the cornfield and the woods. All the Indians had died off or moved on to other locations. The burial site was to be known as the Swinson Graveyard from that day forward.

Tamma died the following October. She too was laid to rest in the Swinson Cemetery.

The number of grandchildren ran high for Listy Ann and Jesse. She finally got the granddaughters she had wished for, though there was not closeness between her and any of those girls.

Zedrick married Catherine from the Pin Hook area also. She was lovingly called 'Aunt Cat' by all the nieces and nephews. Jesse stepped off about nine acres of land located behind the original cabin for Zedrick and his new bride. After four or five years, Zedrick moved to Pin Hook, the area where Catherine had been born, and set to farming on part of her father's land.

Monty married Barbara Horn, sister to Pean, John's wife. Jesse stepped off about nine acres of land adjoining the creek that separated the home place from where the old cabin had stood.

Tom had married a local girl, Fannie Bell, daughter of Ransom Rogers. The Kilby Rogers family had moved into the area down in behind the Pierces several years after the Pierces had established their farm. Ransom was one of Kilby's sons. Tom and his wife built their farm on the Bear Grass road a few miles east of the Garganus farm, starting with nine acres of land stepped off by his grandfather, Jess.

Progress continued for Jake and his growing family. If he found time, he hired out for extra money. In the fall of 1909, he worked for W.B. Allen in his general store at Catherine's Lake, for thirty days at the rate of $1.25 a day. During the month, he made purchases of two hats, five ties, a few stamps, a sack of rutabagas, four sacks of ground peas and one live pig. His bill was $9.80. He had earned $38.95 for the month of work. After paying his bill, he had $29.15 left. On his last day of work, he had brought along to work with him, and sold to W.B., $1.33 worth of meat from his smoke house. He took home $30.48 for his month of hiring out.

Jake fell behind on his 1908 taxes. When he went to pay his 1909 taxes of $6.07 in October, he was reminded of the debt. It was June of the next year before he got them paid. When he learned he had to pay late charges, it made him quite angry. $7.64 he forked out.

A baby boy was born dead to Jake and Clarry, in early winter that year.

Ander Moore, son of Jasper and Miss Marcy, became a preacher by trade while he was a young man in his early twenties. He built and preached in a church house located in his community. He met and married Polly Fisher. Miss Marcy taught Polly the trade of midwifery. Polly took over for her mother-in-law with the birth of Jake and Clarry's baby girl, Roseita. The baby was born in October of 1910. She was called Rosie. It turned out that Rosie was a sickly child all through her baby days and pre-teen years. She cried often from pain in her lower back and stomach. Infection was prevalent throughout her body.

The Rowland Lumber Company bought the railroad that ran out to the Swinson area in 1910 to collect logs, farm products and to continue to haul out turpentine.

Ederd managed to complete and pass the fourth grade before he quit school all together. He was twelve years old. He planned to devote all his time to farming.

Another daughter was born to Jake and Clarry in 1912, named Roxanne. The little thing was also nicknamed to Roxie.

The working of turpentine ceased to operate in 1912. Cotton acreage had increased for each farmer. Cotton brought in more money than turpentine, with less attention and hard labor.

Jake had an account with another storeowner in Catherine's Lake, where he could get supplies if he was out of cash money. In 1913, he paid $10.00 to the owner J.D. McLain. The account was paid in full.

At the age of thirty-eight, Clarry was pregnant again. Jake was thirty-nine. Baby Roxie was only one and a half years old. Miss Polly was sent for, just like she had been since she had taken over for Miss Marcy. She was as good as her mother-in-law, if not better. She always praised God verbally for every blessing that was sent to those she attended.

"Now Missy, you lay dare and push. Iffin you don't works hard, the little un will haft to work dat much harder."

The baby boy was born March 21, 1914. They named him John. He was a pretty little boy though frail and small in size. He lived three days before his death. A few of the neighbors, brothers included, came over to help build the pine coffin. It was a real cold day when he was buried in the Swinson cemetery. There were no more babies for Jake and Clarry.

Each original family had their own private graveyards. A chosen place on their property.

The first American born generation of Swinsons, changed nothing in their way of living. They used the same tools, the same methods of toiling the soil. They raised the same crops and ate the same food. Only the names of the children changed, and, of course, they did not work the pine trees for turpentine.

It was a chilly morning in late October, when Ederd and his brothers, Jacob and Steve, walked out toward the barn to feed up the animals. This chore was always done before breakfast. A heavy frost lay on the ground. It was a very cold, brisk morning.

The cart had been left out from under the pack house shelter and frost had coated the steel rim that covered the wooden cartwheel. A thought popped into Jacob's head as they neared it. "Say Ederd, I bet cha, you cain't lay yore tongue on dat cart wheel dare and git it off agin. I dare you to lick de frost off dat rim," he exclaimed. "I'll bet chu my new pair of Sunday pants, ya cain't do it," Jacob chided.

"Yore pants is too little fer me."

"No dey ain't. Not my newest ones. I'm as big as you are now, around de middle anyhow.

"Go on widge messin. But it won't bodder me a bit if I lick my tongue across it."

"I double dare ya. Jist cause yore bigger and older ain't no sign yore tougher," froth escaped his mouth as Jacob made the statement.

That's all it took for Ederd to walk over to the cart and lean over. A big smile was on his face as he stuck his tongue out and laid the part of his tongue that was out of his mouth against the frost-covered rim. His tongue adhered instantly. No matter how he pulled or twisted, it would not release. Within seconds, his tongue was in severe pain. He rolled his eyes from one brother to the other. "Git mammy! Git her now! Hurry!"

He was a sight for the two brothers to watch and laugh at, until their sides ached. He finally got their attention enough to mumble his request again, for one of them to go get their mother.

Young Steven took off in a trot toward the house, when he saw the trouble his oldest brother was in. He knew she was in the kitchen preparing breakfast.

"Mammy! Mammy!" he literally yelled out, all the way to the house.

His mother met him on the kitchen porch. "What in de name a tarnation are ya hollerin about youngin'?"

"Quick Mammie, Ederd's got his tongue stuck to de cart wheel wid frost. He cain't git it off. Come Mammie, come hep 'em."

She grabbed up her apron tail and hurried back in the kitchen, where she had water boiling in the kettle that sat on the wood cook stove. She reached for the water dipper and poured hot water from the kettle into it.

She joined Steven and took off for the pack house.

By the time she had loped out to where Ederd was with his tongue still stuck to the rim, over half of the water had sloshed out of the pan, and had cooled down some.

"Now Ederd, dis may hurt jist a bit." She tested the heat of the water by sticking her finger in it then poured the warm water, allowing it to run down the rim to his tongue. "What possessed you to do sich a thang son?"

Jacob spoke up, "I dared 'em to Mammie. I bet 'em my new trousers." After another round of laughter he added, "I still got dem pants, too."

As soon as the warm water reached his tongue, Ederd felt pain that he never knew existed. The cold of the frost had burned his tongue and the warm water added to the pain. He pulled away from the rim when the frost melted. He backed away from the wheel with his tongue sticking out of his mouth. "It hurts mammy," his words were barely understandable. Every one had a good laugh, except Ederd.

Ederd balled up both his fists and headed toward Jacob. "You scoundrel, I'll bust yore head open fer dis." At that moment, he realized how much it hurt to speak.

Jacob was so tickled at the sight before him. He took off in a fast run away from his older brother, laughing his head off. "You dang fool. You oughta knowed better dan to do sich a thang. Ain't no pair a pants worth dat. It shore was worth it to me though. And I still got my pants," he sang out as he ran around the group.

Clarry stepped in front of Ederd and cautioned him. "There'll be no squabbling here so early on in de mornin. Come on back up to de house wid me and I'll see to your tongue. You two udder boys git de feedin' done and git yoreselves to de house and git your breakfast eat. Dis is enough foolin round fer dis day. Dare's work a waitin all o' us."

When Ederd turned to go back to the house with his mother, Jacob piped up with, "You dang fool. Ya oughta knowed ya cain't mess wid frost lack dat."

After a few moments thought, Ederd knew his brother was right.

Ederd's tongue swelled up and stayed swollen for the remainder of the day. He did little eating or drinking during that time. The mixture his mother had applied to his tongue was so awful; it had made him forget some of the pain the frost had caused. She didn't tell him what the mixture was made of, but it helped heal his wounded tongue. Having a swollen, hurting tongue was no excuse for him not to carry out his daily chores. His father let him know that right off.

After a day or two, he decided to let it go with Jacob and not beat him up or anything like that. In his own mind, he knew it had been a foolish thing to do. He had figured he could quickly flick his tongue on the wheel rim and then flick it off just as quickly. It had not worked out that way at all, so the deed had been as much his fault as it had been Jacob's. In the end, he had learned a lasting lesson and had a blistered tongue for a while there, plus the loss of a good pair of pants.

Chapter Twelve

The Burnt Shoe was a focal point for the residents of the area. It was common to hear, "Meet me at the Burnt Shoe," or "Just past the Burnt Shoe," or, "You know where it is, there close to the Burnt Shoe." A creek formed at the point of the road where the Bear Grass road joined the road that John and Dave lived on. It made a wonderful swimming hole after a good rainfall.

The Tannery was situated not far from the creek where all shoes were made for the folks who lived in the area. One person in each family learned the art of shoe making, with helpers to do the trimming and final stages of the work. The cowhides were tanned on the site before shoes could be made.

The Tannery was built back in the early 1870s. No name was known at the time for the name of the junction in the road. Late one afternoon, Jess was at work making a pair of shoes when an older Indian man walked up. He sniffed the air a time or two and uttered, "Smell like burnt shoe, umm." Jess related the story to other farmers and the name 'The Burnt Shoe' stuck.

When Listy Ann was 59 years old, back in the year of 1910, she took sick. She had a lot of pain in her side and was almost too weak to carry out any of her chores. Jesse went to Jacksonville and got the doctor to come out and see about her. He diagnosed her illness as side pleurisy.

"The pleurisy? Doctor, what might that be?" Jess wanted to know.

While the doctor bound Listy Ann up firmly from her lower ribs to her upper buttocks, to prevent any movement in her chest area, he answered Jesse's question.

"It's a type of inflammation in the lining of the lungs. Now Jesse, you might as well go on and get somebody in here to do her work. She's not to lift a finger at any kind of labor. It is essential that she rest, and get plenty of fresh air and sunshine," the doctor warned Jesse before he left.

"Where in the world am I gonna find a body to come in here and keep up the house and work around here for us?" he asked the question that afternoon after the doctor left. John and

Monty had come over to pay a visit to their mother and heard the question.

Both the sons thought the same thought at about the same time. Pean and Barbara had an unmarried sister, Mary Eliza, who still lived with her parents. She was 35 years old. John offered his sister-in-law the job.

"Paw I feel lack Mare Lise," her beautiful name had been crushed to Mare Lise, "would be willing to come live here with you and maw and do her biddin'."

"You and Baby Jess, well Paw, I reckon we older boys ought to stop calling 'im baby, since he's 21 years old now, ya two will haft to do a lot of de thangs maw's been a doin', 'til Mare Lise learns how to do 'em," Monty spoke and said his peace.

John went that very afternoon and brought Mare Lise to stay with Listy Ann, and care for her and the household.

Mare Lise caught on quickly to the routine of how Listy Ann wanted things done. She was a hard worker and seemed to never tire. She was a very pretty woman, with a nice shape, that showed through the clothes she wore. It was not too long before young Jesse took a fancy to her looks.

Before six months were over, Mare Lise was carrying his baby. She kept her pregnancy concealed from all of the Swinsons. It was not too hard for her to do so. She wore loose fitting dresses, and her bust line was over large, to help conceal her enlarging stomach. She carried the baby well within her frame and never complained of any discomfort. She kept up with her daily routine. Yes, she was a strong female.

When the baby let it be known to her that he was on the way, she knew what to do. She had helped with the birthing of babies enough to remember the dos and don'ts.

There was a hog pen to the south of the house, across the creek from Monty's farm. She went to that hog pen when she realized her time was near. It was in the late springtime, and the weather was nice. She found a shady spot near the creek and squatted. She pushed herself up from the squatting position with her hands as the baby emerged from her body. The baby reacted to life with no assistance from her. She reached in her pocket, took out a pair of scissors and snipped the umbilical cord. After she tied it off, she laid the baby girl on some leaves near where she squatted. When she passed the afterbirth, she threw it over in the hog pen. She had purposely worn an extra half-slip for the occasion. She stepped out of the slip then tore it in half. She wrapped the baby in one piece of the slip, and laid it back down on the leaves. The other piece, she folded and placed it between her legs, then pulled her under pants up snugly to hold the pad-of-sorts in place. She took one long look at her daughter and walked back to the house to resume her daily activities.

About an hour later, Monty was doing some work in his animal barn and caught a sound he couldn't quite place for a moment or so. He went outside to listen better. He heard the sound more clearly. He started to walk toward the sound. "Dammed if dat don't sound jist like a baby crying," he said aloud.

He found the baby, just like it had been born, laying there on the leaves. She had kicked the wrappings away from her tiny body.

"Damnation little girl, where'd you come frum?"

He ripped his shirt off his back and wrapped it around her. He then scooped up the tiny life and cuddled her in his arms. The piece of slip was too bloody to suit Monty.

He walked on up to his father's house with the baby in his arms. Listy Ann was sitting on the kitchen porch, relaxing in the sunshine.

"Maw lookee, what I done found down by de hog pen," he unwrapped the baby and Listy Ann gasped in disbelief. The baby let out a wail loud enough to announce that she was in attendance.

Mare Lise was in the kitchen and heard the crying. She froze for a moment or two. Then she knew there was no reason to hang back. She had been found out. Slowly she walked out to where Listy Ann sat holding the child.

"Mare Lise, come see this. Do you know anything about this youngin'?"

"Yes'um, I do. I had it. I didn't know what else to do, so I jist left it there. I wuz goin back after a while to see about it."

"When was this child born?"

"Bout a hour ago."

"How in the world did you carry this child nine months and not a soul on this place knew anything about it?"

"I don't rightly know ma'am."

"Mare Lise, who is the father of this girl?"

She tensed up her whole body and wondered if she should be truthful right now, and get it over with. "Well ma'am, it's Jesse. He don't know nothin bout de baby. I never said a word to 'im." Listy Ann knew which Jesse Mare Lise meant, because she referred to the older Jesse as 'Mr. Jesse.'

"Mare Lise, how can you have a baby and simply go on about you business? It took me nearly a month and a half to get back to normal after each of my birthings. Don't you need to go to bed for a while?"

"No ma'am, I feel all right. I didn't have no trouble a tall gitting her borned."

She felt that at any moment she would be ordered to get off the place and take the child with her. She had no place she could go, except back to her parents. She had a feeling they would not accept her after the disgraceful deed she had committed.

She was somewhat stunned when Listy Ann said, "Monty go look up Jesse and bring him here to the house."

Jesse galloped up in the yard on horseback. He jumped off and landed in a run toward his mother. "Yeah maw, what's de emergency? Monty told me to git here on the double, whoose!" he was out of breath.

"Come on over here and have a look at your daughter."

He shot a quick look at Mare Lise who stood close by. Her head was bent so that he could not make eye contact with her.

When he saw the baby, one of his hands automatically reached out to touch it. His mother moved the shirt wrapped baby so his dirty fingers could not touch the little girl.

"Mine? How'd dis come about?" He looked straight at the baby's mother. "Mare Lise, are you sure it belongs to me?"

It infuriated her to hear him ask the question. After the many times she had lain with him since she had been on the farm.

"Jesse ya ought to be shamed of yoreself, to even ask me dat."

"Well I got a passle o brothers."

At that remark Monty, who had returned to the yard, straightened up his shoulders. "Little brother, ya jist might ought to be a little more keerful at what ya say. He knows he's de pa, he jist hates gittin caught." Monty commented.

"Well." Jesse scratched his head and mumbled again, "well."

"Standing there mumbling is not going to do this youngin' any good, Jesse," his mother stated.

"Oh, all right, she's mine." He looked at Mare Lise again. "Why didn't ya say some'um to me afore now? Dis is a hell-of-a bit of news to fall on a man's head."

Listy Ann said, "Mare Lise, come get the baby. Take her in the kitchen and clean her up, she's got scraps of leaves clinging to her body and in her hair. Try nursing her a little to settle her down."

Within two weeks, things were back to normal on the farm with a new baby girl named Belle to love and play with.

Jesse and Mary Eliza did not marry at that time.

In the fall of 1915, Belle took sick. She cried continually, no matter how much her mother or grandmother coddled her. The five-year-old girl had felt bad and been irritable for the past two days. No matter how sick a person was, they were not taken to a doctor unless it was thought to be a matter of life or death. Mare Lise began to worry when the child's fever rose to a disturbing level. She asked the child's father about taking her to see he doctor. He was too busy working in the hay field, mowing. So was the grandfather.

"That youngin'll be all right in a day or two, if you jist go on about your business and give her a good dost of castor oil," Jesse the grandfather remarked.

"I've got to git somebody to take me and her to Cypress Creek to de doctor," she mumbled to herself. She was standing on the back porch of the house. She looked out over the fields and spotted Jake standing near one of the ditches that separated the farms. She took off in a run from the porch.

"Jake! Jake!"

It was a good distance to where Jake was. She was out of breath by the time she reached him.

"Please Jake, wood'ja take me oer to de doctors at Cypress Creek? Belle is so sick and I fear she'll die iffin we don't git'er some help. Please Jake, her fever is too high. Her skin 'bout burnt my hand to touch it."

Jake, being the aggravating scoundrel that he was known to be throughout the entire family, pushed his old felt hat back on his head and rubbed his chin in a fashion that gave her the opinion that he too would refuse to take her. He grabbed his hat and yanked it off his head.

"Whur's Paw and Jesse? How come one uv 'em cain't take ya?"

"I begged and begged 'em both. Dey think I'm worrying oer nothin'. Please Jake won't ja take me?"

After shuffling his feet around on the ditch bank, where he had been shrubbing brush, he told her he would take her and the baby.

"It'll take me nigh on a hour to git my tools put away, and git on oer to yore house. You go on back now and git ready, so's we can git on de road as soons I git dare."

It was nearing dusk by the time they neared the Burnt Shoe on the way back from seeing the doctor. The Tannery had long ago ceased to be used. Only the fallen down remains were on the site. Dark clouds hung heavy in the sky above them. "What ya say de docter said was wrong wid de youngin'?" Jake asked

Belle lay sleeping in her mothers arms. The first restful sleep she had had in several days. The sleep was caused by the medication the doctor had given her. "It's pneumonia, and he said dat if I'd've waited a day or two longer, she'd a died. Thank ya Jake fer savin my baby's life."

Jake looked sideways at her and his nasty, mean old mind began to grind.

"Now I was a thankin ya should oblige me in a way uv thanks," he uttered, with a sneering expression on his face.

When they arrived at the junction at the Burnt Shoe, where they should turn left on Bear Grass road, Jake pulled back on the reins, "Whoa up dare boy." He gently whacked the ropes against the side of the horse to remind the animal who was in command. Jake lowered himself down from the buggy and hooked the ropes around the whip stand. He walked slowly around the back of the buggy and came to a stop beside her where she sat with her head hung.

"Now Jake, ya cain't mean what chu'r astin me to do."

"I mean ever word uv it. Now lay dat youngin down 'n let's git on wid it."

"But Jake ya know what Jesse'll do to me iffin I oblige ja. I don't won't to Jake. Jist git back in de buggy and take me on hume."

Jake took a step backward and smiled at her, "It's time to pay up girly."

She had known she was in trouble the minute the buggy came to a complete stop.

"Please Jake don't be a doin' dis awful deed. Yore the brother of my child's pa."

"Gal git down offen dat seat sos we kin git on about it. Iffin you don't, I'll put you and de little 'um out rye cheer. Do ya understand what dat means?"

It had already begun to drizzle. The temperature had dropped several degrees since the time they had left home earlier in the day. She knew that it would be pitch black dark before she could walk the distance, and it would never do for the baby to get soaking wet and chilled to the bone in her weakened condition.

She laid the sleeping child on the buggy, gently to avoid waking her. She climbed down from the buggy, and stood before him.

"Please Jake. I'm beggin ya. Don't do dis."

He snatched at her hand and missed. The second time he made contact and pulled her toward the thickness of the nearby woods. The leaves had begun to fall from the trees since autumn weather had started to come in. Some of the pine trees had dropped their needles. The ground was covered with the fallen foliage. He maneuvered on over beneath a sweet gum tree to prevent the raindrops from falling directly on them. Jake unbuttoned his overall's fly and drug out his manhood.

"Come on gal, git dem underwear off."

She continued to stand perfectly still, her hands clasped together below her stomach. She had hardened herself to cruelty several years before. She knew it was going to happen, no matter what she said or did.

He took her by the hair on the back of her neck and yanked her head backward. His wet mouth slobbered all over her face. She felt the urge to throw up, but decided she had better not. She saw that he was aroused. She knew the danger she would be in if she deterred the proceedings any longer.

He fell to the ground, forcing her to to go with him. He yanked up her full-skirted dress bottom. He took her with force and hurt. When he was sated, he rolled off her and stated matter-of-factly,

"Git up, n straighten yo'self up."

He arranged his clothes to appear as if nothing had occurred, and returned to the buggy. He yelled out at her,

"Gal will ya come on. It'll be plum dark purty soon now."

Belle started to cry. The loudness of his voice had awakened her. Mare Lise heaved herself up to the buggy seat and sat down. She gathered Belle up into the folds of her arms.

"Hush baby girl, yore ma is here widja now, we'll soon be to de house."

She leaned back against the top of the buggy seat and let her head rest on the padded leather cushion, her eyes closed.

"Ya know sump'um Mare Lise?" Jake broke the silence with his question.

"Yore name fits you right fine, cause ya Lies good gal. No wonder brother Jesse seems to be tarred all the time," he snarled his lips away from his teeth in a nasty grin. "Yeap, you're a mighty fine lay."

She just stared off into the woods. She felt so dirty and demeaned.

"Jake, I wonder if you ever even notice the beauty here in these woods around us."

The words were not spoken, only thought inside her, anything to keep her mind off the awful thing that she had been a part of there at the Burnt Shoe.

Jake tightened up on the reins, just as the horse pulled the buggy up next to the front steps of his father's house. The rain was coming down hard. They were both soaked to the skin, only Belle was dry, she had been covered all during the rain.

"Whoa there fella," he commanded the horse. He looked over at her when she moved to leave the buggy. "Ya best keep your mouth shet, if you know what's good fer ya."

She remained wordless as she clamored from the buggy and ran up on the porch. Only then did she turn back and look at Jake. He turned the horse and buggy around and left the yard.

Supper was on the table when Jake entered the kitchen of his home. Clarry suggested that he change into dry clothes and get washed up to eat.

"I want to git dis kitchen cleaned up afore too much longer. Dis rain has put a scare in me."

All the children were seated around the table. Not a one of them had a thing to say. Each one, in his own right, feared their father with a passion. Even Ederd and Ella, at ages 17 and 16, kept quite around him most of the time because of his actions.

Later on in the night, while lying in bed beside his sleeping wife, his thoughts returned to the afternoon of his sexual encounter with Mare Lise. He got so aroused, that he grabbed and shook Clarry by the arm to wake her.

"Hum...? What's the matter with you Jake? I'm tired and need sleep. Jist leave me alone tonight."

She knew exactly what his matter was. She dreaded each and every time he came near her for that reason. The good had gone out of their marriage a couple of years after they had married. She stayed with him because there was nowhere else to go. Her children lived here. They were the joy of her existence.

He pulled his hand away from her and grunted in an angry tone,

"Ne'er you mind. What I got frum Mare Lise on the way hume frum de doctors office, wuz enough to out do ya anytime." He rolled away from her and eventually slept.

It took her a long time to get back to sleep. Tears filled her eyes, but she dared not make any crying sounds, for fear he would hear.

During breakfast the next morning, nothing was said about the night before. Jobs were assigned for the day. Ederd and Jacob were to finish cutting the trees out in the woods, and then haul the logs up to the woodpile for cutting into firewood for the winter's supply. Jake returned to the ditch bank and got busy with his bush ax. He wanted to complete this one bank by nightfall. As soon as the brush dried, he could get it burned off. One more job finished for the year.

He had been at work about two hours when he heard the rustle of dried grass. He looked up to see Monty and Barbara walking toward him.

"Good mornin, to ya Jake. I see yore at it agin dis mornin," Monty spoke to Jake.

"Mornin'. Yeah, lack ya'self, I never seem to git caught up anymore."

Barbara nodded a greeting to Jake and said, "Well, I'm goin' on up to de house and sit wid Clarry for a spell. Monty, when yore ready to leave, walk on up dare and git me." She gathered up her dress tail and walked off.

When Barbara entered the yard, Ella was busy punching clothes down in the old black wash pot. Smoke billowed out skyward from the roaring fire, built around the pot to make sure the clothes boiled a good long while to ensure getting them clean.

"Mornin' Ella, where's yore maw?"

"Round yander in the chicken yard."

Clarry had her apron tail formed into a pocket to carry the eggs safely to the kitchen. She jumped when Barbara spoke and said, "Well land sakes Barbara, you nearly skeert me to death. I wuz so deep in thought I never heard ya come up on me." She straightened up from the row of nests, and with a loose corner of the apron, she wiped a tear escaping from her eye. After sniffing her nose a time or two, she rubbed the back of her hand across the bottom of her nose, and said, "Come on in de house wid me, I thank dare's some coffee left in de pot."

"Clarry, what's wrong wid'ju dis mornin?"

She set down on the bench that sat next to the eating table. Seldom had she seen Clarry shed a tear. Even when her babies had died, she had done her crying in private. She had a feeling as to why her sister-in-law was in the condition she was... Jake.

"It's de same old thang Barbara. I don't know why I'm a lettin it git to me dis time. I ought to know better by now. I've lived with it for the past twenty or so years." She poured the coffee and sat across the table from Barbara.

"Jake been roamin' agin, has he? Clarry, I put up wid de same mess all de time. Iffin I say anythin' to 'im about it, Monty tries to beat de life outta me, too."

Clarry went on tell her what Jake had said to her during the night before. "Sometimes, I think dat I'd lack 'im better if he'd jist go on and die."

Several days passed before Jake exploded. Barbara had gone home after her visit with Clarry, and related to Monty what Jake had done and said to Mare Lise. Monty in turn had told Jesse. Well, now Jesse got angry, in fact he got real mad. The same day he heard the news from Monty, he met Jake at Jake's hog pen. He let him know first thing, with out even speaking to him, just how mad he was.

"You bastard, I'll git cha fer dis Jake. It jist may take me a while, but I'll fix yore ass." He shoved his hands down in his pockets and turned to leave. "Monty told me what cha done. He got it frum his wife, who heard it frum Clarry. Bragging, were ya?" He left without another word to his brother.

It was about the ten o'clock hour in the morning. Clarry was in the kitchen with Ella and Vinnie. The two girls were getting dinner on the stove, while Clarry stood ironing at the end of the eating table. She had made a pad for the ironing by folding a quilt across the end of the table and covered it with a bed sheet. She had just picked up the flat iron from the top of the cook stove when she and the girls heard heavy footsteps climbing the kitchen porch steps. All three stopped and looked toward the closed door.

The door opened with such force that it slammed against the wall. Clarry and her girls cowered backward in fear.

"All right old woman, you've done it dis time!"

He took steps to get closer to where Clarry stood, still holding the flat iron. He snorted like an animal he was so enraged.

"Put dat iron down!" he ordered.

She turned to place it back on the stove. When she turned back to face him, she was met by a smart slap across her cheek. At the moment, she had no idea why he was in such a foul mood. She automatically threw up her hand to protect her face.

"Jake, in the name of God, what-cha-doin' ?" She wiped blood from the corner of her mouth with her bare hand.

He grabbed her by the arm and began to slap her about her shoulders and on her head. She bent sideways, trying to avoid the strikes.

"Next time ya thank it's any of ya dammed business to strow round to de neighbor wha I do, ya better thank more dan onst old gally." He lost his grip on her arm and she fell to her knees.

She had crawled a few inches when he took her by the hair on the back of her head. She wore a big ball at the nape of her neck. Forcing her to rise to a stooping position, he struck her across the face, back and forth. Her eyes rolled in her head as she strained to keep consciousness. He reached out, grabbed the wooden fireplace poker, and shoved her away from him. He brought the poker down across her back several times, from shoulders to her buttocks. Clarry felt as if she would loose herself in his violence at any moment.

Both the girls were huddled together just inside the pantry door, not daring to make a sound of protest to what they witnessed. Their hands clasped over their mouths to smother the cries of fear they felt for their mother's safety. Ella was sixteen years old and did not have the courage to speak out against her father, no matter what he did, or said.

Clarry's ball of hair came undone when Jake released his hold on it. She collapsed on the floor in a heap. She cried from the pain he had caused. Her hair hung to the floor, covering her face from view. His last act of violence toward her before he left the kitchen was to give her a swift kick to her backside. She flinched only slightly.

"Damn yore sorry excuse fer a woman. One of dese days you'll be outta my sight fer good." He went out, leaving the door wide open.

As soon as the girls knew he was out of sight, they rushed to their mother's side. "Mammy! Mammy!" Vinnie called out in an excited voice. Both girls grabbed her and turned her over, to lie on her back. They too were crying. It was hard for them to tend to her.

Her face was so bloody it was hard to tell where she was injured. The dress she wore was blood spattered across the shoulders and down the front.

"Get a wet rag Vinnie. Wipe her face while I try to hold her up," Ella commanded.

When they completed the job of cleaning her up, the damage they found to her was heartbreaking. Both her eyes were closing from the swelling. One corner of her mouth was busted and seemed to be turning inside out from the swelling. It appeared that her entire face would be black and blue before long. Her long hair was matted with blood. It appeared to the girls to be a miracle that no bones were broken. The place on her behind where she had received the kick was swollen and angry looking.

"Mammy, please help us to git you up and in de bed. Yore about dead dis time mammy. Paw really done ya bad. Me and Ella will be careful not to hurt ya any more." Vinnie sniffed back tears as she pleaded with her mother to go to bed, until she healed.

"I hate dat old man, we call Paw." Ella whispered as they left the room Clarry lay in. At the moment, there was not a more miserable woman in the world than Clarry.

Ella and Vinnie returned to the kitchen and finished preparing the noonday meal.

While dinner was being eaten, not a word was spoken about the awful event that took place a short time earlier. Jake didn't even bother to ask about Clarry. He had to notice that she was not at the table. He ate his meal as if it was a regular meal, with nothing other than work tasks around the farm to speak of. All the nearly grown children sat quietly while they ate. Neither of them seemed to have much of an appetite for the meal. Ella had filled her brothers in on what their father had done to their mother.

Clarry lay in bed, too sore to do much moving around. She could barely see through the tiny openings in her swollen eyes.

"Here mammy, see if you can raise up enough for me to get this fork in your mouth. Paw's gone back to the field," Ella cooed at her mother when she went to feed her the day after the episode.

She moaned as she pushed herself up on one elbow, and propped on two of the pillows Ella had fluffed behind her.

"Child, I don't know how much more of his meanness I'll be able to take. It's gone on far too many years now, and gets no better. He started in on me a couple o years after we married. It's been some long years. If it warn't for you youngin's, I think I'd jist walk off in de woods and ne'er come back." It was the first time she had ever spoken to any of her children about any of her feelings concerning the man she was married to.

"Now mammy, don't talk dat a way. We all love ya, us youngin's do. Maybe he'll die. Then we'll all be better off." She fed forkfuls of food to her mother in silence for a while.

"Mammy, you know sump'um? I been thinkin', if we all leave here, all uv us at one time, we could go somewhere and things maybe would git better, afore he kills one uv us."

"Child, where do ya think we'd go? There's nowhere for us to go. We bound to stay rye cheer."

Ella carefully assisted Clarry to squat on the slop jar. "I'm leaving here jist as soon as I find some man to marry up wid me. I can't stand to witness what Paw is doin to ya."

"Well you know dat Monty is treating Barbara jist like Jake does me. Maybe it's in dare blood to be mean, cruel and hateful."

"Not Uncle Dave. He's kind n lovin' to Aunt Della. I wish he wuz my Paw."

She helped Clarry off the slop jar and while she tucked the covers about her shoulders, continued with her thoughts, "I'll never allow a man to treat me wid what chu git mammy." She left the room in tears.

It took Clarry one and a half weeks to recover enough to get back to her daily work.

Fall eased on into winter. It was a mild winter. Jesse had often pondered on a solution for his revenge toward Jake. He finally decided he had his answer worked out in his head. He began to work on that plan just as the weather started to turn cooler. He needed to have all windows and doors closed in Jake's house for his project. At night, after the family members were in bed over at Jake's, Jesse walked the short distance from his house to Jake's yard. He made sure to take his pocketknife along with him. In his head, he measured the exact spot he needed to drill the hole with the pocketknife in the wooden shutter type window. The window was located to the left of the fireplace from the outside of the house. He wanted the peephole to line up exactly straight from the hole to the bed where Jake and Clarry slept in their room. There was no door between the front room and the bedroom, only an open door frame.

He worked on the hole off and on throughout the cold months, a little each night when he went over there. He accomplished what he wanted by the first week in March 1916. The peephole was big enough for the one eye to see through, up close, but unnoticed by the naked eye at a distance.

He was just biding his time, and patiently waiting for the right time, just as he had through the winter working on his plan of vengeance. He had chosen only the nights when the moon shone brightly to do his drilling with the knife. He would walk over after his own household was sleeping soundly. He always whistled for Jake's dogs as soon as he scaled the rail fence that separated the two farms. He knew that if he entered the yard without letting the dogs know he was about, they would announce his arrival. The dogs of all the brothers knew who each brother was, therefore once he alerted the dogs of his presence it was safe to continue.

"Hey dare old spot, everythang all right up at de house?" He scratched the top of the dog's head, then he and the two dogs walked on up to Jake's sleeping house.

He always stopped when he reached the edge of Jake's yard, to stand quietly for a moment or two. If everything seemed in place, he would amble on around the house where the hole was. On this one night, he stood there peeping in and in his mind, completed his plans.

Returning the next night before the family retired, he stood concealed and watched as the family left the kitchen and entered the house to prepare for bed. He took his place outside the window. The glare from the kerosene lamp provided enough light for him to see Jake and Clarry undress and climb in the bed.

"You bastard Jake, I'm nigh on to fixin' ya." He muttered to himself, as he left the scene, to return home for a good night's sleep.

Jake and the boys had begun their spring work early. Ederd and Jacob were in different fields plowing. Jake worked the section, first in one field and then the other, to loosen up the big clumps of freshly plowed soil. Dust clouded the air they breathed. Ederd stopped his mule and wiped his brow, he then took a big drink of water Rosie had brought out in the field to him, to quench his thirst.

"Thank ya Rosie, dat shore did feel good goin' down my gullet."

The work of plowing the two fields was completed and rows marked off by mid-afternoon. Jake glanced up in the afternoon sky and said,

"Boys, I'll be going off to Wallace tomorrow for fertilizer and more seeds, let's call it a day. By the time we git the feedin' up done and eat our evening meal, it'll be close to bedtime. I'll need a good night's rest for the day ahead uv me."

There was still a little day light left in the day when supper was over. Jake decided he would walk over to his father's house to see if they needed anything from Wallace.

"I'll be back d'reckly," he said to Clarry, on his way out of the kitchen. He failed to mention where he was going.

He opened the door of his father's house without knocking and walked in. He found them all sitting in front of the fireplace, their chairs in a semi-circle. They all looked toward him when he entered. Mary Lise hung her head. She never said one word while he was in the room.

"Evenin' Paw, how ya feelin'?" He pulled up a chair and joined them by the fire.

His father nodded his head in Jake's direction, the customary manner of greeting

Jake held his opened hands up to the fire, to take the chill off his fingers. The days usually warmed up, but the night air could chill a person to the bone, if not warmly dressed.

"Did ya git most o yore spring plowing done yet Paw?" Jake asked more or less to get a conversation started. As he spoke, he glanced over to where his brother Jesse sat. Jake noticed that he had not said a word either.

Jesse, the father, sat with his hands folded in his lap. He sniffed his nose a couple of times and answered,

"We've done what we're suppose to do," not bothering to look at his son.

Jake raked his brogans back and forth across the floor before he spoke again, "Paw, me and the two older boys are gwine oer to Wallace tomorra, fer de purchase of more fertilizer 'n seeds, so's we can go on 'n git de early crops in de ground. I walked oer here to see if I can git anythin' fer you, while I'm oer dare. We'll most likely stay de night dare in Wallace. Sometimes, it seems to take fore'er to git dare and back. Can ya think o anything ya need?"

His father cupped his hand around his long white beard. The beard was an exact copy of his father's.

"Yes, your maw said to me just today, that she was nearly out of salt. You can bring her a twenty-five-pound sack of salt back."

Listy Ann spoke up for the first time and mentioned that she also wanted some white sewing thread.

"Maybe get me four or five spools. That ought to last me a right good spell." She thought of asking about Clarry and the children, but decided against asking. She knew what was going on and could sense the tension in the room, as did the others. It was the first time the two brothers had been together in the company of their parents since Jake had taken Mary Eliza and the baby to Cypress Creek. Instead of saying what she really wanted to say, she added, "Do you think you can do that son? I'll get you a little money before you go home."

The brother, Jesse, sat with his hands folded in front of him, resting on his legs. He felt the urge to reach over and knock Jake out of the chair. To come in their house, acting like a loving, caring brother. He had gotten away with his evil deeds for so many years, he thought there was no end to what he could do and simply go on with his life as if everything was all right.

"Well Jake, old boy, you jist give me de news I been a waiting fer," ran quickly through Jesse's mind. He decided to make a motion to say a word or two, "Do ya think you'll need to stay de night, in Wallace?"

It was the first words Young Jesse had spoken to Jake since their confrontation at the hog pen last fall. Jake took it to mean that things had smoothed out between them.

"The boys need a little time in town away frum all de hard work round de house dare. Dey don't know it, yit but I'm gonna let 'em loose fer de night. As you know, Ederd is so shy and bashful, I doubt seriously he'll be doin much of anythin' other than hanging on to my coattail, but now, that Jacob, he'll see what dare is to do and do it. Do it hard, too."

Jake rose and pushed the chair back with the calves of his legs. "Well, reckon I'll mosey on back oer to de house. I'll send one of 'em boys oer here wid your goods pretty soon after we git back hume." He walked to the door and grasped the knob. "Nite maw. Nite Paw. Oh, how's that youngin', Belle?"

He knew the question would be a dig to both Jesse and Mary Eliza. He went through the door and closed it before either of them could respond.

When Jake and the boys came into the kitchen from taking care of the animals the next morning, both the young men were excited. The father had decided to take them to Wallace with him and had told them so.

"Stomp that dirt offin yore brogans. I jist swept dis floor," Clarry yelled out.

She planned to scrub the floor as soon as breakfast was over. The custom was to sprinkle a light layer of clean sand over the entire area as soon as the floor dried. The sand absorbed grease spatters. When the sand soaked up a certain amount of grease, it was swept out of the kitchen.

"Gawd, mammy! Ya bout skeered me to death wid yore yelling," Jacob exclaimed. The men scraped their shoes and went to wash up for breakfast.

"Clarry, pack up some food that what was left oer frum last night's supper, it'll do. Me n the boys are leaving jist as soon as we finish eatin' here." Jake gave the order, not so much as a request but as a command. There again he failed to mention where they were going, only that they'd be back day after tomorrow.

Jake left the kitchen first and as soon as he was out of ear shot, Ederd explained where they were going, and for what reason.

The children seldom got to go on a trip of any kind. Jake did most of the going. He left Clarry and the children home to fend for themselves, as far as entertainment went. Clarry knew, by the way Ederd was talking, how excited he was to be asked to go along with his father. Her prayer was that Jake would behave himself and not spoil this rare chance for the boys to get out and away from nothing but hard work.

"I'm pleased dat he's taking ya boys along. Wood'ja be keerful while yore in dat town? Folks is different dare dan Jacob an ya been use to."

There was no need for Jake to give instructions on how to feed the animals while he was away, but he did. "And git it done fore night fall." Clarry and the girls had handled things around the place many times before. Jake acted as if not a one of them had enough sense to look out for himself, much less tend to his things.

By good dark, Jesse was standing in the edge of the woods waiting for the lamp light to move from the kitchen to the house. He knew that when that occurred, the entire family would be going to bed shortly. "Not too much longer now," he said to the darkness.

He waited nigh on up to an hour before he walked on up to the yard. He whistled for the dogs when he got close enough for them to hear. They ran out to greet him. After the familiar scratch under the chin, they returned to their sleeping place.

He took his stand close to the closed wooden window. He positioned his face so his eye could look into the room without being noticed by anyone in the house.

The children went on off to bed, leaving Clarry to sit by the dying embers in the fireplace. It was dangerous to leave a roaring fire there for the night. She read a few verses of scripture then removed the pins from her hair. Her hair hung down to her waist when allowed to hang free. There was enough natural curl in her hair to cause it to hang in wavy tresses. By this time, the flames in the fireplace had died down enough to suit her. She used the broom to sweep the ashes from the hearth up into the cooled embers then reached for the lamp. When she got next to the bed, she set the lamp on the side table and removed her dress. It was her habit to sleep in her slip and bloomers.

At the exact moment she left the front room, Jesse climbed up on the front porch at the dogtrot entrance. He then crept toward the front door. Doors were never locked at night. He smiled as he silently turned the knob in order to gain access to the house. He left the door open and quietly took steps to place him so he could see Clarry lift the dress over her head. She stood facing the lamp, which put her back to Jesse. She leaned toward the lamp, cupped her hand around the top of the glass shade and blew out the flame.

Jesse's left hand went around her head and clamped over her mouth at that moment. She did not know who her attacker was. He never made a sound. He realized that if the girls woke up, they would come to investigate. Neither of the girls was afraid of the darkness of night.

With his right hand, he lifted her up and carried her out of the house. On the way out, he hooked his right foot on the door and pulled on it, but left it slightly ajar.

Down the front step, he went with his burden clutched tightly in his arm. Her mouth was still covered with his one hand. The dogs stirred, but caused him no trouble. He walked at a right fast pace for a while, all the while Clarry squirming and grunting. By the time he got to the fence dividing his farm from that of Jake's, he began to tire from the weight of his load. He stopped at the fence and thought for a second or two. Now how was he going to scale the fence with his burden? He had failed to work out that part of the plan beforehand. His Paw had always warned him about being 100% sure of anything. Without thinking too much about it at the moment, he released his hand from her mouth. He needed the hand to assist himself and his load over the fence.

The second her mouth was freed, she let out a scream that alerted every ear in hearing distance. She twisted her head up and looked into his face.

"Jesse Swinson, ya put me down, right dis minute. What in de name a goodness do ya think yore doin anyhow?"

The moon shone brightly, Clarry looked like a wild person, with her hair falling in every direction and her slip half way up her body. She wanted to kill him, if she could only free herself from him.

Getting over the fence was not as easy as he had thought it would be. She kept wringing and twisting every time he made an effort to climb over the fence.

Her screams continued. He had a good hold on her, penning both her arms to her body. Her feet were in a constant motion of kicking, striking him as often as she could make contact with any part of his body.

"Woman, will ya be still. You jist wait 'til I git ya in de barn. You'll have a right ta scream 'n holler den."

He finally got them both across the fence. He paused a moment to catch his breath, "Whoosh!" He took a couple of steps on his way, when he heard the sound of a shotgun roar behind him. At the same time, he felt the blast in his bottom rear. He dropped Clarry and fell forward to the ground.

Clarry found herself in a crumpled pile, half covered by Jesse's shoulder and arm.

"In de name of Gawd, what wuz dat?" she exclaimed in a loud voice. She looked behind her and saw Monty walking toward her.

Monty had been out behind his smokehouse to pee before he retired for the night. Just as he stepped on the top step onto the porch on his way back in the house, he heard the screams and knew instantly who they came from. He looked out over the fields and located the sound. He raced inside the house and picked up his gun, loaded it with rock salt and ran from the house in a fast lope. He ran to the ditch, jumped it, and was on his Paw's land. He was in the field he needed to be in. He raced across the field. If the field had been plowed, he would never have been able to reach his destination in time.

He was winded by the time he got close enough to figure out what was going on. He stood and watched while Jesse tried to maneuver himself and his burden up and over the fence. He heard most of what Jesse said to Clarry, though some of his words had been distorted due to Clarry's screams. He heard enough to figure out what Jesse aimed to do. He raised the gun and took aim at the target he wanted to hit. He waited until Jesse was in perfect range for the shot to be the most effective. He pulled the trigger and watched as the events followed.

He ambled on over to where Clarry sat on the ground. She scrambled to her feet. She yanked at her slip to get it as far down around her legs as possible. Her hair covered her face. With one swipe she gathered it up and twisted it behind her neck in a makeshift ball, then tucked in down in the back neckline of her slip.

"Lawsy mercy, Monty. I do reckon ya've kilt him." She didn't bother to check on Jesse. "Praise Gawd, ya got cheer. Monty, I jist don't know what got in 'im to come in de house and steal me lack dat."

Monty walked up close to where Jesse lay still; face down, in the dirt. He nudged him in the side with the toe of his shoe, "Git up damn ya. You ain't dead yit, Jesse. You jist may be fore dis night's oer. I knowed ya wuz up to somp'um, from de way ya been actin here lately." He propped his arm across the barrel of the gun, while the stock stood on the ground.

Clarry was in a heavy shiver from the chill of the night and the experience she had gone through. She felt none of the cold because of her anger and embarrassment standing there in front of Monty with nothing but her slip on.

"He is dead ain't he? I shore hope he is. I hate dat man. He is one o de meanest things on dis earth, next to Jake dat is." She crossed her arms across her heavy, sagging breasts.

Monty stooped to roll Jesse over. When he did, Jesse moaned from the pain in his butt. His butt was filled with rock salt. He looked up, and in the moonlight recognized his brother. He spat dirt from his mouth and uttered, "Ya've half kilt me," followed by a string of filthy cussing, that was enough to singe the hairs on Clarry's eyebrows.

"Jesse, git up. Ya ain't all dat hurt. I'm takin' Clarry back up to de house. Ya go on up to Paw's and I'll be along d'reckly. Wake up Mare Lise, and let her tend to ya ass."

Monty took Clarry's arm and helped her back over the fence. He then took his coat off and draped it over her shoulders.

"Clarry, if Jake hears bout what went on here dis night it'll be hell to pay"

"Oh! My goodness, I thank I jist tore my little toe off on a root er somethin'." She moaned as she hopped on one foot for a step or two. "Walkin' out cheer barefooted in de dark is rough on my feet."

"Keep ya eye on de cleared part of de path as ya walk along," he cautioned her. "Dare ain't as many snags air."

"I agree wid'ja Monty, bout what Jake'll do to me. He likened to o ruined me last fall when he found out dat I'd told Barbara bout what he done to Mare Lise."

She clutched the lapels of the coat tighter about her chest as she spoke. "He most likely will kill me dis time, for somp'um

I don't eben know about. Monty, what do you reckon got in Jesse to cause 'im to do a thang lack at?"

"Well. I've been keepin' my ears and eyes open, plus a watchin' what's been going on around cheer, all through dis past winter. I caught part of what he said to ya, when he got you oer the fence. His intentions wuz to do to you what Jake did to Mare Lise. I'm prone to thank dis is some kinda revenge, Jesse is gittin' back at Jake for what he done to Mare Lise, and den he had de gall to go round braggin' about it."

"Lawsy have mercy, if dat's it, I'm in a heap o trouble, worries and pain. Do ya reckon dare's a way possible to keep dis night frum 'im?"

They were passing the hog lot at the time. The hogs were grunting and making a lot of noise, moving around in their sleep.

"Well Clarry, we'll haft to see what's goin' on up to de house. If any of dem youngin's is awake, dey'll want to know what's goin' on."

"I pray to my good Lord, dat dey've slept clear through all dis ruckus."

They entered the corner of the yard, where the dogs lay sleeping. One of them raised his head, wagged his tail and lay back down. There was not a sound coming from the inside of the house.

When they climbed up on the porch, Monty spoke, not much louder than a whisper, "Go on in and see how things are in dare. I'll wait out cheer on de porch."

She pushed the slightly ajar door on open, took a step or two and listened. It appeared that all the children had slept through her ordeal.

She turned and tiptoed back to where Monty stood under the porch shelter. The moonlight wasn't as bright as it was out in the open, but they could still see enough to communicate with each other.

"Mebbe, jist mebbe we can git away wid'out tellin' Jake airy a thing bout tonight. You keep quiet bout tonight unless yore forced to speak about it. I'll go on oer to see bout Jesse, and talk to him bout keeping hush on de events of dis awful night." He turned to leave and twisted back around, "Ya go on to bed n try to git some sleep, good night to ya." She handed him his coat before he stepped off the porch.

She went in the house and walked up to the fireplace where the few embers still smoldered. She bent over and dragged the foot tub away from the embers, where she had placed it before going to her bedroom earlier. She pulled a chair up and sat down wearily.

She eased her feet in the water and thought, "It seems like a long time ago that I put the foot tub up next to the embers." She snatched her feet from the foot tub. "Gracious, de water's hotter'n I thought it wuz." She dipped her feet in and out of the water until her feet adjusted to the heat. As soon as she had washed the dirt from her feet, she replaced the foot tub up by the ashes. It was a little hard to see in the house without a lamp, but she crept to her room and fell in the bed. "Lawsy, what a time I've had dis night," she whispered. She lay awake most of the night.

Monty caught up with Jesse at about the time he got to the path that led up to the house. Jesse had walked at a very slow pace. When Jesse realized that his brother had overtaken him, he stopped and turned to look at him.

"Monty, do ya know what cha done to me? My ass is in a pain I've ne'er felt afore. I don't know how I manage to e'en walk. Damn ya to hell. Ya'll rue dis night What I wuz doin wuz none o yore damn business."

"Now Jesse, ya wuz wrong to go and steal Clarry lack dat, no matter how mad j'ar at Jake."

Jesse stared at him a moment and asked, "How'd ja know what I wuz up to, n for what reason I wuz a doin it?"

"I've had my eye on ya fer a while now. It didn't take too much reasoning to figger out what cha wuz up to."

"Can you git ya'self on up the de house? I'll hep Mary Lise pick de rock salt outta ya ass," Monty said and then tossed his head back in a hardy round of laughter. "I always wanted to fill a man's ass wid rock-salt, just to see de reaction of de culprit." He laughed so hard, he could barely talk. "Ya've needed it fore now, brother o mine. To tell ya de truth, Jake needed it more'n ya did." After more laughter he uttered, "Best damn laugh, I've had in a mighty long time."

Mary Eliza met them at the door of the kitchen. She had heard the shot and the noise of their approach. She decided to go on and get up. She figured trouble was on hand. She went to the kitchen and had a lamp lit by the time the men reached her.

"What in de name a goodness are you fellas doin dis time o night?" She noticed how Jesse was walking, "Jesse, wha'cha been up to, to make ya walk lack dat?"

Monty took her by the arm and said, "Come on Mare Lise, we've got work to do. Jesse needs some tending to. He's got a tail filled with rock-salt."

"Rock-salt? How'd dat git in 'im?

"I put it dare."

Not a one in the house had stirred through the fracas. Belle didn't even stir when her mother eased out of the bed.

Jesse had begun to stiffen up by the time they got to work on him. Monty got a roaring fire going in the fireplace to get some heat in the room. They laid him on his stomach on a bench that Monty drug in from the back porch

An iron kettle was placed close to the fire. "Let the water het up a little fore we start," Mary Eliza said.

They pulled his overalls off and when she worked at getting the flap of his union suit down, he moaned when she pulled the material loose from the tiny wounds where blood had seeped into the material.

Monty sat on his legs while she picked the rock salt out with the point of a small pocketknife. At times, it hurt him so bad that he gnawed on the edge of the bench to help ease the pain.

"Mare Lise, fer Gawd's sake do be keerful back dare. I don't rightly know when I ere had sich a pain."

"Is one uv ya gonna tell me how dese shots got in his butt? Iffen you are, bout now is as good a time as any," Mary Eliza asked.

Monty related the whole story to her from the time Jake had bade her to oblige him, to where she now stood.

It took quite a while to remove all the pellets from his hide. "I'm a gonna kill dat Jake Swinson," Jesse moaned the utterance. "Yeah, dat's what I'm gonna do. Jist put him and me both outta our misery."

Monty thought for a moment before he spoke, "Now baby Jess, I been a thinkin' dis situation oer since we been here in dis kitchen. Ya know fer a fact dat he'll kill ya dis time fer shore. Dat is, if he gits wind of what chu've done dis night. Why don't we talk oer de best way to settle dis, rye cheer, rye now. As I said, I been a ponderin' it o'er. Why not let everythan' lay rye whur it tis. Not say a word to a single soul. Cause Jesse, he'll not only kill you, but Clarry long wid'ja."

Jesse fletched his back as a whole and stated, "No by damn, I'll kill the bastard first, myself."

Monty went on the say, "Jesse it's time ya n Jake settled yore differences. There's chillens in both families to consider. Wid Jake dead and ya in prison, who's to care for all dem babies?"

Mary Eliza gouged a little too deep for one of the salt pellets on purpose, to let him know she agreed with Monty.

"If ya don't be more keerful back dare woman, ya mebbe won't be alive too much longer either," Jesse spat out.

"All dis spite and hate and gittin' revenge has gone on long a nuff. It's time to behave lack de grown men dat cha are," she put her two-cent worth in.

The last flick of the knifepoint yielded the final particle of salt from his flesh. She unscrewed the camphor bottle top and poured a small amount in the palm of her hand. Quickly she rubbed her hands together and dabbed his bottom with the fiery liquid. "Whoa! Now ya done it." He rolled and fell hard to the floor.

"Now Jesse, I got to git dis camphor on dem wounds, else dey'll be infection fer shore."

With Monty's help, Jesse got back up on the bench while Mary Eliza continued to dab Jesse's wounds. Monty kept trying to persuade Jesse to take his advice.

"Ya need to think bout Belle, what's to become of her if ya go through wid ja threat and wind up in prison somewhere?" Monty kept trying to convince Jesse to do the right thing.

Nothing was said for a while. It gave Jesse time to think over and consider what Monty had said to him. In the long run, it would be a sight better if the subject could be dropped, even though he didn't really want to drop anything. He hated Jake with a passion, and wanted him to hurt, to feel pain. To kill Jake would only hurt him for a short while, and there he'd be in prison. No, that would never do.

By the time Mary Eliza finished with his medication, Jesse had made up his mind.

"Monty, as much as I hate to let Jake git away wid one more of his evil deeds, I reckon yore right dis time. I'll be a saying nothin', and neither will Mare Lise. But den dare's Clarry to thank about."

"I spoke to her fore I comed o'er here. She's willin' to let it rest, if ya are. None of her youngin's heered a thang."

"How about Paw and maw?"

"I told ja, dey didn't rouse up," Mary Eliza quipped in.

"So, we're to leave it all here in dis room?" Monty asked.

"Ya know dat yore Paw and maw will be a astin' questions, when dey see Jesse limping round here, don't cha?" Mary Eliza stated.

"Yore right, we'd best think of sump'um to tell em. So's our stories will be de same. Got any idees Jesse?"

"No, and I don't want none neither."

After a few moments of silence, Monty came up with a plan. He laid it out before them. "I'll be back o'er here in the mornin', fore maw and Paw git up. We'll go off in the woods for a while, pretend we're huntin'. When we git back here to de house, you've had an accident. You fell over some branches or sump'um. How's zat sound?"

"Good as any."

Monty stepped off the bottom step and turned to watch Jesse descend the steps slowly and carefully. "Go on Jesse, stop actin' lack yore a baby. Git yoreself on in the house n git some sleep. I'll be here early in de day. Be ready!"

He left Jesse standing there in the yard to get himself across over to the house.

Mary Eliza had left them when she patted the last of the camphor on Jesse's rump without as much as a fare-thee-well.

The story they had concocted worked. The folks heard the story about the hunting accident. The hunting trip had occurred too early in the morning for them to see very well. It seemed that Jesse caught his foot on a snarled tree root. When he fell, he twisted his hip. His pain was too much for them to continue the hunt so the two hunters came home empty handed. Young Jesse healed as time passed, with no questions asked.

Chapter Thirteen

In the fall of 1915, Jake decided to try raising sheep. He purchased eleven head from JD McLain, for the sum of $16.50. It took one full year for him to change his mind about breeding and the rearing of sheep. He sold off every head of them to the first buyer he found. He took a loss of five cents a head, not to count the feed and care he had put into the effort.

"I think I'll stick to my hogs n cattle, as fer as animals goes," he made the statement to the man that hauled the sheep off

Ella married Owen Jackson Pierce on July 9, 1916. They went by horse and buggy to Jacksonville and located a Justice of the Peace to perform the ceremony. Clarry went along as witness, because Ella had only turned seventeen on the fourteenth of the month before. Jack, as her husband was called, and Ella had no home, so they lived in a small cabin type house owned by John. They did day work for different farmers for the remainder of that year. Before cold weather set in, they moved to Pin Hook where they found a small farm to work on shares with the owner.

On one Saturday afternoon in late summer, Ederd decided to go a calling on a young lady he had met the month before, over in the Sandy Run area, and had taken a liking to her. Sandy Run was located a few miles southeast of his home.

When all of his work had been completed for the day, on up in the afternoon, he filled one of the washtubs out under the wash shelter and bathed himself. He put on a starched, white shirt and a pair of clean overalls. He shined up his Sunday shoes and donned his best felt hat.

He hitched the horse up to the cart, removed the cross seat and climbed aboard. He stood in the cart bed and held the reins in his hands. He waved good-bye to his family, who stood in the yard to watch the rare occasion of Ederd on his way to visit a lady friend.

"Wait Ederd, I'll go open de gate fer ya," young Steven said as he hopped on the back of the cart to ride the distance to the back gate in order to open and close the gate for Ederd.

As soon as Ederd got horse and cart through the gate, he put the horse in a trot to cover the distance to the road where Dave and John lived.

When he neared Uncle Dave's farmhouse he noticed Buck, son of Uncle Dave, and Arthur, son of Uncle Zedick, sitting beneath the well house shelter. He waved and hollered out a friendly greeting as he passed them, the horse still in a trot.

Buck and Arthur hollered back at him and started to plan a sneaky prank to play on Ederd as soon as he passed them by. The cousins were a few years younger than Ederd.

Dave had cleared new ground and had made fields all the way from his house to the lane that lead on over to Jake's farm. A field of drying stacks of fodder stood in the parcel of land nearest to the lane. Watermelons had been planted in the cornrows and several of the watermelons were still as good as when first ripened. They were concealed from the elements beneath thick clumps of dried grass.

The two young, energetic cousins timed their actions around the time they thought Ederd would be returning. Close to nine o'clock that night, they went to the field of fodder and relaxed by leaning against one of the stacks of fodder that allowed them to keep an eye on the road. From where they were, they could hear the noise the cart wheels made when Ederd slowed down to make a right turn into the lane.

They had gathered up several watermelons and had piled them a short distance from the lane where they waited. Their laughter and fun making kept them wide-awake, though it was past their usual bedtime. It was a bright moonlit night.

"Do ya reckin' he'll kill us if he finds out who done it?" Arthur asked, between giggling spasms.

"I shore ain't gonna tell im if ya don't," more laughter from Buck.

Within the hour of their arrival, the familiar sound of cartwheels bouncing along the dirt road could be heard.

At the same time Ederd turned onto the lane, the boys picked up a watermelon each and dropped them to the ground, cracking them open.

"Ya ready?"

"Ready!"

Ederd stood in a reared back position as he held onto the reins while the horse trotted along the lane. Ederd was filled with warm emotions. It had been a wonderful, fulfilling experience to be in the company of a young woman. It was his first try at mingling with the opposite sex.

When he was about half way the distance of the field, he heard a sound like something hitting the ground to the left of the lane. He looked in that direction and saw nothing, even though the moon provided ample light for night vision. He figured it had been an animal scurrying out of, and away from, the lane. The sounds continued, coming from both sides of the lane. He kept glancing from side to side trying to catch a glimpse of the animals that must have been asleep in the lane.

At about that time a wet cool glob of something hit the back of his head. The top part of his body dipped forward from the pressure of whatever had hit him. He could feel a cool wetness easing down the back of his neck.

"Damn!" He lifted his arms and came down hard on the horse's sides with the reins. "Haw-yah!" The horse was in a full gallop within seconds. The cartwheels bounced and sung out a loud tune of roughness as the cart traveled over the uneven dirt lane.

Those two boys rolled in the field with laughter for several minutes. Before they left the field, they opened another watermelon and ate the heart out of the inside. They cleared away all signs of what they had done, throwing the remains out into the woods across the lane. If Dave, Buck's father, should discover destroyed melons in the field, he would find out what had taken place. The boys knew the beatings they would both get if they were ever found out. It was a tale both of them swore to each other they would never tell until after Dave's death.

Ederd never learned the truth of where the handful of watermelon came from. He strongly figured it had been either one of John or Dave's boys. He allowed it to rest with him, being the only one in his family to know about it. He too knew the punishment that the guilty party would suffer.

The community picnic continued throughout the years. The time of year had been changed to the fall season. The reason behind the change was so the affair could last through the weekend, and by that time of year, all crops had been harvested and the fields could be left unattended for that length of time.

The site for the picnic was located at the Deep Bottom River, near the small settlement of Cypress Creek. The river was simply called 'Deep Bottom.' A sandy expanse of pure white sand ran for over half a mile along the west bank of the river. Each family encampment was set up at the edge of the woods, just past where the sand ended.

The six families that participated disassembled their cook stoves, and took it with them. A table and chairs of sorts was also taken along. Everything they needed for the weekend of camping was packed in a wagon and hauled to the site. Each adult in the family was responsible for his own sleeping place. That is, all except the married men. They shared that of their wives. It was a time to unwind, to relax and swim, and have fun where it could be found.

Of course, there were the animals to be taken care of no matter what else went on. A couple of the young men were picked to do the chore. They went by horseback, to each farm and did the feeding up and watering. Come the next day, another pair of young men was chosen to take the ride to carry out the task.

The picnic of 1916 was a memorable event. Ederd and Chester Pierce, one of Jack's brothers, had been at odds for a year or more. Chester found that he could tease Ederd about the least little thing and get away with it. Ederd was as big and as strong as Chester, but he failed to have the nerve to act as boisterous as Chester did. Each young man was 18 years old. Saturday, a while after the noon hour, several of the young men sat on the bank fishing with reed poles, using earthworms grunted out of the nearby woods for bait. They had caught nearly enough yellow-bellied perch and fresh water bream for the fish fry planned for that night's supper. Chester threw his pole across Ederd's for pure aggravation and the lines tangled.

"Now Chester, ya ort not be foolin' wid my pole," Ederd cautioned, in an irritated voice.

"What's de big man gonna do bout it?" Chester asked, and yanked on his pole. The yank snatched Ederd's pole right out of his hand.

Ederd sat there on the bank for a moment. He looked up to see all the other cousins and friends were looking directly at him. Henry leaned over and whispered, "Ederd, it's time ya stand up fer ya'self."

Ederd arose, brushed the dirt from his legs and walked to where Chester sat. "Say ya want to know what I'm gonna do, do ya?" He bent over and shoved as hard as he could on Chester's body. "Dis is what!"

Chester was in the water before he really knew what was going on. He never let go of the tangled up fishing poles. He stood up in the water and slung his head from side to side to shed the water from his face and hair. He swelled up like a blow toad and threw the poles up on the bank. He came out of the water with both his hands clinched into fists. He swung at Ederd. Ederd dodged and came back with a solid punch into Chester's middle gut. It knocked the wind out of Chester for a moment.

"So ya gonna be de big fighter are ya, huh?" Chester blew a breath of air from his mouth as he asked the question.

"Fight! Fight!" The excited words of exclamation came from one of the smaller children. Most all of the camping party gathered around to observe the fists fly. Ederd placed a well-deserved fist smack into the side of Chester's mouth, drawing blood. Chester staggered and nearly fell. He lowered his head and rushed toward Ederd, liken to that of a charging bull. Ederd swayed in time to avoid the collision. Chester went headfirst back into the water.

Jake and Clarry stood and watched their oldest son who was finally defending himself. They both felt pride in him and neither one dared try to put a stop to the fight. Naturally, they rooted their son on as he continued. Chester climbed out of the water, madder than he should have been.

"Ya dammed Swinson; I'll tear ya head off fer dat." He came to meet Ederd with his fists swinging. Ederd didn't dodge in time and landed up on the ground. Chester fell across Ederd. The two opponents fought on. After about half an hour, they began to tire. The crowd scattered and found something more interesting to fill their time with. Clarry kept her eye and ear tuned to the two spent fighters, who lay on the ground, hugging each other, too tired to do much moving.

Sometime during the afternoon, Ederd worked his pocketknife from his pocket and managed to open it, so the blade showed. A younger child walked by and spotted the blade.

"Look Paw, he's got a knife."

Chester roused up and slipped from Ederd's gripe. He, too, drew his knife from his pocket. They danced around like two bantam roosters, jabbing their knives and both cussing like their elders. Cyrus and Jake decided it was time to get the knives.

"Ya take Chester, Jake. I'll get Ederd," Cyrus said.

Simultaneously they eased up behind the hands that held the knives and upon grabbing the arms, relieved each fighter of the weapons. It maddened each young man to have their weapons taken away, and they went at each other with renewed strength. The fish fry was enjoyed by everyone except Chester and Ederd. They lay in a knotted entanglement, gasping for breath. The two fighter's lay snarled in each other's arms through the night. By morning, Ederd had to pee so bad, that his choice to release Chester, along about daylight, was ruled by the urge.

"Chester, fore I let chu go, I'm tellin' ya, ya ain't to ne'er chide me agin. Cause if ya do, dare won't be no witness to see an' take my knife outta my hand. I'm tellin' ya Chester, if I didn't have to piss, I'd finish you off right cheer."

Chester too, was ready for the change. "Ederd, I promise, frum now on I'll not be a doin a damn thang but be a good friend."

They released their hold on each other at the same time. They stood up and shook hands, then made a dash for the woods. Neither of them noticed the onlookers from the crowd. From that day forward, Ederd and Chester were the best of friends.

The usual time of departure from the campsite was Monday morning after breakfast. When the families left Deep Bottom, there was not one bit of trash left behind.

It was a custom among the local fathers to take their sons up to Kinston, NC, when they reached a certain age, to the whorehouse know as 'Sugar Hill.' Jake had been aiming to get Ederd up there for a year or two and had kept putting it off until he realized that if he didn't get it done, the young man would be old enough to marry. The big day was planned, unbeknownst to the mother and sisters, or so it was thought by the men folk, what was to take place once arriving in Kinston.

"Clarry, me and Ederd, we'll be gone much of de day. We're on de way up to Kinston to see bout a new mowin' machine. Dat ol'un we got is bout wore out." It didn't bother him one bit to let the lie slip quickly out of his mouth. "Jist might be on up in de night when we git home. See to it dat de animals are fed afore dark sits in."

Since Chester did not have a father living at home with the family, Jake took him under his wing, and carried him along with Ederd and himself. Little conversation was shared on the bouncy ride to reach their destination. A glance or two was shared between the two young men, who had looked forward to the day since they had gotten to the age where they heard the stories about 'Sugar Hill.' To tell the truth Ederd was so nervous, he let his anxiety escape when he spoke. He knew that he wanted what his Paw was offering, and had looked forward to the groundbreaking event in his life.

The buggy came to a stop in front of the brothel, located out on the edge of town, down a one-lane dirt street. Each man jumped down from the buggy and Jake tied the horse up to the hitching post.

"Well fellas, ya ready fer ya first hour of what dis world is all about?" He threw back his head in a boisterous round of laughter. "I recall well the day my Paw brung me here. He brung John and Dave, too, on de same day. It was a day to remember for the rest of our lives. I thought Dave was gonna leave us before we e'er got in the rooms. Dat wuz one skeered brother." He took a step or two up the walk and turned, "Well come on boys, what's holdin' ya up? I think I'll git myself reacquainted with one of dem sweet little fillies today, while we're at it."

Two innocent older boys entered the doors of the whorehouse. Two completely happy-with-the-world, glassy eyed young men came out of the building.

Chapter Fourteen

In April of 1918, Jacob and Clyde Pierce, brother of Jack, headed out for Jacksonville. They planned to join the army. Each young man had turned sixteen the month before. Life on the farm held no excitement for either young man. "Paw, I think I'll go on over and enlist in the army. I heered dare's a need fer more fightin' men on de front," Jacob said matter-of-factly to his father, when they had paused at the end of a freshly plowed cornrow in the back of the field. "Me and Clydie, we decided dat's what we wanta do. What do ya have to say bout it Paw?" World War I was well established.

Jake wiped sweat from his brow as he listened to his son express his needs. "Well now son, I reckin' if you've made up yer mind, dare ain't a whole lot I kin do 'bout it. I will haft to say, dat yore still no more than a big youngin. I realize yore as big as a grown man, but ya jist ain't got the years and learning as one."

Jacob and Clyde left the Swinson farm soon after breakfast was eaten the next day. Jacob had been relieved of all his farm duties for the morning since he was on his way to leaving. All of Jacob's brothers and sisters, plus his parents, stood at the gate and waved their goodbyes, as both young men walked the lane toward the Bear Grass Road, where they would turn left and continue with their journey.

Rain had pelted the ground for the past week. Some days it rained all day and night, while other days showers came and went. The ground was saturated with water. Mud holes were spotted here and there all over the farm and along the roadside.

Life went back to normal for those left on the farm, as soon as they turned from the gate and walked away. "I'm gonna miss dat youngin'," Clarry spoke to no one in particular, as they walked back to their daily fare.

It was a good twelve miles to Jacksonville, where the two fellows had heard they could enlist. By the time they got to Chunky Nubbin, an area located in the Harris Creek community, on their route about four miles from home, their pace slowed up somewhat. "Ya know Clydie, I don't think I'll ever go back to dat farm to call hume again. Pa's a mean man. I don't know how much longer I coulda stood dare and watch while he hits on mammy. One a dese days I'm affeared I'd kill im. I may not be of legal age, but I shore do know right frum wrong. Ederd is so meek, he jist takes everything pa does 'n says, 'n jist hangs his head. Pa treats Ederd bad, real ugly. Lack he ain't got a lick o' sense uv his own.

"De way Paw sits out dare in de fields on dat ol stump and orders dem girls to work, no matter how hot tis, or even if dey are sick makes no difference. Jist a sitting dare wid his legs crossed, shaking dat ol long switch at em if dey slows down. I've had de urge to shoot im manys de times. He wuz a doin dat by de time Ella was big nough to chop cotton."

Clyde had a few choice words to add to the conversation. "I ain't got no Paw to be a beating on me, but I don't like staying on dat farm of r's neither. Working from daylight 'til dark every day ain't what I want to do all my life. We're stuck way out dare, so fur frum anythang. All we got is each other. Yeah, I'm going to see what dis old world has to offer me by joining the man's army."

When they neared South West Creek, the water had risen and was halfway up the road, toward the Bullard farm. They stopped in to speak to the Bullards. Everybody knew everybody else in the area from Jacksonville to Cypress Creek, so they were not strangers to the Bullard family. They explained where they were headed. Then Clyde spoke up, "I reckin' we'll have to end our walk right cheer and try another day."

Mrs. Bullard had dinner ready to put on the table and she invited the boys to sit down and eat with them. They were more than glad to accommodate her.

During the meal, Mr. Bullard suggested that if they wanted to go on with their journey bad enough, there was a way. "Both you boys swim?"

Jacob and Clyde looked across the table straight at the man asking the question, with their mouths gaped open, wondering what he was speaking about. "Uh-huh, yessir," came the reply from both of them at the same time.

"If ya want to get on with yore being a soldier, go out yonder to the wash shelter and get one of them big old wash tubs. Take it along with ya to the edge of the water. Strip yoreselves of yore clothes, put the clothes in the tub and pull it along as ya swim across the creek. Now boys, it's a right good ways to swim across with the water up so high and running so fast Tell ya the truth, it's about the highest I've ever seen it. If ya think you can make it across, jist leave the tub over there on tuther side and I can get it when the water goes down."

Both the boys were hunched over their plates while they listened. Jacob sorta pointed his fork at the man and uttered, "Sir, I appreciate de offer. I thank we kin make it across."

When they reached the water, each boy pulled their clothes off, folded them and placed them in the tub. Stark raving naked, they entered the water. It was like ice when they waded in. By the time they got to water deep enough to swim, every thing they had was shriveled up to mere goose bumps.

They entered the edge of town just before darkness took over. They had enough money between them to buy their supper at the cafe, pay for a hotel room and get breakfast the next morning. With a few white lies and bigger fibs concerning their ages, they were soldiers before mid-day. Fort Monroe, Virginia, welcomed them as military men.

In May, a week before Mother's Day, the mailman left a card in the mailbox for Clarry. It was a Mother's Day card from Jacob and the first news they had had from him. The local YMCA, near Fort Monroe had furnished the cards for the soldiers to send home to their mothers.

The war ended before the year was up. Jacob and Clyde remained in the service.

Ederd had borrowed money back the first part of the year to purchase fertilizer and seeds. His father had sectioned off a few acres of the cleared land for him to put in a money crop of his own. After all, he was twenty years old. In the fall when he paid the money back, he realized farming was going to be a hard life, but that was the only way he knew how to survive.

The day after Christmas, Clarry took sick. She ran a high fever and was sick to her stomach. She had the diarrhea and was so weak she could barely get around.

Jake walked in the bedroom where she was trying her best to fluff up the feather tick mattress, so she could finish changing the sheets on the bed. The sheets smelled awful, caused by her high fever and her lying in the bed so much.

"Don't ya think it's time ya git outta dat bed and git to work round here?" he barked at her.

She did not have the energy to respond. When she returned from the backside of the bed to the front near where he stood, he slapped her across the right side of her head. She slumped forward across the mattress.

"Old woman, you answer me when I speak to you!" He snatched her up from the bed and backhanded her several times.

When he released her, she fell back on the bed. He turned and left the room.

She never left the bed again. She died that night in her sleep on January 23, 1919. She too was buried in the Swinson Graveyard.

She left behind a bewildered man with a house full of children. The baby girl Roxie was seven years old. Several of the girls were old enough to take over the household duties, but the mother was sorely missed.

Jake continued his trips to Haws Run. His need for Emma Jenkins never seemed to cease. She had married a commercial fisherman a couple of months after Jake and Clarry had married, neither of their marriage seemed to interfere with their meetings. They had a signal worked out to let Jake know if the coast was clear when he arrived near her house. There were weeks at a time when her husband was away on a fishing trip. All her children, no telling how many of them belonged to Jake, were of school age and gone a big part of the day. If there was a single towel hanging on the clothesline, Jake brazenly rode right on up to the house. If the towel was not there, he turned his mount around and returned home.

In May of that year, Jesse and Listy Ann deeded the nine acres of land that the house and surrounding buildings were erected on, over to Jake. He owned all the property, free and clear. It felt good to have ownership of his holdings.

Ederd had reached an age where he did a little courting of the young girls in the outlaying areas of his community.

In November, Jake was out near the horse lot and Ederd and Steve were raking the last of the hay from the ground pea field. Ederd glanced up to see a young colored man walking across the field toward them. He had emerged from the woods behind the field, east of the farm.

When he neared the two raking hay, he tugged at his felt hat and drug it off his head across his chest. "Good mornin', sirs." As soon as he spoke, he tipped his head forward and kept his eyes on the ground.

"Mornin' to ya, too," Ederd came back with the response. "How ya doin' today?"

"No good sir, I'm here lookin' fer work. Me and my madam are neigh on to starvation. Do ya reckin' ya kin put me to work for a few hours?"

"Go on up yander to where ya see pa, dare close to the barn. Talk to him. Dare's plenty of work round here."

The man turned to leave, then turned around and spoke softly. "I'm Jonas Fisher, 'n Lula, she be my wife." He left while placing his hat back on his head.

Jonas was hired that day. At quitting time, Jake loaded him up with meal, sugar, a slab of meat from the smoke house, collards from the garden, some tobacco for smoking and one pint of whiskey. It would take Jonas days to work off the bill. Before he left, Jake poured him a glass of cider. Twenty cents was added to the bill. "Jonas, bring yore wife on oer here wid ja when ya come tomorrow. There's plenty of work fer her up here around de house. Dem girls will be glad to have her wid 'em."

On Jake's next trip to town, he purchased his first ledger for keeping records of his doings there on the land. The ledger cost him seventy-five cents.

Ransom Rogers was a known alcoholic. He was referred to as the local drunk. His wife had died and he had lost everything he owned. Jake's brother, Tom, who had married Ransom' oldest daughter, Fannie Bell, erected a one room cabin on his property across the creek from his cleared acres. He moved Ransom and the seven children into the cabin. Ransom's older children tended a small garden near the cabin. Ransom helped some during his sober days. Every cent he could get his hands on, he bought moonshine with it, and laid about drunken most of the time.

It was brought to the attention of the community that those Rogers children were starving. Several men of the neighborhood went over and literally chose what child or children they wanted to take home with them, to become part of their own family, Jake being one of those men, he decided on a sixteen-year-old girl, Sina Viola, and a nine-year-old boy, Major. The remaining children were scattered out around the community. Ransom sat in his straight chair, facing the flames in the fireplace. He never said a word to any one of them. He was too drunk to know what was going on.

The reason behind Jake's choice of the children was that he had children about the same ages of Sina and Major. Besides, the more children on the place, the more work could be accomplished in a day's time.

Vinnie was three months younger than Sina, called Sinnie. They bonded and became close friends. There were three to four children in each bed with the boys in one room and the girls in another. Some of the beds quite crowded, since teenagers tend to get larger as they grow. Sinnie and Major fit right into the family within the month, as if they had been born there. It was a welcome feeling to have food in their stomachs on a regular basis.

Jake had made it a habit to wander on over to his father's or brother's property when he needed firewood. "I'll jist let mine grow a few more years 'fore I start cutting on my land." He intended to say the words silently, so neither Ederd nor Steve would hear what he said.

"What's dat ya say, pa?" Steve asked as he removed the crosscut saw from the cart.

"None of ya dammed business. Jist git to work, ya and Ederd, at cuttin' that nice oak tree right o'er dare." He motioned to the tree he intended for them to cut down. "I'll gather literd while you two saw de tree down."

As the boys pulled the saw back and forth, they kept their eye on their father. When he was out of earshot Ederd said, "Steve, I don't feel lack dis is proper. Cuttin' another man's trees down, e'en dough dey are GrandPaw's. Do you?"

Steve agreed with his older brother. He was a mere lad of thirteen years old, with nothing to do but follow his father's command. Even though Ederd was much older and was considered an adult, he too dared not balk against his father, even though he knew it was wrong. The trees were cut and hauled out of the woods along with the literd. The procedure had gone on for several years.

In the spring of 1919, while the father and two sons were in the woods cutting illegally, Steve located a big patch of wild huckleberry bushes. "Ederd, I'm coming back out cheer and pick 'em. They oughta be ripe in bout a week, don't cha thank?"

"I reckin' so."

On the next Saturday, Jake sent Steve over to his father's house on an errand. When the boy arrived at his grandfather's, he saw that one of his cousins, Walter, a boy about his own age, sat on the porch.

"Hey, Walter." He ambled on over and hitched one leg up on the edge of the porch, allowing the other leg to dangle freely above the ground.

"What chu doin oer here dis mornin' so early?" Walter asked.

"Paw sent me oer here to see if GrandPaw is going to town any time today. How bout chu? What chu doin here?"

"I stayed de night. Uncle Jesse n Aunt Mare Lise is gone visiting her mammy and won't be back til sometime dis evening. Grandmaw's feelin poorly and I stayed around so's GrandPaw could tend to things outside."

They continued to talk back and forth for a while, waiting for Jesse to return to the house.

Neither boy noticed as the grandfather walked toward them. "Hey Walter, you goin' hume today?" Steven asked.

"Yeah."

"Come on oer to my house, on yer way hume. I know where dare's a great big old patch of huckleberries."

All the children in the area likes the huckleberries that grew wild in the nearby woods, and went hunting them each spring.

"Whur ya say dem berries are?"

"Right out dare in de woods. Jist across the fence a ways. I spotted em, tuther day when me, Ederd and Paw were cutting wood." He pointed in the direction the berries patch stood.

Jesse had stopped to listen to the conversation between the boys and his ears perked up when he heard where the patch was. He cleared his throat to let them know he was near. "Mornin' Steve. How you doing this great day?"

"Jist fine GrandPaw." He jumped off the porch and related to his elder what he had been sent to do.

"No. I got no plans to travel anywhere this day." He turned to Walter and spoke again, "Son, you can go on home anytime now. I'll be around for a while. I appreciate you helping me out."

The boys left together. The grandfather heard Steve comment to Walter as they were leaving, "Come on, we kin go git dem berries right now."

Jesse went in the house and got Listy Ann situated out on the porch with a quilt draped over the arm of the rocker. "You sit out here for a while in the sunshine. You'll be all right until I return. I need to walk across the field yonder."

By the time he caught sight of the boys, they were climbing the rail fence. He had suspected that Jake was up to one of his evil deeds again as soon as he heard what Steve had said to Walter. He stayed far enough behind the boys that they never knew he was about.

He stayed out of sight until the boys left the berry patch. Walter turned right and Steve turned left when they reached the one lane road that spanned the area from Jake's farm to that of John's. "Bye Steve."

"Bye Walter, see ya 'round."

Jesse walked the woods for a good long time. Nearly every hard wood tree in about ten acres of land had been cut down and hauled off. He was so angry that he could have beheaded Jake. He knew he couldn't do anything about it at the time. He needed to return to the house and Listy Ann. He would take care of the situation on the upcoming Monday morning. Jesse and his family would be back then to be with Listy Ann.

When Jesse reprimanded Jake on the following Monday, Jake denied every word of what his father spoke. "Who de hell filled ya head with sich nonsense? Dat's what I'd lack to know. If yore trees are missin', don't look at me. I ain't cut a damn one uv em," he looked his father straight in the eye while he made the statement.

Jesse figured he'd not let Jake know where he had heard who had cut his trees. In all truth, no one had told him. He knew that Jake would half kill Steve if he learned he was the one that had been overheard.

"Let me warn you Jake, you are going to suffer one of these days if you continue to go on the way you have done for these past years. No one man can do all the ugly, evil deeds you have, and get away with it. I'll tell you another thing. I expect full payment for the trees that you've already made use of." He turned and left the barnyard, where they had been talking.

"Ederd! Steve! Boys come on up here to the yard." Jake had waited until his father was out of sight before he walked up to the house and called his sons.

When they reached the edge of the yard, they were joking and carrying on in a happy mood. "Which one of you youngin's told GrandPaw I was cutting firewood on his land?"

Both of them were aghast. They were shaking their heads from side to side. "I didn't, Paw. I knowed what you'd do to me if I did," Ederd spoke up first. It bothered him that he was treated as a small child.

"Me neither Paw. I wouldn't've done it." In all honesty, Steve spoke the truth. Only after he had said his piece did he recall what he had said to Walter. No way was he going to correct what he had said to his pa. He knew the sting of the whip and the pain of his Paw's hand.

"Well, go on back to yore business. Keep yore mouth shet about where I git my wood, ya hear me boys? Ain't neither one of ya got sense enough to keep yore own tails clean."

"Yes sir."

"Yes sir."

Ederd had begun to resent the way Jake spoke to him and humiliated him around his younger brothers and sisters. Now that Sina and Major were living with them, it seemed to bother him more as time passed.

"One o dese days Steve, I'm liable to crawl that old man and show him jist how much sense I got. Ain't no need fer a man to be so mean and hateful. I don't know why I even bother to love him a tall."

Jake continued to cut his wood from his father's property. He changed the location for the cutting and thought he'd get by with it.

Jesse started taking walks around the wooded area of his property, staying out of sight of Jake's farm. He knew what the walks were for, and one day the walks paid off. As he neared a section of his woods located on the northwest of Jake's land, he heard the low murmur of voices. He crept up close enough to see with his own eyes what was taking place. He left the scene without letting the culprits know they had been caught in the criminal act.

Jesse left his farm bright and early the next morning. "I don't know exactly when I'll be back here to the house. Take care of your maw. Make sure to get her out in the sunshine as early as you can. I'm headed over to Jacksonville to Jarman's stables. I want to see about purchasing another team of mules." He failed to mention that he was aiming to pay a visit to the sheriff also.

An hour after the noon hour, Jesse along with Sheriff Walton, pulled up in Jake's farmhouse yard. He knew the habits of most the farmers around, and timed his arrival to fit his needs. Jake was laying on the edge of the porch, with his head bent up against the post dozing. Ederd and Steve were out in the barn waiting to go back to the fields to work, as soon as their father got up from his rest period. The women folk were in the kitchen, taking care of the dinner dishes. The younger children were scattered about the yard playing.

The racket from the horses entering the yard roused Jake from his drowsing. Ederd and Steve walked up the path behind the horses.

"Jake, get up. The sheriff is here to help me take care of a few things."

"Paw, what-de-hell do ya mean? Bringing de sheriff up here lack dis?" He swung his leg off the porch and stood in the yard.

"Son, I warned you to stay off my property when cutting your wood. Maybe you'll listen to the man here," he motioned toward the sheriff, with his thumb.

The entire family had gathered around to see what the commotion was all about.

"Let's walk out yonder to the barn. No need to air our business here in front of all these youngin's," Jesse said.

After the talk, Jake agreed to pay the seventy-five dollars he owed his father for the wood taken illegally. The sheriff left after a stern warning to Jake. "You're a lucky man that your father is letting you get by without some time in jail. A crime is a crime, no matter who you commit it against."

Jake handed the seventy-five dollars to Jesse before he left the yard. There went every cent of profit he had made from the sale of his pigs and hay. He never said one word to his father as he rode out of the yard. Jake was so mad he could have bit a nail in half. Every family member stayed clear of him for the rest of the day.

He went in the house and cleaned himself up a bit. He quietly walked to the barn, hitched up the horse and rode away without a word to anyone. He was on his way to Haws Run and his Emma.

In the next week's mail delivery, Jake received a letter from the sheriff's office. When he opened the envelope, he found a receipt for the money he had paid his father, along with a warning. It read as follows:

Received of J.E. Swinson in full of all accounts to date this the 17th day of May 1919. I also forbid you and your boys from trespassing, chopping or hacking on any part of my land now henceforth and forever.

Jesse Swinson

The message was notarized. Jake put a stop to his wandering on other people's property to cut his fire wood, from that day forward.

A roving photographer showed up on the farm one nice summer day. Not a one of the children had ever had a picture taken of themselves. Every job of work on the farm came to a stand still when they learned who the photographer was and what he was there for. It took nigh on to an hour for each youngin' to be washed up and into their Sunday-best clothes. The photographer took an individual shot of each off spring, the father, and one of the entire family grouped together. It took nearly two months for the pictures to arrive in the mail to the farm.

In October, shortly after school got started, the building caught fire from a roaring blaze in the small heater. The pressure from the heat blew the flu away from the back of the heater. Escaping flames reached the wall and ignited the dry boards. It was a rather cold morning   All of the students, and Alonzo, escaped with no harm to any of them. The building burned to the ground. Every piece of school supplies went up in the flames.

There was no school for the 1919-1920 term. Plans were drawn up to build a new school, to be called the Garganus School House. The reason behind the name was that Nicklus Garganus donated the land for the site. The building was much larger than the old school, with two rooms, one of the rooms stood empty because there were not enough pupils to fill both rooms. The extra room was used for storage. A large front porch, that was three forth the length of the building, adorned the front of the school. Two outside toilets were constructed behind the main structure, one for males and one for females. A pitcher-type water pump, with a pump bench, stood out in front to the right of the front door.

By the time school started for the 1920-1921 fall term, everything was in place for classes to begin. Alonzo Hewitt continued to teach until Miss Peanie Bryant was secured for the teacher's position. She boarded with Nicklus Garganus and his family. Parents were responsible for the purchase of all books and writing supplies for their children.

Jake went to town one day in November for the sole purpose of paying his taxes. On his way home, he swung by the Simon James farm and bought twenty-five cents worth of mutton. He had a taste for the meat, but not a one of his family cared for it. "Eat it anyhow," was the order handed to everyone at the table. "If taxes keep rising, ya liable to haft to eat more of what cha don't like. I jist paid $21.14 fer last year's taxes, this very day. So all uv ya, shet up n eat."

Chapter Fifteen

A common custom for most of the Swinson brothers was to set up and run a liquor still. Two of the brothers would go together and run the still one year and the next year two other brothers took over. The rotation kept going until the law over took them and put a kink in that means of making money for a while.

In 1921, it was Jake and Monty's year. There were plenty of wooded areas for them to use to set up the still. The location they chose was behind Monty's field. The trees grew thick all around the one spot they chose. Smack dab in the middle of the tree growth, was a good-sized clearing with only one large oak tree standing all by itself. The limbs grew out in all directions from the trunk providing a canopy to shield them from the sun.

"Monty, this shine's gonna be ready in a couple a weeks now. I went o'er to town last week n bought de jars to run if off in. Looks lack it's gonna be a hundred proof likker. We oughta make enough profit to pay off all our debts in the fall."

"Yeah, and I got two bootleggers lined up to transport dat what we don't sell right outta our houses. I agree, we're gonna do all right," Monty responded. They could almost feel the money in their hands. Setting up a still cost quite a bit of money, and the hours of labor, it took to keep it going until the moonshine whiskey was ripe.

Three days before they were to finish with their product, the revenuers showed up surrounding the still. Both Jake and Monty were at the still at the time. They had set down for a few moments of rest. Jake sat on the ground, with his back leaned against the oak tree trunk. Monty was in a straight chair that had been brought to the site for resting in. They were in the midst of a hardy conversation that included loud laughter.

They never heard a sound until, "Stand up with your hands in the air. This is a raid on this illegal still." The command came from one of the federal men.

Monty turned at the sound and his chair spilled him to the ground. Jake's neck stiffened and stretched as he looked around to see where the voice had come from. Both men stood up and lifted their hands skyward.

The many years that moonshine had been brewed and sold out of the Swinson woods, this was the first visit from the government. Oh, they all knew it was illegal to make the liquor. Rules of the law had not prevented them from doing many things that they were guilty of. The only reason Jake and Monty had been caught was someone had gone to the law and reported where the still was and who was operating it.

"I'll find out who brought dese feds down on our necks," Jake mumbled to Monty.

Five agents emerged from the woods with their weapons aimed at the brothers. "Don't shoot us. We'll give ya no trouble," Jake offered up his plea.

"We've got no plans to harm you. Just stand quiet while we get the cuffs on you."

As soon as both men were cuffed, the agents put their weapons away. Two of them entered the surrounding woods and returned with sledgehammers, axes and other wrecking equipment.

Monty and Jake stood and watched as every piece of the still was smashed and destroyed. Even the new jars were shattered. The odor alone was enough to give a person a high from the fumes. All the precious liquid ran off like a heavy rain shower had passed over. Small puddles formed in several low places. The brothers watched and felt like they could cry if only grown men were allowed to cry.

"Monty, this is my last try at making whiskey. But I aim to fix the son-of-a-bitch who turned us in," he no more than whispered. He had no idea what was coming up after the agents finished with their destruction of the still.

"Mr. Swinson," the agent looked from Jake to Monty, "Mr. Swinson."

"How'd ya know our names? Who told ya how to git here?" Jake demanded.

"We have ways of learning things," was all the response he got.

"Now, if you men promise to stand here and let me talk to you, I'll take the cuffs off. Let me warn you, you will be shot if you try to get away."

The brothers looked over to the edge of the woods and noticed three guns pointed at them from different locations. "I don't think I'll be tryin' to make a git away," Jake spoke as the agent removed their cuffs.

"Me neither," Monty came back.

"You fellas should have known you'd get caught in the act sooner or later," Robert, the agent, remarked.

They walked over to where there were seats and all three men took a seat. Robert took out his pad and pencil and started writing.

He spoke as he wrote. "You'll be getting a notice in the mail as to when your court trial will be held. If you fail to show up, the sheriff will be coming to get you. My advice to you is to be there on the date assigned for the trial, and to being on time is of the utmost importance."

After the agents left, Jake and Monty stood around under the tree for a while pondering on what to do next.

"Hell, ain't no use doing a damn thing more out cheer," Monty remarked. They left in different directions, headed for their homes.

When R.G. Yopp delivered the guano that spring, the total cost was $40.00. Jake paid for it in full, with six head of cattle.

Jake took time out of his routine to practice letter writing. The lessons he had gotten from his mother and the Angola schoolteacher, had not included that of writing personal letters. There was a form used that began each letter that went like, "My dear beloved -----, I will drop you a few lines, to let you hear from us. These few lines leave us all about as usual. Truly hope you all the same." Each letter received by a person in the area, and each letter mailed from the area, started with the same greeting. The letter closed with, "From your beloved ...."

One hot day during the early part of June, Vinnie was chopping stove wood. The men folk had hauled the cut logs onto the chip pile and then sawed them into one and a half foot long sections. Vinnie had stood one of the sections on end and had split one section off. She had raised the axe to make her next lick down when Steven ran up, poked his bare foot on top of the block of wood, and said in a rapid voice, "Vinnie, cut my big toe off." Down came the axe. It struck the boy's toe exactly where it joined his foot. The toe snapped off and rolled out on the chip pile. Vinnie could not believe what had just taken place. There was no way she could have halted the thrust of the axe in time to stop it.

Steven just stood there with his mouth gaped open, his foot still resting on top of the block of wood. At the time, he felt no pain. As soon as he realized his toe was off his foot, he let out a scream that was ear piercing. Loud enough, that it alerted every one on the place that something was amiss.

Jake was away for the day so those at the house knew they had to take care of it themselves. Rosie was in the kitchen ironing clothes. Bertha and Sinnie were under the wash shelter working at the dirty clothes.

"Bertha, bring me one of em wet shirts, right now," Vinnie holler out.

When Bertha reached her with the shirt, she wrapped it around the badly bleeding place where the toe had been. It kept bleeding so much that it scared all the girls.

Ederd and Major had arrived at the house by then. When Ederd learned what was going on, he went into action. He knew that Rosie had been in the kitchen ironing. "Rosie go git me one a dem hot irons, right off de stove."

He laid the crying, screaming Steve on his back on the ground. "You girls hold dese legs and arms down, I mean hold em down good 'n tight. Major you help me hold dis foot missin' a toe."

When Rosie came with the hot iron, she handed it to Ederd so he could grab on to it with the holding rag to prevent his hand from burning. "Rosie you set on his stomach." He spoke to Steve, "Now Steve you hush up dat racket. I'm gonna seal off yore foot wid dis hot iron. Den you'll have reason to yell all ya want to."

It was an awful stench when the iron touched the raw flesh. Steve relaxed and was unconscious. When he roused up, his entire foot was bandaged. The pain had subsided to a point he could stand it without crying.

When Jake returned home and heard what had taken place in his absences, he, for once in his life, handled it as a father should.

Later on, in the month of June, Ransom Rogers worked for Jake there on the farm for 28 days. He earned one dollar a day for twenty-seven of the days, less for the half day. His total for the days worked, was $27.50. Ransom's drinking was a very real problem for the man.

In July, Jonas Fisher ditched forty-two yards, extending the existing ditch, for the total sum of one dollar. He removed one stump for forty cents and a few other small jobs for twenty cents.

In July, Major Rochelle worked on the farm for Jake. He made one dollar a day also, for seven days. Then in August, he worked for eight days. Jake paid him with meat, meal, corn, wool, mutton, dried beef and salted down fish.

On July 22, 1922, Ederd took his GrandPaw Jesse in to town so he could apply for the Veteran's pension. The application was approved on August 8 that same year. Jesse had allowed his white-gray beard to grow until it reached half way down to his waistline. He wore his blue chambray, long sleeved homemade shirts, whether it was Sunday or Thursday.

The feud between Jake and Alonzo continued and grew through the years. Nothing serious took place between the two men other than verbal aggravation. When Alonzo married Hattie, she sided with her husband and was more aggressive toward Jake than Alonzo ever was, with her actions and words.

Before Alonzo came to the area, the Swinsons and Pierces had cut out a road caddy-cornered across the back portion of the land that Hewitt bought. The road was wide enough to accommodate a mule and cart. A drainage ditch had been dug out on either side of the road, so the water would drain off when the rains fell. Both the Swinsons and Pierces continued to use the road for years after they were told to cease crossing the Hewitt property by order of Hattie.

One fine weathered, March morning, Jake trotted his horse along the road on his way to the Pierce's and low and behold, the road was blocked with freshly cut trees from one ditch to the other. He politely dismounted and dragged enough of the trees away to continue his journey.

When he made his return trip home, he found an old cart in the space where he had removed the trees. He simply pulled more trees out of his way and went on home.

The annoying of each other continued for nearly a month. Finally, Alonzo dug a ditch across the road, right along beside the different pieces of trash that had built up, in order to stop traffic from traveling the road.

It made no matter to Jake. He was on his horse the day the big trouble started. When he reined up the horse and dismounted, Hattie emerged from the woods. "Damn your hide Jake Swinson, I will stop you frum trespassing on my property one way or tuther. Do you hear me?"

"Woman, jist git de hell outta my way and I'll be on my way." He remounted his horse. The horse pranced around a bit before Jake pulled on the reins to let the horse know to jump the ditch so horse and rider could travel along the edge of the woods, through the marshy area of land along beside the road. At the same time that Jake gave the order to the horse to jump the ditch, Hattie grabbed the bottom of the bridle.

"You ain't goin' no where Mr. Big Shot."

She was so angry she was in a shake. Jake was also good and mad. He pulled back on the reins to cause the horse to rear backward. Hattie held fast and was lifted from the ground. Jake turned the horse around and around in the road. Still Hattie held on. "Stop dis animal rat now, Jake Swinson."

Jake stopped the horse and got off. He held the rope ends in his right hand. "If ya don't let loose of dat bridle, I'm gonna lash de ends of deese ropes across yore back. Woman, ya best heed my words."

She released the bridle because her hands were in a steady ache. She propped both hands on her hips and uttered from between her clenched teeth, "You are the sorriest excuse fer a man dat wuz ever borned. You think you can keep on gitting away wid yore hateful and mean ways in dis community. Well sir, let me tell ya a thang or two. Everybody knows about the evil deeds ya commit. Me being a woman, I can't do to ya what ya need done to ya." She dropped her hands to her sides and her shoulders slumped.

They were standing about three to four feet apart from each other. Jake glared at her as he made a motion to get back up on the horse. Hattie grabbed at his shirtsleeve and snagged just enough of the material to hold on to. "You ain't going no whur 'til we settle dis thang, right cheer and now."

Jake yanked backwards with his arm and she lost her grip on his sleeve. When she tried to get another hold on him, he drew back his hand and slapped her full across her left cheek. It was a hard slap, with enough power behind it to have broken her jaw. She fell to the ground.

She got right back up, madder than a wet setting hen. She brushed dirt from her dress skirt all the way down the length of it, to the ground. When she straightened up, she looked him straight in the eye. With her finger shaking directly at his face, she said, in a cool, calm, collected manner, "Jake Swinson, ya'll regret dis day. Yo'll not be a putting ya hand on me e'er again. Do ya understand exactly what I'm a saying to ya?"

Jake snorted as he mounted the horse. "Jist what do ya think ya can do bout anythang I do? Dat husband a your'n ain't worth two terds being rolled by a tumblebug. Dis road was here long afore you ever set foot back here in deese dam woods. Ain't you nor nobody else gonna stop me frum a usin' it. Hear me good old woman." He looked down his nose at her as he pulled on the reins. The horse galloped off at a fast rate, slinging clods of dirt all over her clothes from the hooves of the horse.   He rode right on past the road that led to his farm and continued over to Haws Run, to make a visit with his Emma.

The Sheriff showed up at Jake's farm Wednesday of the next week. "Mr. Swinson, Hattie Hewitt has sworn out a warrant against you. It seems she is very displeased with some of your actions." He handed Jake the papers stating the date for the trial to be held in the morning of that date. "You'd better be there around nine o'clock. The Judge don't appreciate late arrivals. Court starts at 10 o'clock."

Jake looked down at the papers in his hand. "Now Sheriff, I'm tared a wasting my time running oer yander to dat court house every damn time I turn around. Dat woman ain't nothing but trouble all de way round. Jist tell me, will ya? How can I git outta dis mess without goin' to court oer it. I got too much work here on dis land to be foolin' around, wastein time sitting in a court room."

"There's no way to get out of the fix you've got yourself in this time, sir," the Sheriff faltered a bit before he used the title of respect to Jake. He felt as if the man did not deserve the honor. He knew Jake's record and wondered why the man was not in prison somewhere serving time. He climbed up on his horse and turned to leave, "You'd better be in the court house on time Mr. Swinson. I'd hate to have to come back out here and get you."

On the day of the trial, Jake sat in the courtroom as ordered. He looked over and glared at Hattie and Alonzo. The trial started and the Judge listened to each side of the case. When the defendant and plaintiff were seated in their respective places, the Judge asked. "Jake Swinson, did you slap the plaintiff, Hattie Hewitt?"

"No sir, Your Honor. I never touched de woman."

"Hattie Hewitt, do you have any witnesses to stand up for you?"

"No sir. I do have dis here mark on my face where he hit me dough. The swelling's all gone down now. It's still mighty big sore. Hurts ever time I open my mouth or chew my food."

"Mrs. Hewitt, tell me again exactly what happened. Don't leave out a single thing. Do you think you can do that?"

She went through the entire events of the morning that Jake had struck her. She was tired and aggravated. It seemed to her that the Judge was trying to get her mad or angry or something. She didn't exactly know what he was up to. She had lived so long with Alonzo that she had taken up some of his traits of being slow and responding to a situation in a careful manner.

"I'll ask you again Mrs. Hewitt, where were you standing and where was Mr. Swinson standing when he slapped you?"

"Sir, he was in one ditch and I was in the other one. Jist lack I told you afore."

The Judge rubbed his chin with his cupped hand and rolled his eyes. "Ma'am, how wide is that ditch?"

Her nerves were beginning to react in a way she did not appreciate. "It's wide as any other road out dare in the neighborhood. Why you wanna know how wide de road is?"

"Ma'am, I ask the questions here, you answer."

"Yes'ir."

The Judge leaned back in his chair and quickly brought himself upright again. "Hattie Hewitt, tell me again what happened on the morning Jake Swinson slapped you."

"Dare ain't nothin' else I can tell ya. I done told ja three times dat what went on."

"Just tell me one more time. Don't leave anything out. Try to remember everything as it happened."

When she finished, the Judge looked at her and asked, "So, is he the man with the long arm?"

Hattie looked at him in wonderment. She didn't really know what he meant. After a few moments it dawned on her, what she had done, and done it three times.

"The man known as Jake Swinson could not have laid a hand on you, Hattie Hewitt, if you were in one ditch and he was in the other one. I asked you three different times to tell me exactly what happened. You told me the same story each time."

The Judge looked over at Jake. "You may be guilty of the charge brought against you here today. I'm declaring you innocent of that charge based on what Mrs. Hewitt testified, under oath, to me here this day." He hung his head for a moment or two before he spoke again. "Mr. Swinson, what will it take to compensate the loss of your days work to attend court here in town this day?"

Jake sat up straight in his seat and thought for a few minutes before he spoke. The expression on his face was that of another accomplishment well handled. "Well sir, I think I'd be fully satisfied if you'd award me de tract of land de road in question is located on."

"Mrs. Hewitt I order you to turn the full acreage of that tract of land over to Jake Swinson, this day." He banged his gavel firmly on the tabletop before him. "Case closed."

The tract of land contained about 50 acres. All wooded, filled with prime timber trees. Jake left the town of Jacksonville a satisfied man, proud of himself. He stretched tall while he walked to his horse, where his plans were to head to Haws Run.

Jake and Ederd had put in their first crop of tobacco that year and since it was new to them, their acreage was not too large. "Son let's try it this one year, and see how we make out in the fall, when we sell it." Cotton was still their main money crop. There was a lot of hard tedious work associated with the raising of cotton.

The work put out to get a crop of tobacco ready for market was not an easy task, but seemed to the father and son that it was much easier than raising cotton. About 1 August, they took their first load of prepared tobacco to the Brick Warehouse in Wallace, NC. They sold 216 pounds for $31.92, less $1.64 house fees. Both men were pleased with the money they received. Ederd was allowed to keep 1/4 of the profits.

The court trial for Jake and Monty was held September 7, for their operation of the illegal whiskey still. Both men were found guilty. They were very lucky that all they had to do was pay the court cost. Monty paid $20.03, while Jake's part was $24.86. They had no choice as whether to pay or not. If they failed to pay, they would be hauled off and slapped in jail.

Jake was so pleased with the outcome of the trial, that on his way home he decided to stop off in Haws Run. It seemed as if Emma was the answer for him, whether he was happy, angry, or out of sorts for any reason. Since each brother had rode their own horses to town, Jake told Monty to go on home. He would see him on the next day.

The white towel flapped in the wind as he arrived on the edge of the field. He bravely rode on up to the house, and dismounted. Children were at different locations in the field and about the yard.

The children had become accustomed to seeing Jake on the place at any given time of the day, and sometimes at night. Not a one of them paid him a bit of mind. Those that were old enough knew the reason behind his frequent visits to their home, who he came to see, and for what reason.

Emma sat on the porch. She had a basket of old clay bank field peas on her lap. She dozed from the tedious work at hand. Jake startled her when he spoke, "Emma gal! Wake up my woman. I'm in need of ya in a bad way dis day." He climbed the few steps it took for him to get up on the porch. He sat down in the chair that was empty beside her. He reached over and covered her tiny fist with his tanned, callused hand. He looked her in the eye and asked, "Woman, what's de matter wid you? Why's yore hand clinched up in a fist lack dat?"

She withdrew her hand from his and uttered softly, "I'm with child agin. It's yore'n for shore dis time. Jake, there'll be hell to pay when de old man gits back frum de river. Now dat I'm showin', I can't keep it frum him no longer."

"Damnation Emma. How'd ya let dat happen? I was a thinking ya had passed de age to have any more youngin's."

"Well now, Jake, I thought dat a way for shore, too. I ain't seen no monthly signs for nigh on to two years. This 'un simply snuck up on me or else I wouldn't've let it happen."

"Well tell me dis, how's ya man gonna know now, anymore dan he has through all dese past years, which child around here is his and which is mine? Jist answer me dat woman?" Jake demanded.

Emma placed the basket of peas on the porch floor and arose to a full standing position. "Some men folks loose dare ability to be wid a woman in de way it takes to make a baby. My man has been in de fix lack dat for nigh on to five years now. I'm afeered for my life when he does returns. He's due back in here in bout a week frum now."

"Lord God a mighty, woman. Does he know dat chu been my woman right along wid being his wife? Since fore you married him?"

"No Jake, I don't think he's ever suspected a thang, though he has mentioned at times the different favors amongst our youngin's. I'd jist say to em dat the child looked lack some o my kinfolk frum way back. It seemed to satisfy his curiosity. You n him are colored up bout de same way, wid the same color hair an all."

Jake knew the man they were discussing. He knew him well. He had even bought fish from the man, many a time. He also knew that he was a big, robust man. He had arms to be the envy of many a man from the years and years of pulling and tugging on nets while working his trade out on the ocean and in the river. Jake knew that he did not want to have a confrontation with the man. He was not a small statured species of a man, but he was no match for the likes of Emma's husband.

He then arose from the chair and walked to the far end of the porch. "Well now woman, what are we gonna do bout dis situation? Ya know as well as I do, dat we cain't stop what's goin' on twixt you and me. It's gone on too long."

"Jake, I wont chu to leave dis place and ne'er git yourself o'er here agin. I've lived a life o lies way too long. I kin, and will gone on fer de rest of my life widout de joy you've brung to me dese past years," she looked him straight in the eyes as she spoke. She had lifted up the tail of her apron to wipe the tears from her cheeks as she continued, "You kin go on wid yore life jist lack me. Leave me now Jake, ne'er to return."

"Now woman, ya don't know what yore talkin' about. If dat old man of your'n ain't figgered out anythang through all dese years, he ain't a gonna figger out nothing now. I'll lay low fer a week or so, if it'll make you rest more easier."

"Jist go on now Jake and git offa dis place. You ain't a hearing a word I'm a saying to ya. I'm dreading my man's gittin' home. I don't need to have de worry of ya, showin' up here anymore. Though I haf to say, it's been good Jake, and I have appreciated de money you've handed my way."

Jake walked slowly down the steps and just before he mounted his horse, he turned and raised his hand in a farewell salute, "Don't cha worry woman. I'll be back one a dese days." He rode off with a smug smile across his face.

Just as Emma had predicted, her husband got home exactly one week from the day Jake had rode off with that smirk shown on his face. The husband spoke politely to Emma when he entered the house. She could sense that something was different than when he usually arrived at home from a long working job on the water. He sent the children, those that were inside the house, out into the yard.

"I need to talk o'er a thing er two widge yore mammie."

Emma stood by the cook stove. Her nerves were ready to explode. "Emma," the husband barked her name out.

She turned to face him. "Yes?" She held the big, wooden stirring spoon in her right hand.

"I've knowed for some time now, what chu've been up to. I jist didn't know who de scandral was. Yes, I know yore wid child agin. And I know as good as you do dat it ain't mine." He walked around the table to stand nearer to her.

"I hired me a man to stand watch o'er you and dis here place, oh, bout three months past. Afore I come on home yesditty I rode on o'er to his place. He filled me in on how many time yore other man has called, and a good description of what he looks lack. Now, wife o mine, all I need frum you is his name." He stood very close to her.

Emma's eyes were staring down at the floor. She twisted the spoon around and around in her hand. She knew she'd best come up with the truth. Her husband already knew who the man was; he only wanted to hear her speak his name aloud. "Jake, er… Jake Swinson."

Chapter Sixteen

Way up in the morning, on the day of September 15, 1922, John and his oldest son, Henry, had come in from the field where they had been mowing hay. The mowing machine had quit working properly out in the field, and they had to take it up near the barn where the tools for repairs were kept. They had pulled it up under the shade of one of the large pecan trees where it would be cooler, since it was one of those hot late summer days.

Moments after the repairs began, they heard the familiar sound of hoof beats pounding on the hard, dry, dirt road that ran in front of their house. Each man looked up to see the horse being rode into their yard. The sight they observed was that of an angry man on horseback, with a double-barrel shotgun hung from the saddle.

"Morning, Sir," John tried to act causal, as he and Henry walked closer to where the man had brought his mount to a halt. "How ya doin dis mornin'?"

The horse snorted and pranced about where he stood in the yard. The animal was nearly exhausted from the hard ride he had just endured.

"Won't you get off the horse and water him, there at the trough?" John motioned toward the water trough, located near the barn.

John and his son had a hankering that they knew who the man was and the reason for his state of anguish, though they had never met the man personally. Every man and most of the women, in the entire community knew of Jake's daring escapades with 'his woman' over in Haws Run. All of them knew his day of reckoning would arrive eventually.

The man remained atop his horse, ignoring John's offer. He finally spoke, "I'm looking for the farm of Jake Swinson. Can you point me in dat direction?"

"What might ya be a wantin' wid Jake dis mornin?" John asked the question.

"I'm gonna blow his dammed head off wid dis here shotgun, dat's what I aim to do wid him." He patted the security of the gun.

"What's Jake done to ya to make ya wont to kill de man?"

"He's fooled around wid my woman fer de last damn time, dat's what."

"Well now, yeah, I know Jake and whur he lives. Jist continue on down dis road de same way yore headed. His farm is located bout five miles on down de way dare. You'll come to a lane dat leads off to de left. Follow dat lane and it'll take ya right on up to his yard.

"Thank ya kindly," the angry man spat out as he pulled on the reins and got the horse moving at a high gallop on down the road.

"Pa, dat man's gonna kill Unca Jake. Don't ya know dat? I don't think I e'er seen a man so mad as he is, but do ya know pa, ya sent him way outta de way to git to dat lane dat turns off to de right to git to Unca Jake's place. Ya told him to turn left, not right. Sounds to me lack ya've sent him on down yonder to de Burnt Shoe, n den sent him off toward de Garganus' old field," Henry spoke up, when the horse and rider were out of sight.

"Yeah, I know what I wuz doin, and sayin. You go hitch de mule up to de cart and gallop dat mule all de way o'er to Jake's, and warn em to what's bout to happen. Git a move on son, times running short fer dat wayward brother a mine."

Henry took the lane that ran through the woods of the two connecting properties to reach his Uncle's farm. When he stopped at the back gate, where he had to stop in order to open the gate to pass through, he began to holler for his Uncle. Even his cousin Ederd would do.

By the time he reached the shade of the twin oak trees that graced the front yard, the father and all the children were gathered up to learn what the entire ruckus was about.

Henry jumped off the cart and Ederd led the mule over to the pump bench where a bucket of water was pumped for the animal to drink. "Henry, What's got in ya boy?" Jake asked right away.

Henry related all the details of what had gone on over at his house less than twenty minutes ago. "Pa send me on o'er here to warn ya, dat de man is comin', wid killin' on his mind. Pa, he sent de man on down yonder past de Burnt Shoe to give ya a little more time to do what er ya plan to do," he was nearly out of breath by the time he finished his statement. "What are ya gonna do Unca Jake?"

Jake walked the perimeter of the front yard. He stopped when he reached the corner of the smoke house. "Ederd, you n Henry walk on o'er here." When they reached his side, he uttered quietly. "Boys, I gotta make a run fer it. Henry, you go on back dare by de cart n wait fer me and the younger youngin's to git a few thangs together. We'll be wid'ja d'reckly."

The three of them walked back to where the anxious children were still huddled up, wondering what in the world was going on. "Youngin's, all a ya dat belongs to me, git yoreselves in de house. Change into clean clothes and pack a changin' fer each o ya." The five children he spoke to ranged in age from eighteen-year-old La Vinnia to ten-year-old Roxanna. Sina and her younger brother Major stood there beside Ederd, not knowing what to do or where to turn.

Jake caught sight of their confused state of mind. "Sinnie, will you go to de kitchen n gather up all de vittles dat's been cooked and tie em up in a cloth. We'll need a bite to eat later on."

He turned to his son, "Ederd, I hate worse'n everthang to leave ya lack dis, but if I don't git outta here I won't be a livin' too much longer. When I was in town last week, I was a talkin' to old man Jarman. You know im, the mule trader, with a lot right dare in de heart-o-town. Well, he told me he's got a brother down in Coolidge, Georgia, dat's looking fer a man to farm his land. That's where I'm headed, me and dese younger youngin's are. I'll have to borrow de money to git there frum John, if he'll let me have it, since I ain't got no more'n four dollars in my pocket."

He entered the house to change his clothes and caution the girls to be quick about what he had instructed them to do. "Throw me a change a clothes in along wid yores."

Vinnie spoke up to say, "Pa, we ain't got no suitcases to pack 'r thangs in."

"Strip a couple uv em pillow cases off de pillows and cram de clothes down in dare. Hurry gal, we ain't got all day."

"Pa, why are we a doing dis?"

"Jist hush up yore mouth and do as I say gal, dare'll be time fer talkin' later on."

Jake and his bewildered children met back out in the yard. Sinnie came back with what food she could gather up and handed it to Jake. "Here Vinnie, make room in one a dem pillow cases fer dis food. Now all o ya, git up in de cart."

Ederd stood quite still until his father started to climb into the cart. "Paw, will you step o'er here and speak to me a second mebbe? Paw, ya need to tell me a little bite of what's goin' on. Lack the reason Emma's husband is gunnin' fer ya. I know what cha been up to wid her for years now. What've ya done Paw, to cause de man to come a gunnin' fer ya?"

"Hell Ederd, I got de woman wid child, which ain't nothin' new. Half o what she's got is most likely mine. Only thang is, her husband has just found out bout me and her after all dese years, at dat. Now Ederd, let me git on my way. You take care a yourself and do what you must about Sinnie and Major Dare."

He climbed aboard the cart and sat down beside Steven, who sat in the middle of the cart seat, with Henry up there too, handling the reins. "Tsk, tsk, git up dare mule," Henry flapped the reins against the mule's sides. The mule and cart moved off on down the lane at a slow trot, to gain speed when they reached a straight stretch of the lane.

Jake hollered out, "Major, son run close the gate after we pass through."

The girls in the flat bed of the cart jostled about when the cart ran over the unleveled ground. They waved good-bye until they were beyond the back gate.

Jake raised his arm toward Ederd with his fist clinched and hollered out, "Don't chu forgit de vow GrandPaw Jess made, when he left the shores of Ireland. Tell it to yore youngin's, jist like I did to you."

Ederd looked at Sinnie and said, "Dare goes my Paw, a forty-seven-year old, spose to be a grown man, jist lack a skeert dog wid his tail twixt his legs, runnin' fer his life."

As soon as the fleeing party reached John's yard, Jake jumped from the cart and approached his brother. "John, ya gotta let me have 'nough money to git away frum hear. I need it, n right now too."

John figured there would be a request for cash if Jake did run. "Well Jake, yeah, I got some money ya can have but not widout collateral." He knew from previous dealings with his brother how Jake paid back a loan. "What cha got to put up?"

"Hell John, I ain't got time to go through all dat."

"No collateral, no cash."

"What've I got chu want?"

"Let me think jist a second here." He rubbed his stubble on his chin, as he looked off into space. He all ready knew what he would aim for.

"Tell ya what Jake, sign o'er dat property ya got frum Rachel n I'll give ya de money. I'll hold de property 'til ya pay me back. Dat sound reasonable to ya?"

"Yeah, write up de papers. I'm ready to sign it o'er to ya. I gotta git outta here. I ain't got no deed yit, but what I sign o'er to ya will do 'til I do git one."

When the papers were signed, Jake and his children were ready to leave. Henry had gone to the lot and switched the mule and cart for the horse and wagon to haul them to Verona, NC, where tickets were purchased for the next train that came through headed south.

The cash money John had placed in Jake's hand was an estimated amount, to cover train fare and food for their journey to Georgia. In turn, John received a valuable, fifty-acre tract of land; he felt in his heart that Jake would never redeem, to claim as his own.

Jake left the state of North Carolina, never learning the fact that his very own father had turned him and Monty in for their dealings with the illegal whiskey still.

Chapter Seventeen

Back on the farm, Ederd, Sinnie, and Major just stood there in the yard in wonderment for quite a while without speaking a word to each other, after Ederd's statement about his father leaving the way he did. Ederd knew without a doubt, the predicament they were in. It would never do for the three of them to live there together. After some thought he said to 10 year old Major, "Son go hitch up de horse 'n buggy, den take yore sister o'er to Tom's. You and her stay the night, wid Tom n yore sister." He turned to Sinnie when Major left the yard. "Sinnie, let's me n you git married. Ya'll come on back o'er here early in de mornin'. We'll put on our Sunday clothes and git on o'er to Jacksonville. Major kin go long wid us." Ederd and Sinnie had taken a fancy to each other more than a year ago. Not even so much as a kiss had passed between the two of them. They had taken walks from one farm to another alone, and had sat on the porch for hours to talk through those months.

Sinnie looked at him for a moment and then dropped her eyes to the ground. She knew she had nowhere else to go, and then there was Major to consider. She looked back up at him and said, "Alright, Ederd. I've thought a lot uv you, e'er since we comed o'er here to stay."

Major and Sinnie had only been gone for an hour when Ederd heard the voice of an angry man, hollering an' cussing as he approached the front gate to the farm. Ederd was in the corncrib at the time and stepped out of the door to see the man he had been expecting to arrive at any given moment.

Henry had related the details of what had taken place earlier, when Emma's husband had been to John's. He had told them how his Paw had sent the man off, in the wrong direction, to get to Jake's farm to allow Jake more time to make up his mind as to how he would handle the situation.

Ederd walked on out to greet the man, and opened the gate for the horse to come through. "Mornin' sir, how ya doin?" he spoke, as soon as horse and rider came to a stop inside the fence.

"Not worth a damn. Is dis the farm of Jake Swinson?"

"Well now sir, it used to be, but he don't live here no more. De last I heered-tell, he was gonna share crop a farm down in Georgie."

"It musta been a right quick decision." The horse pranced around on the dry dirt, causing small dust swirls to puff out around his feet. The shotgun dangled against the flank of the horse.

"When and if ya ever see dat man agin, give em a message frum me: if I ever lay my eyes on em agin, he's a dead man."

The horse pranced around a couple of times. The animal was over heated and foamed at the mouth. "I oughta kill ever last Swinson out here," he muttered, while looking straight at Ederd, before he left.

He turned the horse around and galloped away through the front gate. He never stopped to close the gate behind him either. He had not asked for Ederd's name and Ederd had not volunteered it.

Ederd walked on back to the gate, in order to close it. "Whoose!" he breathed a sigh of relief. "I coulda got myself kilt rite dare if I'd a offered him any kind a information or advice. Dat's one time I'm glad I jist kept my mouth shet," he spoke aloud to himself.

What he had said to the man was not a lie, but not exactly all of the truth either. Ederd was more than glad to have that part of the day over with.

It was a beautiful fall morning when the trio arrived in town on September 16, 1922. It took them less than an hour to locate the Judge to do the marrying up of the two. Young Major was the only family member in attendance. Since Sinnie had turned 18 back in February, she needed no older adult to be witness for her.

They walked over to Blake's cafe, just across the street from the Judge's chambers, and ate. The food was brought to the table in different bowls, just like Sinnie would serve the food on her own kitchen table at home. It was the first time Sinnie and Major had ever eaten in a café, right there amongst a room full of strangers. Major could barely keep his eyes off the other people in the cafe during the meal. He thought it was the biggest, and best, treat he had ever had in his entire life. In all actuality, it was the first experience he had had with any kind of event out in the public. Ederd realized that fact, and as soon as the meal was over, he suggested they walk the town over.

When they reached the river, Major and Sinnie both, were nearly overwrought with awe at the sight that lay before them. It was a nice warm day, highlighted with bright sunshine, and a good breeze blowing on them from across the water. "Major, take yore shoes off n wade around in de edge o de worter dare. You too Sinnie. I think I'll jist join ya myself." They frolicked there in the river's edge, for over an hour before deciding it was time to get on the road for home. All their clothes were soaked from their antics of water play.

While they were still in town, they had heard the news. The Roper Lumber Company of New Bern, NC, had burned to the ground taking many of the town's businesses up in flames with it.

Life went on as usual there on the farm except that now Ederd and Sinnie slept together in the big bedroom. It was a lonely time for each of them, until they adjusted to the quiet, with fewer people on the place. The work that had been done by several people now fell to the hands of three.

Word got around the community quickly about Ederd and Sinnie getting marrying. A big party was thrown at his GrandPaw Jesse's farm on Saturday following their wedding, which was only three days later. It seemed as if every Uncle, Aunt, cousin and most of the neighbors showed up for the occasion. Ederd, being the shy person he was, took a good many ribbings throughout the day. A great deal of the conversations was about Jake's latest antics.

Jack and Ella showed up for the gathering. Ella was not one bit surprised to learn what her father had done. "I don't care if he never comes back here."

On Monday morning, two days after the wedding party, Jonas came trudging through the back of the field followed by a young woman who seemed to be somewhat taller than Jonas. Jonas had created a clear lane for walking through the woods from the eastern edge of the Swinson field to his own small farm. Early on, he had brought his bush ax along with him to cut small growth that grew in the single-file-path.

Ederd was rather pleased to see Jonas arrive. He and Major were stacking hay, when they spotted the two nearing the house. They stuck their pitchforks in the ground, near one of the haystacks and walked up to the house to talk to them.

"Mornin' Jonas. I'm right pleased to see ya." He looked from Jonas to the young lady who stood at his side. "Who's dis ya got wid ja today Jonas?"

Jonas fidgeted around a bit and stammered, "Dis be my wife. We ain't been married up but a few weeks now. She be Luler. She be Gideon Fisher's sister. She comed along ober here wid me, hopin' dared be work fer her ober here, too." Lula bowed the top half of her body in greeting to Ederd. Lula was a tall, very pretty, young girl. She wore her hair in tiny, short plaits, pulled back from her forehead. Her complexion was several shades darker than that of her husband. Jonas was the son of a white man.

Now, Gideon Fisher was known for his darkness. He was the blackest man in the area. He was glistening, jet black. If a comparison needed to be made, as to know how black a thing was, it was, "As black as Gideon Fisher."

"Come on, let's sit on de porch and talk a spell. Mebbe Sinnie will bring us a cool cup a fresh pumped worter, d'reckly."

They sat on the porch and enjoyed each other's company. Sinnie joined them after she handed the cups of water to them.

When Ederd finished telling what had occurred during the past two days, all were quiet for a few minutes. Ederd drained his cup of water and spoke, "Jonas, if you still have de need, you kin hep me n Major rite here in dese fields. And Luler dare? She can be a help to Sinnie here round de house n yard."

It turned out that both families needed each other. When Ederd and Major returned to the field, Jonas was by their side. Luler joined Sinnie at work and they soon became fast friends.

Five days a week, the Fishers showed up for work and sometimes on Saturday if the need arose.

A Lanier man came to the farm on Thursday of that week. He owed Jake $7.00 for work Jake had done for him. "Where's ya pa today Ederd? I've come to pay him dat what I owe him." It seemed to Ederd he had told the story of his father's departure enough times that everybody should know about it by now. He told it one more time.

"Well no, I ain't heered a word a dat, but it 'bout time dough, fer dat o cuss to pay up fer some of his dealings. I brung what he said he'd take in payment fer de work he done fer me. I'll jist leave it here wid jew if yo'll write me out a receipt."

It seemed that big blessings came in small packages sometimes, to Ederd. He had been wondering and worrying how he was going to pay the Fishers for their hours of labor. He and his father had used nearly every cent of money the tobacco had brought in, that they had sold the week before his father left.

"That'll be jist fine, Mr. Lanier." He helped unload the goods from Lanier's cart bed. There were two tins of snuff, peanuts, coffee, flour, chewing tobacco, a pair of plow handles, corn meal and a bushel of dried corn, plus $5.00 in cash money. Ederd gave Lanier his receipt and the man left.

When all work was finished late Friday afternoon, Ederd paid Luler and Jonas with supplies from his storehouse located in the pantry off the kitchen, supplied with that what his father had worked for. Luler received $1.25 in cash, while Jonas got $3.00, plus the supplies.

They left the farm laden down with their wares. "You'll see us back here bright n early next Monday mornin'," Luler offered up before they were out of the yard. They walked the two and a half miles to their home, just like they had every afternoon when work was over. They walked the miles to and from the Swinson farm every day that they worked there.

Since Jonas was a half colored man, he had spent his growing up years in the colored community. When he and Luler married, they felt ostracized and unwelcome in the colored community, so they purchased a small farm about five miles from where they had both been born. The farm was located out on highway 53, toward Jacksonville. Actually, their smallholdings were located closer to the Swinson's than to any colored family. Jonas and Luler were no blood kin.

Sinnie knew she was with child by the last of December.

With Jonas' help, both money crops were completely harvested before cold weather set in. As soon as all the cotton was picked, it was taken to market in Wallace, NC.

Two of the first items Ederd tended to with the cotton money were to pay GBD Parker the last payment of $75.00 in cash money that his father owed the man. The other debt of his father's was paid for with one bale of cotton, valued at $54.13. Jake had borrowed the money from Parker to pay for the last tract of land he had bought.

To get a crop of tobacco ready for market took many long hours of tedious work but the difference in the amount of money it brought in was well worth every minute of time. When the last load of tobacco was hauled off to Brick Warehouse in Wallace, NC, and sold, Ederd had paid all his debts for the past year, and all of his father's bills that he had been able to locate. One of the old bills he paid for his father was to settle the guano bill. He paid that bill with six head of cattle.

"It's feels mighty good to have enough money resting here in my overalls bib pocket, and stashed away in the trunk, to take us through 'til next fall," he patted the pocket with pride, while he spoke to Sinnie, as they placed the last items on the storehouse shelf. The shelves were lined with supplies that would pay for many an hour of hired labor when work began in early Spring.

It was a widespread custom to pay work hands with many different kinds of needed items. Many of the hands had no transportation and appreciated receiving what they needed right there where they had worked, as long as a little cash was laid in their hand along with the supplies.

Colored people had continued to settle in by the Moore family farm over on Colored Town Road throughout the years, until there were as many families in that community as there were over in Ederd's section.

In the latter part of 1922, members of the James family from over in Colored Town began to hire out to Ederd. The father, Lenzy, worked for two long days and took home one peck of sweet potatoes, one bushel of Irish potatoes and twenty cents worth of cracklings. His wife Florence worked one full day and took home four and one half pounds of smoked pork meat, forty-five cents worth. One day of the next week, Lenzy worked for five and one half hours and earned sixty-two cents cash. No matter who worked on the farm, Jonas and Luler came most every day.

On January 8, 1923, Ederd paid his 1922 county taxes of $3.20, along with those of his father, for $35.97. He knew that if the taxes were not paid up there'd be more trouble dumped on his head than he wanted to bother with.

The first week of February 1923, Ederd bought a $40.00 money order from the mail carrier. He was placing his first order from the Sears & Roebuck Company mail order catalog. He ordered all sorts of clothing, from socks to felt hats. He hoped he would have enough stocked up in his storehouse to last through the next full year.

Jack and Ella moved back to the area and hired out to Ederd until they could get a farm to work. They moved in with Ederd and Sinnie. Rent and food were free. If Jack worked for Ederd, he earned $2.00 a day and Ella earned $1.75 per day.

Sinnie suffered a miscarriage during the month of January, in 1923.

Ederd received the first news from his father in the form of a letter, dated February 1, 1923. The farm his Paw was to share crop was located at Norman Park, GA, not too many miles from Coolidge. All the family members were doing all right and seemed to like living in the somewhat warmer climate. All of them except Stephen, he was not happy at all with the move. It had taken Stephen a long, long time to recover from loosing his big toe. His sense of balance had to be relearned. At times, he caught himself limping from force of habit.

Soon after reading the letter, he called to Sinnie, "Come sit here wid me a few minutes." He showed her the letter. "Look at de way he writes to me. Jist lack I wuz a ten year old youngin', a tellin' me zactly what to do n when to do it. Well Sinnie, he's gone frum here now, and I tend to do lack you n me want to do, not him. Wid him off yonder in Georgie, he's got no say so. He also mentions here in de letter dat he's married up again with a woman he met from dare round Norman Park. Her name's Elsie Crosby. Well I reckin' she's a Swinson now."

She read the letter and nodded her head in agreement with him. "He wuz a bossy man, I'll haf to go widge dare."

Sinnie was a lovely young woman. About five feet tall, thick dark brown hair that she wore in a bun laying on the nape of her neck, her grayish-green eyes twinkled with a smile most of the time. She was also nicely shaped.

She was a very observant person. She took the time to stoop over and smell the fragrance of a low growing wild flower. She loved to hear a hen cackle when it had laid an egg and fluttered off the nest, bragging on the feat. The sounds made around a farm became music to her ears. Sinnie had Indian blood in her, inherited from her father and on her mother's side, also.

Jack and Ella located a farm in the Verona, NC, area to work. It was early spring by the time they got settled in with their young son, Raleigh, and baby girl Goldie. If Jack found a few days he could spare away from his own crops, he went to Ederd's and hired out to him for supplies and a few dollars cash, to put in his pocket.

Ederd had a habit of lying on the front porch in the shade of the twin oak trees, just like that of his father. The trees had grown to giant size through the years. It was usually hot that time of day. He was known to doze off during the rest period. At 2:00 p.m., the exact time every day, he roused and sat up. He placed his old sweat brimmed felt hat on his head then twisted around to look at the time telling marks carved in the porch post nearest him. The marks had been carved there by his father before Ederd had been born. Each mark indicated an hour of the day.

In Early Spring of that year, Ederd was in a crowd of several of the farmers who had gathered up for a meeting. He over heard his Uncle John telling another person, "Dat sorry Jonas Fisher owes me money. I aim to git it too, if I haf to take it outta his hide."

Ederd moseyed on over closer to his uncle and asked, "How much does Jonas owe you, Unca John?"

"Five dollars, dat's how much."

Ederd pulled his purse from the bib of his overalls and handed John a five-dollar bill. "Does at take keer uv it sir?"

"Yeah, it does Ederd, but ya cain't carry dat man all de time, jist cause him and dat woman of his has set dare sights on you and Sinnie."

Ederd had a feeling deep down somewhere that John envied the faithfulness of Jonas and his wife to himself and Sinnie. John had prospered more than any of the other farmers in the community. At times, he would laud his success in the presence of others.

"Dat's all right, Unca John. Jonas may be a slow worker, and mebbe he don't talk much, but he's a good man, a good worker, too, n I appreciate having em work fer me n fer bein' my friend."

Jonas had started earning $2.00 a day in January and got a raise up to $2.50 by the end of March. Seldom did he collect all his pay in cash money. He took supplies instead, as well as the others that hired out to Ederd. At times Ederd ran low in his storehouse and had to make a hasty trip to town to replenish the shelves. Many items he used to pay the help with came from the land they worked such as hog meat, lard, sausage, potatoes, peas, eggs, wine and fruit.

In October of that year, Jacob returned to the farm to live and work for Ederd in the fields.

One of his first questions was, "Where's Paw and de other youngin's?"

When he had heard the entire story he said, "I figgered he'd git his come-upance one a dese days, but to jist up n leave everthang. Jist lack 'em, to run. Too bad de fella didn't git here afore Paw made his git-away."

Jacob was 21 years old. He earned forty cents a day, plus room and board. He bought his civilian clothes from Ederd's storehouse. When he was paid after 16 days of work, and settled up his bill with his brother, he got to put $2.45 cash in his pocket. "I'll tell ya right now, dis is a heap more'n I had in my pocket while I was in the army." He jingled the change about in the bottom of his pocket. "Yes sir, I'm glad to be outta de man's army."

Ederd got a letter off to his father with the news that Jacob had returned. "He aims to stay wid me and Sinnie, n help me on de land fer a spell fore he strikes out agin," he wrote in the letter.

The first-born child came on a cold, rainy night. December 2, 1923. Ederd had trotted the horse and buggy over to the Moore farm, just like his father and grandfather had done through the years, to fetch the midwife. Miss Polly was kept busy delivering babies for all those who lived in the area, colored and white. At times, she would stay with the family up to three days if it was a difficult delivery.

When she allowed Ederd in to see the boy she said, "Ya've got a good'un here, Mr. Ederd. Listen to de little'un cry. A good set a lungs on dis'un."

Ederd followed suit with the afterbirth, just like his forefathers before him. He was so tempted to have a look inside the bundle of rags before he dropped it in the hole he'd dug for it, but decided against taking the peek. They named the child Cloudie, though the name was pronounced Claudie.

Later on, Ederd, Jacob and Jonas were at the barn feeding the mules a little before noon time while Major drew water from the nearby well for the mules. The working animals were fed and watered three times a day. When Major brought the water bucket to the stall, he said, "I jist seen a man a walkin' down de lane toward the back gate, yonder across de field. I don't know who it tis."

The three of them walked toward the gate, Jonas hanging behind, to see eighteen-year-old Stephen lumbering along, nearing the gate on the opposite side from them. He had a small satchel slung over his right shoulder. He was one dirty, unkempt, pitiful looking young man. With one bound, he cleared the top rail of the gate. "Stephen!" Jacob rushed to him with arms out stretched.

"Steve, my little brother, where'd ju come frum boy?" They hugged each other fiercely. After greeting Ederd and

Major, he handed his satchel to Major and they walked back to the stables.

"Jist whur did ya come frum Steve?" Ederd wanted to know.

"Frum a long ways down south. I been on de road fer nigh on to two weeks. I thumbed n walked my way back hume. I musta walk a third of de way. I slept in ditches, and under trees. I washed my face in ditch water n I ain't had a bath or changed dese clothes since I left de state of Georgie. I stopped o'er yonder to Unca John's. Aint Pean, she gimme a biscuit left o'er frum breakfast wid a cold slab a boiled fat meat in it. She got dat outta de safe. I wuz sa weak, I could hardly git one uv my feet ahead uv de other when I comed up on their place. I'm still nigh on starved to death. Dat biscuit's all I eat in de last two days."

By the time he finished his tale they had completed the chores at the stables and had reached the house. The aroma of what Sinnie and Luler had on the cook stove nearly caused Steven to swoon from hunger pangs. When he opened his mouth, slobber drooled from both corners. They sat at the table and carried on a conversation while the meal was devoured.

The water table was cleared off, and that is where Jonas and Luler sat to eat their dinner. A plate was filled and taken to them. They never would sit at the main table and eat with the family. If Jonas or Luler wanted more food, they sat quietly with their head slightly bent forward and waited until someone at the table noticed. Then the person that noticed arose from the table and replenished their plates until they had had their fill of food. If a person asked Jonas why he and Luler would not sit at the main table, he would only respond with, "It be best dis way."

The week after Stephen's arrival, one of the first cousins, Walter, came over and asked if he could work for Ederd and get room and board with the family. Ederd agreed to let him stay and work. All Walter brought with him was a few changes of clothes and his banjo. Like Jacob and Stephen, Walter earned seventy-five cents a day. Only, Walter had to pay for room and board, thirty-five cents a day, taken from the usual seventy-five cents for a day of work, which left him with forty-cent cash a day. It was home to Jacob and Steven.

There were four grown men, a young boy, a baby and Sinnie living in the house. Sinnie had to do the washing, and cooked all the food, three times a day, with Luler's help, most every day. Trying to keep the house straight was a job on its own. Since there were no screens up at any door or window, chickens had free run of the house and kitchen. On the days that it was warm enough, all the doors were left open. She had tried to train the chickens to stay outside, but they were rather dumb critters.

"They ain't good fer nothin' cept puttin' n de pot, eggs and a course crowing at de break a day."

Now, the dogs and cats never entered the inside of the house through one of the opened doors. Those animals could be, and were, trained to live out-of-doors.

Sinnie entered the kitchen in order to get dinner started. She built a fire in the wood burning cook stove and realized there was very little wood in the wood box. As soon as she closed the firebox door to the stove, she went outside to the chip-pile and returned to the kitchen with a big turn of stove wood. Three chickens had entered the kitchen by the time she got back in there. She dumped the wood in the box and reached for the broom, made exactly like the way her grandmother-in-law, Listy Ann, had made hers.

She started to shoo the chickens from the room. When she crossed over the back door jam, she tripped and fell to the floor. "Oomph!" She lay there a moment before she tried to rise. When she pushed up with her arms, the pain grabbed at her something awful in her lower back. She felt the warmth ooze from her body between her legs. "Luler! Luler!" she called out.

Luler was under the wash shelter scrubbing a pair of overalls, in preparation of getting them in the wash pot to boil. She straightened up to listen more carefully to what she thought had been her name called out. As soon as she realized she had heard Sinnie's cry for help, she went on a fast run to the kitchen. "Lawdy, miss hon-chile, what chu gone n done?"

She leaned over and helped the woman-in-pain up to a sitting position. "Miss hon-chile, what chu doin dare on de flow?"

"I wuz chasin' dem aggravating chicken outta here when I tripped on dat dare jam. Luler, I think I have jist lost a baby." She leaned her weight on Luler. "I only 'spected dat I could be wid child agin."

"Here let me git cha up, n cleaned up, den git cha in de bed for a day or so."

When Luler had Sinnie tucked securely in the bed, she returned to the kitchen and got dinner cooked for the crowd of workers. Her washing duties were completed after the dinner dishes were washed up.

All the men went back to the field except Ederd. He stayed up at the house, tended to Cloudie, and saw to Sinnie for the rest of the day. Sinnie was up and about her usual work in a couple of days.

Walter's brother, Leslie, came over and worked for Ederd from the last week of June on into July. He went home each night. At seventy-five cents a day, he earned $9.00 for twelve days of work. He took part of his earnings in supplies. One can of smoking tobacco for forty-five cents, a straw hat at thirty-five cents, one pair of shoes at $1.75, three packs of ready rolled cigarettes for fifteen cents, and eight packs of Secrets. The rest he took in cash.

In July, Ederd found a note in the mailbox letting him know that eleven cents was due on the mail order from Sears & Roebuck. He had been anxiously waiting for it to arrive. The note also informed him that he could pick up the merchandise at the Maple Hill post office.

He was in need of the supplies to restock his storehouse there in the pantry. When he got home from the post office and unpacked his wares, he saved out the banjo strings and laid them aside to give to Walter later on.

After supper that night, Walter put the stings on his instrument and tuned it up. Every person present sat on the porch and listen to him pick and pluck out one tune after another. Even the baby dozed, as he sat on his mother's lap. They took turns at singing when he played a familiar song. At times, they all sang together.

Their entertainment was what they made for themselves. One of their favorite things to do during their teenage years was to play with the handcart left over the weekends on a spur of the railroad track. As soon as a child got tall enough to reach the handles, he was allowed to take his turns at play on the handcart. Many a mile was pumped on Saturdays and Sundays after the work had been finished.

A square dance was held on one of the farms, in a barn or pack house, at least once a month. The music was furnished by one guitar, one fiddle and a banjo. Of course, there was always swimming when the water was up. At times, they swam in some of the bigger, wider ditches after a big rainfall, but mostly they loaded up everybody in a wagon and went to Deep Bottom. Long walks along the country roads were the number one mode of entertainment. It was not unusual to see fifteen to twenty young folks ambling along on a Sunday afternoon, talking, laughing and generally having a wonderful time.

Ederd received the deed to the parcel of land his father had won in the court case with Hattie Hewitt, in August 1924. It was deeded to his father. He took a few hours off from his own fields, went over to John's farm, and handed the paper to him. "Here Unca John. Do what chu must to git dis straightened out. I doubt chu e'er hear a word frum Paw bout payin' ya back."

In October, Ella came over and stayed two weeks with Sinnie and Ederd. She brought along her two sons, Raleigh and Zollie, and the one daughter, Goldie. At the end of her stay, which was on a Saturday morning, Jack came with the mule and cart to take them back home. She had earned $23.00 during the time she spent with them working for Ederd in the fields. She took some smoked pork meat as part payment for her labors.

Sinnie and Ella cooked a big dinner before they left. It was a rainy day and not too much could be accomplished in the fields. When the meal was finished, the two women cleared the table while the men continued to sit there at the table and carry on conversations. Little Raleigh sat there wide eyed, listing to the stories that held his interest. Six-year-old Goldie sat on her father's knee and dozed. She rested her head against his chest. Raleigh sat on the bench between Jacob and his father.

There were five grown men sitting at the table. Each one of them could curse like a son-of-a-gun. When they were in the presence of the women folk, they toned down the amount of swear words they used. Raleigh's eyes went from face to face, as he tried to keep up with each story and tale. He laughed when they laughed. The babies, Zollie and Cloudie, were in the house asleep in the same bed.

Jonas and Luler had not come over for the day to work, due to the rainy weather.

The rain had put a chill in the air. Sinnie kindled up the fire in the cook stove and got a fresh pot of coffee on to boil. Ella had joined the men at the table and so did Sinnie as soon as she left the stove.

Jacob noticed the eyes of Raleigh darting from one adult to another. He stretched out his leg and rammed his hand down in his pocket. His hand came out with a coin in it. "Raleigh, have ya e'er had any money?

"No sur."

"What wou'ja do wid it, if ya had some?"

The little fellow had never had the chance to think about spending money before. He piped up with, "I'd go ta dat store n buy me a big sack a candy."

Jacob extended his hand out in front of Raleigh. When he opened it, Raleigh's eyebrows lifted in wonderment. "What's dat, Unca Jacob?"

"It's a piece of money. It's all yourn, too," he rubbed the coin between his fingers. "Do ya know how much it tis?"

"No sur."

"Son, dat's a whole dollar dare, a silver dollar at dat. I collected me up a whole handful while I wuz out yonder in Oklahoma, serving in de Man's army. Open yore hand n I'll give it to ya." He flipped the coin over before he placed it in the child's hand. "Let's see here, the date says it twas made in 1922. Ya kin save it or ya can spend it. It's yourn to do wid jist lack ya wont to."

Ederd went over and mowed hay fields for Ed Blake for three and a half days. He earned $6.25. For the use of his own equipment, he earned one dollar for the mower and one dollar for the mule. He worked one day for Blake in cotton. For that, he earned seventy-five cents. He also worked one day on the Blake farm with his mule and section harrow, called a har. For the labor of walking behind the har, pulled by two mules all day long, over fresh plowed ground, he earned a total of $3.50 for his work, the use of his har and for his mule. For five and a half long days, he earned $12.50. For partial payment, he received one bushel of fresh oysters, valued at $1.50 and one half gallon of bean seeds, twenty cents worth. He took home $10.80 in cash money.

William T. Blake had married in years past to his Miss Lucy. They had three sons: Robert, called Bob; Edward, called Ed; and James, called Jim.

Bob, and his wife, Miss Missouri, and his brother Ed and his wife, Miss Nina, and their growing family, had remained on the farm where they had been born. Each took half of the original land purchased by their now deceased parents. Their houses were about a mile apart, each facing the road that passed by their homes. Jim left the area to seek his fortune in another occupation.

News traveled throughout the area by a person walking or riding on horseback from farm to farm. In early December of that year, one of the Garganus boys rode around to let everybody know that an automobile was parked over at the Hewitt's farm.

Within the hour, the Hewitt's yard was filled with curious onlookers. Entire families had shown up. There it sat, a Model T Ford.

Tom Hayes, owner of the car, had driven out to visit the Hewitts. He still lived in the area where Lonzo had lived, before he settled in the local area.

Youngin's stood with their mouths gaped open. Even grown women were amazed at the sight right there before them.

"Do ya reckin' we can touch it?" Sinnie asked Nina.

"I don't know Sinnie. It looks mighty scary." They walked around and around the car, followed by each person there.

Tom Hayes asked Lonzo to sit beneath the steering wheel while he stood in front of the car to turn the crank. When the motor caught, the noise was frightful to every soul on the place who had never seen a car before. Babies and small children scattered and clung to their mother's frock tails. Mules and horses pranced around, whinnying and rearing back against their reins. Most all the men present had seen an automobile when in town or some other place. It was an exciting time, for all residents of the area, to witness the first motorized vehicle to enter the community.

With correspondence through the mail, Jake convinced Jack and Ella to travel to the state of Georgia. "Come on down here and live near us. Dare's a farm not too fer frum ours, ripe for ya to share crop," he had written. "You kin tenant farm a few years n din be able to buy yore own place." He went on to make it sound like the best thing that had come along for the young couple and their three children to take advantage of.

Ella was quite leery of making the move. She knew from previous experiences how her father was. She had no love for the man and dreaded living close enough to him so that he could interfere in her family's life.

It took some doing, but Jack convinced her to go along with her father's suggestion. "Now Ella, dis may jist be what we been a needin'. If we kin settle down in one place n call it hume, it'll be better for the youngin's."

They left in late January by train from Verona, NC. The word they had received from Jake, was to only bring their clothing and personal items, such as they were. Supposedly, the farm located at Ellenton, Georgia, had a small, furnished house. Naturally, they figured that all farming equipment would be on the land in Georgia, just as tenant farms in North Carolina had.

They stored what possessions they left in one of the empty barn stalls over at Ederd's. The stall had been floored and weather proofed.

Nothing was what they had hoped it would be when they arrived in Georgia. There were no cooking utensils, only shabby furnishings and few farming tools.

Ella clashed with her father the second week they were there. "Jack, I'm here to tell ya, I ain't a staying in dis place. I don't haf to put up wid dat man's meanness another day in my life. You jist keep dat old man away from dis house. Ya hear me?"

"Ella girl, we jist got to stay here 'til de crop comes in."

Jack and his small family lived in the state of Georgia just long enough to harvest one crop of tobacco, which was nine months. Jack pocketed his share of the money when the tobacco was sold.

"Ella, pack up everythang ya want to take back hume wid'us. I'm headed to town. When I git back here, I'll have de train fare and a time to leave dis state forever."

Chapter Eighteen

Sinnie owned the first automobile in the area. The car was a 1918 Ford Touring car.

In the spring of 1924, Ederd sectioned off a one-acre tract of tobacco and said to his wife, "Sinnie, dis is yoren. Ya work it in yore spare time. If ya need hep, we're here to hep ya. When it sells, de cash it brings in is yoren. Do wid it what pleases ya."

All through the growing, curing and working up of her tobacco, Sinnie pondered on what to get for herself with the money when her tobacco was sold.

A handbill came in the mail one day about the time she sold the last load of her tobacco. It was an advertisement from the Blythe Motor Company up in Wilson, North Carolina, advertising Ford cars. There were descriptions of new cars and used ones on the flier. Sinnie counted out her dollars for the price of the car she wanted. She had more than enough for the purchase. She secured the money away in a safe place.

On the sixth day of the following January, Ederd and Jacob hitched up the horse and buggy and left the farm before daylight. They were on their way to Wilson to see about buying Sinnie the automobile. "I don't know when we'll git back here, so don't chu worry." Ederd waved goodbye to Sinnie in the predawn light. The price of the used car was $37.50. It was purchased on January 7, 1925.

Now, those two brothers had them a time learning to drive that car. It took most of the afternoon for them to learn enough to start back home with it on the day following their arrival in Wilson. The brothers found the local Sheriff and got a drivers license, free of charge, before they learned to drive. The car dealer advised them to do so.

The horse and buggy had been stabled at the town livery. When nightfall came, Ederd drove that car up to the hotel just like he knew what he was doing.

After a good night's sleep, a big breakfast in the nearby cafe and a five-gallon gas can that they filled with gas, they were up and on the road before dawn the next morning.

Ederd drove several miles while Jacob trotted the horse behind the car. When the car was a mile or so ahead of the horse, the car was brought to a stop and waited for the horse to catch up. Then Jacob drove for a while. They continued the routine until they reach home a little after dark. They had been gone three entire days.

All through the rest of January and February, Sinnie learned to drive. It was the hardest thing she had ever learned to do. It was easier for her to turn the hand crank and get the motor started than it was to get the clutch and gas pedal to work at the same time for her.

Ederd usually sat beside her while she practiced driving. "Girl, my neck is pure t sore, frum ya snatching my head back. Don't try so hard. It'll come to ya fore ya know it."

Sinnie laughed so hard and so often during those driving lessons, she kept peeing in her pants.

"Ederd dis is de most fun I've had since me n Emma used to play on dat old railroad handcart." It was a wonderful time she and her husband spent together, bouncing around the paths throughout the fields.

"It's a wonder you don't joggle that unborn youngin' right outta yore stomach," he remarked, after an unusually jousting trip around the paths.

Sinnie got the hang of driving before too long, and drove around the community, as she needed to. However, it was up in June when she got her first drivers license. The license didn't cost her anything. She and Ederd drove to town, found the Sheriff, and got the license from him. She signed her name 'Sinnie Swinson.'

One Friday morning in late June, Ederd and Sinnie decided to make a car trip down to Winnabow, in Brunswick County. Sinnie's oldest brother, Henry, and his family lived and worked a small farm there. Leslie was hired to come over daily to feed and water the animals.

"Hurry up Major, git wha'cha got to do done so's we kin git on de road. It's a long ways down yonder," Ederd spoke briskly to the young boy. Major threw the last kernels of corn out to the chickens and ran for the house to prepare for the journey.

It would be his first trip anywhere since he had gone with Ederd and Sinnie the day they got married.

"Ederd, you take Cloudie and put him dare in de back seat wid Major." She had agreed for her husband to do the driving, since it was such a long drive.

Major played with, and sang to Cloudie most all the way. That is, until Cloudie fell asleep curled up on the backseat beside him.

It took several hours to reach the outskirts of Wilmington, where they had to cross the Cape Fear River by ferry. When they neared the ferry landing, at the end of Market Street, it was obvious to them that the ferry was in route back from across the river.

Major stretched his neck up as far as he could, "Sinnie, lookie yonder! Dat thangs a slidin' right on top of de worter. Lookie Sinnie!" He was quite excited to witness, for the first time, a vessel moving on top of the water. Major's exited voice aroused Cloudie from his sleeping, and he scrambled up to peer out the window at what the travelers were gawking at.

There were three more cars, a horse and buggy, and one man on horseback waiting for the ferry to arrive, so they too could cross over to the other side.

Instead of Ederd looking for a parking place, he allowed Major and Sinnie's excitement to catch his attention. To see a vessel, what looked like it was skimming along on top of the water, was enough to distract him from what he should have been doing.

"Ederd! My God, look out!" Sinnie took her eyes off the ferry for a second and glance in front of her. Their car was mere feet from the cable guard stretched across the sloped loading ramp.

The ferry lost its place of interest in the minds of the riders inside the car. "Stop Ederd! Stop dis thang."

Ederd applied the brakes. He pulled back on the steering wheel as if that would help stop the vehicle. "Damnation! Hold on, all a ya." If the chain guard had not been securely attached at both ends, and had not been strong enough to stop the car, the car would have plunged right on into the Cape Fear River.

The car stopped with an awful jerk to each person inside it. Cloudie was thrown to the floor, where he let out a wail loud enough to scare his mother. Major hung across the back of the front seat. He too was hurt. His rib cage had banged across the top of the front seat. Ederd and Sinnie seemed to be unhurt.

The crowd of onlookers gathered close by to see if they could help.

One man spoke up, "Sir, since your motor's died, I think we, here on the outside, maybe ought to try pulling you backwards. Don't know that a person can reach the crank from where you're sitting."

The man on horseback attached a rope to the back bumper, and used the power of the horse to help pull while the men folk pushed from either side of the car. When the car came to a stop, secured safely where it should have been in the first place, all occupants got out. Knees were wobbly and sweat formed on Ederd's brow. He raked his hand across his forehead and uttered, "Don't know dust zactly how dat happened." He reached for his child and asked, "Sinnie, ya all right?"

"Yea, everythang seems to be all right wid me." She rubbed her stomach and looked at her brother. "Major you and Cloudie had ya'self a tumble back dare, didn't cha?" she smiled at him, and Major dipped his head forward, while the baby made a little giggle sound.

"Dare fer a minute I wuz skeert, but den I thought it wuz fun. I shore am glad dat cable wuz up dare and dem men wuz here to hep us out," Major replied.

Ederd thanked all those who helped him. "I jist don't know what I'd a done if I'd a been here by myself. I let the excitement of what we saw on de river dare pull my taintion away frum what I wuz a doin."

The ferry arrived and they continued their journey onto Henry's with a grand story to tell once they arrived at his farm.

Later on, a week or so after they had returned back home, a letter arrived from Ederd's sister Vinnie. "Come Sinnie, there's news from Georgie again. Seems lack we are a gittin' a lot of mail frum dare dese days. From what she writes, everybody has got a good crop goin' dis year. Seems lack dey're gittin' to be spread out all around in different places frum where Paw first took em. Every last one uv em are farming, jist lack you and me."

Ederd kept his personal taxes, and that of his father's, paid up yearly. Since Jake still owned the farm and surrounding land, the tax bill came to the farm in his name.

The farm had been doing quite well for Ederd and his little family since his father had left so abruptly. With the help of the hired hands, he could use every acre of the cleared land. He had planned it so there was some product to be sold from the land nearly every week. There was wine; fresh pork; smoked pork; sausage, both fresh and air dried; beef; poultry products; vegetables of varying descriptions; hay; corn seeds; tobacco; cotton; and a few other things. He kept his money in the top shelf of the old steamer hooped lid trunk. The trunk sat in his bedroom. Ever so often, he would go in there and count the dollars, feeling pride in the fact that he was able to farm and make a good go of it. Next to his Uncle John, Ederd was the most prosperous farmer in the farming community. He had furnished the farm with most all the modern equipment available to speed along the work in the fields.

He too, had tried his hand at a whiskey still, the year before. He made a heaping amount of money from the sale of the corn liquor. Oh, he knew it was illegal to work a still, but every man in the area ran a still at one time or another. Ederd had been lucky. The revenuers had not caught him. He felt good when he placed all those dollars earned from the sale of the white lightning in with his other savings, inside the trunk. Each time he counted his money he swelled up with pride.

He was happy with his life. Everything seemed to be going just right for him and his Sinnie, whom he loved dearly. Children were entering their lives to fulfill that part of their union.

The birds were singing and the hens clucked, as they scratched the dirt at the edge of the yard while they taught their baby chicks to forage for food. Sinnie and Luler had cleaned out the bedrooms of the house on a fine warm, April morning. They gathered up all the dirty clothes to wash, which was done once a week.

The wash pot had been filled and a fire built around it earlier. When Sinnie walked out of the house and started toward the wash shelter, she noticed the sounds of a working farm about her. Luler followed close behind her. Both carried an arm full of dirty clothes. Sinnie stopped when she stepped off the bottom step to listen to the music that filled her ears.

"Luler, do ya e'er take a few minutes to hear n look at what's right here round ja?"

"Well no'um, cain't say dat I does."

Little Cloudie played with his toys that GrandPaw Jesse had whittled out for him. He sat in the shade of the twin oak trees.

All the men-folk were out in the fields, at different locations. The friendly swirls of smoke cascaded skyward from the three different fires, scattered along the ditch banks. Jonas was down in the ditch. He threw out shovelful after shovelful of unwanted dirt. It was a farm chore that had to be done each year. Ederd and Major gathered and piled up the dried debris, that had been shrubbed a few days earlier, to be added to the fires.

Jacob, Walter and Steven were each walking behind a mule-pulled plow, turning the soil in preparation for spring planting.

It was midmorning when the sound of a motor vehicle was heard as it came down the lane toward the front gate. Every body on the place stopped what they were busy at, except Jonas. Luler walked over and picked up the baby. She took him to the kitchen porch to rock while the other folks gathered up in the front yard where the shade afforded a cool place to greet company. Ederd sent Major to open the gate for whomever it was.

When the automobile got close enough for them to see who it was none of them were too pleased. "Now what in the name of hell is de sheriff a comin' up here fer? And who's dat wid 'em?" Ederd spoke softly as he asked, so as not to be heard by the two men in the car.

"Mornin', to you all," the sheriff dipped his head in greeting, out of the open car window.

"Mornin' to ya, sir. Won't ya git out n have a drink of cool worter?" Ederd took off his old felt, sweat brimmed hat as he spoke.

"Looks like you got a mighty fine work crew here to help get the farm work done," the sheriff said as he pumped the water off until it cooled.

"Yeah, we're comin' right along sir," Ederd replied.

Walter, Jacob and Steven sat scattered around on the roots of the twin oak trees. They were each rolling a cigarette when the sheriff made mention of them. Their curiosity had their nerves on edge, though they knew they had done nothing to have the sheriff come out to talk to them about.

The sheriff offered the gentleman with him a drink of water. When he replaced the tin cup back on the post near the pump, he wiped he hand across his mouth and said,

"Mr. Swinson, this is GM Jarman," he motioned to the man with him. "Now Mr. Swinson, er, can I call you Ederd?" They had known each other for some time now.

Ederd bobbed his head forward in agreement.

"It seems that your pa has sold this farm to this man here with me," he jerked his head in the direction of Jarman.

Ederd's eyes narrowed and his brow wrinkled. He massaged the sides of his mouth with the thumb and finger of his right hand. "Ah…What?" his hat still in his left hand.

No one said a word for a few seconds. Ederd walked around, he flexed his shoulder blades. The fingers on his free hand played with the ends of his thumbs, where it hung by his side. "What'd ya say to me jist now Sheriff?" he stammered

He could barely speak. His anger toward his father was at the highest point it had ever been. The fool, the damn fool had sold his home right out from under him and his family. Without saying a word to him in the latest letter he had gotten from his father.

"Why, the son-of-a…," he mumbled. The man had pulled some awful deals on Ederd many a time in the past years, but nothing as dastardly as the scoundrel had done this time.

What could Ederd do at this point? Here he was with the responsibility for six adults and the baby. His mind was in turmoil. He put his hat back on then he took it off again.

"Jarman...Jarman, you own the mule lot dare in Jacksonville, don't cha?" Ederd asked.

"That's right son."

"Er...Mr. Jarman, how did dis come bout?"

GM Jarman was an elderly gentleman. He carried an understanding heart.

"Me and your Paw have known each other for many a year. When he left North Carolina and went to Georgia, he has sharecropped one of my brother's farms for the past two years. He found a goodly sized farm, not too long ago, there around Coolidge, Georgia, and decided to buy it. We did all our dealings through the mail service. I received the deed to this farm just last week. I did not know if you knew what was taking place or not."

Neither Ederd nor Sinnie had realized that Jake had taken the deed to the farm with him when he had left the state.

Ederd still couldn't think straight. "Er...er...sir, do ya reckin' we...ah... we kin work out some kinda deal...ah... so's me n de family kin...ah... live here on de place?"

Ederd was so humiliated and embarrassed with the situation that he kept stuttering when he talked. Before the man could answer his question, Ederd walked out into the sunshine and looked out over the fields where he had spent all his life working the soil, from sun up until sun down, the bigger part of each of those 27 years.

Sinnie stood near the front porch steps. She had not uttered a sound, though her heart was breaking for the man she had learned to love dearly. She knew that whatever decision her husband made, she would stand beside him all the way. She rubbed and patted her enlarging stomach where another child grew.

Major sat on the steps behind his sister. The three men who rested on the roots kept looking from one to the other, with only an occasional grunt and a clearing of the throat now and then, to express their concern, rolling and smoking one cigarette after another.

When Ederd walked back near where the two men stood, patiently waiting, he asked again,

"Do ya see anyway ya kin work wid us, me and my wife dare?" he jerked his thumb in her direction, "And allow us to live here? It's all de hume we e'er knowed."

Mr. Jarman shuffled his feet around on the ground as he spoke. "Son, I have no need of this farm and land. Your Paw was in need of cash money. All he owned was this land here. How he handled the deal, I'm right sorry about. I didn't know if you knew about it or not. That's the reason I asked the Sheriff here to escort me out here today. It's enough to drive a man to use his shotgun, when he learns that what he thought was his has been taken away from him. I didn't know how you'd react to the news I had to bring you."

"You don't haf to be concerned bout me doin harm to ya, sir. It's my Paw dat needs a shootin'." Ederd kept putting his hat on his head and taking it off. If it was on his head, he would ram both his hands as deep as he could in his overall pockets, then stretch his hands out away from his legs, as far as the denim would allow.

"Ederd," Jarman spoke and got Ederd's attention, "I feel that we can work out a way for you and your family to live here." He paused in what he was saying to get Ederd's input.

"Sir," Ederd bobbed his head forward, the sign meant for Jarman to continue.

"Do you want to buy this land?"

Ederd found it hard to believe what he had just heard. "Sir, ya mean...ah...you'll ah...ah...sell it to me...ah, right now, here, today?"

"Yeah. We can work out some kind of plan to go by right here where we stand, if you've got a small down payment to let me have today. I'll give you a receipt before I leave. You can come on into town one day next week. We can get the papers fixed up so you can farm your own land."

Ederd was anxious to run inside the house and get the money at that very moment. Sinnie relaxed her rigid muscles and wiped her cheeks clear of tears there where she stood. The root sitters stretched out their legs and twisted about on their behinds. Each one of them rolled another cigarette.

Ederd never smoked or chewed. For some reason he could not stand the taste in his mouth. He would take an occasional drink of whiskey now and again, but he could out cuss all three of the smokers any day of the week. He had held his swearing down pretty good while talking to the Sheriff and Jarman.

"How much will it take to git dis land in my name?" Ederd asked.

"Well son, how much have you got to let me have?"

"Let me git on in de house n count up what I got."

Jarman had no idea the amount of cash the farmer had stashed away within the walls of his home. He was somewhat surprised when Ederd came out holding the cash in one hand and a writing tablet in the other. He had an indelible pencil stuck in the bib pocket of his overalls.

"Will nine hundred cash dollars suit ya til my crop is brought in n took to de market dis fall?" he extended the hand that held the money.

He wasn't about to let on that he had twice that amount still tucked away in the trunk.

Jarman accepted the money as down payment for the farm and surrounding woodlands.

"Yes sir, this will get you off to a right good start. I see you brought me paper and pencil to write the receipt on. Hand it here and I'll get it done. Then you and your hands can get back to work."

Ederd took the receipt and walked over to where his wife stood, a proud smile beamed across her face.

"Sinnie will ya go put dis away fer me?"

When he got back to the two men who still stood in the shade, he stuck his hand out toward Jarman,

"Thank ya kindly Mr. Jarman. Dat wuz a bad feelin I had dare, when ya told me what chu'd comed out cheer fer. I'll be oer in town bout next Tuesday to git de rest straightened out. I shore do thank ya fer bein' de kindhearted man dat cha are."

When the handshake ended, Ederd clasped his hands together and rubbed the palms together. They were wet with sweat.

The Sheriff and Mr. Jarman got in the car and left the farm.

For the next several days, the family and hired hands discussed how the purchase of the farm had come about. When the news spread through the neighborhood, it was the topic of conversation for many months.

Walter's brother Perry began work in Ederd's fields in May of that year. That made nine hands working the lands, in one form or another. Of course, Luler was always up around the house and yard with Sinnie unless they were gathering vegetables from one of the garden patches located here and there on the farm. Walter boarded with Ederd at fifty cents a day.

News arrived on the farm July 5 that Della, Uncle's Dave's wife, had passed away. She was the mother of Walter and Perry. All work ceased in the fields as soon as the news arrived. When Ederd returned from the errand he had been on, and heard of Aunt Della's death, he decided to halt all fieldwork for a day or two.

"We'll be tied up all day wid de funeral n seeing to what needs to be done to help Unca Dave. No need for me to e'en thank about crops. Me and Major can look after the stock. Two or three days won't make dat much difference anyhow."

Before he and his little family stopped for the day, he turned to his cousins, Walter and Perry, and said, "You boys go on hume now. Ya Paw will be a needin' ya dare around de house. Take keer of ya pa fer a day or two now, fore ya git back o'er here to my fields fer working."

On September 6, 1925, another son was born to Ederd and Sinnie. Miss Polly was sent for and she helped the mother through the hard, tiresome delivery. They named him Leon. The custom of boys wearing frocks during their hippin' training days had ceased by the time Cloudie and Leon came along.

When the crop was harvested along about the last of September, Jacob, Steven and Walter decided to catch the train and head down to Georgia. It left a big gap in the household, to have three grown men leave at one time.

By the end of the fall season there was six automobiles in the community. Ederd bought himself a truck, after seeing what the faster mode of transportation could do for his line of work. A second vehicle in the family proved to be handy when the need arose.

Bob Blake saw an easy, quick way to add a little extra to his farm income. He installed a large gas tank and had the company truck come out to fill it up. He bought extra tires and tubes, and stacked them up in his pack house. "No tellin' how much money I can make selling dese three items alone, by havin' em handy when a person needs em."

One of his first customers was Ederd. "How much do ya say I owe ya, Bob?"

"Nine dollars n twenty-five cents fer de tire n tube and two dollars fer de five gallons of gas."

Ederd left Bob's place with a new idea rolling around in his head. As soon as he got home, he approached Sinnie and discussed it with her.

"Sinnie, dare's a empty building right dare on de edge of de water, yonder at Catherine's lake. I think I kin rent it fer nigh on to nothin'. Instead of selling outta de pantry here at hume, why not jist simply operate me a store?"

She thought about his suggestion for the rest of the afternoon. Come morning time she said, "Ederd, you go right on ahead n open up yore store. Wid Jonas, Luler, Major and den dare's Perry, he's still wid us, dis farm will be well taken care uv. Din I kin have de use uv de pantry fer storin' de cookin' supplies and canned goods lack I'd lack."

The store proved to be a successful venture. He emptied out the kitchen pantry and added the articles to other general merchandise, plus farm equipment and items from his own land, to stock the store. Traveling salesmen came by the store to sell their wares, such as fish and oysters, and dishes, silverware and clothing.

Perry worked on through December for Ederd. From September through December, he worked eighty hours, earning $60.65.

Ederd received a letter from Jacob three weeks after he had arrived in Georgia, stating that Rosie's health had worsened and Paw was thinking about returning to NC to take her to a special doctor up in Raleigh. Jacob planned to return with them. Paw needed someone to drive his model-T truck on the long trip. Oh, Jake could drive, but had only been driving a little over a month and felt unsecure to drive alone with a sick girl in the truck with him.

After reading the letter, Ederd remarked to Sinnie, "Well, he's got a nerve comin' back after what he's done around here, even though he warned us not to mention his coming to a soul."

Jake came and went without many people knowing he was about. The doctors found Rosie had only one kidney, the cause of her being so puny and run down all her life.

Jake and Rosie stayed the night of their arrival on the farm with Ederd and his family, and the night before their return to Georgia. No mention between father and son was made of the dirty deal Jake had pulled when he had sold the farm.

Jacob drove them back to Georgia and then caught a train back to NC where he went back to Ederd's to live and work on the land again.

Wally Foy and his wife Mary, Jasper Foy and his wife Lucy, along with Myrtle Davis, helped work on the farm for several weeks during the tobacco-harvesting season. Mary and Lucy earned seventy-five cents a day. Myrtle earned forty cents for a half day, while Wally and Jasper got one dollar per day.

As the farm prospered and grew, so did the town of Jacksonville. A bridge was built across the river to replace the ferry and streets were paved in the main part of town.

In early September, Jesse had taken sick. No doctor was called for a week after he fell ill. Since he worsened daily, Listy Ann decided to get the doctor to come and attend him.

"Your husband has suffered a series of little strokes. His speech will begin to slur more if he continues to have them. Should he have a major one, it will probably take his life."

The doctor took notice of Listy Ann's reaction. He went to her and put his arm about her shoulders. "Keep him as comfortable as possible. Feeding him may become a bigger problem than it is now, but get as much food in him as you can. Keep him clean and move him at least four times a day. It won't hurt if you can get him up and let him sit on the porch for an hour or two a day. You know, if the weather is permitting."

Listy Ann walked him out to his car. "Thank you, doctor. I realize you should have been called before now, but Jesse is still so stubborn about some things. He insisted I not call you, that he'd be up and about in no time."

She stood in the yard and watched his car leave the farm. She continued to stand there for several minutes. She pulled up her apron tail and held it over her mouth. "What am I going to do? Jesse has been my life just about as far back as I want to remember. Those years before him have no meaning for me."

She turned and scanned the area of fields around the house. Each area held fond memories of years past. There at the corner of the chicken yard stood the grape vines, they had set out together the first year of their adventure together as husband and wife.

"After all these years, I still pick grapes from those vines," she muttered to herself.

She looked off toward where the old log cabin had stood, before fire destroyed it. She closed her eyes and visions of the cabin appeared in her mind. The bright, cheerful colors of those flowers she had planted at the cabin that she had cherished so dearly, still lingered in her thoughts.

"Where has all the years gone?"

She walked around to the south end of the house and recalled the day she had brought the gallberry yard broom down across Jesse's shoulders.

How great their lovemaking had been that night, when they had made up. "How I love you Jesse Swinson." She wiped her cheeks dry of tears. It took a lot of sadness to make her cry. To her, this moment right at the present was the most emotional experience she had ever endured.

She knew that Mare Lise was in the bedroom, seeing about her dear Jesse, so she walked on out to the chicken coop to gather up the eggs. Everywhere she looked she saw signs of Jesse's handy work.

She spoke to the empty rack of hen nests, located on the east side of the coop, as she took eggs from them.

"Jesse, how did you get to be eighty-three-years old? And me nearly seventy five?" She glanced down at her much wrinkled hand and arm when she removed the eggs from the last nest. She placed the eggs down in her apron that she had pulled up to form a safe place to carry the eggs. Tears trickled down her cheeks as she walked back toward the kitchen.

Word of Jesse's illness had spread throughout the farming community within a day or two after it began. Seldom was there a daylight hour when there was not a family member or neighbor over to visit with Listy Ann and do what they could to help with her burden. She had had very little sleep since his first symptoms appeared.

Mare Lise tried to relieve her every other night. Even when Listy Ann went to bed, she laid there alert, and if there was any sound from the room Jesse was in, she was up and by his side immediately.

"Now Maw, ya need to go on back to bed. I'll see to his needs while ya rest."

Mare Lise tried to get her mother-in-law to relax a little. It just didn't happen that way. She feared that he would leave her while she was away from him. She remembered too well, how his father Jess had gone from their lives so quickly.

Jesse held on until October 5. It was late in the day. Listy Ann sat by his bed. She held his hand and talked softly to him. He had not responded to anything for the past several days. All at once, she felt the hand she held in hers move.

She sat up straight and leaned in close to his face, "Jesse, can you hear me Jesse?"

His eyes opened and looked straight at her. His mouth opened and she could see that he was trying to form words. "Bris... Bri... Bris."

She lowered her ear next to his mouth and heard her name whispered. "Brister, damn it all Brister, goodbye my Brister."

His last breath was used to let her know of his love for her. He had continued to cuss all the days of his life, no matter how hard Listy Ann tried to get him to stop.

She collapsed across his chest. Loud, racking sobs escaped her. Her heart was broken. She raised her head enough to notice her hand, draped across his middle. She looked at the old wrinkled skin, with age spots covering more than half of it. After sniffing her nose a few times, she lifted up the fingers on that hand, and wiggled them.

"Look Jesse, there's an old, ugly hand laying on you, and it's mine. How did I get to be so old and worn out? Where did all the years go between now and our wedding day?"

She arose and walked over to look out of the window. After she stood there for a moment, she raised her hands up between the light of the window and her face. She turned them back and forth for several turns. It was hard to believe those were her very own hands, spotted with brown age blotches. Gnarled and callused, not the soft, creamy skin of her younger years.

She raked her hand over the top of her head. Where her salt-and-pepper, gray hair was so thin, the scalp could be seen through it. A receding hairline was prevalent. Her eyes were sunk back in her head, with only a few hairs remaining on her eyebrows. Her shoulders were slightly stooped. Her waistline was the only place on her entire body that remained almost the same as it had been when she was twenty. The thighs and calves of her legs were nearly covered with varicose veins. She raised her apron covered floor length frock to look at those legs that Jesse had admired and commented on so many times.

She let the material drop from her hands and walked over to the bureau where she took two pennies from the top drawer. She returned to stand beside her husband.

Mare Lise tapped on the door and asked, "Maw kin I relieve ya fer a spell?"

"No child, no need to now. Jesse is dead."

She turned to look at her daughter-in law, whom she had learned to love as if she were her own flesh and blood.

"Oh." Mare Lise left the doorway and went to relate the news to those who were gathered up on the front porch and in the yard.

Jim, the youngest child of young Jesse and Mare Lise's four children, took it upon himself to spread the news of his grandfather's death, throughout the community.

Mare Lise returned to stand beside the deathbed. "Maw, can I prepare to lay him out?"

"No child, I'll take care of him. You go on and see about the kitchen. I'll need plenty of heated water and there's supper to get on the table. No telling how many'll be here in a short while. Some will bring food, others won't."

When she heard the door close, she turned back to her husband. She placed her right hand on his forehead and with her fingers, she closed both eyes with one downward movement. She then placed a coin on each of his eyes.

"I hate to close your eyes Jesse, knowing I will never look into them again. Why did you go and die before me anyhow? I'm too old and worn out to be left here without you."

Her tears had ceased to flow. She pulled the bed covers all the way off his body and began to undress him. He lay there in the bed they had shared for so many years with nothing on but his long, flowing, white beard, which reached mid-way his chest. She combed the beard with her fingers, as she had done for so many years.

"Jesse, I have loved you since that first day I laid my eyes on you, there on the streets of Clinton. My heart is breaking to see you laying here in this state."

She pulled the sheet up to cover the lower half of his body and went to get water for bathing him.

Work had already begun out near the sawmill area, at building the coffin to lay Jesse's body in. Neighbors and family members had started gathering up on the porches and in the yard.

By the time the coffin was ready, Listy Ann had Jesse prepared, ready to be placed in it. The coffin was placed upon two sawhorses in the front room, for open viewing by anyone who chose to.

The funeral was held in early afternoon of the next day. It was a beautiful warm day. Young Jesse had ridden horseback to the south-west area to get the young Primitive Baptist Minister, affectionately referred to as Preacher Hill Edwards, to come out and hold the services.

Every soul in the entire community, including most of the colored friends, attended the funeral. One freshly dug grave waited for the body of the last Swinson who had been born across the oceans. The size of the Swinson Family Cemetery continued to enlarge.

Listy Ann was the last person to leave the gravesite. She stood there for nearly half an hour before she turned and walked to the buggy where Jesse and Mare Lise waited for her.

"Let's go on back home Jesse," she uttered.

Chapter Nineteen

The first insurance Ederd ever bought was car insurance. The policy was to cover his truck and Sinnie's car for one year. The fee for both vehicles was a flat ten dollars. He purchased the policy from the Pilot Life Insurance Company out of Greensboro, NC, on November 3, 1926.

Ederd established a bank account pretty soon after he realized the store was going to be an asset to himself and his family. During the span of February 1, through April 24, 1927, he wrote fifteen checks, the largest for $88.08, and the smallest for $1.71. At the end of the each month, he depleted the account, making the check payable to himself, so the last check for the month's expenses was always to him. He kept the same account for each month's use.

Clydie Pierce began to work for Ederd on the farm in March. He, too, took the biggest part of his earnings in supplies as payment for his hours of work. Ederd brought Clydie's order from the store at the close of the workweek, after he had closed the doors of the building for the weekend. "Thank ye, Ederd. I jist don't know what me n de o lady wou'da done if ya didn't let me work fer ya. It's mighty hard times ober dare at our place. Uh-huh, we appreciate it kindly." The order consisted of fish, oysters, dye, snuff, tobacco, liniment, meat and one sweater. As usual, there was always a small amount of cash handed to the worker.

When the weather warmed up, Clydie's wife, Dessie, commenced to work for Ederd, also. She spent most of her time with a hoe, chopping out row after row of crops in different areas in the fields.

Of course, whoever worked in the fields ate the noon meal with Sinnie and the children. Luler was there to help with the cooking and the work around the house.

"Sometimes I feel lack dis work I do here in and around de house will ne'er end," Sinnie made the statement to Luler one day as they prepared a big pot of chicken and pastry to go along with several different vegetables.

"I knows what chu means hon-chile."

When all the planting was completed, Jacob told them at supper that he had decided to return to Georgia. "I met a gal when I wuz dare de last time, by de name of Pearl Castleberry. She lives on a farm wid her folks dare near Moultrie. As you know, Vinnie n her husband, Heywood, works a small farm not too fer frum de Casselberry's. Well, me n Pearl, we took a fancy to each other and I'm a heading back dare to marry up wid her." I'll be a leavin' tomorrow as soon as ya git my pay to me Ederd.

The day after Jacob left, Ederd said to his wife, "I reckon we'll not be a seeing much a him frum now on. I spose it's time he settled down n quit traipsing up and down the road."

Perry showed up to work for Ederd as soon as he heard that Jacob had returned to Georgia.

Monty's wife, Barbara, died that year. She had only been sick a short time when death took her. She too was buried in the Swinson Cemetery. The once small graveyard was growing larger, with so many family members passing on.

The mailman delivered a letter to Ederd the first week of August 1926. It was from his brother-in-law, Heyward Batts, down in Moultrie, Georgia. Heyward informed him that Jacob had married his cook as he, Jacob, called his wife Pearl. They were getting established on a farm nearby and they all planned a trip over to Quitman for the weekend coming up, to spend the two days and two nights with Ederd's father. All was well with all his family members now living in Georgia.

In the four years that Jake had been gone from North Carolina, Ederd had never made a trip down to visit his Paw and siblings. At present, he had no plans to ever make the trip. He could live his life without the aggravation of being in the same vicinity as that of his father.

He kept getting letters from his father and siblings, keeping him up on the doings of one another. Most of the letters were about marriages, births, and how farming was down in Georgia compared to North Carolina. He seldom got a letter off to his father. He did try to keep in touch with the sisters and brothers. He had recently received a letter from his sister Vinnie, who lived with her husband Heywood in rural Moultrie, Georgia, where they were tenant farmers.

Walter, Perry's brother, showed up on the farm in September. "Do you reckon ya kin give me a few days work, Ederd?"

There were plenty of sons still left on Dave's farm to carry out the work over there. Dave and Della had only had two daughters and the rest of their children were sons. Any time any of the young men in the area, not desperately needed on their own father's land, would seek work elsewhere.

Ederd kept the store open five days a week so, on Saturdays, he was free to hire out to those farmers that needed him or his farm equipment. He mowed hay all day on some Saturdays. He sat and slept at tobacco barns and cured tobacco from Friday night through late Sunday afternoon many a weekend so the owner could carry out another chore. He liked the idea of collecting money from many different sources.

Walter boarded with Ederd the three days he worked for him. He paid fifty cents a day for his food and lodging. Perry worked on through the month of December. He continued to go home at night, to return early the next morning.

"As long as I feel like walking o'er here I don't aim to be a paying fer room and board."

By the year 1927, the boll weevil had gotten to be such a pest in the cotton fields that Ederd made up his mind to cease planting the crop.

Eders e made the statement to his wife early January that, "Not one cotton seed do I plan to drop in de ground, ever again. All de back breaking hours it takes to git it to de stage of the bolls and den dem dam weevils eat most of it up."

He had worked a small field of tobacco for several years, including that which Sinnie had claimed each year.

"I do believe baccer is where de money will be in de future."

By the end of January, the three tobacco beds were seeded and covered with cheesecloth covers. Running along the inside of one of the beds, collard, cabbage and tomato seeds were sown to be transplanted in the garden areas as soon as the weather permitted. When a warm day arrived, the cheesecloth covers were rolled back to allow the sun to get to the seedlings.

"Oh how I hate dis work a pickin' baccer beds," Sinnie stood up from her crouched position in the center of the bed. She stretched her entire body then sat back down on the board that spanned across the bed.

Luler sat on the board near her. "Sinnie, hon-chile, you might orten to git on back up to de house. Dat youngin' yor're carrying inside ya belly don't much lack bein' crammed up so." Luler had never had a child, but she knew a woman needed to take special care of herself while pregnant.

Ederd was beginning to tire of being a store operator. Through the more than one year he had run the business, he had stayed away from home many a night. From three to four nights a week he went toward home as far as his first cousin Ida and her husband, Murriell Brown's, farm, and located not too far from his business.

"Ya know Ida, workin' every wakin' hour of my life has got to be tiresome to me. Wid Sinnie due to have dat third youngin' most any day now, I been a thinkin' 'bout selling out, so's I can stay round de house a little more. Everythang is going right good dare on my land."

He found a buyer for all the merchandise and cleared out his personal belongs. He worked out the rest of the week for the new boss and left the store after closing hours on Friday.

When he arrived at his home, he found several neighbors and family member in and around the house.

"The first one to greet him was Emma Garganus, Sinnie's first cousin on her mother's side. "Ederd I wuz a hopin' dat you'd git here fore de baby gits here. I been oer here since right after dinnertime. She's having a right smart hard time gitting dis one borned. Miss Polly's in dare wid her now. Been here longer dan me."

Ederd made a motion to climb the steps to enter the house. "No need fer ya to eben thank bout going in dare. Miss Polly'll run ya outta dare. I go in dare now and den. Thangs are all right at de present," Emma cautioned him.

Folks gathered up at the home of a new baby coming into the world just like they did for a wedding or a funeral. Ederd walked out to the pump bench, speaking to this one and that one on the way. He pumped a bucket half-full of water and reached for the homemade lye soap. When his hands were covered with suds, he rubbed them all over his face, and then gave his face a refreshing dousing of water. Henry walked him to the kitchen where several local women had a 'barn notching' meal spread out on the long eating table.

"Well lady folks, I'm as hongry as I've ever been. I shore am glad to see every one of ya."

Most of the adults stayed way on up into the night before returning to their homes. A few stayed the night to sit up with Ederd and help with the two small boys, in case they should wake. Of course, the boys knew nothing of what was taking place. They only knew what a great time they had had with so much attention from all the company.

The baby arrived midmorning, April 22, another boy to sit on Ederd's knee and be diddled when it was old enough. He was recorded in the family bible as Floyd.

Fannie Bell returned the next morning to tend to the needs of Sinnie and her three young boys. Luler had sent word by Jonas the day before that she was sick in the bed and shouldn't be around her hon-chile and newborn baby.

Ederd renewed his driver's license in May. He was quite aggravated when he learned he had to pay twenty-five cents for it.

"Beats all I e'er seen, fore ya know it, we'll be a paying for worter."

Ederd's first cousin, Leslie, and Sinnie's first cousin, Emma, showed up at the farm early one beautiful Friday morning.

"Hey Ederd, spose ya n Sinnie can go wid us to town? We aim to marry up dis day."

Ederd rubbed the stubble on his chin and looked at his wife, who had just a few days earlier gotten out of her birthing bed. She nodded at him in agreement.

"I don't see no reason why not. It'll take a little while here for us to git ready. Since Jonas n Luler 's all ready here, dey kin look adder thangs til we git back."

Leslie unhitched his horse from the cart and let him loose in the lot where Ederd's horse and mules were. He smacked the horse's rump and uttered,

"Go boy. When I return, your master will be a married man."

Sinnie knew she could not be gone too long a time away from the baby. Since he was breast fed, her breasts would be too filled with milk if she stayed away too long. She figured five to six hours would be all she could stay gone. Moreover, Floyd may have a hunger pain or two. Of Course, Luler knew how to feed him broth and use a sugar tit.

The wedding party left by the front gate at nine o'clock sharp. They returned at about one thirty, to find the yard filled with family and neighbors. Jonas had taken it upon himself to get the news of the marriage to the adjoining farm. It was a glorious afternoon. Leslie and Emma spent their honeymoon night with Ederd and Sinnie.

Different ones worked for Ederd throughout the summer. Among them was Sinnie's younger sister, Lubbie, who had married Martin Gainey, an older man with two daughters. Martin was prone to drink excessively. An illegal moonshine still was operated in the area by one or another of the residents at all times, affording Martin white lightin', to be had at his disposal.

Lubbie was expecting her first child in November.

Martin had bought a few acres of land from Tom and had erected a small coastal Carolina cottage on the road frontage of the property several hundred yards from Tom's residences.

Lubbie worked out of necessity to help feed herself and two stepdaughters. She worked at wrapping tobacco from June 1 through September 1, earning eighty-five cents a day. So did Emma, and Annie Jane, one of Lubbie's stepdaughters. They worked right along with Lubbie. The three continued to work at grading the tobacco until the last load was ready for the market. Pay for grading tobacco was ten cents an hour. There was always a huge dinner for all workers in the middle of the day, free of charge.

Lubbie continued to receive the biggest part of her pay in supplies such as items grown on the farm, and a few commodities such as salt, sugar, coffee, and oil for her lamp. Ederd allowed her to share that what was in Sinnie's pantry. Only Lubbie, Jonas, and Luler were privileged to receive supplies as part payment for work, no one else.

Another letter arrived on the farm from Heywood Batts in August of 1928. He and his little family have moved over to Hartsfield, Georgia, to tenant farmland there.

Clydie and his wife Dessie worked as a team through most of the tobacco-harvesting season. Clydie worked in the field cropping, while Dessie was at the barn, wrapping.

Ederd worked for Clydie one day at cropping tobacco and earned $1.35 for the day's work.

Ederd received a letter from the Eagle Warehouse in Kinston, North Carolina, in early October. The letter urged him to take his tobacco to their warehouse where he would receive top dollar for the sale of his crop. Opening day for sales was slated for October 5.

Ederd had already sold his first cropping at a warehouse in Wallace, North Carolina, but decided to try Eagle's for a promised higher dollar. When the tobacco crop was completely sold, Ederd had made up his mind to enlarge his tobacco acreage the following year. He thought back to the plot of land that Sinnie had first grown tobacco on, and where they were today.

On November 12, F.W. Kellum drove up on the farm with an insurance pitch that Ederd found hard to resist. When the National Life Insurance Company agent left the farm, Ederd had paid him $16.43 for one-year worth of life insurance. The policy was for $1,000.00.

Ederd missed the hours of work he had put in at the Catherine's Lake store, but found no extra time due to a full schedule on his land. He still managed to sell products made on the farm quite often. After killing hogs that winter, and finished with the smoking of the meat, he found he had enough to sell Bob Blake 105 pounds of the meat and 56 pounds of lard, plus he sold Bob's brother, Ed, $15.00 worth of lumber, that he found no use for at the moment. His total income for the month was $40.83, not bad for the times.

It was a happy day in November when Lubbie delivered her first child, a baby daughter whom they named Gertrude, in memory of one of Fannie Bell's daughters who had died earlier. It was a good name, so why not use it again.

Chapter Twenty

It was a cold Saturday night in January, when Ederd and his little family returned home from a night of gaiety, fellowship, and good food. Uncle Dave had thrown the party. To start with, the guests gathered up in the pack house for dancing. There had been square dancing along with other types of dance for those who chose to dance at a slower pace. Local musicians furnished the music at no cost to Dave.

A young pig had been roasted over a hole in the ground for most of the day. After a couple of hours dancing, the crowd was ready for the food when it was brought into the pack house and served.

Children scampered and played around the edge of the dance floor, keeping well out of the way of moving feet and legs.

A big wood burning heater had been set up in the corner of the pack house for warmth. All the babies were bedded down in the area near the heater.

There was drinking of moonshine on the outside of the building. When a round of dance stopped, men could be seen hurrying out for a nip. Seldom did a man drink to the point of not functioning properly at one of the affairs.

When the party seemed to be ending, Ederd stood up and invited all who would come, "We're having a ground pea shelling o'er at our house next Saturday evening, uh, and night. Well, for ever how long it takes to git 'em shelled. I hope most uv ya will be dare."

Soon after Ederd shut the door, Sinnie got her baby boys tucked away snugly in bed and joined her husband in the fluffy feather tick that had belonged to her father-in-law.

Major got his own self to bed.

Sinnie told Ederd she was with child again that night. "It should be a coming around de second week in July. I shore do hope dis one is a girl. Don't cha thank it'd be right nice to have a daughter to stay wid me here about de house?"

"Yeah, I shore do."

They made love before going to sleep that night.

Ederd had started paying Major a monthly salary when he reached the age of sixteen. He earned $10.00 a month while he lived and worked with Ederd and Sinnie. Ederd purchased all of Major's clothes and other needs, just as if he was his very own child. Major enjoyed his older teenage years and had become a trusted, hard working member of the family. He took to smoking early on, and there again Ederd bought the cigarettes for him at fifteen cents a pack, and loose leaf Prince Albert smoking tobacco, for thirty cents a can.

Ederd and Major were out in the woods one early spring morning, where they sawed pine trees down for firewood. Each tree was left where it had been felled. It would lay there until all the needles turned a dull yellow, not quite brown. The color was an indication that the wood of the tree was safe to use for firewood. Allowing the pine tree to cure up to that stage, meant the tars in the tree had subsided and left a good quality of wood to be used for many different needs.

Close to the middle of the day, they decided to go on up to the house for dinnertime. After securing their tools, and coating them with a good coating of kerosene, they headed out of the woods.

"Damnation to hell and back!" Ederd exclaimed.

Major looked up and around. When he saw nothing out of the ordinary he grunted, "Hump?"

Ederd sat down on a stump nearest him and lifted up his right leg.

"Jist look what I gone and done. Rammed my foot in dat old piece of literd sticking outta dat root dare," he pointed toward the obstacle. "I think it's gone all de way through and stuck in my foot." He worked the boot off and discovered the literd had torn a good-sized rip in his instep. Blood had soaked his sock by the time he saw it.

"Now ain't dis hell to pay. De first time I e'er wore dese boots and dey are pure-tee ruined. If it ain't one dam thang lately, it's another. What good is one boot? Dis means I'll have to put out money fer a nudder pair."

He rattled off another string of profanity that got Major tickled.

"Laugh, dam ya. It's me dat's a bleeding and out more money."

All men wore knee-high black rubber boots when entering the woods or other areas that posed a danger to a person's feet and legs. It gave protection from danger along with keeping the feet dry when the ground was muddy or wet.

Later on in the season, Ederd and Sinnie got a chance to buy the old Cooper place from his father, the present owner. He wanted $60.00 for the twenty-five acres, more or less. The property abutted a portion of the southeastern section of land Ederd all ready owned. He figured purchasing the acreage would enhance his holdings. He went to the trunk where he kept his cash money and upon counting it, discovered he had nearly run out of cash. He knew without looking that his checking account had dwindled to near on to nothing.

"Sinnie, where'd all our cash money go to?" he asked, when he reached her on the porch where she looked and picked mustard greens. "I had no idee we'd spent de majority uv de money. I reckin' we been a puttin' out more dan we been a puttin' in. Frum now on, we best build up our cash fore we go a spendin' again. Dat means we gotta think about hirein' less help here on de land until we build up our money again."

He left her and walked on out to the barn, to return shortly. "Sinnie, I been a thinking. I'm going on o'er yonder to Unca John's and see if he'll lend me de money to pay fer de Cooper place. I'll be able to pay him back fore de year's o'er." He cranked up the truck, and after backing up to turn and head in the right direction, he leaned out of the truck window and said, "I'll be back by de time ya git dem mustard greens on de table."

He returned home later than he had planned. The family still sat at the eating table, though they had finished eating, when he walked into the kitchen. Of course, Jonas and Luler sat at their usual place to eat at the water table.

"What took ya so long, Ederd?" Sinnie asked as she stood to fill his water glass.

"Unca John would only lend me half de money, so I went on o'er to Bob's. He lent me de udder half. I'll go tomorrow n get a money order to mail off to Paw." He answered her while he washed his hands then sat down on the end of the bench, as head of the household. "I tell ya, I wuz skeered fer a while dare, whether or not I'd git the money."

As the custom had begun back in the days of the 1890's, illegal whiskey stills were in operation on one of the Swinson's farm every year, sometimes more than one. As long as one of the stills was not reported to the authorities, a moonshiner could make a good profit from their efforts.

Ederd decided it was time for him to try his hand at the profession of making moonshine whiskey. It cost quite a sum of money to get the operations in working order. He felt that, in the end, he would get all his investment back, plus a handsome pocketful of cash to line his money pouch that was always present in the pocket of his bibbed overalls.

He worked his hidden still daily, located right in plain sight if a person happened to be in eyesight. The still was in the kitchen part of his home, near the fireplace. He told nary a sole about the still, that is, except Sinnie, Jonas, and Luler. Of course, they knew because Jonas helped with the work involved in running the still.

Ederd thought to himself when planning to make money the illegal way, why waste all that heat out in the woods somewhere, when the wood used to make the fire could serve two purposes: cook the corn mash and heat the kitchen at the same time.

There was never anyone invited into the kitchen to set a spell or to eat a meal with the family while the still was up. When company came, they were entertained in the house part of the building.

When the first batch of likker, so the locals called it, was ready to sell, he and Sinnie were loading the jars into the bed of the pick-up truck. The batch of jars was few in number, being it was the first run off.

"The next batch will be mebbe four times as much as dis'un," Ederd said.

Just as Ederd placed the last jar in the bed of the truck, preparing to make delivery of them to his costumers, they heard the all too familiar sound of a vehicle coming down the lane toward the house.

Before Ederd could get the tarp out and cover the jars, Perry was getting out of his truck right there beside where Ederd and Sinnie stood. Now, Perry had taken a strong liking to the taste of moonshine and found it very interesting to see all those jars ready for drinking.

"I see what's kept ya so quiet n busy of late, Ederd," he uttered with a sheepish grin on his face. He walked nearer to the truck bed and peered in closer at the jars, "How much ya astin' fer a jar?"

Ederd knew at that moment he may be in for a little bit of trouble. The last time Perry had been over and asked for work, he was a bit too tipsy to have done the work properly, so Ederd had not hired him. It had made Perry angry. He had needed money at that time for the purchase of more likker. Today was the first time the two men had seen each other since that event.

Perry seemed to be completely sober while the three stood and carried on their conversation.

"Dis your first run off Ederd?"

"Yea Perry, it tis."

Ederd caught the glint in Perry's eye and figured right then that if anyone turned him in to the law it would be his first cousin Perry. Perry knew about how long it would take to get the next run off in jars and ready for sale.

He walked around in the yard a few steps before saying, "I'll take one a dem jars right now."

When the second batch was ready, Ederd jarred it up and stored it in the corner under the water table. His plans were to get it loaded early the next morning and be off the farm by good daylight.

He had carried about two dozen jars to the truck while Sinnie stayed in the kitchen to move the likker jars closer to the door and get their breakfast started.

There was enough daylight to see your way around pretty good. Just as Ederd straightened up from releasing his hand from the jar top, he glanced up to see three men standing near him, all strangers to him.

He didn't have to be introduced to know who they were. Without a doubt, he knew he was caught.

He dipped his head in greeting, "Mornin' to ya," he spoke as if nothing was wrong.

How the men had gotten that close to him without him hearing one sound, he did not understand. Not a one of the dogs had aroused and given a warning that strange people were approaching.

Sinnie heard the voices outside and cracked the front door of the kitchen open enough to see what was going on out there where the men stood. She closed the door as quietly as she had opened it. She stood close to the door and listened to the conversation between her husband and the federal agents.

She and Ederd thought to themselves, at about the same time, that Perry had done his deed for the day. They both felt in their hearts that he had reported Ederd and his still.

"What chu fellas doin' out so early dis morning?" Ederd asked. He pretended to have no idea of what they were in his yard for.

One of the agents walked over and stood by the truck bed. "Mr. Swinson, you know why we're here. This cargo you have loaded here is illegal whiskey. We've been searching the woods here around your farm for some time now. We have not located the still yet, but knew about when the whiskey would be ready for sale. So we have been right out yonder in the edge of the woods waiting for you to load it up." He pointed in the direction he wanted Ederd to look.

"Would you mind telling me where you got the still hidden?"

"I ain't got no still sir," was the answer.

"Come on fellas." The agent said. "Let's get this taken care of so we can get out of this cold and back to someplace where it's warm."

It didn't take the three men very long to smash every jar of the whiskey to smithereens. They crashed the jars downward on the giant oak trees root, right there beside where the truck was parked. Pieces and shivers of glass covered a big portion of the ground around that side of the oak trees. Illegal whiskey began to puddle on the frozen ground as it ran from the tree roots.

As the men turned to leave the yard, the one that had spoken before said to Ederd, "The sheriff will be out to see you in a day or so."

When the federal agents were out of Ederd's, sight he walked into the kitchen.

"Well Sinnie, that'll teach me to try makin' a livin' another way from now on. I've had a feelin e'er since Perry paid us dat visit dat wuz a gonna happen."

She nodded her head in agreement, "Uh-huh, me too. What chu gonna do wid dese jars ya got left here in de kitchen?" Sinnie asked as she placed the pan of biscuits in the oven.

He got himself a cup and poured the steaming, boiled coffee from the pot that sat on one of the back eyes of the wood burning cook stove. The stove was a four-eyed low standing appliance with a full sized oven beneath the eyes. It also served as an aide to the fireplace to add to the warmth of the kitchen. During the hot months of the year, it seemed to warm the kitchen up more than a body wanted to stand.

"I'm a gonna sell ever last jar uv it. And I aim to git it done fore night fall sets in, dis very day."

When Ederd paid his court cost and fine he had cleared four dollars from his experience of running an illegal likker still.

Later on in the year, Sinnie's youngest brother, Elbert, began to do day work for Ederd, it was in July. He was still almost too young and little to accomplish any big task. He was a trusty little fellow and aimed to please. Ederd kept an eye on him through the day's work and Major helped him with jobs that seemed to get the best of him. Any amount of money young folks could make there in the area was greatly appreciated. His earnings were seventy-five cents a day. Elbert called his sister Fannie and her husband Tom's farm, home, along with an older brother, Pete. The next to the oldest brother in the Roger's family, Abbie, had ventured on out of the community, seeking work other than farm life. He found his place up at Roanoke Rapids, North Carolina.

Lubbie's oldest stepdaughter, Beulah, who had married Henry Rogers, Lubbie's oldest brother, worked July and August at wrapping tobacco on the farm, at ten cents an hour. She too looked after the welfare of little Elbert.

A letter arrived in the mail from Ederd's father, down in Georgia. Ederd called to his wife to come join him on the porch steps and listen while he reread the letter to her.

"What do you think he means when he ask me to sell his land? I know of no land he's got to sell, do you Sinnie? Well anyhow, he wants $2,000.00 for it."

Sinnie wagged her head and uttered, "No Ederd I know nothing bout no land ya pa's got. I thought dis farm n de old Cooper place was all uv his holdings. Well a course dare's de Hewitt acreage, but Unca John's holding dat."

He read a portion of the letter again. "Listen, right cheer he mentions dat Unca John was interested in buying it. Maybe Unca John knows sum'um I don't. Tell ya what, I'm going in yonder and go through everythang in dat old trunk n see what I kin find. I don't know why I ain't done it fore now."

Sinnie went on back to her chores around the house and Ederd headed for the trunk. Way down at the bottom he found a deed to a section of land located between his Uncle Dave's property and that of Ederd's. It was a right good-sized piece of land, too.

"Now dat I thank about it, I know why I been a paying taxes fer Pa every year since he left here," he muttered as he went to look up his wife again.

"Sinnie, do ya recall me a grumblin' bout paying dem tax bills of pa's every year? Wid out puttin' too much thought in why de bills kept on a coming. I jist figured pa owed em from years past. I gotta start keeping better watch on what I'm a doin."

"What's dat ya got in ya hand dare Ederd?"

"It's a deed for dat tract of land pa wants me to sell fer him. Well I reckon I'd best mosey on o'er to Unca John's and see if he still wants de land. If not, I'll try to sell it to another man." He walked out to the pump and pumped off the water until it cooled. After drinking, he said to Sinnie, "Do ya reckon we'll e'er be shed of dat man and his troublesome ways? De sooner I git dis took keer uv, de sooner he'll be off my back about it."

In late August, a notice came from the National Life Insurance Company, notifying Ederd that if he didn't pay the $11.90 due within a limited time, the policy would run out. He let the $1,000.00 life insurance policy elapse then turned right around and bought another insurance policy to cover the tobacco barn. Naturally, he purchased it from another company.

Ederd made his mortgage payment on the farm, with the first load of tobacco he sold in the fall. With the second load, he caught up his 1927 taxes to the sum of $11.23.

"De way prices keep going up, I wonder sometimes if farmin' will be a way of makin' a livin' later on in our lives. Do ya realize how costly things has got since you n me married up, Sinnie?" he mentioned causally to his wife, while they picked dried field peas that he had planted in the middle of the cornrows, back in late spring when he had laid the corn by.

He was a little late with paying his debt back for the money he had borrowed from John and Bob to purchase the old Cooper place. He sold off timber to a sawmill company in late December of the year before. The money coming from the sale of timber allowed him to pay both men.

"I thank ya Unca John fer de loan when I needed it. How much interest do ya say I owe ya on de money?" He grumbled all the way over to Bob's farm about the amount John had charged him.

He left Bob's farm feeling quite a bit better. Bob had not charged him a cent of interest

"Dat's right kindly of ya, Bob. You n de Misses, Miss Missouri dat is, come on o'er bout de middle of de day Sunday and take a meal wid us, me n de family."

"Thank ya kindly, Ederd. It'll be our pleasure."

All married women in the area, outside the blood relative circle, were all called Miss, then whatever her given name was. All adult relatives were called Uncle, Aunt, or Cousin, such as Uncle Tom, Aunt Lubbie, and Cousin Dunnie.

Ederd tried to go see his grandmother, Listy Ann, at least every other day. She was getting on up in age and felt poorly most of the time. She did little more than sit on the porch and daydream about her past. That is, if the weather permitted. She was just too feeble to do any of the work around the house anymore. At times she would blurt out a statement as if she was twenty-five-years old again, giving instructions to one of the boys when they were little tykes.

"Grandmaw, I got a letter frum Rosie yestiddy. She wuz astin' bout chu. She got herself married to a fella named Willie Casteberry. Dey're workin' a farm fer a man dare not too fer from Paw."

"Who? Who's Rosie?" Listy Ann scratched around the side of her mouth as she asked.

"My sister Rosie, Grandmaw. Don't chu remember Rosie?"

"I'll tell you what I do remember. Jake is still lost in these woods around here somewhere."

Ederd had heard the story enough times to know what she spoke of. He also knew it would be no more use talking to her today. She had mentally ventured off from the present.

He stood and leaned over to kiss her cheek. "Grandmaw, I gotta git on back to de house. I'll be back in a day or so."

His grandmother leaned sideways in her chair and lifted the right cheek of her hinny, which allowed a large amount of gas to escape her bottom that made a very loud noise. Her eyes opened up wide, she then dropped her head.

"OOH!" She looked back up at Ederd sheepishly and remarked, "I'll tell you one thing for sure I can still do, that's fart, fart, and fart." She relaxed and slumped against the back of the rocking chair, her eyes closed.

It was so out of character for Listy Ann to do such a rude thing in public, and then to use those words to define what she had done. It amazed Ederd there for a moment, to realize what had just happened. He threw back his head in a hardy round of laughter.

"Bye Grandmaw."

When Ederd walked past the barn on his way out, he ran into his Uncle Jesse. He tried to avoid the man as much as he could. Ederd had no time to mess around with that Uncle. It seemed to Ederd that Jesse had too many devious ways about him. Since he and Jesse were somewhat close in age, Ederd simply called him by his name. "Afternoon to ya, Jesse," he bobbed his head and kept on walking.

"Whoa, wait up dare a minute, Ederd," Jesse spoke and walked on out to the path where Ederd stood.

"What's yore hurry? I want to talk to ya bout dat ditch dat runs yonder through de fields. Ya ain't shrubin' and ditchin' good 'nough. All dat trash comes a washin' through when a big rain comes n clogs it up when it reaches my ditch."

"Now Jesse, yore a dam liar, yore a balled faced liar and ya know it. Me and Jonas clean out dem ditches every spring n burn off every stick of trash. Why do ya want to cause trouble all yore dam life? If ya ain't got nothin' good to say to me, jist keep yore dam mouth shet while I'm around," he left Jesse standing there with a look of startled surprise on his face. It was not like Ederd to defend himself very often.

While Ederd walked home through the fields, he recalled the money he had earned from the sale of the timber he had sold. He had deposited the majority of it in his bank account, enabling him to write a check for the products he bought from the Raleigh man, who was E.H. Garganus at the time. The order for the day came to $2.45 for the four items, which were coconut shampoo, vanilla flavoring, Anti-wool and a package of chewing gum. The Raleigh salesperson came calling once a month to the farm.

The weather was extra hot for early July 1929. Ederd and Sinnie sat on the front porch on a Sunday afternoon, late in the day. They reminisced of their life together on the farm. Baby Floyd was on his father's knee. Ederd diddled the child, causing him to nod off in sleep. Major entertained the two other boys beneath the wash shelter.

Luler had arrived early in the morning to prepare the noon meal. She didn't usually come over to work on Sunday, but since Sinnie was heavy with her fourth child, Luler felt like she couldn't stay away more than half a day at a time. Sinnie's babies were Luler's babies, too. Luler loved Sinnie as if she were her own kin.

Company had shown up to eat dinner with them that day, Emma and Leslie, plus Henry and his wife Dunnie and their two-year-old son, Burris.

There was always plenty of food put on the table, so if unexpected company dropped in, all that had to be done was add a few more plates around the table.

Later on in the day, when all the company had gone home, Luler left after cleaning up the kitchen.

"Now hon-chile you take keer whilst I'm gone. I be back here bright n early come moanin' time," she offered up before she walked out of the yard.

"Ya know Ederd, I'm really blest to have a friend lack dat woman dat jist left here. I love her as good as I do any sister I got."

A sound from the wash shelter caused them both to look that way.

"Cloudie git yoreself down frum dare!" Major shouted the demand to his five and a half year old nephew.

The young boy had climbed the stepladder that leaned against the wall, clear up to the top and was reaching for a hand tool. The tools were stuck in the crack between the back wall and roof of the wash shelter. The tools ranged from hoe, ax, pitchfork, shovel, and bush ax. Some of the tools were doubled in number.

"You beat all I e'er seen youngin'. Into everthang no matter how high it tis."

Major reached up, took a firm grip around the boy's waist, and lowered him to the ground. He gave the seat of Cloudie's pants a swift smack, which sent the child into a wobbling walk. Neither a sob nor a whimper left his mouth. He was a tough little fellow and took most things in his stride.

"Ya better behave yoreself boy. Ya know you ain't spose to be a climbing up dare. Sometimes ya pay me no-taintshun a tall Cloudie."

Leon, almost four-years-old, stood with big eyes watching the proceedings going on about him. Major took the ladder and laid it on the ground next to the wall.

"Now den, climb all ya want to, both of ya." Ederd have ya noticed how mischievous dat oldest youngin uv ours is?" Sinnie asked.

"Uh-huh, I shore have, and he's a gonna git worse if folks here bouts don't quit pickin' at him. Every whur the youngin' goes or even here at home, folks, specially our kin, is a teachin' him out uv de ordinary thangs he shouldn't be a learnin' at de age he is now, or fer dat madder, when he gets older."

Cloudie had learned a few choice words from his father and other cussing men in the community. He used them on occasion, too.

The twin oak trees that stood in the front yard provided shade for the entire front of the house and most of the front yard. It was cool where Ederd and Sinnie sat. A gentle breeze rustled through the leaves, creating a peaceful, calm atmosphere.

The baby growing inside Sinnie's body twisted and turned in such a manner that Sinnie stretched her torso up as far as she could.

Ederd noticed and asked, "Are ya all right Sinnie? I know how bad dis heat is on ya."

"Yeah, I'm as good as I can git fer de shape I'm in. It won't be much longer fore dis baby comes into dis world. And dat won't be too soon to please me."

Yes, it was a peaceful Saturday afternoon for Ederd and his family. They felt secure and happy with their lives and their surroundings.

Ederd looked over at his wife and commented, "I don't think I've e'er told ya I love you Sinnie. I realize we married up under somewhat strange conditions, but I've learned to love ya so much." His smile was a sheepish one. His eyes showed an expression of tender care for her.

Her head dipped a little forward when she replied to his loving remark. "And I love you Ederd."

The story continues in *Skeet Apples*

Glossary

a mudder	mother	er	ever
afeered	afraid	er	or
agin	again	fer	for
aint	aunt	fillies	pretty girls
air	there	flow	floor
are's	ours	frum	from
ast	ask	fur	far
astin	asking	gally	girl
at	that	Gawd	God
atall	at all	ground peas	peanuts
bout	about	gwine	going
barn notchin	big, large	haf	have
cain't	can't	haft	have
cha	you	har	harrow
cheer	here	heered	heard
cheer	chair	hep	help
chillens	children	het	heated
chip pile	kindling pile	hippin	diaper
chu	you	hume	home
chu've	you've	I'd uv	I would
chu've	you have	Idée	idea
chur'n	yours	Iffen	if
comed	came	'im	him
d'reckly	directly	J'ar	you are
d'reckly	soon	Ja	you
dang	mild curse	jew	did you
dat	that	jist	just
de	the	keerful	carefull
dem	them	kilt	killed
den	then	kin	can
den	then	knowed	knew
dere	there	lak	like
dese	these	lawsy	Lordy
dey	they	likened	almost
dis	this	likker	liquor
dis'un	this one	litered	fat pine
eben	even		kindling
'em	them	Maw	mother

mebbe	maybe	weren't	was not
messin	messing	wha	what
'n	and	whur	where
nigh	near	whur's	where is
ober	over	wid	with
oblige	thank you	wid'ja	with you
oblige	agree to sex	widge	with oyu
oer	over	wood'ja	will you
offa	off of	worter	water
ole	old	wouldnt've	would not have
onest	once		
orten	ought	wrapping	Tying tobacco leaves
our'n	ours		
passel	a lot		
Paw	father	wuz	was
pure-t	really	yander	yonder
purty	pretty	yes'um	yes ma'am
reckin	reckon	yestiddy	yesterday
rite	right	yit	yet
rye	right	yo'll	you will
shet	shut	yore	yours
shore	sure	youngin	youngster
sich	such	yourn	yours
skeert	scared	zackly	exactly
slang fer ya	all purpose word	zat	that
slang fer you	connective		
some'on	something		
sump'un	something		
sur	sir		
taintion	attention		
tarred	tired		
thang	thing		
tis	it is		
tomorree	tomorrow		
tuther	the other		
un	one		
uv	of		
warn't	was not		

Other Fine Books From Righter

*4 Women b*y E. B. Alston
And Deliver Us From Evil by E. B. Alston
*Barefoot Girl b*y Hilda Silance Corey
Black Soldier of Mercy by Joseph E. Brown
The Emerald Necklace and Other Stories by E. B. Alston
*David McGregor's Diary b*y Ian Fletcher
The Deal of a Lifetime by E. B. Alston
Hammer Spade and Case of the Missing Husband by E. B. Alston
Hammer Spade and the Diamond Smugglers by E. B. Alston
Hammer Spade and the Merchants of Death by E. B. Alston
Hammer Spade and the Midnight Treader by E. B. Alston
The Historical Architecture of Warsaw North Carolina By Charles F. Ainsley
Immersion by Steven Kornegay
Itsy Rabbit and Her Friends-Itsy's First Adventure by Mary Noble Jones
Itsy Rabbit and Her Friends-Itsy's Giant Leap by Mary Noble Jones
Kate's Fan by Elizabeth Silance Ballard
The Kingdom of America by E. B. Alston
The Last Chance Bar and Grill by E. B. Alston
The Last Voyage of the Dan-D by E. B. Alston
The Mid-Life Crisis of Paul Revere by Ian Fletcher
Passages by Gussy Knott
Telling It Like It Is by E. B. Alston
Three Letters From Teddy and Other Stories By Elizabeth Silance Ballard
Those Whom the Gods Love by E. B. Alston
Whoopin and Hollerin in Onslow County by Hilda Silance Corey and Elizabeth Silance Ballard

Printed in the United States
114374LV00003B/126/P